ColorBlind

June 2011

Greg and Ca-a-a-a-rol ~
What crazy fun we have together! You both are such good constants in our life — steady, eddie friends who are crazy about Jesus! Thank you for so much — assisting at book signings, playing drums at book signings 😊, believing in me. Love you to pieces!
Melanie
Ps. 119:32

ColorBlind

*A preacher's daughter finds
God's love and hope
in the midst of racism
in the 1960's South*

Melanie Meadow

RA Publishing
Clarksville, Tennessee

Copyright © 2011 by Melanie M. Meadow

All rights reserved.
Published in the United States by RA Publishing., via Create-a-Space

Library of Congress Control Number 2011905551

Cover design by Dawn Lombard
Piedmont Ridge map by Teresa Elder

This is a work of fiction. Names, characters, places and incidents either are the products of the author's imagination or are used fictiously, and any resemblance to actual persons, either living or dead, businesses, companies, events or locales, are coincidental.

ISBN 978-0-9829120-0-3

For the four men in my life;

my father who painstakingly milked cows
for more than sixty years,
my pastor husband who knows quite a bit about
church planting,
and my sons who run Coon Creek behind our house.

Forward

I am a different white girl now than I was forty years ago, although I still haven't "arrived." In the late 1960s, my family had a brown maid, Henrietta, who came to clean and iron once a week. I had brown friends in school, but we never attended church together, never shared potluck dinners, never spent the night at each other's homes. We liked each other, even loved each other, but we were separate.

Today, color doesn't register the way it once did -- not because I've been educated through a post-graduate degree, not because I'm living in a commune or even because our society has become more accepting. I'm different in my thinking and living only because of Jesus Christ. He is the only one who changes hearts.

The character Sam Rhodes was a man before his time, but his dream of a group of different colored believers living in community was a worthy one of which, I think, many people today would approve. Sam knew this could only be achieved through the love of Jesus.

May we choose to love in the same way as we live out our lives.

Melanie Meadow, March 2011

Piedmont Ridge, South Carolina
1968

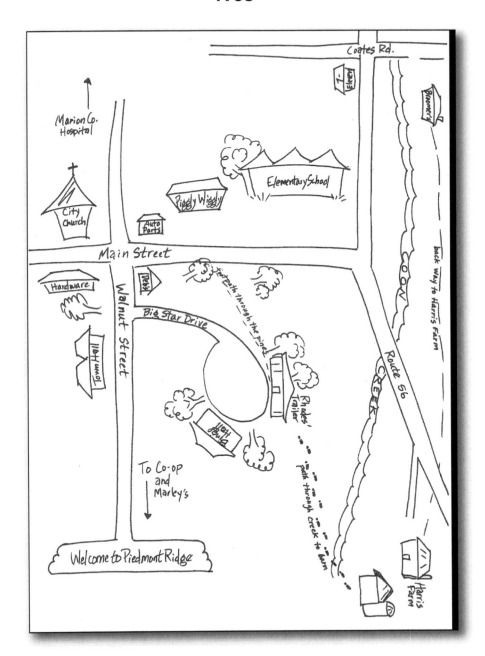

Chapter 1

Mildred

I was born old. Leastways, that's how I always felt.

"Leave her alone, Laura Lee. The child can't help it if she'd rather listen to adults than play with tow-headed boys like her Cousin Jimmy," Daddy always said. And he was right.

When Mama had her famous, neighborhood bridge games, I crammed myself against the corner of the card table with my bony knees popping the table legs as I strained to see fan-shaped hands of hearts, clubs, diamonds and spades. Mama always tried to shoo me away so she could be free of me for a while, but I never left. Bridge was never boring; Cousin Jimmy almost always was.

Talk around the bridge table that summer of 1968 was all about Hurley's Mill and the possibility of layoffs coming. Mama had said Mr. Hurley was awful nice and took care of his own – not to worry. But for once in her life, Mama was wrong. Daddy got laid off a few days later.

Hurley's Mill was *everything* to Prosperity, Georgia. Most everybody from our church, my uncles and cousins all worked there Monday through half-day on Saturday. The go-home bell would ring and you could spot a mill worker a mile away. Slow-walking to his house, tiny brown pellets dribbling from pants cuffs, he left a sort of bread-crumb trail. None of us were rich from the mill, but we got along okay.

But I'm rambling on without saying nothing, that's what Daddy would say. I talk too much.

To get to it — Daddy was doing fine at the feed mill until he came home one night looking all downcast. Mama saw the difference right off and the two of them went into the bedroom and shut the door tight. I always knew that was a bad sign. It didn't take me long to find out the feed mill wasn't just laying off – it was shutting down. For that week, it was real bad in town. Lots of men didn't know what they were going to do, lots of families were afraid. And I was too, which is why Mama and Daddy reminded me to trust in the Lord. Now, I may be twelve years old, but I learned all my Sunday school verses and I knew that trusting in the Lord was the way to go. So I did it. I just trusted and went on about my business, all the time praying that Daddy would find another good job in town and all would be well. I felt pretty confident in my prayers. Then the world came crashing in.

"Laura Lee, I've had a revelation!" my Daddy announced with certainty.

It was one of those hot, sticky, impossibly sultry, July days in Georgia, and Mama and I had just finished shelling the last bucket of butterbeans. Daddy had been out at the church with Mr. Fitzwater, one of the elders, and the front door busted open, revealing Daddy's face lit up with passion and fire. I don't think I had ever seen him that way and it scared me a little. Mama paused with her hand in the bean pot. I sat as still as an owl on a branch – eyes wide, ears perked.

"Fitz and I have been talkin' and I'm convinced that losing my job was the *exact* thing that had to happen."

Mama smiled hesitantly and nodded but said nothing.

"Don't you see? This is the perfect opportunity to throw myself into the ministry that the Lord has been speakin' to me about. I've always felt I'm supposed to be workin' full time for the Lord, and now I have the chance. Plus, you know the mill house reverts back to the company. Who knows what they'll do with this whole row of shotgun houses?"

"But, how…?" Mama began.

"I know. I know. I had the same questions," Daddy interrupted like he knew exactly what she was going to ask. "How can we do that? What about the money? What church would ever consider hiring a feed mill worker? But Fitz says there's a need for a new work in Piedmont Ridge, South Carolina. He's got some friends up there and they want something new and fresh and are lookin' for the right man to come aboard. Fitz says they don't give a hoot if the pastor has education at seminary. They just want to know he's the man the Lord has called.

"Laura Lee, I gotta tell ya," Daddy sat down, "I felt the presence of the Lord fly all over me when Fitz was talking. I just know this is right. I'm not an emotional man — you know that — but think of it! Think of the possibilities!"

Well, I can tell you right now, Mama *was* thinking of the possibilities. *All* the possibilities. And she didn't look any more thrilled than I did at this prospect. Piedmont Ridge, South Carolina? What in heaven's name was in Piedmont Ridge?

I gotta hand it to her, though. My Mama was a rock. She smiled a big, wide smile and lifted her shoulders with a sigh. "Well, Sam, this is news." She stood up from her chair, carefully placing the bean bowl on the floor, and walked over to Daddy. She hugged him and kissed his cheek and suggested he go get those potatoes out of the root cellar for supper, and maybe we could all talk about this some more later.

Daddy had no idea what hit him as he obligingly rose to gather his bucket. His eyes were glazed with a bewildered look. But I knew Mama. She was buying time, and sure enough when he walked out the back door, the smile faded, the lilt in her voice disappeared and the light in her eyes vanished.

"That Mr. Fitzwater has gone puttin' more ideas in more men's heads and here he goes plantin' something in your Daddy," she said, even though I don't think she was really talking to me. "I've seen that look in Sam's eyes before and it's a look to be reckoned with." Mama continued talking to herself, and I knew enough to keep quiet. I'd learned a lot that way. If you keep perfectly still and don't even breathe loud, grown-ups most often forget you're in the room. That's how I was privy to finding out that Cousin Martha *had* to get married to that Sells boy. I don't think Mama and Aunt Mamie ever figured out that I'd heard the whole story.

So I sat real quiet-like, watching and waiting. Mama picked up her bean pot and slipped into mumbling about Mr. Fitzwater. She walked toward the kitchen but must have thought about me at the last minute, because she whirled around to face me, apron lifting like a ballerina's skirt.

"Mildred Juniper Rhodes. You are not to discuss this with anyone outside this house. Do you understand me, girl?"

"Yes'm."

"It ain't no business of nobody's to know what goes on here, and especially when your Daddy's goin' off on some wild hair. It's best we keep this one inside 'till we can talk him down. Do you hear me?"

"Yes'm.

"Not even Beth Ann. You can't say anything to her either. Her Mama is on the social board at church, and Lord, if she catches wind of this, we'll be packed and off to Piedmont Ridge before you could swat a gnat." Mama's apron whirled again, swinging erratically as she marched toward the kitchen, bean pot keeping a melodic rhythm to her steps. I heard the screen door slam as Daddy brought in the potatoes and decided it would be a good time for me to escape to my treehouse and do some thinking on my own. I liked knowing what's going on, but sure didn't want to be inside when it really hit the fan between Mama and Daddy.

The screen door slapped lightly as I stepped onto our front porch where the brightness of the hot July sun seemed to bake me as I came out of the shadows. Our white, clapboard house was neat, although somewhat dingy. It matched the houses on our left and on our right to the letter. Mill houses. The only difference was the types of flowers planted by its owners or maybe the holes in grass covering in the yards. Mr. Mosely next door had big circles of dirt mixed with short, greenish-brown grass. Covering the dirt in bold, black sections were grease and oil, remnants of the half dead cars that were brought to life in his yard. For our piece, we contributed daffodils in the spring – hundreds of them lining the porch and around each side. They were Mama's favorite. By now, though, they had become burned twigs and sticks, buried beneath azalea bushes and pine needles.

I squinted, staring up at the sky, wondering what would become of this day. As my gaze dropped back down to the dirt road running in front of our house, I spied Martha Claire ambling down the street. She was munching on a raw corncob and held another one in her hand. She waved an enthusiastic greeting and picked up her step as she drew near.

"Hey, Mil, what 'cha doing?" she said, corn tumbling in her mouth.

"Nothin'."

Her sharp, brown eyes weren't fooled.

"Wanna go to the treehouse?"

"That's where I was headed," I answered briefly, pondering my next move. Martha Claire was awful perceptive. Some of the old folks in Prosperity didn't think much of the colored folk, but I didn't pay attention to their notions. If Martha Claire was any indication, there were more colored folk in Prosperity who knew what was what than white folk. Her black, shiny braids flapped as she led the way to the treehouse.

Our "house" sat tall in one of the few hardwoods behind Mill Row. There wasn't nothing fancy about it; only a few slats of two-by-fours nailed to a limb here and there that formed a ladder. But the oak was situated behind a huge cedar tree; in fact, the tree sort of wrapped around the oak. If you didn't know to walk into the cedar pile, you might not find the treehouse steps —- and certainly not our sitting spot.

Martha Claire reached it first and put her extra corncob in the bucket on the ground. We climbed up slowly, bit by bit until we reached our favorite seats. Then Martha Claire pulled up the rope, bucket clanking hollowly against the trunk of the tree. As she grabbed the corn out of the bucket, she turned toward me offering the ear and questioning me with those vivid black eyes of hers.

"Want it?" she asked.

"Naw." I still wasn't sure what to do. Mama told me not to tell anybody, but she specifically mentioned Beth Ann, who I wouldn't tell anyway. She didn't specifically mention Martha Claire. And besides, Martha Claire being colored and all, she wouldn't have any contact with our church folk. I just felt I needed to unburden myself somewhere, and Martha Claire should be pretty safe. I sighed deeply, the weight of it all settling heavily on my shoulders.

"Well, come on girl, spill it," she said. "Makes no sense to keep somethin' so caught up in you. I can tell you's about to pop." Small bits of corn kernel flew as she spoke. "You know treehouse rules. You gots to tell all or don't enter."

She was right. Our well-known Mill Row Treehouse Rules held that no secrets were kept from members and nothing that was told behind those dark branches would be shared outside the woods. There was no question about it now. I had to tell; and Mama would just have to understand — or better yet — not find out at all.

"It's Daddy. He came home from Mr. Fitzwater's all excited about being a preacher in some dumpy church in South Carolina."

"Nuh uh," Martha Claire shook her head fiercely. "Yo Mama not gowna abide by that, is she?"

"Of course not!" I declared. "Only…well, you know how Daddy can get if he's got a bee in his bonnet. Remember last year when he wanted to plant those blue potatoes in the garden and Mama was dead set against it? She told him she'd be the laughingstock of the whole neighborhood. But Daddy was determined and sure enough, those blue potatoes came in right in the middle of the summer."

"Uh huh," Martha Claire's eyes rolled at the remembering. "There was yo Daddy gatherin' up them blue potatoes and everybody was a'laughin'. Yo Mama was pretty hot with him, I remember. Y'all wuz the only ones with blue potato salad at the Fourth of July picnic."

"Right." I agreed heartily, still wincing at that memory. "It didn't matter what Mama wanted 'cause he was so dead-set on plantin' them."

Martha Claire leaned over and flicked a tree ant off my sleeve. The breeze blew lightly through the leaves, lifting our sweat soaked blouses off our backs.

"I'm scared it's gonna happen that way again. He's got that look in his eyes."

"But why come he'd want to move all the way to South Carolina?" Martha Claire continued. "They ain't nuthin' up there that we don't have down here. He could help out Reverend Rawlins at yo' church anytime. He don't need to be movin' so far."

I sighed deeply....again. "I don't know. He said something to Mama about his lifelong dream and God callin' him to step out and how maybe losing the mill job was all in God's plan." I shifted on my board, suddenly wishing I hadn't told Martha Claire what was going on. This was almost worse than thinking by myself. "Anyhow, I just got to have a little time to think, that's all. Mama'll probably talk him out of it by tomorrow."

"Humph!" Martha Claire rolled her eyes again. "I don't know about all that, but I do knows that when Daddys gets their minds made up, ain't no stopping um." Martha Claire knew about that because her Daddy made up his mind to leave her Mama three years ago and they hadn't seen him since. Mama would always use words like "low-down" and "good-fer-nothing" when anybody mentioned Martha Claire's daddy. I had to say I agreed with her. No man should leave his wife and four young'uns without food or money. Martha Claire did lots of odd jobs after school during the week to make extra money. Lucky for them, though, none of the Mathis' worked at the mill. At least they wouldn't be affected by the shutdown.

"Whooo-eeeeee! "Martha Claireeeeee!" The sounds of Martha Claire's Mama echoed around our treehouse. "Suupppperrrr! You'd best git yo'self in, ya hear?"

"Yes'm!" Martha Claire shouted back. She leaned back and threw the half-chewed corncob against the base of a magnolia tree about twenty feet away. It split open, cracking in two and spilling corn kernels over the ground. She pulled herself up by a top branch and gathered her skirt around her waist. As she slowly felt her way down the ladder, she glanced back up at me, a mixture of pity and – something else – in her eyes.

"Yo Daddy. He be a good man," she said. "Jus' pray to the Good Lawd, and he'll do the right thing." She paused. "But I sho' hopes he don't take you to South Carolina. Lawd! I hear theys lots of rednecks up that way. Plus I'd miss you too much."

Martha Claire's eyes smiled and her white barrette reflected the subtle beginnings of a sunset dropping below the trees. As her foot stepped softly on the pine-needle covered forest floor, she unhitched her skirt, smoothing it out as she spoke.

"'Course you could be kinda like Moses in the Bible. Tryin' to get to some new Promised Land. But, Lawd. I jus' cain't see South Carolina as somebody's Promised Land."

"Martha Claire Mathis? You best git yo'self in right now, ya hear?"

"Comin'!"

She spun around one more time.

"I'll see ya tomorrow?"

"Okay." And Martha Claire was gone, bare feet flying on the sandy ground. I knew I needed to be getting back home too, but I didn't feel any closer to having this figured out. The air began to get a little heavier, a little cooler and I slipped out of the tree. My steps made almost no noise as I began to walk slowly back toward Mill Row. Dinner sounds crept out of houses, hasty goodbyes were being called down the end of streets, the rich smell of cooked stringbeans drifted near my nose — and all I could think of was change and how I hated it. In my mind, I dug my heels in tight, clinging to the ground of Prosperity, Georgia, and swore I would never, ever forget it — even if my Daddy hauled me to some God-awful South Carolina town. Miz Betsy's tabby cat padded up, slowly circling my legs as I tried to walk, its tail hooking around my ankle.

No. I'd never forget. And no one could make me.

Chapter 2

Dot

Dot Harris's '58 Chevy pickup maintained the steady speed of thirty miles an hour as she passed the Piedmont Ridge City Limit sign. Much to the chagrin of teenage drivers, thirty was the peak speed Dot ran the rusty, blue truck – not because it couldn't handle higher speeds, but because she was never in a hurry. Dot was never late. Never had any cause to speed, according to her.

Her glass milk bottles clinked in the back as the truck humped over the pavement change, but Dot didn't hear the familiar sound. Her mind wasn't on deliveries this morning, which in and of itself was odd. As Piedmont Ridge's primary deliverer of fresh milk, Dot had plenty to keep her preoccupied. Feeding up, bottle collection, the eternal, never-ending milking, morning by morning, evening by evening. It was hard work for any man. But Dot wasn't any man; she was one woman and had held it together by herself for ten years, ever since Tom died.

She flipped the blinker down as she eased into a left turn, which would take her to the 7- Eleven on Coates Road. This morning was July 28, Leslie's birthday. She couldn't shake it, that reminder every year. She'd spent extra time cleaning the barn this morning, gave the hogs extra food. Took special care with the bottle cleaning. She did anything to keep her mind preoccupied, but like water seeping through a cracked pitcher, Leslie's birthday wouldn't go away. She would be twenty-four today – wherever she was.

I'll bet she's a knockout, Dot mused with a tiny smile. *And probably is as ignorant of that as she always was.*

Tiny Leiper was out tinkering on a broken gas pump as Dot

rolled into the store parking lot. He raised his grease-stained face long enough to throw up a two-fingered wave and went back to work. Dot shifted the truck into park and heaved out her wiry, but strong frame. She clumped to the back in her tall milk boots, pulling the tailgate down to slide the crate closer. Used to be that she would jump into the truck bed at each delivery stop, but she wasn't a spring chicken anymore and had begun to ease up on her body. After all, she was on her own. Nobody around to take care of her in her old age.

Dot snorted under her breath as she considered this. Nope. She didn't know of anyone in Piedmont Ridge that would hold her hand into old age. Didn't used to be that way, but yesterdays were just that – yesterdays.

"Mornin' Harris," Tiny's son Lloyd greeted her as she lugged her crate through the glass doors. "Mighty fine morning, ain't it? Reckon you heard the news about the fire over at the colored church?" Lloyd ran ahead of Dot, talking over his shoulder and kicking empty boxes out of the pathway to the refrigerated section.

"Nope," Dot grunted under her load. "Wasn't on the radio this mornin'."

"Naw, just heard it myself," Lloyd shifted the last box, clearing a spot next to the milk section for Dot's crate. "Pete Griffin was in here just a bit ago. Said somebody done set a cross on fire in the colored church yard outside of Pecan Holler. Ain't heard much about that kind of thing going on round here in a long time. I hate it," he shook his teen-age head sadly. "Makes my heart sad somehow."

Dot offered Lloyd a brief smile as she slid open the refrigerated door and began moving older bottles to the front and newer ones toward the back.

"It should make your heart sad, Lloyd. It oughta make all our hearts sad."

.

Chapter 3

Mildred

Old Mr. Mosely once told me if I wanted to remember something really clear, like I was seeing it all fresh in front of me, that I should stare at it for ten seconds, then close my eyes and paint it in my head.

"Mildred, are your eyes botherin' you?" Mama asked from the front seat of the car.

"No, ma'am."

I opened and squinted shut, opened and squinted shut.

"You sure?" she looked at me with concern.

"Yes, 'um."

I opened my eyes and it was gone. Our dingy, lovely, perfect, old house on Mill Row. Gone. I shut my eyes again, real tight. Could I still see it? Was it there?

I was half buried under mounds of clothes, dishes, towels and sheets in the backseat of our 1964 Chevy Malibu on the way to the God-Awful Place, as I had begun to call it. Daddy had an old hay trailer jimmied on the back of the car which made me feel like I was dragging low in the rear. Mama and Daddy sat in the front seat, windows down, hair blowing wildly and not talking much. Mama hadn't been talking much since that day earlier this month when Daddy had his revelation.

Our clothes were stuffed in nooks and crannies, old chests, dresser drawers, empty feed sacks from the mill. Somehow, we had managed to cram all our possessions in our car and trailer, but I knew my heart was in Prosperity.

Beth Ann had come to the house that morning, carrying a bag of fresh peaches, tears streaming down her cheeks. She and her

Mama tried to put on a brave front, but they both left our porch just a' bawling. I think Mama and me were all cried out. My eyes hurt from three weeks of crying myself to sleep, and I just don't think I had any water left. I could tell Daddy felt sorry for us. He kept following Mama around the house, trying to help out or be extra-nice to her – and to me too, but it just didn't seem to help much. I could hear her crying late at night when my sobs ran dry. I think she tried to muffle her cries in the pillow, but I knew Daddy could still hear her from his living room chair.

One night, when I was going to talk to Daddy about leaving, I rolled out of bed and stomped toward the living room. Before I could march myself in there, I had to stop short. Daddy was on his knees by the chair, and he was crying too. And he was praying real hard.

"Oh Lord, am I really hearing from you? Listen to my wife, Lord. Listen! Why would you ask me to do something that hurts so bad. Why, Lord?" Daddy buried his face in a pillow and cried more. Part of me wanted to race back to my room and cover my ears. But the other part of me – the bigger part – had me rooted to the doorway.

"Lord, you know I've committed everything to you. Me, my family, my life. But why do you want to hurt the ones I love? I need to hear from you again. Would you have me take this job in Piedmont Ridge? Is this really you, God?"

Daddy broke down again, muffling his tears in the chair seat. But the oddest thing happened. The room, which was already dark and still, became sort of heavy. I just don't know how else to describe it. I didn't see any angels or nothing, but a heaviness fell over the room – sort of how I felt when Mama tucked me into bed real tight during the winter, with layers and layers of heavy quilts.

I felt it right away. Daddy must've too 'cause he stopped crying and got real still. I held my breath. Then, it passed, whatever it was. Daddy seemed better and I figured it was time to sneak back to my room.

My earlier stomp switched to tip-toes as I eased down the hallway. Lucky for me, I had memorized the squeaky board toward the right of the hall and I fell into bed unnoticed, my mind filled with questions.

Not long after that, Mama seemed somehow to pull it together and have enough presence of mind to give some of her special items to her friends. To Beth Ann's mama she gave her favorite pink scarf. (I think she had secretly wanted that scarf since Mama found it on sale three years ago.) To Martha Claire's family, she gave all our extra food – beans, bags of flour, just about everything. Mama told Martha Claire's mama that we just didn't have the room to carry all these supplies and we could always buy more in South Carolina, but I knew we *did* have room and we didn't have much money to do any buying. But Mama would never let on about that. Miz Mathis cried silently as we brought in bag after bag of food. The tears streaked her strong, dark face, leaving lines of chalky residue. Three of her children stood behind her, holding tight to her apron. And Martha Claire? Well, even though she's colored and all, I think she was the hardest thing to leave. My best friend, really, but don't tell nobody that. Wouldn't seem right somehow for my best friend to be colored.

Fields of tan-colored corn stalks raced past the window as I thought once more of Martha Claire's parting words.

"Now Mildred Juniper, don't you forget me." Her intense gaze willed me into remembering. "And don't you forget neither that the Good Lawd, He know what He doin'. He wouldn't be sending you to that redneck place without His Holy Ghost walkin' alongside you. You best write me some letters, and read His letters to you in the Good Book. I jus' know He gonna take good care of you."

She ended her sermon with a strong, tight hug and a hard look into my soul. Ever since Martha Claire's hero, Martin Luther King Jr., had been shot and killed last April, she'd gotten awful serious about things. I decided I would honor her wish; I would never forget her.

"Ready for some lunch, Mil girl?" Daddy called out.

"Yes, sir," I responded. Mama just kept staring out the window. She had been terribly quiet for days – and pale too, come to think of it. Seems like we had gone past a million corn and soybean fields. One after another with a small town interrupting the flow every once in a while. Daddy spotted the truck stop with a diner hooked to the side and pulled the light tan Malibu into a vacant space. The doors creaked open as we shuffled out, hot and sticky, tired and dirty.

"Well, this oughta do us," he said, a quick smile flickering across his sunburned face. Daddy came around to our side of the car, locking the doors and cracking the windows so as to keep the heat from roasting us when we returned. "Earl always said this was the place to stop. May not look so good, but the food's supposed to be outta this world." He watched Mama carefully as he spoke, willing her to be happy. Mama glanced up at him with a half-smile and sighed deeply. She stretched her arms out to the side, accidentally pulling her red-checkered, sleeveless shirt from out of her waistband. She quickly re-tucked, pinning the shirt tail under the waistband of her khaki peddle-pushers.

Daddy grabbed Mama's hand, tugged on my arm and led us toward the M & P Truckstop Cafeteria.

For a truckstop, the burgers weren't half bad. I didn't think I'd write Beth Ann about it, though. I'd never hear the end of it from her. Mildred enjoying a burger at a truck stop! I figured Martha Claire would probably be thrilled to just get a burger, so I wouldn't write about this part of the trip to her either. It'd be best not to.

Daddy had just finished swallowing another big draught of the M&P's famous sweet tea when Mama started to look all flushed. She asked to be excused pretty quickly, then patted his hand briefly – sort of one of those "it'll be alright dear" – pats and headed to the bathroom. Daddy let her slide out of the booth, a look of mild concern on his face.

I studied Daddy while we waited for Mama to return. Beth Ann always said he was good looking and it wouldn't be long before all my girlfriends would have crushes on him. I think she already had a crush on Daddy but didn't want to fess up to that. I had to admit, he was handsome. His probing blue eyes would get this clear-blue color when he was sad. Almost hurt you to look at them. Then, they'd get a darker, moodier blue when he was angry. He had thick black hair that had begun to recede somewhat. I heard him complaining to Mama just a few weeks ago about them "widows peaks" creeping in. But, it didn't matter to me. He still was just as handsome as he'd always been as long as he had Mama picking out his clothes. Daddy was born color blind – had the hardest time matching up his browns and blues. Today's jeans and plaid shirt seemed fine, though.

Once when I was listening to Daddy talk with Mr. Fitzwater on the front porch, Mr. Fitzwater had asked Daddy why he and Mama didn't have no more kids than just me. "Sam, you and Laura Lee oughta keep on havin' them young'uns," he had said with a half laugh. "You both are so pretty, you oughta keep the line going." Daddy had quietly laughed in response and changed the conversation real quick. I knew he didn't want Mama to hear any more about that 'cause she couldn't have no more children. They hadn't gone into details with me about all that, but Cousin Jimmy did let on one time that his mama said my Mama was real sad about that. She was just thankful to the Lord they had me around. I would have liked a brother or sister, I think. Although Beth Ann sure put up with a lot from her little brother.

"Mil?"

Daddy broke into my thoughts.

"Yes, sir?"

"How you feelin' about moving up to Piedmont Ridge?"

I tried to keep my voice steady and straight. I was still thinking that Daddy taking us to the God-Awful Place was completely against the Good Lord's will, but I didn't want to let on.

"I'm good with it, Daddy." My smile was up, perky and intended to appear honest. "I think we'll have a real good time there."

God forgive me – I lied.

"That's my girl," he said. "I knew you'd be okay."
No doubt about it. It was worth the lie. The waitress leaned in to pick up our dirty plates as he reached out and grabbed my hand.

I think me and Mama knew there was a time to convince and a time to refrain from convincing. (I don't think that's in the Bible, but it ought to be.) Even though Mama and me hadn't said it to each other, this just felt like one of those times to refrain. If Daddy believed we should be hauled off to God-knows-where, then I would lie and pretend I liked it as long as I could.

The song on the jukebox switched. "Now here's to you, Mrs. Robinson, Jesus loves you more than you would know – oh, oh, oh." As the song floated over the truck stop booths, I wondered who Mrs. Robinson was and did she even know Jesus?

"Mil, your Mama oughta be out of the bathroom by now. Can you go check on her?"

"Yes, sir." I inched my way out of the booth, my bare legs sticking to the red plastic seats. The "Ladies" arrow pointed toward the back of the kitchen galley. A pay phone jutted out from the wall next to the door. I tried the knob, but it was locked. So I knocked. Nothing. I knocked louder. Still nothing. I banged and kicked, still nothing. Maybe I passed her somehow and didn't notice. I came back to the table where Daddy still sat all alone. He looked up at me, surprised, I think, at my quick return.

"She alright?"

"I don't know. I knocked on the door, but there was no answer."

"There wasn't?"

"No, sir."

Daddy's frown deepened as he pulled himself out of the booth and led the way back to the Ladies Room. He knocked and banged and yelled too, but nothing.

"You wait here, Mil. I'm gonna get the manager."

It couldn't have been more than two minutes but it felt like two hours before Daddy returned. He was half pushing, half dragging some sorry-looking truck stop kitchen boy holding a key. He waved at me to follow.

"I'm sure my wife went to this bathroom, I told you. Something's happened. Hurry up!" Daddy was at the same time polite and demanding, propelling the boy toward the locked door. I quickly shifted to the side to let him to the keyhole. He glanced up at me as he squatted by the knob, his acne-speckled face coloring deeply at the "Ladies" sign.

"Ma'am? Ma'am?" he called out feebly.

"Laura Lee? Honey? Are you alright?"

The boy slowly pushed the key in the lock and turned it. As the click echoed in the hall, Daddy barreled past him, calling out as he entered.

I waited, afraid of what was in there. "Call an ambulance. She's unconscious."

The truck stop boy flew back to the telephone as I hesitantly stepped onto the pink-tiled floor. Daddy was on his knees, holding Mama's head in his lap. Her eyes were closed, her clothes still perfect, but there was a small trickle of blood dripping down the left side of her head. And then the room got *really* hot, and dark, and fuzzy, and cramped – and it went black.

Poor Daddy. There he was with both of his girls passed out on the truck stop bathroom floor and nobody around to help him. He told me later that he just yelled a lot at the kitchen boy, waited impatiently for the ambulance and prayed to Jesus when he wasn't yelling at the boy. I thought that sounded like a good plan.

I finally came to about the time they were strapping Mama into the stretcher. She still hadn't woke up and Daddy's face looked all pale and white. He had my head in his lap and when I opened my eyes, I could see him staring hard at Mama. His hand was cradling my head and rubbing my temple, and it felt really good. Real peaceful. But I knew I couldn't just stay there. The room swam around as I lifted myself up and the picture of two ambulance men rolling Mama over the tiled floor fuzzed into focus.

"Mil?" Daddy leaned over to look in my eyes.

"Huh?" I mumbled, still feeling pretty groggy.

"You passed out, baby," Daddy stroked my cheek and tried to smile. "Do you think you can get up and go to the hospital with Mama?"

"Yes, sir."

I pulled myself up by grabbing on the porcelain sink attached to the wall. Daddy supported me from behind, and suddenly I was standing. He whisked around and picked me up, heading out of that bathroom as fast as any middle-aged man carrying his daughter could. He wanted to jump in that ambulance with Mama, I could tell. But I reckon he figured we'd need the car. So he threw some money at the cashier and lugged me out to the parking lot. Clouds were rolling in on our beautiful August day. As he carefully placed me in the front seat, I watched his face, wantng to see signs of hope – or at least a knowing of what was going on. Did he have any idea? I know I didn't. But seeing Mama like that…I don't think I'll ever get over it.

Nighttime comes quick when you've had a trying day. If that wasn't a saying on a plaque somewhere, it oughta be. By dark, Daddy and me found ourselves in Mama's hospital room, using woolen blankets to make up a bed on the chairs. The doctor said only an overnight visit was required, that Mama would be just fine, she was plain worn out. Right now she resembled an ice princess, all pale and beautiful, and it was hard to believe things would be normal again. This wasn't the way I pictured this day turning out.

Daddy found me a pillow and turned out the lights. As I nestled down in the covers as best I could, he sat – staring at Mama as she slept. His crystal blue eyes were clear and intense. I fell asleep watching him hold her hand, the sounds of machines rocking me like a lullaby.

"Mil? Mil?" Mama was standing at the open door, her head peeking around the screen. Flies were buzzing on the porch and the sun slanted through the trees. It was late afternoon, everything felt hazy and distant, but her voice was an insistent whisper.

"Mil? Honey, I need you. Can you come over here?" I tried to stand up from the swing and walk toward her, but her face began to sway and dip. And that voice. It seemed far off yet in the same room.

"Mil. Wake up. I need you."

And suddenly the porch on Mill Row vanished and Mama floated away from the screen door. She was back in the white-sheeted bed, leaning off the side waving to me while whispering as loudly as she could. "Mil."

"Ma'am?" I struggled out of the dream.

"Come here, honey, I need you to grab that water for me. I can't reach it and I'm parched."

Daddy was snoring in the fold-out chair on the other side of Mama's hospital bed. So I tiptoed over to her, taking the quart-sized cup with me as I went. She grabbed it and gulped three or four good swallows before she smiled weakly at me. Then she patted the empty space beside her. "C'm here and sit with me a while, alright? Mornin's here, but I want your Daddy to get some more shut-eye."

The hospital was making slow wake-up noises and I caught the smell of eggs cooking mixed with ammonia. I eased up on the bed with Mama and cuddled in closer. I knew we would be leaving today 'cause the doctor told us all late last night. Mama looked better this morning, but I still wouldn't say "fresh." She hadn't looked fresh for quite a while, come to think of it.

"Mil, I need to talk with you some before your Daddy wakes up." She put her arm around my shoulder and pulled me close. I still had on that pink shirt with the stain, but Mama didn't seem to notice. She was always particular about my appearance. "A lady must always look the part," she'd say, usually while wiping jelly off my cheek. But today wasn't about me.

"Dr. Moore says I'm going to have to rest – a lot – when we get to Piedmont Ridge. Now I argued with him about that, told him I had a husband and a little girl to take care of, and he insisted that the two of you would be alright. But I just don't know…" she trailed off.

I drew in a breath to let her know that, of course, we could handle it, but she didn't wait for my answer.

"You see, he says I'm sufferin' from exhaustion,'" she smiled weakly. "So you may have a few more chores to do for a while, but

I'm not going to stop being your Mama, and the very best one I can be. You are my precious little girl and I will always take care of you – no matter what Dr. Moore or anyone else says."

Well, I can tell you I was sure glad to hear that. Maybe everything would be alright after all.

"And then there's your Daddy," she sighed, glancing over toward him again. "He's full- tilt forward on this church thing, and nothing's going to do but him starting a work in Piedmont Ridge. And we're going to have to help him make this happen – or at least, help him try to see his dream come true." Her hazel-green eyes peered intently into mine as if she was trying to read my thoughts. Did I agree? Was I on Daddy's side too?

I gave her my most reassuring look. "Mama, are you saying we girls need to stick together and help out Daddy?"

Her eyes twinkled. I think she may have been laughing at me – but she answered so sincerely, I wasn't sure.

"That's exactly what I'm sayin'. Let's stick together and help Daddy and each other. Alright?"

I thought about that a while. I was already hating the "more chores" part of this plan, but I couldn't see any other way. I couldn't forget about school. I was supposed to start the sixth grade in a few weeks. How would Mama manage with me gone?

"Mama. Do you think you're gonna be sick a long, long time? Like maybe even weeks?"

"No, honey. I won't be sick a long, long time, Lord willin'. But the doctor is telling me I have to rest a while."

Daddy began to stir and it was perfect timing as far as I was concerned. I was beginning to feel a little teary, but I knew I had to be strong. I couldn't cry now. Maybe not ever. Maybe I could never cry again in front of Mama or Daddy because Mama needed me to be strong and Daddy needed me to be solid, not a wimpy little girl.

I decided then and there to do away with tears. I could do it. I could be strong and tough– and if the tears ever tried to squeak out, I'd just find me a bathroom and get myself together before Mama or Daddy saw me. After all, Martha Claire had gotten to where she didn't cry that much anymore. She cried an awful lot when her daddy snuck out and left, but after a while, she didn't cry as much. She got real strong. And this was nothing like Martha Claire's trial. I still had my Mama and Daddy. Sure wish I had Martha Claire here too. She'd be a real big help in a time like this because there was so much I didn't understand.

By lunchtime we were back in the loaded down Malibu, dragging that trailer, with corn fields flying by a mile a minute. The wind tore through the open windows, carrying in the fierce smell of chopped corn husks mixed with Johnson grass. Somebody, somewhere, was cutting corn for silage.

"Mil, could you let your window up just a smidge?" Mama requested from the back seat.

I obligingly cranked the window up halfway and glanced back to make sure her hair wasn't blowing.

This was the only part of this repeat of yesterday that was different. Now Mama was on the back seat – all stretched out on top of clothes and bags – and I sat in the front with Daddy, my hair whipping against my cheeks. I wished I had been a fly looking in and seen all the sameness, not having to know that, really, everything was different. Moving to Piedmont Ridge was hard enough. Now I felt like somebody was gonna call out a letter, finish the word and my neck would be strapped on a stick hangman's noose.

"Not much longer, girls," Daddy rang out. "We're entering the South Carolina upcountry. I expect it'll be another hour or so."

I smiled serenely at him, thinking, *Whoop-dee-do!* Mama didn't open her eyes. I think she had fallen asleep. Wish I could disappear too. With every passing field, Prosperity and Martha Claire and Beth Ann slipped farther away. I felt sick in my stomach just thinking about it all.

I reckon I was tireder than I thought, what with the clink, clink, clink of the trailer lip banging on the tire, the wind whipping loudly through the window crack and Daddy's AM radio station playing. I fell asleep, my head lolling against Daddy's shoulder.

Later I woke dry- mouthed and foggy as Daddy nudged me gently.

"Mil? D'ya want to see the town for the very first time? We just passed the 'Welcome to Piedmont Ridge' sign."

I forced myself to open my eyes real wide. That usually gets the sleep out. And sure enough, Daddy was turning left down a street decorated with tall silver street lights and glass- covered store fronts.

A True Value Hardware sat on the right corner. Daddy probably already filed that away in his mind. Looked like about three-to-four other small shops sitting next to it. There wasn't a flock of people walking along the sidewalks, but enough for me to see that most of them were white folk. That struck me as odd.

Daddy pulled up to the first intersection, and while the light was red, he pulled out his directions. "I know I'm supposed to turn right at a light to get to Elder Crenshaw's house. Just can't remember if it's the first or second light on Main," Daddy said to himself. I continued looking around, only half listening. The Piedmont Ridge City Church was situated right here on the corner, and what an important looking building it was! Stained glass windows that must have reached clear to heaven, or close enough. Tall columns on the front, pure red Carolina brick, crisp white sidewalks, and even a special parking place for the pastor right near the front of the church.

As I scanned the outside, the front door swung open and out stepped one of the most beautiful women I'd ever seen – well, besides Mama of course. She had blonde hair twisted on top of her head in that new fashion, and she was laughing so I could see her clear smile and sparkling eyes. I stared, engrossed, but the traffic light changed just then and Daddy figured this was where our right turn came in.

As he swung wide, I craned my neck around to watch as the beautiful lady in her hot pink suit grabbed the hand of the man beside her. He was dressed fancy for the middle of the day and looked to be as happy as a fox in a henhouse.

Then Daddy hit a pothole and I was back on track. We were going slowly down Walnut Street now and Daddy was looking at mailbox numbers. "Try to find Number 413, Mil. That's Elder Crenshaw's house and his wife's the one that's got the key to our house."

I pointed quickly to the left and Daddy swung into the driveway before I could even speak. We were facing a plain, white-sided house with a nice flower bed. Mama would appreciate that, I thought, but Mama was still sacked out in the back. I figured Daddy decided seeing Piedmont Ridge for the first time wasn't a big enough deal to wake her up.

"Stay here. I'll only be a minute. I'll let you get acquainted with these folks later, alright?"

Daddy popped the car door open, and I settled to wait. Daddy's "minutes" were always way longer than he said. The street itself looked clean, well-kept, but certainly not rich. Not like that City Church building or the houses behind it. Elder and Mrs. Crenshaw must not have an awful lot of money and probably no kids. I didn't see any toys on their place.

Daddy was talking with her now. She was a tall lady, gray-haired and thin with a quick smile. She waved at me enthusiastically and I waved back, not so enthusiastically. I don't think she noticed. I saw Daddy making motions with his hands, and I figured he was explaining where Mama was (since you couldn't see her, all laid out in the seat like she was). Miz Crenshaw's face got sad and then you could tell she was making those "poor little Mildred and her Mama" sounds. I could almost hear her clucking out in the car. Then Daddy motioned to go and she got all happy again, grabbed his arm and disappeared. She returned a few seconds later carrying a tinfoil plate covered with plastic wrap. Daddy smiled again, waved and came back to the car with a satisfied look on his face. He handed me the plate, slamming the door shut behind him.

"Mrs. Crenshaw made chicken and dumplins today and said she's got plenty to share." Daddy smiled jubilantly. "Now that's hospitality, ain't it Mil? We'll have chicken and dumplins and cornbread for supper." He started the car with a look that said "I knew moving here was the right thing to do."

It was only a few minutes later that Daddy pulled up in front of a trailer on the end of a cul-de-sac, at least that's what he called it. Just looked like a dead-end road to me and it sure wasn't pretty. At least it was a double-wide trailer instead of single-wide, but the siding was brown with a combination of dirt and weathering. Darker brown shutters hung off the windows on the front and there wasn't a real yard to speak of.

"Laura Lee'll have this place looking top notch in no time," Daddy said confidently as he parked the car. I smiled vaguely, turning in my seat to survey the area.

"What's that?" I asked, pointing to a deserted-looking building next door. Hanging at the top on cheap canvas was a faded sign that read: Bingo Every Wednesday Night.

"Well, that's gonna be the church, Mil."

You could've knocked me over with a feather. Church? I wanted to yell. Church? No, a church is what we just passed on Main Street. This is a bingo hall. A dirty, mouse-infested (I was sure of that) bingo hall! Underneath that sign was another faded sign that read: Big Star Grocery. So, the grocery store/bingo hall was going to be the church? Oh, I could tell fitting into school in this town was going to be a whole lot of fun. I could just hear it now. "There goes the girl who lives next to the Bingo Hall." "No, she doesn't live next to it. She goes to church in it!" My heart sank at the prospect. Our first day in Piedmont Ridge wasn't looking good at all.

Daddy threw a feed bag full of clothes at me and pointed to the front door that he had just unlocked. I guessed he was gonna let Mama sleep while we unloaded the bedframes. He must want a ready-made place to lay her before he woke her up. I sighed deeply. Might as well get started; I had a feeling the inside of the double-wide would be just as bad – if not worse – than the outside. Daddy said something about Elder Crenshaw coming over later and I figured somebody would need to unload and clean up. Wouldn't be Mama. I threw the bag over my left shoulder, took one more look at the Bingo Hall and walked through the door. The God-Awful Place was living up to my expectations.

Chapter 4

Dot

"Blasted door's jammed again," Dot muttered as she heaved against the Piggly Wiggly side delivery door. She put her shoulder to it and leaned in heavily – thud, thud, thud. Suddenly, the door swung in and a frizzy, red-haired woman with milky pale skin stood solidly blocking the way.

"What tha...oh, it's just you. Well, what 'cha waitin fer? Get on in here with yo' milk." Eunice Thornapple, stockroom manager of Piedmont Ridge's Piggly Wiggly, turned on her heel and stomped back into the store. Dot ignored Eunice's curt welcome and grabbed the last full crate on her truck. The Piggly Wiggly was the last of her Tuesday deliveries and Dot was glad – for lots of reasons. She was tired, foremost, and Eunice drove her nuts. A combination that pushed Dot into moving in a more speedy manner than usual.

Dot trod through the well-stocked back room, easing between boxes of Charmin tissue and Bounty paper towels. Eunice stood near the swinging doors leading into the store, berating a teen-age girl wearing a "Hi, I'm Your Cashier" button. The girl looked close to tears as Eunice continued her barrage.

"...and if'n ya can't get it in yo' head that we can't be pullin' stock outta boxes at yo' beck 'n call, I'll have to talk to Mr. Hammond 'bout your seemin' inability to comprehend how a grocery store works." Eunice dragged the word comprehend out as she stretched her vocal chords. "Now git back up front and take care o' the customers. They's always number one, 'ceptin' on pulling out fresh stock. You got to make 'um take what's on the shelf. Hit's the only way to run a bizness."

Eunice turned toward Dot before the girl began to escape, her words continuing to overflow – a stream of unconscious thought. "Lord. What kind o' help Mr. Hammond done brung in here? Like you kin tell somebody to wait while good ol' Eunice digs around in hundrets, I mean, hundrets o' boxes to find some woman's favorite smellin' soap. Good Lord!" Eunice threw up her hands. "What's tha world comin' to?"

Dot attempted to move past Eunice, not wanting to be pulled into any sort of a scene that involved her. She almost made it. Almost.

"Oh, Harris. I been meanin' ta ask. You been gettin' any extree milk? We been sellin' out o' yo' milk two days afore you bring more. Can you up yer deliveries to one more crate?" Eunice trailed Dot as she walked through the swinging doors into the refrigerated section of the store. A few customers were in the dairy section, but the afternoon rush hadn't begun yet. Dot placed the crate on the floor and began to unload.

"I reckon I could bring you another six gallons per delivery."

"Six, huh? Couldn't up it ta twelve?" Eunice pulled the pencil from behind her ear, turned the lead point toward her scalp and scratched vigorously.

"Nope. Don't have enough producin' right now. Might could in a couple of months," Dot said.

"Oh, awright. Guess that'll have to do. But when those cows start puttin' out the milk, you put us first on yer list, ya got it?"

"Right." Dot tried to keep her answers as brief as possible. Eunice was one of her least favorite people. But she didn't have to worry because Eunice's assistant Johnny chose that ill-fated moment to bring in the carrots to stock. Eunice lit into him like a fly on honey.

"Hey, I see you got carrots. What happened to that other box o' carrots I left beside the outside door?"

Johnny, who seemed to be way too old to be taking orders from Eunice, looked mystified.

"What carrots you talkin' about?"

"Mr. Boyer's carrots, that's what! I left his second box of fresh carrots by the door this mornin' fer you to bring in, and I ain't seen it since. If you put 'um out already, we been sellin' heaps o' carrots." Eunice looked searchingly at the carrot selection. "You caught up ta listenin' to them radio dramas again? I swear on sweet Mary's grave, I'm gonna send that radio o' yourn in tha garbage heap..."

"I never saw no carrots by the back door," Johnny interrupted.

"What?"

"No, ma'am. Weren't no carrots there when I come in this morning." Johnny stated with certainty. "And I ain't listened to no drama t'all today."

"Well, I'd like to know where they gone to. You best go check with Billy Joe when he comes back from tha bank. Tweren't nobody here but me, you and Billy Joe. Mebbe he brung 'um in and put 'um somewheres." Eunice's anger dissolved as quickly as it came.

"Yes'm."

Dot continued stacking bottles of milk on the shelf while Eunice trailed Johnny back to the stockroom. She found herself breathing more freely, reveling in the shroud of silence that seemed to fall anytime Eunice left a room. It occurred to her that if she started parking out front, she might could avoid Eunice altogether. Next delivery, that's just what she would do.

Chapter 5

Mildred

The sun peeked through slanted blinds, leaving deep shafts of shadow and light across my bedspread. It was a miracle, really, that I found my bedspread among all the clothes, blankets, sheets and towels we unloaded the night before. But here it lay – a little torn and tattered, but a comforting reminder of home, my real home.

We'd had a busy few hours unloading and setting up beds, but thanks be to God – or maybe just Miz Crenshaw – the ugly, soiled trailer was as neat as a pin on the inside. Don't get me wrong, we shuffled over frayed, ratty carpet, suffered in August heat with no air conditioner, and stacked plates in cabinets with no doors. Good thing Mama was out of it. "Tacky," she'd pronounce with a huff. Maybe she wouldn't notice for a while.

I decided to lie still a minute before facing this Monday – the start of a week. What kind of week would it be? Daddy slid boxes across the floor in the kitchen, probably looking for the frying pan to cook eggs in. Eggs were his specialty – any kind of eggs you liked. Scrambled, over-easy, omelet. He was the egg-man. The sun was warm in its patches that spread out like a striped bathrobe – warm and enfolding. As I stared at the pattern, my hand rubbing over and under the fat stripes, I thought about the dark and the light, the black and the white. And then I remembered last night.

Elder Crenshaw had indeed visited after he got home from his job in a Piedmont Ridge logging camp. As you would expect of a logger, he was big — really big — tall with lots of hair. Hair on his head, his face, his arms. I'll bet he even had hair on his back, but I sure didn't want to think about that! Yuck. Martha Claire used to talk about how hairy-backed men made her nauseated, and I agreed.

The big surprise of the night was Elder Thomas, the one Elder Crenshaw brought with him.

They had arrived just after we finished licking our plates from Miz Crenshaw's chicken and dumplins – a truly wonderful feast. Even Mama was able to shovel several heaping spoonfuls down before she fell back asleep. Daddy was tucking her into their recently made-up bed when I heard the knock on the door.

"Go ahead and get that, Mil!" Daddy yelled from the back room. "It's probably Elder Crenshaw."

So I obediently – and I accent that "obediently" part, because it had been a hard day and I sure didn't feel like being obedient anymore – anyway, I obediently opened the door and there was Mr. Big Hair Crenshaw. Standing behind him in the shadows was another figure that I couldn't quite make out.

"Why, hello there, child. You must be little Mildred Juniper," Elder Crenshaw said in a boisterous voice. If it could've sounded hairy, it would have. He was pumping my hand faster than a bicycle pump the whole time he talked. "So pleased to meet 'cha and have you'uns comin' to Piedmont Ridge. The Lord's got a work to do here. A mighty big work! Where's yo' Daddy?" I couldn't find my voice.

"Er, he's uh…" Luckily Daddy entered the room declaring, "Mildred, honey, let Elder Crenshaw in. Let's don't keep him standing outside."

As he entered the trailer's living room where we had two turning fans that pushed the heat from one side of the room to the other, the man in the shadows followed Elder Crenshaw. I'm not sure who was more surprised, me or Daddy.

The stranger stood tall, a twiggy black man with a quick smile. His teeth shone like bright, white stars, highlighted by the darkness of his skin while his warm brown eyes said a kind, gentle "hello" to me before he ever spoke. When he did, his voice was quiet and soothing, like a creek running steadily in the heat of summer.

"Howdy, there, Mr. Rhodes and little miss." He tentatively held out his hand to Daddy. Daddy immediately took it and shook hard.

"Why…hello there. Who do I have the pleasure of meeting?" Daddy asked.

"This here's Daryl Thomas," Elder Crenshaw busted out. "Or, I should say, Elder Daryl Thomas."

A dead silence entered the room then. Drop dead. The no-breathing kind of silence. It was as though the world froze. Then Daddy broke through the ice, God bless him. It was getting awful embarrassing.

"Elder Thomas. Well, what a pleasure to meet you," Daddy offered his hand, shaking even more vigorously this time.

"I, ah, apologize Pastor Rhodes, fer us not lettin' ya know that you wuz a'comin' up here to watch over a body of believers that's mixed up. A little colored. A little not," Elder Thomas began with a wry laugh. "We didn't think of it as deceitful…just tryin' to be careful and wise. As shrewd as serpents, ya know? We just felt like you couldn't make an informed decision on whether God's callin' you to this body until you met this body. All of us. All types o' folk."

Daddy looked like he'd been blasted by a tornado. I wasn't any help either. I know my mouth gaped open, and I think even Martha Claire would've been floored by this development. We all knew our places in this world, and the colored and white folk didn't mix when it came to the gospel. We learned and worshiped in our churches; they worshiped and learned in their churches. And never the twain shall meet.

Daddy had this plastic smile fixed on his face, and I knew he must have been frantically trying to find a way to recuperate without promising anything.

"Well," he had managed to croak out, "this *is* a surprise. I had no idea…" At this, Daddy looked sharply at Elder Crenshaw who didn't quite meet Daddy's gaze. He oughta feel pretty rotten, I figured. Dragging a man and his family all the way up here under false pretenses. "Why don't you fellas find a box or bucket to sit on and let's share a cup of coffee and talk. We might as well hash this out and see what the Lord might be saying." Daddy grabbed a five-gallon bucket as he spoke and tossed it toward Elder Crenshaw. Guess he was making him sit on the bucket. Served him right. That bucket oughta be pretty uncomfortable after a while.

"Mil, why don't you fix up some coffee for us, then head on back and keep your Mama company, alright?"

"Yes, sir." I compliantly moseyed toward the kitchen, ears tuned to the living room. I didn't want to miss a bit of this! Daddy telling these guys they were crazy and that we'd be leaving for Prosperity as soon as possible. Ha! The look on Martha Claire and Beth Ann's faces when we drove back into town would be priceless. Best get a move on, though, school would be starting up soon.

I spooned out five large tablespoons of coffee into the stainless steel basket and set the percolator on the stove. Daddy always liked it strong, and as I listened, I banged pots and pans loudly, figuring Daddy would think I was awful busy and not able to hear a thing. Elder Crenshaw's voice drifted around the corner.

"Now, Sam. I hope you're not all upset with me, but I just knew once you got to Piedmont Ridge and met all these special folk, you'd know you was the man for this job, for this church."

Daddy must have made some sort of interrupting sound because Elder Crenshaw began talking again real fast.

"What we're askin' you to do is meet us, walk among us, get to know us a little and ask the Lord what He would have you do. It wouldn't make no sense for you to pile up yo' beautiful family – especially that sickly wife of yours – and turn back to Georgia. There ain't nothin' left there for you anyhow. You need to hear from Jesus on this, and we're sure you're the man. We prayed and prayed...."

"Yes, sir, we have," interrupted Elder Thomas. "We done spent many a night together, in each other's houses, asking the Lord who He would have to lead this mighty peculiar body of believers. After three days of heavy prayer, we got the phone call ..."

"Out of the clear blue sky..." blurted Elder Crenshaw.

"...from Mr. Fitzwater sayin' he had a man searchin' for his place of ministry. The more he told us about you – bein' a mill man, a hard worker who understands the plight of the workin' family, a man of God – we just felt in our soul that the Lord was callin'

Sam Rhodes to be the preacher at Piedmont Ridge Community Church. Do it really matter to the Lord whether we are black, white or polka-dotted?" Elder Thomas almost yelled that last part. Well, yelling for him. He was such a quiet man that getting a little loud seemed a big thing.

The room suddenly felt serious and still and the sounds of coffee perking sounded like a giant, boiling cauldron. I made lots more noise, grabbing what mugs I could find stacked on top of one of the boxes in the corner. Seeing a box top, I put cups, pot and sugar packets on it and carried it into the living room. All three men sat facing each other, Daddy on a box, Elder Crenshaw on his bucket and Elder Thomas on the floor. I set the coffee in the middle of them.

"Thank you, honey," Daddy said without seeing me. "Head on back to your Mama now and see what she might need."

I walked down the narrow hall and entered Mama and Daddy's room where I had found her awake by that time. We played Crazy Eights until the two elders left. She never asked me what was going on and I had never said.

But this morning, a warm, peppery smell from the kitchen lured me out of my room. Once again Daddy had served up the best eggs in the South.

"Wonderful, Sam," Mama said, her pretty coral fingernails looking chipped and scratched. "Whoo-ee, I'm fuller than a bee on honey." She rubbed her stomach, but Daddy and I saw she only ate about three bites. Her smooth hair was swept up from her neck in a makeshift ponytail.

"Mildred, honey, think you can help me wash this mop of hair today? I'm 'bout tired of feeling greasy and dirty."

"Yes, ma'am."

"Why don't y'all pull out the necessities in the kitchen and bathroom and get things a little straighter. I can't hardly stand the mess. Then after lunch, you two can hunt down a grocery store, grab a few things – like shampoo – and get on back home." Mama smiled weakly. It looked like all those orders wore her out, and I reckon they did 'cause while Daddy and me unloaded boxes and stacked dishes, Mama slept in the chair.

When lunchtime rolled around, we all realized a trip to the grocery was needed, so Daddy and me packed up to find it. We left Mama in front of a sunny window while Daddy steered toward the Piggly Wiggly. He said he figured it'd be a good time to get a layout of the town and show me where Piedmont Ridge Elementary School was located. We pulled out of our dead-end street onto Walnut and hung a right to go back toward Main Street. Then we turned right on Main and went only a half of a block to the Piggly Wiggly. A little farther down on the left was the school.

"You know, Mil. I think this loops like a horseshoe. I'm thinking if we take that footpath there," Daddy pointed to the right as we swung into the Piggly Wiggly parking lot, "we'd end up in our dead-end circle."

I decided not to comment on that "dead-end circle" and how well the name fit, but I could see he was right. A winding, dirt path ran through the woods, right across Main Street from the grocery, and ten-to-one, it'd end up at the trailer. Guess that meant I'd be walking to school too – if we stayed. Daddy hadn't let on yet what he decided last night and I was too scared to ask.

He eased the Malibu into a space near the front of the bulletin-covered glass window, squeezing tightly between a newer model Oldsmobile and a really old, beat-up truck. I think it must have been blue once, but now was mostly rusty. Cartons stacked in the back read: "Harris Dairy Products," and I saw dirty oil cloths and *The Piedmont Ridge Views and News* wrapped together on the front seat. The car door slammed shut as Daddy met me on the sidewalk.

"C'mon honey. Let's see about getting us some groceries and finding those favorite cookies of your Mama's. Ginger spice, right?"

I nodded as he stepped on the threshold and the automatic door swung open, cloaking me with a delicious cool blast. I sure was missing air conditioning. Daddy got the buggy while I squeaked behind him in my purple, Converse, high-top tennis shoes. Mama would've been really ticked off at me if she noticed I was wearing high tops and shorts. But she didn't notice and Daddy never paid attention to those things. Figured I should get away with it while I could.

As we swung around into the dairy section, we almost ran up on an old woman stacking milk jars in the cooler. She was the strangest looking thing I ever saw. A fisherman's cap hung down around her ears while straight gray hair stuck out at the sides. It looked like she had on men's pants, drawn up tight around her skinny waist, with an oversized, blue men's shirt tucked in. Her pants were stuffed into black, plastic knee-high farm boots – the ones with the orange treads. Mama would have been rolling her eyes by now. There was no Piggly Wiggly tag on her shirt, so I knew she didn't work here, but obviously she was stocking milk for some reason. As she turned around, she glanced up and I caught a glimpse of the most piercing, startling eyes I'd ever seen. For about three seconds, I felt like she saw into the depths of me, then she reached for another bottle and turned her back to us.

Daddy didn't seem to notice anything out of place as he grabbed a half-gallon carton of milk and moved down the aisle. A silver double-door that led to the storerooms swung open suddenly, and a frizzy-haired lady screeched out, "Harris? You through re-stockin' yet? The 7- Eleven's callin' and they says they outta yo' milk too. Best head on that way!"

I turned back toward the old woman, who actually didn't look that old when she stood up straight, and saw her nod briefly to the Piggly Wiggly lady. She didn't seem to move any faster, though. I don't know that I would have either.

"Whoa! Excuse me, little lady," an overweight, balding man practically ran me down.

"Mil, watch where you're goin'," Daddy chastened.

"'Scuse me," I mumbled, ducking under Daddy's arm.

"Weeee-ll, and howdy there," the man continued, "don't believe as I've met you folks. You new to the Ridge?"

Daddy's million-dollar smile lit up his face as he extended his hand. "Shore am! I'm Sam Rhodes and this here's my daughter, Mildred."

"How'd ya do," I said.

"Pete Griffin's the name," he said, returning Daddy's handshake with energy. "What brought y'all to this part of the country?"

"Well, the ministry actually." Daddy responded. I could tell this was going to be one of those boring parent/grocery store conversations, so I casually turned back toward the woman at the milk ... Harris, the frizzy-haired lady had called her. She was still there, but looked to be about to run out of milk in her crate. Since she wasn't looking at me, I continued to watch her out of the corner of my eye. She was odd, but interesting. I'll bet Martha Claire would be able to figure her out better than I could. She was so good at knowing people by just watching them.

I hadn't been paying much attention to Daddy and Mr. Griffin, but suddenly I caught a word that snagged my attention.

"...daughter about your girl's age..." Mr. Griffin was saying. "You goin' to Piedmont Ridge Elementary next week when they start up?" he asked me.

"Yes, sir."

"Well, little Mildred, you just look up Violet Griffin. I'll bet you two will become good friends." Mr. Griffin began to push his buggy past us, still talking. "What church did you say ya'll are comin' to work with?" He really didn't give Daddy a chance to answer. "My family has been elders and deacons in the Piedmont Ridge City Church for come near hundret years, now. We love the Lord's people. 'Course you're always welcome to come a'visitin us too, ya know?"

"Why, thank you, Mr. Griffin," Daddy said politely.

"Oh, just call me Pete," he said as he squinted his eyes, searching the shelves behind us. "Now tell me again what church ya'll gonna be at?" This time he actually waited for an answer.

"Well, I'm looking at the pastor position at Piedmont Ridge Community Church."

Mr. Griffin's intense searching on Aisle Two stopped right then and there. All thoughts of canned beef stew went right out of his head; I could tell. He turned – very slowly – back toward me and Daddy.

"Did you say the Community Church?"

"Yep, I did. Do you know of it?" Daddy asked.

"Somewhat…" Mr. Griffin hesitated. "Do *you* know of it, Mr. Rhodes?"

"I'm just learning," Daddy laughed, but a little strained if you ask me.

"Mr. Rhodes," he was all seriousness now. "You are aware that Piedmont Ridge Community Church, well, that they's coloreds at that church?"

I glanced back toward Harris. Sure enough, she was just finishing up and was close enough to hear this. Luckily, I didn't see anyone else in our vicinity. This was going to get ugly.

"Excuse me?" Daddy said, his voice rising. "If you mean, do I know that some white Christians and colored Christians have decided to worship together, bringing into this segregated town a picture of what the true gospel is about, then I would say, I do know about that."

Whoa, boy. Here it comes. Daddy's face was turning red. I began to press against his leg with my arm, trying to move him down the aisle, a move I was sure Mama would approve of.

"Don't start yo' high falutin' talk with me, Mr. Rhodes," Mr. Griffin's bald head broke out in a slow sweat, while the squeaky pitch of his voice rose higher.

"It's people like you who mess things up in society. Everybody knows their place; everybody's happy with their place," Mr. Griffin took a breath to continue, then seemed to remember I was there. He lowered his voice – as if I couldn't hear.

"Coloreds are coloreds. You can't change 'um and I can't change 'um. They are slow, clumsy and not real bright," he said, pointing to his head. "They don't know their left from their right and belong with each other – not with white folk. Mr. Rhodes, if you go to tryin' to change the code of this here city, you gonna regret it. I kin promise you that!"

And with that final say, Mr. Griffin heaved his buggy around us, plowing around the end of Aisle Two. He was in such a huff that he didn't see the front end of another buggy rolling in from Aisle Three. With a crash, they collided. An embarrassed colored lady peeped around the Fritos display. With an loud, "Humph!," Mr. Griffin pulled around her and rolled away. The three of us stared at one another, wide-eyed. Part of me wanted to laugh, but it wasn't the time.

Behind me, I heard boxes shifting and I turned in time to see Harris lift her empty milk bottle crates. We exchanged glances – and in the middle of that serious, unsmiling face, flashed a quick smile and a wink. When Daddy grabbed my arm to pull me on down the aisle, I followed with my head tucked low, praying to God I wouldn't see any kids who heard that conversation. So much for easing quietly into Piedmont Ridge.

Chapter 6

Dot

Dot heaved three wooden milk crates into the back of her truck and let them clatter into position, wedged against each other snug enough to keep from flying out. It was a lucky throw and that was a good thing. Dot was in no mood to stack neatly. Her ire was raised; subsequently, her blood pressure was probably topping out.

That jerk, Pete Griffin, she fumed. *The spots on a leopard never change. A body would think that any man who had lost his own wife to a bad heart would have more compassion on others, but somehow Pete must have missed the day of that lesson.*

She slammed the truck door so hard that pieces of rust flew off the tailgate. As she turned the key, the engine caught with a shudder, and she slammed it into gear. Wheeling out of the Piggly Wiggly, she noticed a Georgia license tag on the Malibu parked next to her.

Must be the girl's car. Humph! I'm betting the Rhodes family won't make it in Piedmont Ridge for long. Not with the likes of Pete Griffin and his sort running loose in town.

Dot turned her truck down Main Street, heading toward the 7-Eleven. She was running deliveries backwards today – she liked to change things up every once in a while. Only one more milk delivery and she could get out of town, back to her farm and her peace and quiet. Dot's family of fifteen Holstein cows, one bull, four pigs, fifteen laying hens, one rooster, twelve cats and three no-good dogs would be waiting to be fed. The Harris Farm was only one mile from the center of town, but with a place the size of Piedmont Ridge, that put her far enough in the country. At this time, her

54-acre spread was safe from developers or even close neighbors. Nobody wanted to live near a crazy old lady.

And yet, Dot mused as she coaxed the truck into third gear, she couldn't help but feel sorry for another stupid soul like Sam Rhodes who might think he could help or change people around here.

She had learned the hard way that a lot of Piedmont Ridge's old money families couldn't be trusted, and Lord help you if you try to befriend the coloreds! Or switch churches. Or denominations. Or do anything to knock against "The Establishment." Or, heaven forbid, die and leave no money to your church. The voices still echoed in her memory.

"This here's the church your papa's papa helped establish. The church of your forefathers. What do ya mean there's no money left for the church in Tom's will? He was a deacon! The only thing we can figure, Dot, is as his wife, you had somethin' to do with that."

Easy, Dot old girl. You haven't thought about that stuff for years. Let it go. Let it go.

She inhaled deeply as she passed by Powell's barren cornfield, the dead brown nubs of stalks looking like rows of marching men. She wasn't sure why she had smiled at the lost-looking girl in the purple tennis shoes. That stringy brown hair, wide blue eyes and those lanky, colt-like legs. Maybe she reminded Dot of Leslie. She shrugged, quickly dismissing that line of thought, choosing to dwell instead on the obnoxious, hypocritical Pete Griffin.

If we want to keep this town small, we oughta set up Pete at the welcome center, Dot thought with a smirk. *He'd run a bear away from her honey. Somebody ought to tell that Pastor Rhodes, ought to warn him, let him know what he's steppin' into. There's more than one Pete Griffin out there. Plenty more. Wouldn't be her, though. None of her business. Even though she'd read that passage in the Bible just that morning about taking one another's burdens and being one in Christ.*

She pushed the thought out of her head.

The 7-Eleven's unevenly paved parking lot loomed ahead and Dot eased into her spot – the last parking space on the right.

Looked like Floyd was working the register again. Dot sighed. She hated dealing with Floyd. He was such a nice kid. Maybe Eunice had her good points. At least with her there'd be no chit-chat, no compassion, kindness or humor. Oh well. It was the last stop. Ten minutes and Dot would be back on her dirt-covered driveway, any thought of Sam and Mildred Rhodes banished from her mind.

Chapter 7

Mildred

August 21, 1968

Dear Martha Claire,
    So far Piedmont Ridge is looking pretty bad. I guess Mr. Fitz told your Mama about my Mama and her sickness. We spent a day in the hospital, but it sure felt longer. Remember you said this could be our Promised Land, like Moses in the Bible? I sure hope not. Moses had to have it better.
    You won't believe what Daddy's got himself into. The church up here has whites AND coloreds in it. I'll bet your hairclips are flying out just reading that. My teeth almost dropped on the floor. I just never figured grownups would do something like that. It'd be like us being in our treehouse and having church too.
    Oh well. I'll let you know more later. We live in a trailer, it's pretty nice I guess. And I haven't seen anybody other than Mama and Daddy and some people at the grocery.
    Mama says to tell your Mama that she's doing fine and that we miss you already. We don't know what Mama's sickness is, but it mostly just makes her tired all the time. I've been cooking and cleaning a lot. You know how that is!
    Love and Best Friends Forever,
                      Mildred Juniper

p.s. Our address is 4 Big Star Drive, Piedmont Ridge, South Carolina

I licked the envelope gently, so as not to cut my tongue. I hated it when that happened. I figured I'd best get a note to Martha Claire quick-like, since I hadn't wrote her since we left Prosperity. I hoped the Lord would overlook that little lie about the trailer being nice. I figured it would be nice as far as Martha Claire was concerned, plus I didn't want to worry her.

Daddy and I had scooted on home after loading up with lots of Peter Pan peanut butter, jelly, bread, milk, cereal and some Cokes. I could tell Daddy hadn't been doing much of the shopping before now. I helped him a little, tried to grab some green beans and fresh apples, but I'm afraid I wasn't good for much. The new Little Debbie Oatmeal Cakes got me, and Daddy said he needed them as much as I did. We had discovered them only a few weeks before and we were hooked.

So when we entered the trailer, knocking against the recliner and waking up Mama, we both got what-for when she saw Cokes and Little Debbie cakes peeking out of our crinkled Piggly Wiggly bags.

"Looks like leaving the two of you to get groceries is gonna be my undoin'," she said ruefully. Her normally neat hair was tousled and her eyes were puffy from sleep, but she was still the same Mama. "As soon as I can get myself some energy, I'm gonna whip this house and you two sweet-toothed bumpkins into shape."

"Laura Lee," Daddy grunted as he lifted his three bags to the already overloaded counter. "I'll pay to see the day when you can rein Mildred and me in and break us off Little Debbie cakes. Right, Mil?"

I laughed as Daddy tossed me the twelve-pack across the room. "Yeah, Mama. I just don't see it happenin'." I popped open the plastic and took a big bite of pie, white cream squeezing delightfully between my teeth. Mama just rolled her eyes.

"Well, I can see Piedmont Ridge has a Piggly Wiggly. Anything else interesting in town I need to know about?" Mama shifted in the recliner, turning her question toward Daddy. I watched him carefully out of the corner of my eye. This was gonna be good. He stopped stacking cereal boxes in the cabinet and waited for a second, staring at Mama as if weighing his options. Finally, he spoke slowly and carefully.

"Yeah, Laura Lee, there is. Mil and I met some town folk..."

"Oh?" Mama interrupted with interest. "Will I like them?"

Ho, ho, this was getting good.

"Guess you'll have to decide that, honey." Daddy still hadn't started stacking those boxes again which tipped off Mama.

"Did something bad happen?" her eyes shot quickly to me, looking me up and down. Uh oh.

"Mildred Juniper! You didn't wear those purple tennis shoes to the store, did you? With *shorts?* Heaven forbid! Sam! You didn't let Mildred leave the house looking like that, did you?"

"Looking like what?" Daddy asked, eyeballing me with confusion.

"Good Lord. There's no telling what people are gonna think about us now. Mildred. You knew better!"

Mama's face was getting all red and I knew it was time to use a well-known tool of mine – redirection.

"Mama, it wasn't my shoes that was the problem, was it Daddy?"

Daddy gave me one of those "Thanks-A-Lot-Mildred" looks, and Mama swung her head back to Daddy.

"What, Sam? Tell me. Is the car alright?"

Daddy groaned. "Yeah, the car's fine. I was trying to tell you, Laura Lee, but you kept interrupting."

"Interrupting what? Honestly. If you people don't start talking, I'll… I'll…well, I'll just…" Poor Mama. I think she realized again just how sick she felt right then, that she couldn't really do anything, and her face turned sad all of a sudden. Daddy saw it too and put the cereal boxes down.

"Mil?" he said, walking back into the room.

"Sir?"

"Why don't you head to your room for a few minutes and let me talk with your Mama, okay, honey?"

"Yes, sir." I padded through the two-inch carpet back into my room and shut the door. That's when I decided to write Martha

Claire. I had success on dodging the purple tennis shoe issue but didn't want to push it by trying to listen to Mama and Daddy — then get caught. Besides, I already knew the story and didn't figure Daddy to add much more to it.

I was glad he'd decided to tell Mama. Even though she'd been out of it for the past two days, she still needed to know why we'd be leaving Piedmont Ridge and heading back toward Prosperity. Well, I assumed that's what we'd be doing. I know Daddy talked big to Mr. Griffin, but there were so many things wrong in this town already, and had we even been here twenty-four hours yet? Nope.

'Course, Daddy was anything but predictable. Maybe I'd better pray. Martha Claire would say that was a perfect thing to do.

I hopped up from my writing desk and knelt beside the bed. Grabbing my favorite pillow that read: "Property of Mildred – No Boys Allowed," I hugged it as I laid my head on the bed. Beth Ann's mama had cross-stitched it for me a few years ago and I always slept with it. You needed to be humble to talk to the Almighty, but I also figured He wouldn't mind if I was comfortable.

Lord, you know that me and Mama have been obedient and followed Daddy to this town. And you know there's some nice people here like Mr. Thomas. But, Lord, we just don't belong here. Plus it looks like there's not many other people who want us around. That Mr. Griffin seemed nice until he realized we like colored people. Lord...please convince Daddy this isn't the right place for us. Convince him that Mama's sick because of this foolish thing. You've got to, Lord. I just don't know that I can handle...

"Mildred! Daddy hollered from the living room.

"Sir?"

"Come here for a minute. Me and your Mama want to talk with you a spell."

That was fast, Lord!

I hot-footed it into the living room, stepping over boxes stacked up on the left side of the tight hallway. Maybe we would just load them back up.

As I came in the room, I noticed the warmth of the afternoon sun shining through the window on Mama's face. It made her look real peaceful-like, more so than she had looked since we left home. The fan was on again and the front door held open with a stick to keep the air circulating, but it didn't seem that hot. Daddy patted his lap and I came and sat down with him since he and Mama had the only two chairs in the room.

"Mildred. I told your Mama about our run-in with Mr. Griffin. Then we took some time to talk about what's happened in our family since we left Prosperity three days ago. Can you believe it's only been three days?" Daddy asked, squeezing my shoulder.

I shook my head.

"We've prayed about it and talked some more and we feel like we need to include you in our talking. I've been setting on my decision to stay or not ... and praying a good bit. And I feel like the Lord's leading me in a direction - as does Mama."

I glanced over in Mama's direction and saw her nod her head briefly. She gave me a quick smile then closed her eyes again to listen.

"But before I tell you what we're thinking, you tell us what you're thinking."

Well, that sure caught me off guard. This was the first time ever that Mama and Daddy included me in family decisions and the cat got my tongue. I just stared, stared, which made me madder than anything.

"Do you have anything to say, Mildred Juniper?" Mama questioned me softly and I realized she had been listening to every word.

"Well, I..."

"Hm?" Mama tilted her head and the sunlight struck my face with its full power. I blinked and shielded my eyes.

"I, uh, I guess I just don't know." Don't know? For heaven's sake. Of course I knew we should go back to Prosperity, but for the life of me, the words wouldn't come out. Daddy didn't wait any longer.

"Your Mama and I have decided that, even though it may be hard, we are gonna stay here a while and see where this mule takes us. There's nothing left for us in Prosperity, and the Lord isn't telling me to leave, so I reckon we'll stay. Right, Laura Lee?"

Mama nodded and smiled, carefully concealing any real emotion. My eyes widened, and I'm sure my face flushed like it always did when I was upset. Mama, sick as she was, noticed right away.

"Now Mildred, let's hang in with Daddy and see what surprises the Lord might have for us 'round the next corner." Her words were right but they didn't sound very convincing to me. Daddy didn't notice.

A darkness slid into our bright, sunny room. Daddy, obviously assuming all was well, moved me off his lap, got up and began making comfort noises to Mama as he straightened her pillow. Then he asked about fixing her a Coke. All I knew is I couldn't take it anymore. I saw the front door open and jumped up, tripping over a bucket on my way out.

Daddy called, "Where're you going?"

I jumped off the front steps, skipping three in mid-air, and bolted toward the woods in the back of the trailer. I pretended my purple tennis shoes were Aladdin's flying carpets as I raced down the hill into a gully filled with pine and cedar trees. There had to be a place I could go to escape.

Chapter 8

Dot

It was close to five o'clock when Dot sputtered into the shed beside her house, parking her truck between stalls and hay bales. *Five o'clock and still feeding to do before milking,* she thought.

Floyd had tried that chit-chat stuff at the 7-Eleven, but Dot didn't fall for it. She had answered in monotones, head turned toward the coolers as she stacked. He finally had given up and Dot was pleased. She didn't have all day to gab, didn't even want to. Her animals were waiting.

As soon as the machine-gun spurts from her muffler were heard, chickens, cows, dogs and cats came to life. Their siren call had sounded; food was on the way.

Dot lifted her lean, muscle-laden body from the truck seat with a sigh. Hauling full milk bottles was beginning to wear and tear on her. She'd increased her monthly supply of Ben-Gay from two to four tubes and figured she smelled like old people now. But the relief to her aching muscles at night was worth it. Her animals didn't care anyway.

"Hello, 'Lizbeth, you ol' mule, you," Dot affectionately scratched hard on the forehead of an aged Holstein. "You know I'll find that soft spot." A black-and-white twin shuffled up and nosed Dot's hand off of Elizabeth, pushing aside the other cow. "Ah, Jane, you goat! Your jealousy's gonna be the end of you one day." She put the newspaper on her truck hood and leaned further into the stall, scratching both cows vigorously.

A voracious reader, Dot had enjoyed naming other animals after some of her favorite characters — Beth, Joelle, Meg and Amy — four more Holsteins, and nothing like Little Women. Her Three Musketeers lay sprawled on the front porch as she stepped over them and through the screen door. Only Aramis lifted his head to make sure it was Dot. Porthos and Athos didn't crack an eyeball.

Useless hounds. If I didn't love 'em so, they'd be gone to Huskies' bird dog farm for resale.

She didn't pull out a key because she didn't have one. The front door always stayed unlocked at Harris' place. She figured her 12-gauge shotgun would stop anyone if she was home. If she wasn't home, folks could take whatever they wanted.

She dropped *The Piedmont Ridge Views and News* on a metal-legged kitchen table and plopped down in a chair to pull her work boots off. She made quick work of unlacing them, stacked them neatly by the back door, and walked out on the back porch to slide into her black, plastic milk boots.

Years of steady routine made her actions almost rhythmic and dance-like. She leaned over, stuffed her pantslegs into the upper part of the boots and grabbed a handful of corn as she straightened up and opened the back screen door. "Chick, chick, chick," she called, and a dozen or so hens and two roosters came scurrying from all parts of the yard. She tossed the corn to her left as she firmly stepped down a well-worn trail to the back pasture. A right turn to the pig pen and three shovel-fulls of slop out of the barrel only took her three minutes. She wanted to be finished before dark.

Time to set out the grain in the trough and call in the girls to get this milking done, she thought. Her "girls" – the other eight Holsteins that were easing up from the back pasture – knew it was time for relief. Their bags hung precariously low to the ground as they stepped toward Dot's small but neat milk barn. They, too, moved in perfect rhythm, part of their afternoon dance. They lined up obediently at the gate to the barn, waiting patiently for their turn to be milked, fed and turned out for the night.

As Dot shoveled grain into the feed troughs, she felt the familiar rub of Bartholomew as he twisted his thick, orange tabby cat tail around her calf. She bent down to scratch his ears, being sure to catch his favorite spot behind the right one. He purred loudly and jumped up next to her on the wooden fence rail that surrounded the outside of the barn.

"You cat," she said lovingly. "What would I do if you didn't help me feed up every day, hmm?"

He answered with another twist of his tail, turning his body around again for another run of Dot's caresses.

"I don't have all day to rub a no-good, lazy cat," she continued. "You hear Beth mooin' over there? If I don't deal with the girls, you won't get any supper. Now come on and let's get moving." Dot placed the shovel back against the wall of the feed room and walked around the barn toward the gate. Four or five more cats scattered around her feet, knowing that milk time for her meant supper time for them. By the time the excess milk was poured into the cat dish, all twelve should be home. Bartholomew was a homebody, but her other "disciples," Matthew, Mark, Luke and John had a habit of roaming. Often in the morning, she would find an offering of a dead baby rabbit or mouse on her back doorstep. She always felt a little sorry for the rabbits, but the more mice they found, the better.

Dot's top-of-the-line pipeline system had been cleaned and sanitized this morning after the early milking. The suction tubes hung neatly on their platforms, ready for another job. She flipped the outside power switch, turning on the pump action that would pull the milk from the cow's teats, through piping and into her 500-gallon milk tank in the adjoining room. Tom had always insisted they have the best in milking gear and Dot had continued his tradition by switching to the pipeline method a few years earlier. She was painstakingly careful to keep it all cleaned, oiled and primed, and it had paid off.

Beth mooed gratefully as Dot swung open the gate, letting three cows in at a time. Since she was down to only eight milkers right now, she ought to be finished and cleaned up in an hour.

Chapter 9

Mildred

I tore through the trees with no thought as to where I was going. Ducking and dodging saplings and overhanging limbs, I ran as fast as I could — away. It was only a few minutes before I realized I'd best slow down before I fell. The hill behind the trailer dove straight down to the base of a gully. My steps slowed and broadened as gravity shot me faster downward to where a small creek wound across the bottom.

I stopped, panting at edge of the water. A waterfall the size of shoebox dribbled slowly over a few stones — not much more than a trickle here. I sank to my knees, dipped my hand in the water and cried a gullywasher. Tears for Mama. Tears for me. Tears for Georgia and my treehouse and Martha Claire and Beth Ann, for Prosperity Elementary School that would start its classes without me. For everything. I must have sat there for thirty minutes or so; it felt like years. So much for not crying anymore.

The constant trickle of the creek made a steady background for the crickets, whip o' wills and bluejays to sing along. Every once in a while, I'd hear a crack of a twig or the sudden swish of a limb and I knew the squirrels were busy in the trees above me. Maybe I could just stay here forever, far away from Piedmont Ridge.

I dipped hands in the clean, cold water and splashed off. I was glad I couldn't see my face. It was sure to be all splotchy and red. Martha Claire always said my blue eyes turned a pretty crystal color when I cried, but I never noticed. I puffed up so bad that I never wanted to check in a mirror. Once I washed off, I stood up.

The creek wound snake-like through the gully and a barely used trail ran alongside it. Most likely it was a deer trail. I saw a few tracks on the other side of the creek and glanced back toward the trailer and Big Star Drive. I couldn't see either one anymore, but knew which path would get me there. I didn't feel like going back to the trailer.

My eyes started to scruntch up again, tears threatening, but I forced myself to stop. My tear ducts hurt and that was a sure sign it was time to stop crying. Mama would say I'd cried enough tears to float the ark and maybe I had.

Stepping on a large, flat stone, I jumped to get to the other side of the creek to begin walking the trail. I knew the proper, Christian thing to do right now was to pray, but I sure wasn't in the mood. Truth be known, I was mad at God. Don't know when I'd be ready to talk with Him again, but it wasn't right now.

A gentle breeze blew off the water, cooling me down on the outside, but my insides were just gathering steam. It just didn't seem fair that Daddy had the right to upset our family like this. Granted, he had asked for my opinion, and I hadn't given it ... but he oughta know. I mean, what in heaven's name had happened since Prosperity that might have changed my mind about this place?

Oh, I know. He must've thought that cheery encounter in the Piggly Wiggly made me want to stay.

I angrily pushed a branch out of my way. "Sarcasm doesn't become you, Mildred Juniper." Mama's voice rang in my mind.

"Well, I don't care," I muttered, stomping around a stump. "I'd just like to tell them both that they are being selfish. Grown-ups! Always got to have things their way. They aren't the ones who've gotta go to school and face Violet Griffin and other girls in the sixth grade. I'm sure I'm gonna get the 'Favorite New Kid at Piedmont Ridge Elementary' trophy. Yeah. I can see that comin'."

The creek wound more to the right and I could see a clearing through the trees. Looked like it flowed right into somebody's pasture. I decided to walk on and investigate, still burning in anger and a sense of being right. Maybe I would just keep on walking. Maybe I needed to run away for good. I could hitch a ride back to Prosperity; I'll bet Beth Ann's mama would let me live with them.

My feet began a steady rhythm. Wanna go home. Wanna go home. Wanna go home, they seemed to say. I started humming it in my head as I walked faster and faster. Wanna go home, wanna go home...

Moooowhooooo ...

Some animal's baying slid right into my song. Come to think of it, I'd been breathing through my mouth because of an awful smell. What was that?

I looked up the rise to my right and saw several black and white cows coming out of a concrete barn. A gate was open and they were ambling toward that open pasture. Looked like four of them, no, there were five, six, seven, eight. Eight cows. The sun was running away, too, down the horizon faster than I expected. The cows cast long, leggy shadows on the ground and I saw the outline of a person walking to a gate, latching it soundly after the cows moseyed on into the pasture.

There was another rough trail going up from the creek to the back of that barn, and several cedar trees were spaced in such a way as to make a good hiding place. If I snuck up quickly, I could hide under that cedar nearest the back door and see what's what.

Well, I knew Mama and Daddy would not be happy with me spying, but right now, I didn't care what they thought. I was free for a minute, and this looked like an adventure. Who knew? Maybe there were some kids living here. Maybe God even sent me here.

Yeah. That's what I'd say if I got caught. God must've led me this way. Hard for them to fault that — especially Daddy. He knows all about God leading him weird places. Besides, if I kept on going to Georgia, he'd never know about this anyway.

My decision made, I hotfooted it up the hill, quietly, always placing myself behind big shrub-like bushes. My heart began beating harder, and I'm not all that sure it was just the running. I felt my breath come in shorter spurts and tried real hard to breathe quiet. It seemed like an eternity, but I finally made it to a spot of dirt under the cedar and found I had a pretty good view of the inside of the barn. It helped that it was all lit up.

Looked like there was just one person working. He was picking up strange-looking, four- pronged machines and dipping them in a bucket. Then he moved and did another. Cats meandered around his feet, and he kept stopping to pet one with the hand that wasn't holding the machines. I stood up a little to try to see around him. Surely there were other people here, and right when I stood up, he turned around, looking in my direction.

"Shoot!" I hissed under my breath. Diving back into my crouch. I held my breath, not moving a muscle. I couldn't see his face, but his head turned my way for a second, then he turned back around and grabbed the next machine.

"Phewwwww," I let my air out slow. That was close. It spooked me so bad, though, that I was ready to head back to the trailer (God forbid I ever start calling it home.).

Suddenly seeing Mama and Daddy didn't seem so bad. Maybe I'd run away another day, but I knew I'd have to wait until this man moved to another part of the barn. I'd be too much in the open if I tried to back down now.

He spent another five minutes on those machines, then took his bucket and dumped the water out next to the gate. He looked familiar to me somehow, which was odd. It wasn't like I knew anybody in this town.

Finally, he turned the lights off in that area and went through a door into a more enclosed part of the barn.

"Wait a sec, Mil, give it time," I whispered, trying to encourage myself. The sun was getting low, and I was gonna have a hard time finding that trail up to Big Star Drive in the dark.

I spun around and began walking when I heard a voice like the trumpet blast from heaven.

"Those woods are gonna be awful dark. Sure you want to go back down there?"

The hair stood up on the back of my neck, and I somehow turned around without moving anything on my body except my feet. That voice had frozen me into an ice statue — and it wasn't the voice of a man!

Chapter 10

Dot

The look on the girl's face was pure panic. Dot immediately saw it in her eyes – and the question: "Do I stay or run?"

Mildred paused, hesitating, long enough for Dot to work on coaxing her.

"You're that girl I saw in the Piggly Wiggly today, aren't you?" Dot began loping slowly down the hill. "You and your Daddy just moved into town? I saw you standing with him as he talked with Pete Griffin, that ol' codger." Dot snorted and shook her head as if to say she couldn't believe the way Pete acted. Mildred stayed frozen in a position to run, but Dot could see her body relax just a hair. She decided to continue on the same train of thought.

"Yep. It's tough movin' to a new place. I oughta know. Done some moving myself in my life, but it always turns out right if you just hang in there. Where you living?"

Mildred was in a dilemma. She knew better than to talk to strangers, but this woman wasn't really a stranger. She even remembered her name — Miz Harris. And she seemed to be one of the nicer folk in Piedmont Ridge. Besides, it'd feel rude not to answer.

"We ... uh ... we're livin' in a trailer next to the Bingo Hall," Mildred answered quietly.

"The Bingo Hall?" Dot's eyes squinted, trying to remember. "You mean next to the old Big Star Grocery? Good Lord, A'mighty, I figured that area was closed up. They running a Bingo Hall there, are they?"

"Well, the sign says 'Bingo', but Daddy's gonna start a church there." *Good grief*, Mildred thought. *What are you doin? Gonna tell this old lady your whole life?*

"A church, huh?" Dot said, easing up closer to Mildred now, feeling the trust of the girl. "Well, that's alright, I reckon. You know, sun's goin' down pretty quick. Why don't you let me drive you home? You don't want to go back down Coon Creek. It'll be too dark and I bet your Daddy's getting close to wondering where you are."

Mildred's eyes glanced at the sky and quickly returned to Dot. The old lady was right. The sun was half hidden already, and it'd be dark before she found the path up to the trailer, maybe even before that. As much as she hated to admit it, Miz Harris was right. Mildred was stuck.

"Yes'm. I guess that'd be alright."

"Good," Dot said definitively. "Let's head up to the house so I can pull on my boots, and we'll get you home quicker than you can say scat!"

As Mildred watched the small, lanky Dot Harris climb the hill toward her concrete blocked milk barn, she wondered what she had gotten herself into. Daddy wasn't gonna be real thrilled about her riding with a stranger, but maybe more forgiving than if she'd tried to walk the creek back home. Harris turned back around, "You comin'?"

Mildred shrugged off her concerns and decided it was do or die. Yep. She was coming. She huffed up behind Harris, who didn't seem winded at all, and followed her around the barn. Surprisingly, Mildred saw neatly manicured, well-worn paths winding through the back yard. A path to the barn. A branch off from that path to a pen of some sorts. Smelled like pig. Mildred spotted a curly tail around a corner. Yep. Pig, but it was obvious Miz Harris wasn't the typical, throw-stuff-anywhere, farmer. There were wildflowers growing in a large, circular bed near the back door of her house.

"Come on in for a sec," Dot said as she opened the back screen door. "Got to get these boots off and slip on my others. Think you ought to call your Daddy and let him know where you are?"

Mildred entered cautiously, her wide blue eyes taking in the small room with stacked shelves laden with jars of every sort of vegetable and fruit. Canned tomatoes, green beans, butterbeans, peaches, apples ... and okra. Mildred's nose wrinkled.

"We don't have a phone," Mildred answered, slight embarrassment crowding her face.

"Not a problem. We'll just jump in the truck and be at your house before you'd get to dialing good."

Milk boots shed, work boots back on, Dot thumped into the kitchen to grab the truck keys that dangled from a wooden knob above a black telephone. It sat solidly on a small hall table.

"Let's head on out the front door; it'd be quicker," Dot said over her shoulder. Mildred continued to follow through the small, immaculate house. She saw an old, black leather recliner positioned by the front window with an enormous stack of books on its right. A tattered ottoman sat cock-eyed in front of it and cream-colored lace curtains lifted and paused as Dot pulled open the front door. Odd, Mildred thought. Miz Harris didn't strike her as a lacy kind of lady.

Three dogs slightly stirred as Mildred stepped onto the wooden front porch. "Watch out, Porthos," Dot said irritably, stepping over the bloodhound. "Got to get around these dogs. I'd hate for them to be displaced or anything." Mildred followed suit, stepping over the big dog. He never lifted his head, but she thought she saw one eyeball lazily pop open.

They continued, single-file, in a fast pace to the shed where Dot's double-headlighted Chevy truck was parked. Mildred was a little afraid to venture farther. Looked to her like the truck might be holding up the shed. But Dot forged on, jumped into the driver's side and slammed the door with energy. Mildred moved to the passenger side and found she couldn't get the door open. She pulled, pulled harder, then jerked with all her eighty-five pound strength. Nothing.

"Oh, yeah. Sorry 'bout that," Dot said, leaning over the seat. She expertly lifted the latch and the door swung open. "Thing's been broken from the outside for a few years. Never had any use to get her fixed. Nobody ever rides with me." Mildred looked into her face, wondering if that made Dot sad, yet Dot didn't seem at all perturbed by her revelation. Inwardly shrugging, Mildred pulled the door shut and prepared for the ride home.

As the truck lumbered out to Route 56, Mildred let her head hang out the window, relishing the feel of fresh air blowing through her sweaty hair. Dot noticed the girl leaning out, turning her face toward the wind, and didn't say anything. She didn't know what problems ailed her. Who knew what ailed young people these days? Dot returned her attention to driving, telling herself that she didn't care to know her problems.

Mildred loved the feel of the air and looked to the ground, watching the wide, white- painted lines weave around clumps of grass that were growing beside the road. She wished she could ride forever, that she wouldn't have to face Mama and Daddy and that Miz Harris would take her farther and farther away.

They were passing the Piggly Wiggly within a minute and Dot turned left onto Walnut, sure of where she was going. Big Star Drive loomed ahead before Mil could blink, and Dot swung the pickup down the isolated road. The dim light bulb at the front door of the trailer was already lit for the night as they approached. Several cars sat in the driveway, and Sam Rhodes' head popped out before Dot had geared down to a stop. He ran his fingers through his hair, pinning the long bangs back in an effort to see better who was pulling in. Mildred took a deep breath and opened the door.

As he spotted the purple tennis shoe easing out from the side door, Sam bolted out, skipping the three steps to the path and raced toward the truck.

"Mil? Mil?" he yelled as he crossed the yard. "Is that you, baby?"

"Yes, sir," Mildred squeaked out as she was embraced and swung around. Dot sat in the truck, watching with interest.

"Where've you been?" he asked rapidly as he placed her carefully back on her feet. "Me and your Mama have been worried sick! Don't you ever do that to us again, you hear?"

Mildred hung her head in shame. She had been so wrapped up in her own world, she never really thought about how her Mama and Daddy must've been feeling. Sam looked around, gazing curiously into the truck.

"Ma'am? I appreciate you bringing Mildred Juniper on home. It's not like her to run like this..." Sam again pulled his hand through his hair, unsure where to go from there. Dot felt for him.

"Oh, that's alright," she said. "I'm Dot Harris. Mildred and I met up at my farm. She's been fine, no harm done."

"Well, we're new in town and I reckon Mil might've gotten lost in her exploring."

Mildred didn't speak, didn't look at Dot or her daddy. The silence felt heavy and awkward; Dot took that as her cue.

"Yep. I'm sure that's what happened. Anyways, I got to get back to my animals." Dot pushed the floppy fisherman's hat back off her forehead, put her truck in reverse and eased out of the driveway before Mildred had a chance to really say thank you. She watched the rust flake off again as Dot pulled away.

Chapter 11

Mildred

Dot's leaving felt abrupt to Mildred, and she wished she wouldn't go.

"Come on in. I gotta let the others know we found you," Daddy began walking toward the front porch stoop.

"Others?" I dragged my feet, dreading what was coming. "What others?"

Daddy turned around slowly, looking a little older than he had when I left, and stared at me like I'd grown three heads.

"Well, what'd ya think we'd do when you didn't come home? Just wait on you to make your way back?" His voice began to rise a little. "I hollered for you and walked back behind the trailer a ways but didn't know which way you went. So we called Elder Crenshaw, who brought Elder Thomas and his wife. We were about to go out searching for you. I gotta tell you, Mil, this wasn't the way I wanted our first real day in Piedmont Ridge to go. I'm glad you're home, honey, but you haven't heard the last of this." Daddy spun around to the front door where I could see a short colored lady peering through the curtain. "Come on."

It was hard to think clear. I took my time as I headed toward the trailer, trying to decide on my plan of action. I knew I needed to explain how I came up on Miz Harris and how time got away from me, but explaining was going to be hard with those church people here. Daddy held open the screen door for me to walk into the living room. It was a sorry sight that greeted me.

Elder Crenshaw, his big hair in an even bigger mess than last night, stood in the doorway of the kitchen with a flashlight in his hand. Elder Thomas stood on his right, apparently ready to fly out the door to come find me. Honestly, they looked like Andy Griffith and Barney – if you take away the color difference. But the sight of Mama sitting in her chair caught my eye. Shame washed over me when I realized how I must have frightened her. Still, nothing had changed, and I just felt torn in two and mixed up and... Mama held out her arms and I gave in to them. I ran over to her, falling beside her chair and, seeing her tears, couldn't hold back my own.

I vaguely heard sounds of the door shutting and Daddy's voice out in the yard, soothing, kind and apologetic. Mama kept "tsking" and handing me Kleenex after Kleenex. When Daddy came in a few minutes later, I felt somewhat better and had a stack of dirty tissues on the table. Mama's eyes looked tired, red-rimmed and I realized again how my short disappearance had upset her. I was trying to get rid of those crying hiccups when Daddy pulled up a bucket and sat down next to us. I lay next to Mama, crammed in between her and the arm of the recliner.

"Mildred Juniper, what do you have to say for yourself?" Daddy asked.

"I don't know."

"Where have you been?"

"I ran down the gully to the creek to think. Then I took a trail by the creek, but I got distracted by this cow and farm and then I saw this man milking cows, only it wasn't a man, it was really a woman. And she was milking and she saw me and ..." I realized I was rambling, but didn't know how to shut it off. "And she hollered at me and it ended up being Miz Harris, that lady stacking milk bottles that we saw at the grocery store today?"

Daddy and Mama just stared at me. So I went on.

"Anyway, she told me it was too late to walk back home – and it was – and she said she'd bring me home. And I figured it wasn't like she was a stranger, after all, and it'd be better if I rode with her than to get lost on that trail. She was real nice and had lots of animals and a nice house." My words trailed off awkwardly.

"Mildred. Your Mama and I realize you're upset with our decision to stay in Piedmont Ridge, and we wanted to give you some space to think and pray. But we feel you took advantage of that today and broke our trust in you. Not to mention, you did a very dangerous thing. Don't you understand that you could be lost right now or worse?"

Daddy's blue eyes intensified and bore into mine. I saw that I had hurt them, but it didn't change the way I felt.

"Yes, sir."

"Well, I'm not sure how we're going to handle this. You'll have to be punished in some way, but I need to sleep on it," Daddy mused. He looked at Mama. "Maybe your Mama and me can talk some later."

Mama flashed her wonderful, peaceful smile. "Mil, honey, why don't you go get your pajamas and hop in the tub? Your Daddy and I'll talk things over and, after all, tomorrow's a new day, isn't it?"

I looked at both of them and fell in love with my Mama and Daddy all over again. As I eased off the chair and walked back toward my room, I heard their voices begin to mingle, rising and falling, and thought how crazy I was to even think about running away. Why would I ever leave them? How quickly I had forgotten my vow to be the helper that Mama needed, to stick with her while Daddy was on his rampage to be a preacher. I remembered that verse that talked about how Jesus set his face like flint to go to Jerusalem where he would be crucified. Well, I, too, could set my face like flint, to make it as long as I needed to in this God-Awful Place.

Chapter 12

Mildred

The next day was Friday, only five days away from school starting, and I was getting more and more jittery by the day. But this morning, Daddy took away the jitters by doling out my punishment. It could have been way worse. I reckon Mama must've talked Daddy down some because all I had to do was plant daffodil bulbs. Mama had insisted that even though it wasn't the proper season to plant, we put in bulbs and hope and pray that the Lord would draw them out of the ground come spring. My prayer was different than Mama's. I just prayed we wouldn't be there to see them if they did grow.

So Daddy and me again hopped in the Malibu – this time destined for the local farmer's co-op. Elder Crenshaw told Daddy it was a far piece out Walnut Street, so we hung a left at the stop sign and followed the road for a few miles.

Piedmont Ridge was such a little bitty place. Prosperity at least had a Dairy Queen where I could get my favorite double-dip cone, chocolate and vanilla mixed. I hadn't seen anyplace like that in Piedmont Ridge. When Miz Harris drove me through town last evening, I had spotted a line outside Deb's Chicken n' Such that stretched near to Piggly Wiggly across the street. But nobody coming out of Deb's was licking a cone. Probably just sold fried chicken.

Daddy bumped over a railroad track that ran right beside a one-roomed, clapboard building. A crooked wooden sign reading "Marley's General Store" hung on the side and underneath, painted in terribly faded red paint, were the words, "Fresh Ice Creme." I'm figuring Mr. Marley may not have finished his schooling, and by the looks of Marley's, I'm not so sure that whatever was there would be all that fresh. Still, might be worth a try.

"Daddy?" I alerted him to the store as we passed.

"Hmm?"

"Marley's store says it has ice cream. You think we could try it on the way back from the co-op?"

Daddy glanced at me, his eyes registering my presence, but I wasn't sure he heard what I said. He looked really tired this morning, even though we all had gone to bed early the night before. There were dark circles under his eyes. His black hair was clean and still wet from the shower — still it was tousled, wind-blown, I guess. But he kept running his hands through it, too. That didn't help much.

"Ice cream? Well, maybe so, Mil. We'll see."

And I lost him again. He turned back toward the road, deep in thought. I still felt guilty that I had brought all this on him – I mean, the dark-circled eyes and all. Mama was extra tired this morning, too. We left her sleeping in bed. She had given the orders on the number of daffodil bulbs to get – at least 100 – and fell back in bed. I didn't figure we had money to go spending on daffodil bulbs, but Daddy must've thought it was important. Maybe that was why he was so quiet. Maybe it was money.

We had gone about three miles from the town limits when we saw the Marion County Farmers Co-operative on the left. Seemed like thousands of pick-up trucks, tractors and trailers sat every-which-a-way in the parking lot. Since it was dirt, there were no real spaces anyway, so Daddy pulled the car in as straight as he could. Several old-timers were sitting out front on rocking chairs that had price tags stuck to the legs of the rockers. I didn't expect they'd be buying them. Daddy nodded politely as he approached the door. A chorus of "Mornin's" rang out as the old guy on the far left spit a stream of wood-colored tobacco juice into the dirt beside him. I immediately checked the ground in front of me. There were few worse things than stepping in fresh tobacco spit, even if you did have shoes on. I padded on past.

A familiar smell hit me the minute we entered and it took me back to Georgia. Seed, feed, sack-cloth smells. I breathed in deeply, closing my eyes. This was almost ecstasy. Daddy headed straight for the bulb section, which actually surprised me. I knew he could spend days in a store like this – in fact, I was already prepared to be bored, but he acted like a man on a mission, so I followed.

"'Scuse me, ma'am?"

A colored lady wearing a red vest walked briskly toward us.

"Yas, sir?" she questioned — polite, but busy.

"Would you happen to have any daffodil bulbs on hand?"

"Hmm. We just might....you do know that this ain't the time to be plantin' no daffodils. It's best to plant those later in the fall." She spoke with an air of authority bred from years of co-op experience. I was a little awed by her. Daddy sighed and smiled.

"Yes'm, I realize that, too. But we're new in town and my wife just won't be settled until we can get some daffodils planted around the house. I'm just doing the best I can to make her happy."

She smiled widely then, her deep dimples making her round face look complete.

"You's a seasoned husband, then, knowin' how to make yo' woman happy. Come on back in here and let's see what we kin round up fer ya."

We dutifully followed her into a back room that was cooler than the rest of the store. Cardboard boxes full of bulbs, seed and other co-op type items covered the floors and shelves. The co-op lady leaned down and began inspecting the unlabeled bulbs. I suppose all tags had fallen off by this time. Daddy and I hung back, letting her browse freely. Finally, she stood up groaning and stretching her back out. She still had a smile on her face though.

"Found 'um. They's prob'bly close to two hundret in here. How many ya thinkin' ya need?"

"Well, Laura Lee wants one hundred. How 'bout that? How much are they anyway?"

Mary Rose – her nametag read – scratched her head.

"Seems like these oughta be on sale, left over from last season, don't cha know. Let me check with the manager. I think we kin work ya a deal."

"Oh, that'd be super." Daddy sounded relieved.

"Come on this way and I'll find a boy to count out your bulbs." Mary Rose was off in a flash, down the aisle, talking as she walked.

"Y'all new in town? What brought ya to the Ridge?"

Isn't that the question of the week? I thought. Here we go again. I began lagging behind, looking for anything on sale in the co-op to preoccupy me from the coming storm. Daddy must've had similar thoughts 'cause he wasn't as quick to respond as he had been in the Piggly Wiggly.

"We moved up from Georgia for the work."

"Yeah? What kind o' work?" Mary Rose picked up the loud speaker microphone. "Mr. Anderson, Mr. Anderson. You needed in the front. Mr. Anderson." She plopped the mic back by the cash register and turned to face Daddy squarely. I had the feeling he wasn't going to be able to dodge Mary Rose.

"Um. Church work." Daddy started looking intently at the screws on the shelf beside him.

"Really?" Mary Rose looked interested. Then a light lit in her face and her smile grew even larger – which I didn't think was possible. "Hey. You ain't Mr. Rhodes, is ya? You comin' to the Piedmont Ridge Community Church?"

I ventured a look at Daddy. I knew we were done for, so did he.

"Well, sure, that's right. That'd be me. Sam Rhodes," and he held out his hand to her. You would have thought Mary Rose just won the Reader's Digest Sweepstakes. She completely pushed Daddy's hand aside and swept him up in the biggest bear hug you ever did see. Mary Rose was almost as big around as she was tall, and I think she lifted Daddy's feet off the ground. He grunted, turned red and politely tried to unhook her arms. It was hysterical. I began giggling, just couldn't help it.

"God bless ya, Mr. Rhodes. Oh, I'm so thrilled to meet 'cha. Wait'll I tell Stew that I gots to meet the new pastor before he did.

Oh, he's gonna be fit to be tied. Ha!" She let out a giant whoop and let Daddy go. He desperately tried to restore his dignity while Mary Rose was looking past him...and eyeballing me! Oh Lord.

"And who might you be, you precious thang?" She moved closer. I began to move behind Daddy.

"Mildred Juniper," I whispered.

"Why, honey chile, you is the spittin' image of yo Daddy. Come here and lets me give you a hug," and Mary Rose tackled me from the side, sweeping me up into the grandest, most fulfilling hug I ever got. She smelled like honeysuckle, garden tomatoes and cow feed all mixed together. It was truly lovely. If I hadn't been half smothering to death in her bosom, I would have liked to stay there. Mary Rose felt safe and I hadn't felt very safe for days. All too soon, the hug was over and I reeled back like Daddy did, trying to straighten my clothes.

Daddy found his voice again.

"I take it you belong to the Community Church?"

"I sho does, Pastor Rhodes. My Stew and me been part of the church for well-nigh two years now. 'Course, we been meetin' in folks' homes and all. Havin' you come on full-time and gettin' the ol' Bingo Hall is 'bout more than we all can fathom. We been feelin' the Spirit o' the Lawd movin' in a mighty way..." When Mary Rose said "mighty," it felt like a breeze blew through the co-op. She meant mighty! "We been prayin' and seekin' and callin' out to tha Lawd for His will and His power to come to Piedmont Ridge. Pastor Rhodes. We think you is the answer for us and for this town. It's a mighty thing, you comin' all the way from Georgia, and I don't mind tellin' ya that I'm 'bout as excited as a body can get."

Mary Rose's face was full of life and passion, and her hands almost knocked down that store mic several times as she spoke. There was no way to doubt her sincerity. She was pretty overwhelming, but I liked her. Daddy did too. It felt good to be needed, wanted and even prayed for.

A boy about my age, wearing one of those red co-op vests, ventured toward Mary Rose with a question on his face.

I wondered if he was her son.

"'Scuse me, Miz Mary Rose? Mr. Carter's askin' if it's too late to plant his fall lettuce and I don't know what ta tell him."

Mary Rose swung toward the boy, joy marking every movement, and grabbed him by the front of the vest.

"Gregory! Do you know who this is?"

Gregory looked at me and Daddy, confused.

"No'm."

"This here's Pastor Rhodes and his daughter Mildred Juniper. What do ya think about that?"

Gregory's face changed quickly, realization lighting his features, and he turned toward Daddy with a quick smile, hand extended.

"Hi, Pastor Rhodes. It's good to meet 'cha. My daddy's Daryl Thomas."

"So you're Daryl's boy, Gregory. Well, what a surprise! Your daddy's been saying some awful nice things about you. And I believe you and Mildred are close to the same age, Mildred?" Daddy turned my way. "Can you say howdy to Gregory?"

"Hi." I smiled and slid a little more behind Daddy. Gregory was taller than me and even skinnier. I didn't think that was possible for anyone, least of all a boy. His black curly hair was cut closely to his head, and – come to think of it – he had that same beautiful smile as his daddy. His skin was a chocolate brown and I immediately thought Martha Claire would have a fit. She always hated it that her skin was so dark.

"Hi, Mildred. Nice to meet 'cha."

Gregory didn't seem shy at all, but he did seem persistent.

"Miz Mary Rose. I'm sorry but Mr. Carter's waitin'. When's the best time to plant fall lettuce?"

"Oh Lawd a' mercy, that man goin' drive me crazy. He always forgettin' thangs. He too old to be doing a garden. Let me go to him. Gregory, I need you to go count out one hundret daffodil bulbs for Pastor. They're in the box, far back right corner. Next to the corn seed. And when Mr. Anderson gets here – if he ever gets here! – ask him to give them a deal, alright?"

Mary Rose spun toward the front of the store.

"I gotta go, but I'll see you'uns real soon. Ha! Stew is gonna be so mad!" And Mary Rose left, laughing out loud and stomping every other step. Daddy began following Gregory.

"She always like that?" Daddy asked.

"Sir? Oh, Miz Mary Rose? Yes, sir. She always happy, always laughin' 'bout something. She and Mr. Stew always helpin' people out too – one way or ta other."

"Mr. Stew?"

"Yes, sir. That'd be her husband. They call him Stew on account of him makin' the best catfish stew in Marion County." Daddy grinned at that.

"Oh yeah?" he said.

"Yes, sir. You'll see." Gregory turned and winked. I smiled back. I decided I liked Gregory and maybe he would be a friend. He helped us lug our bulbs to the checkout desk where an overweight, red-faced man stood behind an old cash register.

"They got a hundret bulbs, Mr. Anderson," Gregory said, huffing and straightening up.

"Anythin' else we can get you folks?" the manager smiled, ignoring Gregory who turned and skipped away like the wind.

"No," Daddy paused, "well, maybe some of this chap stick." He picked up a clear golden tube out of a brown shoe box on the counter. "Coon Creek Critters' Lip Balm? Never heard of it. Is it any good?"

Mr. Anderson's face broke out into a smile, revealing only one missing tooth. "It's the best stuff you'll ever find. Why our own Dee Whipple makes it out of her beeswax. All local, ya know, but quality. Ever since I started usin' it, my lips never get chapped."

I started to look carefully at his lips when he said that, but I realized pretty quick that part of his lunch was still trapped between his teeth. Instead, I investigated the floor.

"Good enough," Daddy answered, unperturbed by Mr. Anderson's teeth. "We'll take three."

.

Chapter 13

Mildred

I honestly didn't think this many daffodil bulbs could fit in our puny little trailer yard. Mama told me to keep them in the front area, with trails of bulbs going to each side. She wanted an extra cluster around the tin, silver-painted mailbox and two large groups on either side of the front stoop. Daddy handed me the shovel and told me to have fun. It wasn't long before I realized just how harsh my punishment was. I had already spent three hours in the August sun – digging, burying and refilling – and I was only half-way done. I looked up again at the empty blue sky, hoping for one teensy weensy cloud to cover me over, but it was no use. I couldn't buy a cloud today.

"Mildred, come on in for supper. You can go back to work after you eat," Daddy hollered from the inside of the trailer. With the door wide open and a fan rotating at the entrance, there wasn't a need to walk outside to call. I stood up, wiped the sweat off my face – again – and began trudging inside. I understood this weather. The heat wouldn't break until nightfall and that was an hour away. Every once in a while, we'd hear a roll of thunder from somewhere far off, but nothing ever surfaced here.

I pulled off my tennis shoes at the door, catching a whiff of fried bream. Elder Crenshaw had brought a fresh batch over earlier in the day. "Fish so good it'll make you want to slap yo' Mama," he had said with a laugh and a wink. I didn't know about all that, but I could tell Daddy had used his special seasoning. Hunger rolled around in my belly as I rounded the corner in the kitchen. The fish, home-cooked French fries and hush puppies were neatly stacked in a row on our counter. Daddy smiled broadly and handed me a plate.

"You get to go first tonight, Mil. You've been workin' the hardest."

Well. He was right about that. Mama smiled from her chair. Daddy had already set up the TV tray beside her, but her plate wasn't fixed yet. I guess he meant it, so I loaded up.

We all piled in our living room, digging into the fish like we hadn't eaten in weeks. Even Mama ate more than usual. I sat on the floor, plate resting on the overturned bucket, legs crossed under me. Mama and Daddy were talking church talk. I was so tired I let my mind wander until I heard Daddy say something about tonight.

"What's happenin' tonight?" I managed to get out between bites. Daddy paused for a moment, apparently remembering I was in the room.

"Just the elders coming over to talk about our first church service in the Bingo Hall."

I thought on that a minute.

"Don't they want to hear you preach or somethin' before they pay us money and give you the job?" Actually that thought had just occurred to me and it gave me a faint spark of hope that hadn't been there two minutes ago. Daddy taught a few times at Friendship Bible Church in Prosperity, but I'd never paid much attention. After watching him a minute or two, I'd go back to reading or writing notes to Beth Ann. I had no idea if he was a good preacher or not...but maybe he wasn't. If they didn't like him, they might fire him before he got started good. I felt my heart lift. Then leaving wouldn't even be my fault.

"They already heard me speak lots of times." Daddy absentmindedly pulled a piece of a bone from between his teeth.

"What? How?"

"Reel-to-reel tape recording, of course. Fitz recorded my messages and sent them on up here. They already know how I preach." My face fell, but Daddy didn't notice. "So they're coming over to talk to me and your Mama. I figure you got enough daffodils to plant that you won't be bothered by us. They oughta be gone by the time you finish up."

"What about the black/white thing? I didn't think you wanted to be in a church with coloreds and whites."

"What makes you think that?" Daddy glanced up but didn't seem perturbed by my question.

"You seemed awful surprised when you saw Elder Thomas – but not in a good surprised way," I dragged out the word good. Before Daddy could respond, Mama laughed and interrupted.

"I figure that's why the Good Lord made your Daddy color blind, Mil."

"Very funny, Laura Lee," Daddy said, rolling his eyes, but I giggled, noticing his clothes actually matched tonight. Mama must've helped. "You don't need to worry your pretty little head about that, Mildred. God's color blind, too," Daddy stood up, taking his plate to the kitchen.

"Now, they oughta be here in about thirty minutes, so come help me get the kitchen cleaned."

"Mildred," Mama spoke.

"Ma'am?"

"Be sure to tidy up after your Daddy in the kitchen and make it look homey in there. Sometimes these men don't rightly know how to fold the dishtowel or wring out the washrag," Mama smiled. Her color looked better this afternoon, so I felt better while Daddy pretended to be offended and huffed off.

"How's planting them daffodils going?" Mama's green eyes lit up with interest as she leaned forward in her chair. I picked up her half-empty plate from the TV stand while answering.

"It's hot – real hot – but okay."

"I just can't wait to see them in the springtime, Mil. Just picture it." I hesitated in my walk, watching Mama's tired face suddenly look alive, bright, eager. "We'll have beautiful, yellow daffodils leading the way to our home, like a signpost or a single trail in the woods, promising hidden beauty around the corner..."

"Yeah, only this trailer ain't beautiful."

Mama's face fell and her shoulders sagged. Me and my big mouth.

"Mama, I'm sorry, I..."

"No. It's alright, Mildred. Go help your Daddy now." And Mama laid back, closing her eyes. I couldn't believe I said that. What was the matter with me? Mama found one thing that made her happy and I snatched it away. What kind of a daughter was I?

I joined Daddy at the sink. He didn't notice my silence and handed me the drying towel. He washed and I dried while Mama slowly eased down the hall to the bathroom.

It only took a few minutes to get the place tidy. We still had boxes stacked everywhere, but they were stacked neatly. Mama came back in, wearing the same house dress but with some rouge on her cheeks. Her hair looked nice, pulled back tight the way she liked it. It looked a whole lot better since we washed it yesterday! She had a pink scarf tied around the ponytail, and if she wasn't wearing bedroom slippers and a robe, she'd have been beautiful. Gravel crunched in the drive, and Daddy slipped over to the front door to shift the fan so the elders wouldn't trip as they came in.

Elder Crenshaw walked in first, smiling and grabbing Daddy in a giant bear hug. Then Elder Thomas entered in his quiet way. His handshake looked firm and strong, and he caught my eye and walked over to me first.

"Mildred Juniper, I hear you met Gregory today at the co-op," his voice peacefully rolled out.

"Yes, sir."

"Well, I hope you don't mind, but I brung Gregory along with me tonight. He wasn't busy and was lookin' fer something to do."

About then, Gregory entered the trailer looking a tad more shy than he had earlier in the day. I was about to explain to Elder Thomas that I appreciated that, but I had daffodils to plant and wouldn't be much fun to play with when Gregory spoke up.

"Hi Mildred. I'll bet you gots lots o' daffodils to plant. Thought I'd come along and see if I could help," Gregory smiled a smile as perfect as his Daddy's and his eyes twinkled. I know they did. I didn't know who had told the Thomases about my fate, but obviously the cat was out of the bag. Still, it was nice of Gregory to come and I didn't want to be rude. I smiled back and thanked him, figuring it'd go faster anyway with two working. Gregory and I moseyed back outside while Daddy ran around trying to find places for everyone to sit. I wondered why Gregory's mama didn't come since she was here the night before, but I didn't want to ask that yet. You never knew about some people, what might be going on, and I wasn't one to jump into a lot of questions before I knew what was what.

That late summer evening cool-down had begun in the last hour. It was the time of day when the temperature gauge still read 85 degrees, but it felt cool compared to the 98 degrees of a few hours before. I hesitated, enjoying the feel of the outside, then groaned as I walked toward the bulb box.

"What is it?"

Gregory must've heard me.

"Oh nuthin'. I'm just tired of plantin', that's all."

"Yeah. I reckon you are. How many more ya got?"

"About half."

"Ah, we can knock that out in no time." Gregory's positive attitude stopped me short this time.

"Aren't you ever grumpy?" I asked impatiently. Gregory just laughed.

"Sho I am. Remember that Mr. Carter I was talkin' about at the co-op today?"

"Uh huh." I grabbed a bulb and pushed it in the ground.

"That man gets on my last nerve. He calls me 'Boy' and acts like I ain't got no sense at t'all." Gregory picked up the shovel and started digging – hard. "He tells me to 'Get this' and 'Get that' and 'Take this to my car' with not nary a thank you." He stabbed the shovel into the dry dirt.

"Why don't you tell Miz Mary Rose 'bout it?"

"Oh, she know it. He treats her 'bout as bad."

"How come?" I stopped planting for a second, watching Gregory's face change. He stared at me.

"What d'ya mean, how come? Why do you think?"

I dropped my eyes.

"'Cause you're colored..."

"Heck, yeah, that's why!" His eyes blazed and his gentle countenance hardened, then grew soft again. "Don't you know how folks treat us colored people, Mildred? It's ain't that easy bein' a Negro, ya know."

"Yeah, I know," I said, thinking of Martha Claire. And suddenly it seemed very important that Gregory knew that's not how I was. "But I don't think that, Gregory."

His laugh returned – as bright and clean as ever. "I know that, Mildred Juniper, else yo' Daddy wouldn't be my pastor."

And that was when it all changed for me. It was like I heard this "click" in my head, or maybe the changing of a gear. Whatever it was, I was different. Gregory's laugh felt like refreshing rain on the dry ground of my soul, and all the energy I had built up over having to move and running away and meeting rude people in grocery stores – all that energy started to fade away like clouds at sunset.

But I didn't put all that together 'till later. Right then, I just laughed with Gregory. We laughed and laughed like I hadn't laughed since I was with Martha Claire.

When the last bulb was covered up, my legs felt like rubber bands. The grown-ups were still talking inside the trailer, but I noticed someone had turned on the porch light. Gregory and me stumbled toward the stoop and plopped on the top step. Hands washed in the water hose next to the door, we felt about as clean as we could. I sat in the quiet, feeling tiredness in my bones. Gregory, on the other hand, was quite alert.

"Been over there yet?" he asked, jerking his head toward the Bingo Hall.

"Nope. Why should I? It's locked, ain't it?"

"Yeah. But it's got a big picture window. Let's go look inside," he jumped to his feet.

"Hadn't you been in there already?" I was in no hurry to stand.

"Naw. Come on, Mildred," he grabbed my arm, hauling me to my feet. Boys! I took a last glance at the trailer. Daddy's face could be seen clearly through the front window, his brows furrowed. He obviously was asking a question. Didn't look like they were winding down at all.

"Oh, alright."

I trudged along, crossing the dead-end circle and walking through the large, empty parking lot of the Bingo Hall. The building looked dark and gloomy and I shivered in spite of the heat. Gregory ran on ahead and reached the windows before I did. Cupping his hands over his eyes, he peered into the darkness eagerly. I joined him, staring intently into the room. I could barely make out a large, empty front area. Styrofoam cups littered the floor and a few tables were spread around. Nothing of interest here. Gregory must've thought the same thing 'cause he cut it to the right side of the building. It wasn't as well-lit and I hesitated.

"Mildred, come on!" Gregory insisted. I dragged along behind, not feeling so good about this. I didn't like the dark.

He ran around the side, disappearing from my view for a second. I tagged along and rounded the corner, almost running smack into him. He had stopped on the edge of the building. His chocolate face looked a little pale in the light from the streetlamp and he was crouching behind an old dumpster.

"Shhhhhhh!" he hushed me quickly. I skidded to a stop, not breathing.

"What is it?" I whispered.

"Don't know. Saw somethin'." Gregory crouched lower and I did likewise. We stared together toward the long, dark shadows that framed the back of the building. I couldn't hear or see a thing. After a good thirty seconds, I ventured to speak again.

"Well, what did you think it was?"

"Quiet," he whispered, raising his hand to motion silence. It was then that I saw what had shushed him. A stooped-over man stepped out from the woods, turning back for a second to fasten a rusty bike to the tree beside him. He lugged a well-used brown paper grocery bag that looked full and heavy. Suddenly, he glanced our way sharply, as if he, too, heard an odd noise. Gregory and me held our breath. After staring intently for several seconds, he looked toward the back door of the Bingo Hall. His crusty face seemed worn and tired and very dirty, but his eyes were sharp and alert. I had the feeling he wasn't as old as he seemed.

He reached the door and nudged an old brick with his foot. It slid away from the base of the door, which allowed it to simply fall open. He moved again, the bag shifted awkwardly, and some onions dropped out. Odd thing was, the onions still had dirt on them. Then a carrot rolled out as he leaned down to pick up the onions. Obviously, his bag was full of fresh summer vegetables but not all were store bought or even sold at a roadside stand. I didn't know of any stand that would sell onions without cleaning them off a little. The carrots seemed fairly clean. Gregory looked at me, raising his eyebrows. He had noticed it too.

We looked back just in time to see the door shut quietly. Sounds of chirping crickets returned and it was as though nothing unusual had happened. Gregory jabbed me in the ribs and we ran back toward the trailer quickly and quietly, making sure not to cross front of the windows.

We covered the parking lot in less than a minute, falling in a heap behind some bushes next to our front stoop. Then we peered out and stared intently toward the Bingo Hall, gasping for air.

"Who – do – you — think that – was?" I managed to eke out.

"Got no idea," Gregory panted. "But I'll bet he's got no place to live."

"Ya think he's dangerous?" Fear crowded my mind. After all, I was the one living only a few steps away.

"Naw, but it's a real mystery, Mildred," he said, standing to his feet. "You've got a mystery at the Bingo Hall and I want to solve it."

"You've read too many Hardy Boys books," I stated.

"Naw...next time I come over in the daytime, we're going explorin'," Gregory declared.

"We can't do that," I said emphatically, "we've got to tell Daddy and your daddy. They can find out what's going on."

"We cain't tell them," Gregory declared. "Then they'll kick 'im out and he'll have no place to stay."

"My Daddy won't," I insisted.

"He won't have a choice. You know, Mil. They's all sorts o' city and county rules 'bout livin' in places you ain't supposed to. Yo' Daddy'll tell somebody, then before you knows it, they'll come and throw him out – or worse! Put him in jail!" Gregory's face worked up the more he considered it. "We gotta keep this to ourselves."

"But..." I hesitated, not sure what other argument to make, but I didn't like this secret road Gregory was going down. "I've got to tell. What if he is dangerous? Then we could get killed or something." Gregory stared at me like I'd lost my mind.

"Killed? Killed?" he repeated. "Mil, that old man couldn't kill a fly. Let's just give it a day or two, okay? I'll snatch some food from Mama's kitchen in the morning and bring it over to that back door. I'll guarantee he'll get it and be glad. Maybe we can be his friends, then get 'im some help. I just need to think. You gotta promise me you won't tell. Not yet."

"I don't know..." I was weakening and Gregory knew it.

"Oh come on, Mildred, you..." We heard the sound of parents moving toward the front door. We hurried from behind the bushes, appearing innocent and hard-working by the time Daddy stuck his head out the door.

"Oh, there you two are. Gregory, 'bout ready to go home?"

"Yas, sir," Gregory flashed his smile and watched his daddy walk out on the stoop.

"So Sam, we'll be lookin' at a start-up in two weeks, the last Sunday of August. That'll give us time to advertise and promote and let folks know. Let's meet agin in a few days..."

"Absolutely!" Elder Crenshaw's voice boomed from the interior of the trailer. "We need to pray and fast for what the Lord's gonna do on our start-up Sunday. How 'bout gathering after church this Sunday? Sam?"

The grown-ups continued their planning while my mind went back to Gregory, who was by this time winking at me profusely.

Elder Thomas walked toward his car, still talking with his arm around Gregory's shoulders.

"See you later, Mildred," Gregory said loudly. "Let's play again together – real soon!" He pointed toward the Bingo Hall, smiling a broad smile as he sat in the front seat. My stomach turned.

Daddy came out and put his arm on my shoulders as Elder Crenshaw got in his car. He kept on talking and yelling out his car window the whole time he turned around in the driveway. Then he hollered going down the road. I looked up at Daddy who was trying to control his laughter.

"I'll bet Tom Crenshaw has a hard time sittin' in the stillness and presence of the Lord," Daddy remarked as we walked toward the house. "Wonder what it takes to get him quiet?" Daddy chuckled, pulling me into the warmth and security of the dirty brown trailer at the dead end of Big Star Drive.

Chapter 14

Dot

Dot might have forgotten about school starting that morning if she hadn't heard "Slick Willie" on WUWP-AM reminding parents to get their kids to the bus stop fifteen minutes early. Her late '50s model radio crackled and sputtered each time the pitch of his voice elevated.

"Goooooooood mornin', Piedmont Ridge. And gooooooood gracious! Can you'uns believe that we got us here another school year taking off? My own Lucy's son, Nate, will be out there fer the first time this year. Yep. Got me a grandson headin' directly over to the Ridge Elementary. Good luck to all the young'uns listn' in this mornin'."

Dot only half paid attention as she double checked the back left teat on Meg. The holstein had caught it on the barbed-wire fence last week, and although it was healing nicely, Dot didn't want to assume all was well. She prodded and squeezed, watching Meg's gentle, black-and-white face. The cow merely glanced at Dot before returning to her grain.

"Atta girl, Meg," Dot said, stretching up slowly. "You look to be pretty well near healed. We'll be milkin' on that side in a few days." Slick Willie's voice continued to rattle through the barn.

"..and don't 'chu be forgettin' to find your own tube of Coon Creek Critters' Lip Balm at the Marion County Co-op – your one-stop store for all your farmin' needs. Now, ya know, Piedmont Ridge folk, it seems like only yestyday that my own children were headin' back to school. My how time flies..."

And suddenly Dot was in another time, standing at the front door, holding out a brown lunch bag filled with sandwiches for

Leslie's lunch. And Leslie was there, looking like she always did in Dot's memory – tall, lanky, freckled, serious yet not, sad yet happy. Always a paradox, was Leslie, especially for a little girl. When Dot and Tom had found Leslie – or rather, she found them — she had been only six years old. Yet Leslie had seemed more mature than many thirty year olds Dot knew. As the years passed, Leslie grew in stature, but her heart and spirit stayed the same. The same, simple, profound girl that had stood on their doorstep, saying that she was gonna be their daughter now. Very matter of fact, she had been, and the years had begun to roll in earnest – from fall to winter, to spring and back to summer. Leslie had been there, growing, learning, carrying lunches, hauling hay to the barn, and always laughing, loving and spreading sunshine every place her foot landed.

"...now my grandkids are gettin' on that bus this morning," Willie's voice eased back into her consciousness, jolting Dot with the truth again.

Nope. No grandkids for Dot. No Leslie. Not even Tom anymore. Nothing but her animals.

The veil fell back over Dot's eyes as she willed the memories into their hole. She pulled Meg away from the grain, pushing her broad backside out the barn door into the pasture. She'd found that moving and getting back to work always kept the memories at bay — at least most of the time.

Chapter 15

Mildred

Diary Date:
August 25, 1968. A day I will never forget.

I stared hard at my entry, wishing the date said something different. Anything would do. It could be August 27. Then the first day would be over with. Or maybe July 25. No, didn't want to go back and relive the past few weeks. It'd be better if it was just later – any day but today.

Mama had insisted I have one new school outfit before we left Prosperity, and I wore it today. That, at least, was somehow satisfying. We had run to the J.M. Fields Department Store and found a pair of navy blue pants and a matching blue-and-white striped cropped top. I felt a little like Shirley Temple, but I was at least presentable, although I bet some of the girls would be wearing those new skinny jeans. Mama said no to those.

My hair was pulled back on the side in a matching blue barrette and I wore flat brown sandals. *I'm wearing a new outfit,* I wrote quickly. *Hope it brings me luck.*

"Mildred, we need to be heading out the door," Daddy's voice interrupted me and I hurriedly grabbed my book bag, notebooks and pencil case, tossing the diary back under my bed. My stomach knotted up and I wasn't sure if I was gonna make it or throw up on the road. My face must've looked like I felt 'cause Mama stopped short when I came in the room. She had forced herself up and made a sandwich for my lunch. She said if a Mama couldn't make her daughter a sandwich for her first day of school, she wasn't fit for anything. She looked tired, but held out my lunch box triumphantly.

"Well, Mil, I did it. You've got the best peanut butter 'n jelly sandwich made in Piedmont Ridge, South Carolina!" Mama's eyes glistened with pride. "Come here, honey, and give me a hug."

I leaned into Mama's arms, wishing I could just stay there. She felt soft and warm, but a little bony, and she smelled wonderful, like fresh daffodils. She pulled me back and looked me up and down. "Sam? Doesn't Mildred look beautiful today? She's just got to be the prettiest gal at Piedmont Ridge Elementary." I felt my face grow hot while Daddy eyeballed me.

"Not a doubt in my mind that you're right, Laura Lee," Daddy exclaimed. "And I get the privilege of driving up with her — in the golden chariot. Come, my dear, it awaits your presence." Daddy waved his arm toward the door and the waiting brown Malibu. Some chariot. Mama giggled as I grabbed my box from her hand. "Have a wonderful day," she said, walking slowly toward her chair. "I'll be praying for you all day. I know you're gonna love it."

"Thank you, Mama," I said, hurrying out the door. If there was one solid thing I knew about today, it was that Mama would pray. That gave me comfort.

Daddy shut the car door when I slipped in beside him, taking care not to slam my new pants in the crevice of my door. As I flopped back into the seat with a loud sigh, Daddy slipped the car into reverse, talking as he turned his head.

"Mil. I've been up early praying for you today." Daddy flashed me a grin as he shifted the gear column to drive. "Praying that the Lord would give you the right teacher, put you in the right class, just that you would love this school and find your place here. I know it's been hard on you, coming all the way up here and having so much change in so little time." His crystal eyes darkened. "It's been hard on us all, but we're alright, aren't we? We've got friends already, your Mama is looking almost perky this morning. I think everything's gonna be real good here once we get our feet good n' wet."

I heard everything Daddy said as he was driving. Honest. I did. But it was hard to concentrate on it all with that giant green and gold "Piedmont Ridge Elementary" sign bearing down on me. I knew I needed to be grown-up about this and nod and say something like, "Yes, sir. God's just real good and He is taking good care of us." But nothing came out. I still wasn't sure God was real good. And I suppose peanut butter and jelly did count as nourishment, and I know all the starving children in China would be happy with it, but we sure weren't living what I'd call a bountiful sort of life.

The Malibu eased in toward the front of the school. It looked a lot like my old school, same red brick, one story – sort of all stretched out like. It had these flat awnings that followed the sidewalks from one part of the school to another. The wooden sign, other than being painted school colors – also had a horse drawn on it. Maybe they were the Piedmont Ridge horses or something. Daddy shifted into park and turned toward me in his seat.

"Well, Mil. You ready?"

I don't reckon I was real comforting to Daddy 'cause he sighed hard, smiled and leaned over to kiss me on the cheek. "Come on, honey. Waiting always makes stuff like this harder."

I opened the door on the end of my life. My sandaled foot stepped on pavement, and I looked down, knowing that I'd never set foot here again, that I was going to enter that place, mix in with those hundreds of kids milling around and never be seen on this earth again. It was all over.

Then Daddy came around the car, carrying my lunch box, and took my hand. It felt safe. Comforting. Solid. Sounds of kids calling out names of friends they hadn't seen all summer echoed through the doors as we walked toward the entrance. Girls and boys swept by us, rushing through the doors like it was the last call for Noah's Ark. I began to drag my feet, knowing I hadn't seen one face that I knew. Daddy pulled harder and we entered.

The first thing I noticed was the walls. They weren't limegreen painted concrete like it had been at Prosperity Elementary. In fact, they didn't even look like walls. Gorillas, huge butterflies, giant snakes and lizards were weaved in among tall green trees and root systems running along the baseboard. It was the most brilliant jungle scene I'd ever imagined. Even Daddy drew in his breath and stopped mid-stride.

"Good Lord, Mildred. This is really something." I guess I looked the same way, and I knew we were blocking traffic flow, but we couldn't move. Some of the trees were painted right up to the ceiling and beyond, the leaves – that looked so real they might fall on me any minute – grew into the light fixtures.

Daddy and me probably looked like tourists by now. We gawked, and that must've been what triggered a teacher-person to come to our rescue.

"Good mornin'," her voice rang out, full of sugar and sunshine. "I'll just bet y'all are new to Piedmont Ridge Elementary. Am I right?"

I tore my eyes away from the wall and had my first look at Miz Dingle — a vision I'll never forget.

It was her bosom. The first thing I noticed, I mean. It was big and hanging down low. The glasses dangled on a string of pearls, bump, bump, bumping each time she spoke; it didn't help matters. Her robin's egg blue sweater stretched tightly over another sweater, but both were short sleeve, because it was late August and hotter than a dog on a hunt.

When I looked up, I found the most alive green eyes I'd ever seen. They sparkled, her smile added to the warmth coming from her face. She had a pile of white hair, tied up in a tightly wound bun, sitting firmly on top of her head. Her flower-patterned skirt wrapped around her ample waist, completing the vision of Miz Dingle. She was perfect in her "teacher-ness," and I loved her immediately. I nudged Daddy.

"We sure are new," he held out his hand, smiling broadly. No woman in her right mind could dismiss Daddy's charm. Miz Dingle fell victim right off – I saw the blush creeping up her cheeks — but she still had her senses about her. She shook his hand and took stock of me. Her sweeping glance didn't miss a thing, and suddenly, I was even more glad I was wearing my blue outfit. I self-consciously felt for my barrette. Still positioned correctly.

"Welcome to our school. What is your name, dear?" she waited expectantly. I cleared my throat, determined to be as mature as she expected me to be.

"Mildred Juniper, ma'am. Mildred Juniper Rhodes. Sixth-grader. Out of Prosperity, Georgia."

There! Surely that was more than sufficient and very, very professional. I glanced toward Daddy who looked proud. Miz Dingle only seemed startled.

"Mildred Juniper Rhodes out of Prosperity, Georgia? And in sixth grade? I do believe I have the honor of meeting my first new student of the year," she said. "I'm Miz Dingle, and your name is on my roster." Almost magically, she pulled a clipboard from her side and set her glasses on the end of her nose. "Yes. Here you are. Oh my, this will be so much fun." And she almost had me believing her, but then an incredible clash of noise began barging its way into our conversation. Someone knocked my back hard with a lunch box as they dashed by, chasing another student down the hall.

"Slow down, Harley!" barked Miz Dingle. I had no idea that sort of sound could come out of her. She turned back toward Daddy, all smiles again.

"Mr. Rhodes? Why don't you ease on into the principal's office right there to your right?" she pointed to a door covered with jungle leaves. Peeking out was a red printed sign, acknowledging this important place. "If you don't mind, I'll go ahead and escort Mildred to her classroom. Mr. Cummings will bring you down later on to see where we are so you can pick her up this afternoon. Promptly at 2:30," she was now speaking over her shoulder, grabbing my arm and gently, but firmly, guiding me down a hall that was less painted and more school-ish. "We'll see you then."

I watched Daddy disappear into the principal's office with a smile and a wink and turned around just in time to keep from plowing over a girl about my age with the most perfect blonde curls I'd ever seen.

"Mornin' Miz. Dingle," she practically curtsied while I watched in amazement. She reminded me of one of Beth Ann's china dolls with the round, blue eyes.

"Why, welcome back to school, Violet. Did you have a fun summer?" Miz Dingle managed to stretch down far enough to give her a hug.

"Oh, yes'm," Violet gushed. "Mama and Daddy took the boys and I..."

"The boys and me," Miz Dingle corrected. Violet didn't miss a beat.

"...to the beach and we saw real, live dolphins!"

"Well! I certainly hope so!"

"Ma'am?" Violet questioned.

"I said, I certainly hope they were live."

I looked at Miz Dingle carefully. She reminded me of Daddy but that was all lost on Violet.

"Oh, never mind, Violet. I'd like you to meet Mildred Juniper Rhodes. She's new to Piedmont Ridge and will be in our class. I know you'll be the best of friends."

Violet finally noticed me, which was awkward. Would we be friends? I had no idea what to say, so I waited. Violet hesitated, then smiled oddly.

"Oh yeah," she drawled. "I remember you. My Daddy says your Daddy's gonna lead that colored church."

"Violet!" Miz Dingle stopped in her tracks, right in front of Room 32.

"Well, it's true." Violet carelessly tossed her curls. "Daddy says it's bad enough that they got the vote and are gettin' better jobs than white folks. He says they's no sense in worshiping with them in the churches. What's the world comin' to? That's what my Daddy says."

Why, oh why, wasn't the floor opening up so I could fall in? By this time, a steady stream of sixth graders had lined up behind us, waiting for Miz Dingle to unlock the classroom. I could only hope they hadn't heard, but even if they hadn't, I knew the news would be out soon. My stomach turned and I felt like I might throw up.

"Violet Griffin, I forbid you to speak anymore of this," Miz Dingle spoke quietly but firmly as she pushed open the door.

"Please welcome Mildred to class as a fellow student – nothing more and nothing less." She flipped the overhead lights, revealing four rows of evenly placed desks. Each one had a name card taped at the top and one new pencil and eraser. Any other time, this would have been terribly exciting. Today, it was the nice part of a really, really bad dream.

Violet moved aside to let the other kids pass and whispered in my ear, "Welcome to Miz Dingle's class ... blacky."

Her perfect, black-pattened shoes clomped as she walked away. Luckily, Miz Dingle pointed to an empty desk and I made a headlong dash to it, keeping my eyes on the floor so no one would see the tears welling up.

Chapter 16

Dot

Seeing Sam Rhodes wasn't what Dot expected as she pulled her Chevy around the back of Piedmont Ridge Elementary. Gallon milk jars clanked and rattled as she eased over the worn pavement. Myrtle, the school's head cook, preferred cooking with milk "straight from the cow," so Dot delivered several gallons once a week during the school year. Usually, she didn't see children or parents on her run, but she was beginning to realize the Rhodes weren't usual.

Sam saw her almost simultaneously and wheeled the Malibu around, jerking to a stop beside her.

Good heavens, she thought, *he can't even get the car stopped before he's out of it.*

"Miz Harris, Miz Harris," Sam jogged up to the driver's side door, sticking his head in her open window as she tucked the keys into the front pocket of her overalls. "I'm so thankful I saw you here. I've been wanting to chat without Mildred around and wondered if you had a minute."

Dot shrugged, sighed and eased out of the truck, looking as though she didn't care, knowing in her heart, she did.

"I just had to thank you again for taking care of Mil, bringinger home – just being so kind to her. She's had a real rough few weeks, and to be honest she needed a friend."

Dot pulled herself up to her full five-foot, four inches and straightened her fishing hat.

"Look here, Mr. Rhodes. I was glad to help the child, but I got no time to befriend a little girl."

"Oh no, no, Miz Harris," Sam leaned against the truck hood with a half smile, his blue eyes sparkling. "I'm not saying you need to be Mil's friend, I'm saying you were her friend and Laura Lee and me are so grateful. We'd love to have you over for dinner as soon as we're more settled in.

Dot was silent. She turned her back to Sam, striding to the truck gate. Jerking at the chains holding the gate, she then laid it down flat, grabbed the truck frame and heaved herself up.

"Here. Let me help with that." Sam swung around, but Dot stopped him short with her outstretched hand.

"No, thank you, Mr. Rhodes. This here's my job and I reckon I'll do my own work till I'm tossed in a grave somewhere."

Sam nodded and stepped back.

"Well, we'd sure love to have you over," he repeated, watching her closely. Dot shifted the crate and stood up on the truck bed, stretching out her back.

"It's appreciated, Mr. Rhodes. But I don't know that you want me over at your place. Seems like you've already cracked open a kettle o' worms in this town. You don't need me around to mix it up and make it worse."

"'Scuse me?"

Dot gave Sam a wry, tired smile.

"It's this simple, Mr. Rhodes. People around here call me Harris. Not Mrs. Harris. Not Dot. I'm the milk lady. Nothin' else. I live alone. I work alone. I like it that way and so does everybody else. I do my work well and take care of what's mine." Dot squinted in the sunlight, then pulled the bill of her hat a little lower. Her eyes were shadowed, covered.

"I'm the eccentric old woman who lives out on Coon Creek. Friendship just isn't anything I want or need."

Sam met her gaze, unblinking.

"I see."

Dot eased the crate off the bed of the pickup.

"Miz Harris?"

She glanced up.

"Everybody needs friends. Everybody needs a family. When you find that out, come see us. We'll have an empty chair at our table, waiting on you."

Sam turned and walked slowly back to his car as Dot picked up her crate and walked to the door marked "Employees Only." She rang the entrance bell with a free finger and didn't turn to look as Sam Rhodes drove away.

Chapter 17

Mildred

Dear Mildred:
*   I guess you know that by the time I got your card, Mr. Fitz done filled us all in on your Mama's hospital stay? I'm sure glad to hear she's doing better. Mama says to tell her we are keeping her in our prayers. Mama put her name on Mrs. Geldarht's Sunday school prayer list and if you remember right, that was the very list Mr. Johnson was on when he had that big healing with his skin sickness. Anyhow, I know that will help.*
*   It was real nice to get your letter, but I got to tell you the best news before I tell you what's going on in Prosperity. Ha! My news really means I won't write you any news cause I can just tell you in person.*
Are you wondering yet?
*   Well Uncle Goose has got to go to the stockyard next weekend to sell some calves. It just so happens that stockyard is in Exeter, five miles outside Piedmont Ridge!! Can you believe it? He says he's gonna ask your Daddy if we can spend the night at your house on the way back. Yep. I said WE! Mama says I can go.*
*   So I reckon I'll see you soon, Mildred Juniper. Then I'll tell you all about home. I pray to Jesus every day for you.*
*   Love,*
*   Martha Claire*

I folded Martha Claire's letter, written on pink kitten stationery, and then unfolded it again. Re- reading the words more slowly this time, I let my book bag dangle off my back and slide to the floor. *"Spend the night at your house..."* My head swam. First, I'm gutted at school, now joyful emotions climb up into my throat. I flopped hard on my bed, feeling a breath of life blow back into my soul. It would be so good to see Martha Claire again. Her letter may not take away the sting of Violet Griffin's words, but it sure helped.

My school day hadn't improved after Violet's welcome. She spread the word about me quick enough, and I sat alone at lunch and was ignored at recess. The only saving grace, besides Miz Dingle, was all the neat stuff we had in our classroom. A real microscope, a pet hamster, the Reading Center with more good books than you could shake a stick at. I moaned, knowing I could've been happy there.

"Mil?" Mama's call echoed through the wafer-thin trailer walls.

"Ma'am?"

"I'm waiting for you to come tell me about your day. What's taking so long?"

Mama had met me at the door when Daddy dropped me off; her eager gaze driving me away. I had grabbed the letter from Martha Claire and raced to my room, buying time to think. How much do I tell Mama and Daddy? Luckily, Daddy was so preoccupied with fixing the screen door that he didn't grill me on the way home. He practically coasted into the yard, barely letting me jump out before speeding away to True Value Hardware. I wouldn't be as lucky with Mama.

"Comin' Mama. I'm unpacking my book bag," I yelled back.

What to do? If I tell Mama about Violet, it'll only upset her, which she doesn't need. If I don't tell her, I'd feel like I was keeping secrets, which I don't need. Third choice. I could tell Mama a little, but not the whole story. I moved further into the room and hung my pants on a hanger. Yesterday's blue jean shorts lay on the floor. I grabbed them up, slipping them on quickly. Yep. The third choice felt the best. Swinging open my door, I carried Martha

Claire's letter with me.

"Mama, guess what?" I attempted to sound carefree. "Martha Claire says she's comin' to Piedmont Ridge." I eased into the living room, carefully plastering my smile.

"Really?" Mama's eyes twinkled.

"You already knew, didn't you?" I jumped on her lap – as gently as I could. "That's not fair! You didn't tell me!"

"Of course I didn't. I wanted it to be a surprise."

"Well, when do they come?"

Mama shifted, sliding me beside her. "I think next weekend," she said. "They should come in Saturday night and be here for Sunday service. Your Daddy hopes we'll be in the Bingo Hall by then."

"Really?"

"There's just so much to do before your Daddy can start services there, and I'm no help," Mama pushed her hair back, smiling sadly. "But we're getting ahead of ourselves here. How was your day, Mildred? Did you like your new school? Make any new friends?"

"Yes ma'am. Well, the school is really neat. Did Daddy tell you about the jungle walls?"

"He sure did."

"Miz Dingle is great, and her classroom has pets and books. Oh, and we got a new pencil and eraser. So it was...nice."

"Nice, huh?" Mama looked at me carefully.

"Yes, ma'am." I thought quickly. If I didn't keep her preoccupied, she'd move on to that new-friend question. I got up to get a glass of tea.

"Mama, you didn't tell me we should be in the Bingo Hall in two weeks. How's Daddy gonna get the place ready?"

And, I thought, how's he gonna be when he finds out about Gregory's homeless "friend" living there?

"I'm not sure," her forehead wrinkled thoughtfully. "Elder Thomas and Debbie said they'd bring a work crew over this weekend. I'm sure you and Gregory can help too. And who knows? Maybe I can make sandwiches and tea. I am still tired, though."

Mama laid her head back on the recliner.

"I can't help it, I just wish we weren't here, Mil. Do ya think if we were still in Prosperity I'd be sick?" Ice chinked in my glass, but Mama didn't seem to hear it. "I'll bet Marsha's bridge club started back in its full rotation. They'll probably pull that ol' Elsie Miller in to fill my slot. Lord, that woman wouldn't know a trick if it slapped her in the face. And the smell of Georgia pines. Oh, that sharp, freshness – better than gardenias in the dead heat of summer. It's just the simple things, really, that you miss. Rain slapping on the tin roof. Mr. Jamison's crooked front porch. Miss Bertha's pound cakes. Gaddie's honey from her hives. Sometimes I wonder if I can even bear it, and my little girl ..." Mama's eyes moved toward me.

"My sweet girl comes home from school saying little, but not saying an awful lot. And I'm just so tired, so dad-blamed tired. If I can just keep smilin' for your Daddy and not let him see it." She closed her eyes and I realized she'd heard Daddy pulling in the yard. His door slammed and feet stomped on the front stoop. I wondered how much more Mama would have said if he hadn't come home.

Honestly, if it hadn't been for Miz Dingle and her Reading Center, I don't know if I'd have made it through the week. But I did — I also had the help of Charlotte and Wilbur and Fern in "Charlotte's Web." Working with Fern to keep Wilbur from being butchered somehow took me away from the stage I was acting on. Plus, Violet and the other popular girls seemed to hate reading. On the blue pillow in the back corner, my back propped next to a bookshelf, I was safe.

So Saturday finally rolled around and Saturday morning cartoons were laid aside. According to Daddy, it was cleaning day. Since Martha Claire wasn't due in till next weekend, Daddy knew I was stuck. Luckily, Gregory was coming with his Mama and Daddy. I was pretty anxious to find out what had been happening with the homeless man. In fact, my stomach was knotted up about the whole thing, so I found myself stirring my cereal a lot.

"Mildred Juniper. I've never seen you wait long enough for your Rice Krispies to get soggy. You feeling alright?" Mama looked at me carefully. She'd been doing that a lot lately.

"Yes'm. Just sleepy, I guess." I responded with a smile, hoping to put her at ease. Daddy had been dashing back and forth from the car to the store to the trailer all morning. An assortment of buckets, mops, brooms, sponges and detergent bottles littered the front stoop. I think Miz Mary Rose and Stew offered to loan the co-op's power sweeper which made Daddy practically slobber. They promised to be here with the rest of the crew by 9 o'clock. It was 8:07 and I still stared at my Rice Krispies.

Suddenly, a persistent knocking on the back window pulled me out of my thoughts. I glanced at Mama. She hadn't heard, and Daddy had just left the driveway for "one more quick trip to the store." I eased over and peered through the blinds.

Gregory was hopping up and down on the septic tank in the backyard, tapping the window at the peak of each jump. What was he doing? I shook my head in a vigorous "no," trying to keep him from continuing. His white teeth flashed and big, brown eyes sparkled as he pointed further down the trailer toward the bathroom window. I shook my head again, glancing toward the living room. Gregory only jumped higher and harder, refusing no for an answer. Then, his sneaker slipped on the side of the tank and he fell backwards. I let out a quick gasp.

"What is it, Mil?" Mama called from the living room. "You alright?"

"Yes, ma'am. I, uh, I just gotta go to the bathroom." I let the blinds fall quietly back into place and dashed down the hall. Locking the door quickly, I whipped up the shade, unlatched the window, stood on the commode and poked my head out into the warm, morning sun. Gregory lay on the ground, moaning.

"Are you all right?" I hissed. "Are you crazy or something? You could've broke your leg!"

"No way, Mildred Juniper. I knows all about the ins and outs of septic tanks. Heck! I been using ours as a slide my whole life. Anyway, got your attention, didn't I?" He smiled mischievously, but I refused to believe he fell on purpose.

"Oh, whatever. Why in tarnation are you banging around the back of the trailer anyway? If you hadn't noticed, we got a front door."

"Because, silly, I need yo' help with Ol' Homeless, but I didn't want yo' Mama to know." Gregory stood up, wiping off his backside.

"You don't have to roll your eyes," I replied hotly. "How 'm I supposed to know? Just read your mind? Besides, I told you I don't want to have nothing to do with that man. It's your problem."

"Oh, come on, Mildred," he began to beg. "I've been leavin' him some of Mama's cookin', but I hadn't talked to him yet. I got to talk to him today, this mornin', *right now!*"

"Shhhh!" I hissed again, glancing back toward the locked bathroom door. "Mama'll hear you." Gregory took a deep, calming breath and straightened up tall in his overalls.

"Look, Mildred, if we..."

"We?"

"Yeah, we! If we don't warn him that the cleanin' crew's comin' today, he'll get caught. Then they might throw him in jail. That just cain't happen."

"OK. Fine. Then go warn him. You don't need me."

Gregory moved closer to the bathroom window, staring up with huge, pitiful eyes. I felt my heart begin to weaken.

"But I do need you, Mildred. I need a lookout so's I can sneak into the back. Look. All you gotta do is whistle three times if'n you see anybody. Then you can sneak back home and nobody'll ever have to know you was even there. It'll buy me some time with Ol' Homeless."

"But how do I get out of the house without Mama and Daddy knowin?" I added, in spite of my good sense telling me not to fall for this.

"I'll come round to the front door and ask yo' Mama if you can go explorin' with me until my parents get here. You know she'll let you."

"I still haven't eaten my cereal," I mumbled.

"So? I'll wait five minutes. Come on, Mil. Pleasssssssseee?"

Oh, good Lord. How was a body supposed to stay strong and say no when you got a face like Gregory's staring at you? He looked like a puppy, desperate and hungry.

"Oh, all right. But only a whistle and I'm gone," I said with determination.

"It's a deal. Oh, thank you, Mildred Juniper. Ol' Homeless will probably thank you too."

I just shut the window. I didn't want any thanks from Homeless. I didn't want to talk to him at all. The bathroom door banged open as I hurried back to the table.

"Everything alright?" Mama hollered from the living room.

"Yes'm. Just eatin' my cereal."

The knock came on the front screen door when I was picking up my bowl to down the last of the milk. Gregory's eager face peeked through, smiling broadly at Mama.

"Mornin', Miz Rhodes."

"Why, good mornin' Gregory. Is your Mama here, too?" Mama peered around him.

"No ma'am. I come early to see if Mildred Juniper could go explorin' with me a little afore we start cleanin'. Could she?"

Boy, did he ever have the charm turned on. I saw right through it, but Mama was fooled.

"You wanna go play with Gregory for about thirty minutes, Mil? Your Daddy ought to be back by then and I'll have a little time to put on some more coffee for the work crew."

I glanced at Gregory with raised eyebrows, but Mama didn't see that.

"Yes ma'am. That'll be great."

"Good. Don't go too far, you two."

We lumbered out the front door as Mama was pulling herself up from the recliner to move toward the kitchen. Gregory waited until we were out of earshot before he opened his mouth again.

"It ain't no better?"

"What?" I had no idea what he was saying. My mind was over

run with all the horrible things that could go wrong.

"Your Mama. Her sickness ain't no better?"

"Oh," I considered that as we walked toward the Bingo Hall. "Maybe some. I don't think she could've gotten up to make coffee a week ago." Gregory sure had a way of ruining a perfectly good day.

Our feet hit pavement and I stared at the concrete-blocked building in the morning sun. There was no sign of Ol' Homeless – not even his bike hidden in the back, but that didn't phase Gregory. I pushed my hair out of my eyes — frustrated. Seemed like it always bugged me more when I was worried up about something.

"So what's the plan?" I ventured.

"Well, I'm guessin' Ol' Homeless is still here, even though his bike's missin'. It ain't been here a few mornin's this week, but them food bags I been leavin' are still disappearin'. Why don't you stick to our hidin' place near the dumpster, and I'll go knock on the side door."

"You just gonna knock? Like it's a regular house or somethin'?" My eyes must've bugged out because Gregory laughed at me.

"Dang, Mildred. You need to do somethin' 'bout yo' nerves. It ain't no big deal. I don't reckon he'll eat me."

"Yeah, but he could be an escaped convict — you know? Someone who robbed a bank and had a big shoot-out. I heard about people like that. Or maybe he fed his children to wolves or..."

"Lord a'mercy, girl. You got rocks in yo' head?" Gregory's eyes cut sharply at me. "You been readin' them 'National Enquirer' magazines at the store, ain't you? You got to stop messin' with that junk. It'll taint yo' mind every time."

The shade of the dumpster broke a little of the morning heat and we squatted together, checking the perimeter one more time. Back toward the trailer, all was quiet. Daddy wasn't home yet and there was no sign of other church folk driving up. The back of the Bingo Hall was as deserted as ever.

"I reckon it's now or never," whispered Gregory. I think the awful quietness of the place had actually gotten to him. "Now, remember Mildred. Three short whistles."

"Do I whistle if somebody drives up to the trailer? Or only if people are walking over here?"

Gregory looked at me with newfound respect. I could tell he hadn't thought of that question and maybe I redeemed myself from some of that robber talk.

"Give me three whistles even if it's just somebody drivin' into yo' yard. I might need the extra time."

"Okay. But remember, three whistles, then you're on your own. I'm sneakin' back home."

"Deal." And we shook on it.

When Gregory began tip-toeing to the side door, he looked like he was barefooted on the Sahara desert. One foot up, one foot down — knees high and a long pause between each step. The squirrels in the pines made more noise hopping from branch to branch. Finally, he reached the door and crouched down, looking back my way. The sunbeams shot through the trees, throwing slanted lines of light around him. For a moment, he looked almost angelic, and I wondered if Gregory's mission was more than just an idea on his part. But then he tried the knob and it turned! He pulled open the door and disappeared — just like that!

I let out a gasp. Where was the knocking, for goodness sake?

The noisy silence of the woods grew and I suddenly realized there was no way Gregory would hear one whistle from me, much less three. I was too far away from the door. I'd either have to wait here, go home or get closer. My lips felt dry and cracked as I contemplated my choices. I softly attempted a practice whistle, just to get a feel for it.

"Pttbb." Pathetic. I tried harder. "Whrrrrrr!" Wobbly, but sufficient. I knew I had to move toward the door, regardless of how stupid that was! Now that I was in, I couldn't desert Gregory, but it sure was mighty tempting. Stupid boy. Now look what he had done.

After a quick glance back toward the trailer, I crept out from my dumpster shield and drew close to the Bingo Hall wall. I followed Gregory's trail as quietly as I could.

I reached the door, which was now open about three inches, and squatted, peeking into the crevice. There seemed to be a little light, but not much. Maybe if I pulled it open just a hair, I could ...

Before I could even move a little, the door slammed open, hurling me back on the pavement. I felt my shirt slide up on my side and the harsh, stinging of road rash on my back. Then the full weight of Gregory fell on top of me and the warm sunshine disappeared in a cover of Gregory's body.

"Oouuff! Ouch! What in the good Lord's name? Oh! Lord. Mildred! Run! Get up, Mildred. Run!" and he was off.

I barely knew what hit me. Sharp pain was shooting from my back, my lip felt funny and by the time I could focus, all I saw was Gregory's backside running toward the trailer — in full view of anybody who wanted to look. The side door to the Bingo Hall was swinging open, showing a complete view of all its secrets, and I didn't see anything to cause alarm. Gregory kept running.

I jumped up, figuring Gregory must've had good reason, and began to dash after him. I could still hear him hollerin' all the way from the trailer. He reached the front stoop at the exact same time his Daddy drove into the yard, and here I was still in the parking lot. I ran harder, breath wheezing, back stinging, toward Gregory, the trailer and safety, and to heck with nobody knowing what we were doing.

Gregory collapsed in the front yard, panting and crying all at the same time. I reached him just as Elder Thomas did.

"Gregory, son, what's the matter?" Elder Thomas leaned over him, looking him up and down. I stood behind him, breathing hard, holding my side. With the pain coming from my back, this better be good!

"Man...bingo...door....dead," Gregory spit out the words, pointing all the while to the Bingo Hall.

"What? Slow down, boy. Now, say it again."

"The man, the homeless man at the Bingo Hall, he's dead!" Gregory shrieked out the word "dead," his eyes widening and mouth quivering. Dead? Inside the door I just was looking in? A dead man?

Chapter 18

Dot

Dot checked the bottom of her milk boots before she yanked open the door of True Value Hardware. She was so intent on getting rubber washer replacements for her milking machines that she'd left home immediately after the morning milking. Saturday was her repair and maintenance day, and she had no time to waste.

The sight of Harris in her boots, floppy hat askew, men's pants belted tightly around her waist was as common as the sun rising and setting in Piedmont Ridge. No one noticed as the bell jingled her arrival. Percy was focused on a customer at the front desk, and Dot knew the washers were on Aisle Three. It wasn't until she located them that she heard her name. She lifted her head, a question brooding in her vibrant blue eyes.

"...Harris might be willin' to drop 'er off on her way home," Percy was saying. Frowning, Dot shook her head. Nothing aggravated her more than presumption.

"Oh, Dot Harris?" the customer's voice echoed. "Is she here? We've run into each other a couple of times."

Can't be, thought Dot. *Just can't be.*

"Yep. Saw her head down Aisle 3 jus' now. Hey! Harris! You still 'ere?" Percy's graveled voice carried over stacks of nuts, bolts and drawer pulls. Dot considered not answering, but knew the only two ways out were blocked by the register. *Must be God's way of gettin' a laugh,* she thought.

"I'm here," she answered, stepping out of the aisle.

Sam Rhodes smiled broadly — looking as pleased as a bird dog on a hunt, thought Dot.

"This 'ere's Sam Rhodes..." Percy began.

"Yep. I know that," Dot interjected. Percy hesitated, sliding his thick glasses back up his nose as he looked at the two of them more carefully.

"Right. Well, Mr. Rhodes needs his new ladder dropped off over at the old Bingo Hall and Bill's out on another run. Thought you might hep him out?"

"Reckon I can," Dot said matter-of-factly. She turned towards Sam, motioning to the blue Chevy in the front parking spot. "You can jus' throw the ladder in the back while I get these washers rung up. I'm in a rush."

Sam smiled at Dot's turned back, winked at Percy and picked up the ladder without speaking. As he maneuvered out the door, Percy totaled Dot's purchase and handed her the receipt. Dot picked up the bag and strode out the front door without another word. As Percy watched her slam the truck door and putter off down the street with Sam Rhodes trailing in his brown Malibu, he scratched his head, wondering what ailed her this morning. Then a customer walked up with a broken faucet.

Dot maintained her reasonable thirty miles an hour as she drove to the Bingo Hall. Easing toward the Rhodes' trailer, she saw Daryl Thomas in the yard leaning over something - or someone. He seemed to be agitated, yelling toward the trailer porch. It was a boy stretched out on the ground, pulling Daryl's arm and crying frantically. Dot sped up just a hair and pulled into the yard with Sam easing in behind her. Laura Lee stood at the trailer door still in her bathrobe, looking disheveled, worried, but still young and ... somehow ... strong.

"Sam," Daryl Thomas was saying, "seems like we got us a commotion o' some sort. Mildred Juniper's not sure what's wrong and Gregory's rantin' and ravin' 'bout somebody dead in the Bingo Hall."

As he spoke the word "dead," Gregory wailed louder and began rocking back and forth on the ground. Dot heard it all through her open window and found herself out of the truck and in the yard.

"Dead? In the Bingo Hall?" Sam's steady voice masked the intensity in his eyes. He stooped quickly to check on Mildred, who was sitting on the ground, pale and shaken. Laura Lee pushed past Debbie Thomas at the front stoop, determined to get down into the yard.

"She'll be okay, honey. Just a blood rush or something, Sam said to Laura Lee. "We need to get on over there and see what the fuss is all about."

Dot watched it all – detached, yet somehow woven into the scene. Ladder forgotten, Sam waved toward Daryl and the two began trotting toward the Bingo Hall with Dot trailing two steps behind them.

Although the children couldn't have entered the deserted building by the double-locked front doors, Sam swept by quickly, checking the locks. Sure enough, they were fastened tight. The trio continued on a run-trot around to the side of the building. The door that Gregory had stormed out of minutes before hung open against the concrete wall.

Sam sped up, rushing through without hesitation, and Daryl followed with Dot behind him. It was only a few seconds before they found a small, light-filled room on the left side of the hallway. Obviously, it had housed an office – the three-legged desk and two splintered chairs spoke of years of payrolls and accounts received. Yet instead of layers of dust, the room was spotless. One chair was pulled to the desk, neatly placed. Boxes of fresh carrots were stacked near the windowsill, and a few personal items – soap, toothbrush, comb – were carefully nestled in a tin bucket by the door.

Dot caught the scene in less than three seconds. By the time she entered, Sam and Daryl were kneeling over a solitary figure stretched out on the floor. From her vantage point, Dot only saw long, thin legs extended in an awkward position. Brown, soiled boots flopped to each side.

"Do you get a pulse?" Daryl spoke first.

"I think so. It's faint, though." Neither realized Dot was there until she shuffled closer. Sam glanced up as she spoke.

"Check his pupils. Are they dialated?" she asked.

Sam peeled back the eyelids. "Can't tell. He turned toward Daryl. "Can you get to a gas station and call an ambulance?"

"Consider it done." Daryl bolted from the room while Dot squatted down beside the man, looking closer at his face. Suddenly, her knees jerked and she swore softly. Sam looked up from his watch, fingers still on the man's wrist.

"What is it?"

"Nothing. It's only..."

"What?"

"Well, if my eyes aren't going bad, this could be Bobby Caldwell, though I haven't seen him in about thirty years. It's hard to tell with that scraggly red beard."

"Was he a friend of yours?" Sam asked, laying the man's hand gently on the floor.

"Friend?" Dot tilted her hat back thoughtfully. "I suppose you could say that. Really. Bobby was everybody's friend – if you liked a good-natured drunk. It wasn't until his drinking killed his family that he changed. After that, he wasn't a friend to anybody in town."

Sam rocked back on his heels – thoughtful – and began to pray silently. Dot found an old blanket and covering the man gently, sat down to wait. Within minutes, they heard the shrill rolling of sirens.

"I'll go out and meet the ambulance if you'll stay here," Sam said.

"No problem," Dot replied, wondering if this dead man – who wasn't really dead – was going to die.

The gray ambulance with cat-eyed taillights wheeled into the parking lot. Its course through town caught three other vehicles in its wake, creating a sort of ambulance-chasing party. It didn't warm Sam's heart.

Lord, what about all this? Is it just a distraction to keep us from fixing up the church? Or is this part of your plan?

The drone of the siren magnified the silence from the heavens, so Sam trotted toward the first man out of the ambulance.

"He's over that way!" Sam pointed toward the side door as two more met at the back of the ambulance to drag out a stretcher.

"Does 'e 'ave a pulse?" the driver asked, grabbing a bag and slinging it over his shoulder.

"As best as I can tell."

Daryl ran up then as the other vehicles began emptying out. Piedmont Ridge had found its Saturday morning entertainment. An older man clad in dingy overalls climbed out of a truck while a lady trailed him. A young, slick-haired man with a star-shaped badge pinned to his waistband leapt out of a two-door car, and Pete Griffin sauntered out of his older model Cadillac. Daryl simultaneously deflated and cringed at that sight, and Sam didn't have to wonder why.

Pete's gaze flickered over Sam, then lingered on Daryl. Ignoring both of them, he moved toward the deputy.

"Heard the call on my shortwave radio. Anythin' I can do to help?"

"Don't know yet, Pete. Jus' stay back fer now and we'll let ya know."

Sam vaguely noted the conversation as he led the ambulance man toward the Bingo Hall. Daryl stayed right on his heels, doing his best to avoid breathing any of the air around Pete Griffin.

Once they reached the room, Sam and Daryl backed away. Dot stepped to a side, but she was the one questioned. Sam watched it all with interest – but not surprise. He was an outsider and Daryl was colored. In a town like Piedmont Ridge, they were in the same camp. Dot answered the questions as best as she could.

"Was he alone when you found him?"

"Yep. Best as we could tell."

"Has he said anything?"

"Nope."

"How'd you find him?"

"I didn't. The kids did."

"What kids?"

Sam stepped up. "It was my daughter, Mildred, and Daryl's son, Gregory." All action stopped as they gazed at Sam.

"Well, we'll check into that later," spoke Deputy Houston Fields from the doorway.

On the count of three, the ambulance men shifted him onto the stretcher. Pete stuck his head in the door, took in the scene and glanced at the stretcher. His eyes widened and mouth worked soundlessly for a moment. Finally, he was able to speak.

"What tha...? It can't be. It jus' can't be."

Dot snorted, rolled her eyes and tried to find a way out of the room.

"It *is*. It's got to be. Bobby Caldwell. Don't cha see, Harris? I'm right, ain't I?" Pete's narrow eyes fixed on Dot, sweat glistening on his forehead.

"Well, what if you are right, Pete? What 'cha gonna do about it?" Dot stood solidly, hands on her hips. Sam listened, ears tuned to what was going on behind the words. No one else, except maybe Daryl, seemed concerned with the conversation.

"Do about it? Well, good God, woman! We need to let folks know he's back! He cain't jus' expect to waltz back into town after what he done. He ain't welcome here."

"Who died and made you the gatekeeper of Piedmont Ridge?" Dot tossed back. "Bobby Caldwell didn't break the law, and as far as I'm concerned, he oughta be able to come home anytime he wants to."

The stretcher rolled out into the hall, but neither Dot nor Pete seemed aware.

"Home? Ha! Did you say, home? The last time Bobby had a home in this town, he let it burn up – with his wife and babies in it! He ain't got no home, Harris! He done seen to that. He ain't got no home in the Ridge!" Pete turned on his heels, chasing after the stretcher, trying to fill in the young deputy on the sordid history of Bobby Caldwell.

Suddenly the little room felt eerie and quiet, and Dot, Sam and Daryl found themselves staring at one another.

"Seems to me Pete Griffin needs to learn a little about grace,"

Sam noted.

Daryl nodded, head lowered, eyes on the floor. "That he do. That he do."

Dot turned and walked out into the bright light of a sticky, August morning, wondering what on earth made her follow the men into the Bingo Hall. Was she losing her mind?

Outdone with herself, she walked through the crowd, pulled the ladder from the back of her truck and propped it against a tree. Slamming her truck door hard, she saw Sam and Daryl move toward the deputy. *Let them deal with it,* she thought. *I'm done.*

She revved the engine and backed out of the yard. It was Saturday and she still had repairs to make. Bobby Caldwell's reappearance – just like the Rhodes family – was none of her business.

Chapter 19

Mildred

A week later, I still couldn't believe I'd missed it all. Ambulance, deputies, the "Mystery of the Bingo Hall" – it was all there, right in my front yard, and there I sat stuck with Mama and Miz Debbie at the trailer.

Gregory had been useless ever since we had gone inside, but once I heard Ol' Homeless was alive, I had been itching to get out there. Mama and Miz Debbie would have none of that! You'd have thought I was getting over the chicken pox the way they were carrying on. Keeping me away from people, forcing me to lie down. It liked to have done me in.

When all the folks cleared out, Daddy came back in the trailer, took one look at me and pronounced me healthy enough to help clean the Bingo Hall. Life just wasn't fair. He did tell me, in no uncertain terms, that we'd have a big talk about what I was doing in the Bingo Hall to begin with.

I had glared at Gregory who was sitting at our kitchen table, sipping on an Orange Crush. He grinned at me apologetically and shrugged. I had known better than to listen to his ideas, and now he had dragged me into a kettle of hot water. I knew that Mama and Daddy always said I make my own choices – who to follow and who not to – so I was gonna get it. But I'd still let them know about Gregory's persuasive ways, if only to get some of the frustration off my chest.

Daddy waved a broom my way.

"C'mon Mil. Excitement's over for the morning. Time to clean."

I knew better than to argue, so I grabbed the broom and followed Daddy across the yard, back to the Bingo Hall.

It hadn't been such a bad day, I reflected as I wiggled in my straight-backed school desk. We had worked like dogs, but it still beat being here.

The giant wall clock with long, black hands read 3:05. Only ten more minutes and I could escape. And since it was Friday – and Martha Claire was due in tomorrow morning – it would be a true escape. For two whole days, I could forget about Violet Griffin and Mary Beth Connelly. Mary Beth glanced up at me even as I thought about her. Uncanny. She smirked, pinched her nose like I stank and looked back at her drawing.

Miz Dingle had asked us to sketch our house as a fun way to end the school week. Even her amazing 500-colored pencil set couldn't whet my appetite to draw our trailer on Big Star Drive. I had raised my hand and asked Miz Dingle if I could draw any house I had lived in and she said, "Of course." So I picked Prosperity and was just finding the brightest yellow in the box for the daffodils that had lined our front porch when Mary Beth gave me the look.

I sighed.

3:07.

Eight more minutes...the bell would ring and Daddy would be waiting at the door, ready to drive me to the Marion County Hospital. He promised that Friday, after school, he'd take me to see Ol' Homeless at the hospital – I mean, Mr. Caldwell. Daddy had been to visit every day since Saturday, coming home with daily reports. Sunday, Mr. Caldwell had been "almost alive." Monday, he was "looking better." Tuesday and Wednesday, he'd been "pulling out of it," and finally, Thursday, he had "turned the corner."

"Laura Lee, he's gonna make it," Daddy had yelled, banging through the door Thursday afternoon. "Bobby looks great and the doctors say he can be released in a couple of days."

"What did they ever decide was wrong with him?" Mama was so beautiful, standing at the stove with her rose-colored housecoat on. Her chestnut hair curled damply around her ears, steam from the stove producing a thin line of sweat on her brow.

"They're figuring malnutrition was most of it. Course, he's covered with cirrhosis of the liver after so many years of heavy drinking. Reckon the two things together made for a bad day."

"You know, Sam. He reminds me of my Daddy – such a sad story and all," Mama had said. "Part of me feels awful sorry for him, but the other part wants to shoot him for what he did to his family – leaving them to go drinking while they got burned up in a fire. It's awful. At least my Daddy didn't burn us up while he was doing his drinking. But I sure can sympathize with people in this town who haven't forgiven him for what he did. Forgiveness for that kind of thing is a long time coming."

Mama chopped the potato she was peeling right in half when she said that part about shooting Mr. Caldwell. I'd heard some of her stories about Grandpa Mitchell, and I'd always been glad that he was dead before I came along. Never told Mama that, of course.

Mama almost never brought him up in conversation. From the starts and stops of talking over the years, I'd picked up that Grandpa Mitchell was known as a drunk way before Mama was born in 1934. He had been too young to fight in the "big war" – World War I – but not too young to lose his older brother, Henry, in that war. Aunt Maud had whispered to Mama one time that Grandpa never got right after Henry was killed. The only way he could numb the pain, said Aunt Maud, was by drinking. All I knew was that being a kid wasn't fun for Mama, and Daddy came along and rescued her.

Like he always does, I thought, watching the last seconds tick off the clock. A smothered giggle to my right pulled my attention toward Russell Simpkins. I was just in time to see him put a live lizard – at least that's what it looked like – in Mary Beth's pencil case. He quietly zipped it shut just as the bell rang.

"Class, don't forget to read one newspaper this weekend and bring it to school on Monday," Miz Dingle ordered from her pulpit. I always thought she looked more like a revival preacher when she stood solid like that. As large as her podium was, it still didn't hide her body all the way.

"I would prefer you to bring at least one article covering the election – there should be plenty to choose from."

Violet raised her hand, of course. "Miz Dingle? My Daddy says we can't even allow any propaganda about Richard Nixon to enter the house. My Daddy says he's nothin' but one of them flaky Californians that don't know their butt from a hole in the ..."

"Violet!" Miz Dingle interrupted. "There will be none of that language in this classroom."

Violet's mouth said, "Yes, ma'am," but her eyes were laughing.

The bell clanged from the hallway and the mad rush began. I took my time, knowing that Daddy would be backed up in school traffic. I wanted to watch and see if Mary Beth found the lizard.

Russ and John William had the same thought because they were dawdling. Russ was actually straightening his desk, which should have been a dead giveaway to anybody watching. Miz Dingle, preoccupied with another student, was clueless.

I squatted to adjust the books under my desk when Mary Beth unzipped her case to slide in her favorite, two-toned pencil that read "A+ Student." Out leapt the lizard, straight into the pocket on the front of her blouse.

"Ayyy...eeeeeeek!" she screamed, swatting frantically at her shirt. Miz Dingle glanced up and frowned, apparently irritated at being interrupted again.

"Help! Help! It's on me! It's in my shirrrrrt!" Mary Beth howled. The pencil case went flying across the room as she twisted and jumped, leaning over trying to roll whatever it was out of her shirt. And, God help me, I couldn't help it. I laughed. The more she moved, the more I laughed. Her arms were flailing like chicken's wings as she squawked around the room. Miz Dingle rushed over to try to calm Mary Beth down enough to see what was in her pocket. By this time, I had to sit down to keep from falling down. The room was in chaos. Tears streamed down my face and I couldn't catch my breath.

"Mary Beth! Be still for a minute," Miz Dingle sputtered, reaching her hand toward the bouncing, jiggling pocket.

"I can't! I can't! It's alive!" Mary Beth squealed.

Miz Dingle finally grabbed Mary Beth's arms to hold her still. The pocket bulged to one side and a blue-tailed lizard leapt out, hit Mary Beth's desk and rolled to the floor. It was wedged under a crack in the wall before you could say "jackrabbit." Mary Beth's tear-stained face registered shock, and suddenly I realized that the only sound left in the room was my laughter. I shut up real quick and turned to find Russ and John William.

Vanished. Gone.

I turned back toward the scene of the crime, suddenly waking up to what this must look like. Miz Dingle had her no-nonsense, you-disappoint-me, expression on. I felt the color drain from me.

"You!" Mary Beth pointed, fury lining every crease in her face. "You did this! Mildred Juniper Rhodes, you will live to regret it!" she ground through clinched teeth.

"I did not!" I refuted adamantly, turning toward Miz Dingle. "I didn't, Miz Dingle. Honest. I don't even like lizards!"

Cold eyes peering from behind matted blonde hair, Mary Beth didn't buy it. Miz Dingle pursed her lips, then sighed deeply as if she were a judge handing down a tough verdict.

"Well, it certainly doesn't look good, Mildred, but without proof..." She turned briskly back to Mary Beth. "Come along, Mary Beth. Let's get you cleaned up. And Mildred," she turned back toward me, glasses bouncing on the chain around her neck, "I'll be keeping a sharper eye on you from now on."

Mary Beth smiled hatefully, then set off with Miz Dingle to the girls' bathroom. I gathered my things quickly, realizing Daddy was probably waiting for me now. My joy at Martha Claire's visit, at seeing Mr. Caldwell in the hospital was all but gone. A new dark cloud hung over me at Piedmont Ridge Elementary School. It wasn't the only dark cloud. I'd been living with them for weeks now, but I had a feeling it was going to get worse — much worse.

I had to tug the car door three times to finally get it shut. It almost always stuck when it got really humid.

"Hey Mil. How was your day?" Daddy smiled at me while he moved the lever into gear. He wore a nicely ironed plaid shirt tucked into some brown pants. I knew Mama had patched the knees, but you really couldn't much tell. I thought he looked very handsome.

"Oh, it was alright, I guess."

"Just alright?"

"Yes, sir."

"Well," he apparently didn't want to pursue that any farther. Don't blame him. My days had been just "alright" for weeks and weeks now. "It's gonna get better now! Weekend's here and Bobby is looking forward to meeting his rescuers. Elder Thomas is picking Gregory up from school too, so both of you can meet him at the same time. Sound fun?" Daddy's blue eyes sparkled with the surprise of Gregory.

"I suppose so. But Daddy? Why are you so nice to Mr. Caldwell when he burned up his family. Even Mama don't like that."

"Doesn't."

"Sir?"

"Doesn't. Even Mama doesn't like that."

"Oh, so how come?" We turned right at the Piedmont Ridge City Church heading out in a new direction of town to me. I'd never been down this road before.

"Well. The Lord calls us to care for widows and orphans, and Bobby is a widower."

"Yeah, but he killed his wife."

"No, Mil. He certainly didn't murder her with intent. It was an accident and he wasn't at home. He didn't kill her, though lots of people in Piedmont Ridge would like to say so." Daddy wiped his hand across his head like he was exasperated or something. "I look at it like this, Mildred. Jesus died for our sins, right?"

"Yes, sir."

"Well, would you say Mr. Caldwell's drinkin' and not taking care of his family was a sin."

"I reckon so."

"Well, then, did Jesus die for his sin, too?"

"Uh huh."

"Exactly. So if Jesus has forgiven me for my sins, which are pretty dog-gone bad, I'm thinking He'll forgive Bobby for his sins. Now. If Jesus can forgive Bobby, I sure don't see why I can't. I'm not Bobby Caldwell's judge anymore than you or anybody else in town is. All I know is Jesus calls me to love people and help point the way to knowing Him. Seems to me very few people in this town love Bobby – and I don't see anyone pointing the way to Jesus. So I reckon I'll do it."

Daddy hit the left blinker before he began easing into the hospital parking lot. "Besides," he cut a grin at me, "I really like him. He's a nice guy. You'll see."

Gregory was jumping up and down near an empty parking place, rolling his arms like he was directing Daddy into park. Good grief. He was so goofy sometimes. I still hadn't gotten over him dragging me into this mess, but I had to admit he was the most fun I'd found in this town.

"Hey Mildred Juniper," he cried out, running over to the car. "We gonna meet Ol' Homeless face to face! Hot dog! I can't wait. Wonder if he like our vegetables." Elder Thomas walked up a little slower, placing his hand calmly on Gregory's head. He was always calm, I thought, looking at him. Something about him made me quiet and at peace. His eyes were like deep pools of water.

"Come on, boy," he chastened gently. "Let the folks get outta the car before you start gabbin' on like that. Afternoon Pastor," he shook hands with Daddy as he walked around toward the three of us. "Reckon we got us a big day today. Mebbe Mr. Bobby will want to join us walkin' on the road with Jesus?"

"You never know, Daryl." We walked together toward the glass doors, excitement in the air. I wasn't even sure why, but it felt like God was up to something and I might get to watch.

The air-conditioning took my breath away as the glass door rolled shut behind us, but even the fresh feeling of air on my face couldn't take away the stink of a hospital. I wrinkled my nose and tried to breath through my mouth without letting on. Mama would expect me to be grown-up acting, and I knew ladies didn't hold their nose. 'Course ladies carried hankies to put their delicate noses into, and I sure didn't have anything like that.

Daddy walked straight down the main hall, turning left under the signs that read: Rooms 112-119. Elder Thomas, Gregory and me sort of lingered behind, and I noticed some folks clearing the way for us. Gregory and his Daddy were watching the floor instead of where they were going. People stopped to stare. Well, really, white people stopped to stare, and I didn't see many colored people. There had been an older man sweeping the front walk when we came up, but other than that, this seemed like a white-sort of place. I knew, though, that Piedmont Ridge didn't have a black hospital, so I supposed coloreds were treated here, but where? Daddy paused in front of Room 115 and knocked lightly. I lifted my head to straighten out my back and have good posture. That's another thing a lady always does; she walks well.

"Yeah?" a graveled voice hollered from the room.

"Bobby? It's me, Sam. I've brought some visitors."

"Well, come on in then. Don't stop up traffic out there."

Daddy pushed open the door and turned back to motion the three of us to go first. I hesitated. Elder Thomas smiled kindly and led the way. Gregory followed behind, all his earlier excitement had floated away by now. Confound that boy. He could never make up his mind.

If Daddy and Elder Thomas hadn't been so sure they were conversing with Mr. Caldwell, I'd have thought they got the wrong room. This surely wasn't Ol' Homeless? Where was the beard? The gritty, grimy clothes? This man looked half-way normal, except for that big, bushy head of hair. But his face was clean now, and without the beard I could see a deep dimple in his chin. He looked nice. Old, but nice.

"Well," he drawled, squirming up in his bed. "This must be Miss Mildred and Mr. Gregory, my rescuers. It shore is good to meet you both. Your pa's done told me so much about you, but I already knowed you were some good 'uns." Mr. Caldwell held out his hand and I hesitantly walked over to shake it. Gregory cowered behind me like a dog caught in the henhouse. Elder Thomas firmly pushed him forward.

"And I'm just supposin' that I've got you two to thank for some tasty vittles that were laying outside my door last week. Would I be right in thinking that?"

I waited for Gregory to explain, but since he wasn't moving at all, I figured somebody best step in.

"No, sir," I replied, "not both of us. Gregory is the one who brought you the food. I was ..." I glanced at Daddy, hesitating. "I was too scared to do that but Gregory wasn't."

I swear I think Gregory was blushing under that brown skin. Mr. Caldwell seemed to realize I'd made him uncomfortable.

"Well, thank you, Gregory," he said again. "My stomach is really thankful!" And he laughed a hard laugh, revealing missing teeth on the bottom row. Gregory suddenly thawed out, moved forward and sat on the edge of the bed.

"I jus' figured that a homeless man would be pretty hungry, and my Mama makes the best buttermilk biscuits in the whole world," he began. "It wadn't hard to do. I just got extra helpins and put it outside your door on my way to school in the mornins'." Gregory looked up at his daddy. "Sorry, Daddy. Hope you don't mind."

Elder Thomas flashed those white teeth of his, laughing almost as hard as Mr. Caldwell. "Mind? No, son. I don't mind."

And then we all got comfortable and talked together. It felt like Mr. Caldwell was already a part of the family, and I found it hard to remember that he killed his own family. This poor, old man didn't look able to do such a thing. Besides, like Daddy said, Jesus forgave my sins and Lord knows, I have plenty of those.

The afternoon sun was beginning to cast short shadows into the room when another knock sounded at Mr. Caldwell's door. Wanda Broomer's flushed face peeked into the room and her hesitant face broadened into a wide smile as she caught glimpse of Daddy and Elder Thomas. Without waiting for a "Come in," she shoved through the door, hauling something tempting in a tinfoil plate. "Mr. Caldwell," she breathed, as if she'd waited her whole life for this moment. "I done brought you some homemade cinnamon rolls, and I guarantee this hospital can't handle the smell of 'um, much less the taste. And they're all for you!"

Miz Broomer had been at the Bingo Hall Saturday, helping clean for the opening Sunday. Her husband had dropped her off, then picked her up and all I had seen of him was a camoflauged hunting cap and the back of his pickup. I gathered he didn't approve of church, or maybe he didn't approve of Miz Broomer cause he wasn't here now either.

"Good heavens, Wanda," Daddy breathed in the aroma of the rolls, "I think you've outdone yourself."

"Sho 'nuff," Elder Thomas agreed.

Miz Broomer blushed ruby red and grabbed the rolling hospital tray in one swift move. "Now, come on here, y'all. Enough of this. We got to eat these things before they git cooled off. Mildred Juniper? Run out to the nurse's station, honey, and tell them we need us some napkins in here." I headed quickly for the door. "Oh, but don't tell 'um what for, now. Just tell them Miz Broomer needs some napkins real bad. Real bad. Got it?"

"Yes, ma'm."

"Uh huh. That's right. You get them and we'll get this here tray set up..."

I left Miz Broomer talking to herself and a room full of men staring at her tinfoil plate. The nurse's station was down at the other end of the hall, and I took my time walking down there. Not that those cinnamon rolls didn't smell great, it's just that I wanted a little time to think. Daddy had been talking with Mr. Caldwell about him going on and living in the Bingo Hall, I mean church, from now on out. And Mr. Caldwell could help pay for that by doing yard work and keeping the church cleaned up on the inside. Seemed like a good deal for Mr. Caldwell. He really appeared to be harmless enough, but I wondered what the rest of Piedmont Ridge would think.

As I carried the thin napkins back down to the room, I knew I was avoiding the truth: Piedmont Ridge would not be happy about Mr. Caldwell staying and certainly not happy about him living for free in the new church.

Chapter 20

Dot

Dot overheard snippets of conversation all week as she delivered milk. Seemed like everyone was talking about Bobby Caldwell – the old-timers retold his story over and over, and the younger folks rolled their eyes and shook their heads. Dot kept telling herself she didn't much care. Of course she felt sorry for the man, but he was of no concern to her, and if it hadn't been for that dad-blamed ladder, she wouldn't have to fight to keep from picturing him, lying on the floor, looking half-dead. She shook her head as if to throw out the image as she rinsed off the last of the crook-necked squash in the kitchen sink.

Fall was approaching; her favorite time of the year, but she sure hated to see the end of fresh vegetables. Dot had canned twenty jars of green beans, more than twenty jars of butterbeans and frozen more creamed corn than she cared to count. She was well-stocked for fall and winter, but still enjoyed fresh corn on the cob and tomatoes every day. Nothing like good vegetables to keep your system flowing, Dot considered, then smiled vaguely as she remembered Leslie with the first tomato of the year.

It always began in early June. Leslie would rise at the crack of dawn even though school was out. She would make her way to the garden, tiptoeing slowly over dew-sodden grass. By the time Dot was at the kitchen sink pouring water into the percolator, Leslie was examining every green tomato on each plant. Her amber hair would catch the rays of the morning sun, reflecting variations of color and light. Dot always knew when the first tomato was beginning to ripen because Leslie would leap high into the air, then run sailing through the screened door.

"Mom!" she would cry. "It's almost here. I see a bit of orange, and I'll bet you some fresh catfish that I'll be eating my first tomato sandwich in three days!"

Dot finished scrubbing the last squash and looked up, staring out the window, half expecting to see Leslie.

But no. It was the wrong time of the year. There were only a few tomatoes left on the bushes. The plants were almost completely withered now, and weeds had overtaken the black-eyed peas. Fall was on the way, and Leslie hadn't been in the garden for twelve years.

Dot stacked the squash next to the stove. She figured she'd pan fry them for supper.

Twelve years – how time had flown and she still kept going. When Leslie's biological mother came and carried her off, Dot thought she wouldn't survive. She and Tom held each other long into the night – for many, many nights – crying for Leslie. For her return. For what had been and wouldn't be anymore. She had written letter after letter, reminding Leslie how much they loved her and wanted her back. That they would wait until she was old enough to leave, and she could always come back to Piedmont Ridge, always come back home.

But Leslie never wrote back and she never came.

Two years later Tom had fallen dead in his tracks. He had been on his way back from milking and dropped right there in the middle of the path, only two years after Leslie had left her. Her heart and soul had still been recovering, and then the good Lord – because He had to be good – had taken Tom.

Oh, Dot had lost faith for a while, but she couldn't work the land and see the power of God's existence day in and day out and not remember that, indeed, God was good.

She sighed and reached for the degreaser bottle. The stove fan and light were a mess, so she sprayed the oven hood and scrubbed fiercely.

She had an awful lot of questions to ask when she finally did make it to heaven, see Jesus, and meet up with Tom again. But she didn't figure anybody down here could answer those questions, and she sure as heck wasn't going back to any church to try to find out. She had her memories. She had her God – on her own terms. That was enough.

The stove hood sparkled again, and Dot remembered those dirty milk bottles in the bed of the pickup. She really needed to get them down to the barn sink for cleaning. She was running low on bottles and the cows were producing more milk than usual. She may even have enough milk this week to up Eunice's order at the Piggly Wiggly.

Chapter 21

Mildred

Martha Claire and me sat together on the back row. There were only five rows of metal folding chairs in the church "sanctuary," and the center aisle had pieces of styrofoam cup embedded in some of the cracks. But even though chairs were sparse, the back row was still the back row – and it felt good sitting there – almost rebellious. We could whisper freely. Gregory kept eyeballing us from the second row, but I wasn't paying any attention to him. He could meet Martha Claire after the service. For now she was mine...although she was kinda driving me crazy.

"Mildred, who's that over there?" Martha Claire's deep brown eyes stared unblinkingly at Miz Mary Rose and Stew.

"Oh, that's the lady I told you about from the co-op. Remember?" I whispered.

"Yeah." Martha Claire giggled. "The one whose bosom almost smothered you to death."

"Uh huh. That's her."

"How 'bout her? Who's she?" Martha Claire pointed to Wanda Broomer, first row, center.

"Miz Broomer. Expert cinnamon roll maker."

"Right," Martha Claire dragged out the word like her understanding of Miz Broomer was way more than meets the eye.

"You have got to stop this," I whispered furtively. "Daddy's gonna notice and we're gonna get in trouble."

Daddy had been going on now for almost an hour. You'd a thought his first Sunday message was a time to introduce himself to the whole world, not just the smattering of people sitting here in the Bingo Hall.

Besides us, Miz Broomer, Miz Mary Rose and Stew, and the Thomas family, there was one other family. Daddy had introduced them as the Lewises from down toward the hospital road. They were friends with Miz Mary Rose and – I had to say – their three little kids were actually pretty good, not whiny or anything. They looked to be about two, three and six years old. No one to play with there.

Mr. Caldwell was still in the hospital, but since he'd be living here, I figured he'd be coming to church too. So I counted seventeen members, including us and Mr. Caldwell.

I sighed. Not very impressive numbers. Martha Claire swung her head at me, shushing me with her eyes. She had a lot of nerve after all that whispering she'd been doing.

Martha Claire and me had been inseparable since she and her Uncle Goose had arrived yesterday afternoon. Uncle Goose was happy – he'd gotten a good price for his calves – and the celebration had extended to our house. Even Mama was sitting on the front row this morning, although Daddy practically had to carry her here. She was determined to be here for his first Sunday. Mama still had her doubts about Daddy's call of God. I think I might be the only person who she let on to, but I knew it. I glanced up at her now, sitting straight and tall in her only good dress. The green floral. I liked it cause it matched her eyes. Daddy bought it for their anniversary three years ago. The green dress only came out on extra-special days. It was all for Daddy.

He was sweating pretty hard now. The doors were propped open with concrete blocks and a big fan was blowing to beat the band. Still, it just didn't do much for this heat. I had drops sliding down my back, too.

Suddenly I noticed it had gotten real quiet. I didn't catch what Daddy had last said, so I set myself to listen better, then Miz Broomer hesitantly lifted her hand.

"I'd like to pray, Brother Sam," she stammered, "for our church and our town." And she did. After Miz Broomer, others lifted their hands and prayed out loud for God to bless Daddy's church and bless us and bless Piedmont Ridge. Then Miz Mary

Rose stood up, her large presence loomed even bigger in the significance of the moment. The air seemed to crackle.

"Lord," she began, "we know what peoples are already sayin' in this town 'bout coloreds and whites goin' to church together. We hear the whispers. We can feel the looks, the stares, the hatred that's sent our way." Several "amens" dotted Miz Mary Rose's prayer.

"Well, we're here to say that we knows You love whites and You love the coloreds and all folks worshippin' together. And we say it's an honor and a privilege to be persecuted for Your name's sake – just as You was, our Lord. It ain't fun, Jesus, but we choose this day to walk in Your ways, wherever that leads."

The chair creaked and groaned as Miz Mary Rose sat down heavily, as though the prayer had worn her out.

Martha Claire leaned over in the stillness, her sackcloth dress scratching my leg. "I sho do like her," she whispered. "You don't know what a person's made of until theys have to stand up fer somethin'. I think I know what Miz Mary Rose is made of." She sat back in her chair, a knowing smile pasted on her lips.

There she goes again, I thought, acting like she knows everything.

It always amazes me how fast people can go from praying to eating. Before Daddy ended his last "Amen," Miz Debbie was in the back of the room directing Elder Thomas on table set-up duty. Our first Sunday was "Bring a Dish" day. Somebody opened the door to the back office, and sharp smells of fried chicken and homemade macaroni and cheese woke up every tastebud I had. My stomach growled as Martha Claire and me walked up to check on Mama. She really wanted to stay and eat, if she could hold up. Martha Claire had laid hands on Mama's head and prayed out loud for her health this morning. I don't think I could ever do that – just pray out loud. But nothing like that ever flustered Martha Claire. She always said she was just talking with Jesus.

"How you feelin', Miz Rhodes?" Martha Claire skipped up the

aisle. Mama saw us together and smiled. "Martha Claire, I do declare, you look more like your Mama every day. And I believe you've grown a foot since we left Prosperity."

"Mama, we've only been gone six weeks," I reminded her.

"I know, darlin', but it sure seems longer somehow, doesn't it?" We smiled together. A knowing, woman-to-woman sort of smile.

"Yes, ma'am, it does."

Daddy swept up then, free from chatting with Miz Broomer. I could tell he was excited about the first day, but he also looked a little sad – or maybe just thoughtful. I glanced over toward Miz Broomer, but she was already putting serving spoons into dishes, her red, polka-dotted sundress looking like a table ornament.

"Laura Lee, what do ya think? Can I move you up to a table and fix you a plate?" Daddy's eyes begged her to say yes. Mama flashed him a bright smile and nodded, but I could see she was pretty tired. I wondered how long she could keep up her imaginary world of all is well. Martha Claire was watching carefully too.

"Great. Let me help you up. Mil?" Daddy turned toward me and Martha Claire. "Why don't you girls see if you can help Miz Debbie? It looks like Gregory might need a friend." Mama laughed as we all turned toward Gregory. His Mama had loaded him up with two pies and a pot of beans – then she stuck an apron over his arm and had him carrying it all to Miz Mary Rose who was holding out her arms, directing Gregory as he approached. He turned and glared at me, begging for a rescue.

"C'mon Martha Claire. It's time you met Gregory anyway. It'll be an experience; I can promise you that."

We were easing into mid-afternoon – our stomachs ballooned out with chicken, beans, watermelon, rolls and every dessert you could imagine. The grown-ups had straightened and closed up the leftover food to keep the flies from hauling it off, and Gregory, Martha Claire and me were itching to go exploring. I had promised Martha Claire I would show her the creek, and Gregory had been wanting to spy on Dot Harris ever since I told him about her barn and cats. I wasn't real keen on that idea but didn't want to look like a chicken either. I probably could count on Martha Claire, though. She was a real stickler for every kind of honesty and probably wouldn't allow Gregory to drag her into spying or eavesdropping. Course, it was up to one of us to get permission. I opted to ask Daddy. He seemed preoccupied – more so than Mama – in fact, he was getting ready to walk her back to the trailer. All the others were still sitting around talking, except the Lewis'. They had to take their three-year-old home for a nap.

"Daddy, can I take Martha Claire down to the creek? And can Gregory come too?" I smiled my widest smile, trying to show as many teeth as possible. He glanced up, and Mama put in quickly, "Not in your best dress, you're not!" Amazing how quickly she sounded well.

"Oh, no ma'am. Me and Martha Claire were gonna change."

"Martha Claire and I."

"Yes, ma'am."

Mama and Daddy exchanged one of those looks, then Daddy waved to Uncle Goose. He was leaning back in a folding chair, laughing hard at something Miz Debbie had just said. Uncle Goose had the body of a No. 2 pencil, and his afro stretched out tall and wide, giving him the funniest looking eraser head I ever saw. He stopped laughing long enough for Daddy to explain our plans.

"I reckon we got time, Sam. I got to get outta here in a couple o' hours to make sure Martha Claire's in school tomorrow. You know Sally'll have my hind end if I don't get her home in time."

Daddy laughed, signaling me on. "Go ahead, young 'uns. Don't be gone more than an hour, you hear?"

"Yes, sir," we chorused, dashing out the open door. Only an hour – time was wasting.

"I'll race ya down," Gregory called out, zipping past me and Martha Claire on the steepest part of the hill.

"He's a crazy black boy," Martha Claire stated, matter-of-factly. "He always like that?"

"Worse," I muttered, trying to keep from sliding into Martha Claire's heels. "You know if it hadn't been for him, I wouldn't have been dragged into all that mess with the homeless man. It was Gregory who wouldn't leave it alone." A few rocks tumbled into the water as we approached the creek. "Always had to be leavin' him food or sneaking over there. I was as scared as a hunted deer."

"But it worked out alright, didn't it? I mean, if Gregory hadn't been so pushy about it, you'd never found Mr. Caldwell in time. Then he would o' died – a lonely man in a bingo building, not knowin' anything 'bout how much Jesus loves him." Gregory was already crouched down, looking for tadpoles. I propped my hands on my hips, catching my breath. Martha Claire looked sideways at me. "Right?"

"Yeah, I guess so."

Much as I hated to admit it, Martha Claire had a point. Still, it would be wise to keep an eye on Gregory; he was what my Daddy called a loose cannon.

"Hey! Lookit! That's the biggest pole I've seen in .. Forever!" Gregory had a stick in the water, pointing out a whopper of a tadpole.

"Yeah, sho is a big 'un," Martha Claire's eyes searched all around. "This is a real nice place, Mildred Juniper. Real peaceful and quiet. Almost as good as our treehouse in Prosperity, but not quite."

Martha Claire smiled lightly, punching me in the arm, but I just couldn't laugh with her. It hurt my heart too bad. This place wasn't anything like Prosperity, and it didn't matter how peaceful it was, it wasn't really home. I squatted to watch Gregory's tadpole hunt because I didn't want to cry in front of Martha Claire – or heaven help me – Gregory. About the time I got situated, Gregory leaped up like he had a bee in his britches.

"C'mon, Mildred. Show me how to get to Miz Harris's place. Didn't you say it's not far from here?" Gregory was looking up and down the creek, trying to figure out which way to go.

"No, it's not far, but she might not like us snoopin' around, Gregory."

"We won't be snoopin', jest being neighborly and friendly-like. After all, you and her got to be good friends now, right?"

"Well, I don't know that I'd say that..." I trailed off helplessly, feeling myself being tugged at again. My eyes searched frantically for Martha Claire, but she had already wandered off a ways, checking out the creek rocks. Gregory seemed to instinctively know what I was trying to do, and – drat him! – he headed me off at the pass.

"You don't care, do ya Martha Claire?" he hopped over her way. Martha Claire looked up.

"Care 'bout what?"

"'Bout walking down toward Miz Harris's farm."

"Naw. It's all fine with me," she looked back down, and Gregory smiled at me triumphantly.

"But it's not just walking down there," I shot back, "it's...it's..." Martha Claire glanced up again, squinting in the light of the sun's rays.

"What is it, Mildred? Somethin' wrong?" She stood up, waiting.

"No, I don't reckon. It's just that I don't want to appear to be snoopin'."

"Oh," she shrugged. "That won't happen 'cause we just won't snoop. Now, which way do we go?"

Defeated.

I pointed up the creek, and Gregory leapt ahead and was off like a rocket while Martha Claire and me came along more slowly. She was awful quiet – and I wasn't in the mood to chat.

It only took us about ten minutes of creek wading to get to the place where I had first seen Miz Harris letting out her cows. I didn't think it was milk time yet, but it should be close. I always heard folks milked their cows a couple hours before dark

Right ahead was a slanted curve in the creek, and just when Gregory was rounding the corner, we heard a sharp cry of pain. I wasn't at all sure it was a person. Gregory stopped and stared back at us, eyes and mouth wide. Martha Claire and me froze in our tracks too, but she jumped to it when we heard the second cry and lots of creek splashing. Martha Claire was past Gregory and around the corner before we thought to move again.

"Mildred, come quick!" Martha Claire shot out. "I needs yo' help."

Gregory and me unfroze at the same time and dashed around the corner, feet splashing in the six-inch deep water. I almost stepped on Miz Harris's leg, I came racing around there so fast.

"Hold up there, girl," she snapped. "I don't want to lose a leg."

Miz Harris sat on a rock, one leg stretched out in the water and another wedged in between a large rock and the bank of the creek. Her ankle and foot were completely hidden, and it appeared she couldn't pull it out of the crack.

"Oh, Lord," Gregory gasped. "What done happened to you, Miz Harris?"

"Well, son, I would think that would be apparent," she gazed at him calmly. "I caught my dadblamed ankle in this crevice and can't seem to get it out."

"Are ya hurtin' bad?" Martha Claire was feeling up and down her leg, concern evident in her eyes.

"Not so bad I can't stand it."

"What do we do?" I asked.

"Now, there's a good question. I've been sitting in this creek bed for about an hour ponderin' that one," Miz Harris scratched her head thoughtfully. At first I thought she was making fun of me but realized she wasn't. She was just as stuck as we were.

"How 'bout I go fer help?" Gregory asked, already backing down the creek bed. I stared at him in irritation. He was building a solid reputation of being no good in a crisis.

"No need for all that. Just help me get my foot out," Miz Harris said.

Martha Claire, a formidable opponent in stubbornness, wasn't about to let that go.

"No, you're right Gregory. You go get help. Mildred Juniper and me'll try to git Miz Harris freed up."

Dot Harris looked at Martha Claire in surprise. I had the feeling not many folks had the last say with Miz Harris. Either way, there was nothing more to be said there because Gregory's splashing was all that was left of him.

"Here, Mildred. See if you can wedge that stick in between the big rock and that smaller one. Right there, see?" Martha Claire pointed. "I'll count to three, you use it like a lever, and I'll try to rock this stone at the same time."

Honestly, Miz Harris looked too tired to fight with Martha Claire. She must've been out in this heat more than an hour. Her hat was off and her gray hair frizzed out like a clown. Sweat and mud were caked on her face, hands and arms, and you could tell she'd been working real hard to try to get herself free.

Martha Claire began counting.

"One, two, three!"

I wedged, Martha Claire rocked – trying to pull the stone sideways, and Miz Harris grunted, heaving backwards. Sweat broke out on my forehead immediately as I pulled with all my strength. It didn't feel like it was going to be enough and I was just about to let the stick down when Miz Harris shifted and the foot slid out with a sucking sound. She fell backward on the creek bank and I fell backward into the water! My backside slid into a deep spot and water coursed over my face as Martha Claire howled with laughter. Even Miz Harris managed a smile.

"It's not funny," I said, wiping my eyes. "I could a' been hurt."

"Jest yo' tailbone and pride," Martha Claire hooted. "That's all that's hurt." She had mud splattered all over her face, but I didn't laugh at her. I told her as much, but Martha Claire didn't care. She just kept on laughing until she began to realize Miz Harris was lying there pretty still. We both got up, me dripping all down my legs, and walked over to where she was all stretched out.

"We's sorry, Miz Harris," Martha Claire began, "I jest fergot myself fer a minute. You alright?"

Miz Harris cocked one eye at both of us and muttered something.

"Ma'am?" I couldn't make it out.

"I said, it's a good thing I'm not dying! You two would've missed the whole thing."

I felt ashamed right then and Martha Claire did too, but Miz Harris didn't seem perturbed.

"Come here, both of you," she said. "Give me your shoulders and I believe we can make it to the house." I glanced up the hill and wasn't so sure she knew what she was talking about, but she was back in charge and even Martha Claire didn't argue this time.

We somehow pulled her upright, then Martha Claire took her left side and I took the right. Miz Harris pulled, wrestled and dragged her way up that steep hill, determined to get to the house. I was pretty amazed, although she still looked a little white around the gills to me. Every once in a while, I'd catch Martha Claire's look and she was thinking the same thing. Neither one of us knew what to do with an old lady in a heap on the hillside.

So it was a blessed relief to hear a vehicle rolling into her driveway as we closed the pasture gate. Daddy came running around the corner with Elder Thomas and Uncle Goose fast on his heels. Miz Harris, for once, didn't seem to mind all those folks around her. Daddy and Elder Thomas took over for us while Uncle Goose ran up to the back door. We all trudged into the kitchen while the men gently set her in a chair at the table.

"Well, good grief, Miz Harris," Daddy began, catching his breath, "what in the world happened?"

Miz Harris wiped her brow, breathing hard. "I reckon I slipped when I was laying out the food for the coons and my right foot got wedged firm. Couldn't budge it. Good thing the kids came along when they did."

She actually smiled then and it changed her whole face. I mean, Miz Harris was still old, but she seemed – I don't know – almost pretty somehow. Daddy just kept right on.

"We need to call the doctor and get him over here..."

"Nope." Miz Harris stated firmly. "Don't need the doctor. I know it's not broken; I can tell. I've got a sprain. Nothin' a little bandage and a few days of being easy on it won't fix."

"I think we oughta call him anyway and ..."

"Nope. I said no doctor." Miz Harris looked at Daddy fiercely. Made me kinda wonder what she'd do if he just pushed right past her and called the doctor anyway. Martha Claire had melted into the background on the other side of the room and watched. Gregory must've stayed with his Mama.

"Well, alright. But where are the bandages and we'll get that taken care of." Daddy looked around the kitchen.

"No time to bandage now," Miz Harris said matter-of-factly. "I've got to milk. Just hand me that cane over by the door, and I'll get that done. Cows don't wait. You've all done plenty and I'm grateful. You can just be on your way." Miz Harris moved to stand up as Elder Thomas floated over in his calm way. He lightly placed his hand on her shoulder.

"Miz Dot?" his voice was like summer rain. "Now, you know we ain't gonna let you go milk them cows. I milked cows for ten years for Mr. Carpenter up Turkey Creek Road, and I don't believe I've forgot a thing. Me and Goose right here'll go milk them cows. You jest stay put."

Uncle Goose nodded his head, his afro bouncing up and back, up and back.

"No, Daryl," Daddy said. "Actually, you and me are gonna milk those cows. Goose and Martha Claire got to hit the road." I heard Martha Claire's moan clear across the room. She always hated to miss out on an adventure. "Goose, you take Martha Claire in my truck on back to our trailer. Tell Debbie to give us a couple of hours and come on back to pick us up. And Mildred?" Daddy looked my way.

"Sir?"

"I want you to stay with Miz Harris, help her find her bandages and get her cleaned up, you hear?"

"Yes, sir." I looked at Miz Harris to see how she was taking all this ordering around, but she had leaned her head back in her chair, her white face giving nothing away.

"Right," Uncle Goose spoke. "Sounds like a plan. Martha Claire? You best say yo' goodbyes to Mildred Juniper. We need to git on back to Prosperity."

Martha Claire and me met in the middle of the room and shared a hard hug goodbye. There was just too much to be said, so she pulled back, made a goofy face and said, "I'll write ya on our way home and mail it tomorrow. Alright?"

"Alright." I smiled, sad to see her go but knowing she had to.

She hugged my Daddy and Elder Thomas, then whispered something to Miz Harris. Martha Claire patted her on the hand and then she and Uncle Goose left out the front door. Daddy and Elder Thomas were out the back door, and Miz Harris still didn't say a word. I wasn't sure what to do, so I sat down at the kitchen table with her.

Just me and Dot Harris.

Chapter 20

Dot

There was only one thing worse than the pain in Dot's right foot – people being pushy and taking over her life. She hated the thought of Sam Rhodes and Daryl Thomas in her barn with her cows, but Dot knew she couldn't do a thing about it. Her ankle was swelling rapidly, and the pain made her vision cloudy. She cracked open one eye to see a blurry Mildred Rhodes staring at her across the table.

"Ice," mumbled Dot.

"Ma'am?"

"I said, ice. I need ice on my foot, now! It's probably already too big to get outta my boot," Dot leaned forward to try to pull the milk boot off her foot. "Grab a pail from the back porch – right next to the door – and fill it with the broken up ice in the freezer next to the back door."

Mildred jumped to her feet, moving toward the porch while Dot gingerly eased her foot from its black, plastic casing. The boot thunked on the floor as she leaned back again, closing her eyes against the nausea that welled up in her stomach. Mildred glanced over at her as she grabbed a small, tin pail. Dot's face was ashen.

Quickly, Mildred found a half-gallon carton of chopped ice in the freezer. She grabbed it out and poured most of it into the pail. As she scurried back across the floor, she hesitated to speak. Dot's eyes remained closed.

"Just put the bucket here, Mildred, and I'll drop my foot in," Dot heaved up again, pointing to the base of the table leg. "Why don't you head into the bathroom and check the medicine cabinet for a sturdy roll of gauze bandage. Should be on the second shelf."

Dot slipped her red, swollen ankle carefully into the ice, shifting it around to completely cover both sides. Mildred watched silently, then walked around to the bathroom.

As she flipped the lights, she was surprised to find a pastel green-colored tile laid against walls painted creamy beige. Mildred wasn't sure what she expected, but this feminine room wasn't it. Family portraits were placed neatly on the walls with other photographs propped on a small, half-table. Fragrant soap filled the room with a delicious, flowery aroma, and it was clean enough to eat on the floor. Mildred was impressed.

"Do you see it?" Dot called weakly from the kitchen. Mildred opened the mirrored medicine cabinet, spotting a tight roll of gauze on the middle shelf.

"Yes ma'am."

Gently closing the door, Mildred caught a glimpse of herself in the mirror — of mussed-up brunette hair and a dust-smudged face. Her Daddy's blue eyes blinked back at her – clear and dependable. As she turned to leave, she saw a black-and-white picture on the half table. She stopped and picked it up.

A younger Dot Harris smiled broadly, her brown hair pulled neatly into a bun. Next to her, a thin, angular man draped his arm loosely over her shoulder. The curious smirk on his face was almost hidden by the rim of a straw hat perched crookedly on his head. Standing in front of them was a girl who looked to be about Mildred's age. She picked up the frame to examine her more closely. The girl stared back at Mildred, almost defiantly. Her chin was slightly lifted as she rested one hand on her hip. In the other hand was a bunch of freshly picked wildflowers. Her slight smile betrayed her kindness. Mildred could tell this girl had a mind of her own.

Ice chinked and clunked in the bucket in the kitchen. Mildred carefully placed the picture back and hurried into the kitchen, carrying the bundle of adhesive bandage.

An hour later, Dot sat in her recliner, foot neatly bandaged and propped on pillows, face and hands washed clean from the grime and sweat from her fall. Mildred had just returned from checking on her Daddy and Daryl's progress. It wouldn't be long before they would be heading home. After all, Mildred had school in the morning.

Mildred was washing out the ice bucket in the kitchen sink when Dot called from the living room.

"I have a proposition for you, Mildred."

Quickly drying her hands on the embroidered dishtowel, Mildred came into the room.

"How would you like to make a little extra money this week?"

Mildred's eyes widened. "Oh, yes ma'am. That would be super."

"I reckon I can get my morning milking done on my own, but the afternoon's gonna be a little hard with the pasture work I need to do. If you could come over after school and be my legs for a few days, I'll be glad to pay – if it's alright with your Mama and Daddy, of course." Dot paused, eyeing Mildred carefully. This wasn't an offer she carelessly threw out. She'd been thinking hard about it for the last hour, not wanting to ask, but knowing she needed the help. Of course, there was something about this girl. Something.

"I'm sure they won't mind. I could be here by three o'clock." Mildred's eyes danced with the prospect.

"Well, we'll need to ask. Isn't your Mama on bed rest? Won't she need you too?" Dot had been hearing trickles of information on the Rhodes family on her milk deliveries.

A shadow briefly passed over Mildred's countenance. "I don't think so," she said hesitantly.

"What exactly is wrong with your Mama?" Dot questioned, almost gently, but Mildred's face flamed in response.

"There's nothing wrong with my Mama," she snapped. "I'd best go check on Daddy again," and she was out, slamming the screen door shut behind her.

Dot frowned thoughtfully. Farm lesson No. 1 for Mildred

Rhodes was not slamming the door. There was no telling what lesson No. 2 might be.

Chapter 21

Mildred

    I hung my head out the window as Miz Debbie drove us home, hair slapping my face, leaving stinging prints across my cheek and neck. The wind blew away the emotions of the last hours, leaving me feeling weak and tired, and the night air was beginning to turn crisp, almost like fall. Sweater weather.
    I couldn't believe I had to go back to school tomorrow while trying to smother my excitement about starting my first real job on Wednesday. Daddy had convinced Miz Dot to let Elder Thomas cover the milking for one more day, so my job would only last half a week, but Daddy had given permission for me to help. Yet looking ahead, I had to calm down because tomorrow morning, before the rooster crowed three times, I would face Mary Beth Connelly, Violet Griffen and – Miz Dingle. It highly perturbed me that my beloved Miz Dingle didn't trust me anymore.
    Hanging my head out a little farther, I sucked in air with deep, steady breaths. I already missed Martha Claire.
    "Mil, is your door locked?" Daddy questioned from the other side of the front seat. I punched down the lock button and stuck my head back out again. The tires droning on the pavement could have lulled me to sleep any other time, but not tonight.
    Miz Harris had bugged me by asking about Mama. I'm not sure why, but it crawled all over me. It wasn't any of her business – and anyway, I hated answering those questions. Miz Dingle had nailed me at the cafeteria door last week, talking about the upcoming PTA meeting.
    "I sure hope your Mama can make it, Mildred," she had said

innocently enough. Then she added, "Is she doing any better?" I wasn't sure how much Miz Dingle knew, plus I had no idea how to answer that.

A bug popped me on the forehead and I drew back in, feeling carefully around my hairline. No mushiness. Guess it didn't splatter. Daddy was talking to Miz Debbie in the front seat, something about the sound of their motor and how long had it been since they changed the oil. I moved back out the window.

I had told Miz Dingle that Mama was better, and really, she was, but she still wasn't my Mama. I left my Mama in Prosperity, in a tiny, white feed mill house, setting up bridge games and humming in the kitchen. My Mama read her Bible every morning – extra time on Saturdays to study the Sunday school lesson. She made dozens of extra, extra chocolate chip cookies for me and Beth Ann and whoever else dropped in. She was dressed neatly every day and would never be seen in her bathrobe.

I felt the tear slide off my cheek in the wind and leave a quick, drying mark. I hadn't even realized I was crying. It was all well and fine to swear off crying about the whole thing, but sometimes it just snuck up on me. I tried to keep Mama on the back burner.

But she never really was ... on the back burner, I mean. She was like a big, boiling cauldron right on that front, right eye of the stove. Always in my sight. Always worrisome. I'd been doing all the stuff a good daughter should do in this case – cleaning, helping Daddy cook meals at night, playing rummy with Mama and Daddy before bed and laughing at all the right times. But it was hard, so very hard to keep smiling and not fall apart.

When would Mama come back?

I thought again about that question right before bed when Daddy reminded me that he and Mama would be out of town all the next day. She had a doctor's appointment and I was to walk to school through the shortcut path. He handed me a five-dollar bill and told me to go by Deb's Chicken on the way home to pick up supper. We hadn't splurged on eating out since we got to Piedmont

Ridge, and I was excited. Mama screwed up her face and looked at Daddy with a question darkening her green eyes.

"Are you sure she's old enough to do all that on her own, Sam? We can always pick up the chicken on our way back into town."

My heart dropped as I turned toward Daddy. He was sitting at our borrowed kitchen table paying bills and barely glanced up as he answered.

"It'll be a big help, Laura Lee. Neither of us is gonna feel like waiting for chicken at Deb's after driving half the day. Mil'll be fine."

Mama, stretched out in her chair with a romance novel in her lap, apparently decided this wasn't a battle worthy enough to warrant a fight. She shrugged and picked up her book. Inwardly, I leapt for joy. This should make school fairly easy tomorrow. Plus, a doctor's appointment meant more news on Mama's sickness – maybe good news.

Next morning I was out the door at 7:15 on the nose. It usually took about ten minutes to get to school through the shortcut path. I had found that no other kids walked this way and that suited me fine. Mary Beth and Violet had been pretty quiet since the lizard day, but I didn't trust their silence one bit. I knew something was coming, so the fartherest I could stay from them, the better. Miz Dingle didn't seem to treat me any different, but I could feel a tall, brick wall between us. She tried last Friday to ask me my favorite thing about the book I was reading, *Little House on the Prairie,* but it all felt fake to me. I mumbled something – don't even remember what – because I knew she didn't really care.

Daddy's crisp five-dollar bill sat firmly in my back pocket as I came out of the path, right across the street from Piedmont Ridge Elementary. I waited till the crossing guard waved me on and skipped up the steps, my ponytail popping my shoulder. A huge, homemade yellow poster greeted me as I reached for the handle. Decorated in fall colors, it showed a turkey, a pretty weak sketch of a pilgrim and an Indian teepee. Bold letters across the top stated:

Tryouts for Piedmont Ridge's Annual Thanksgiving Play
Tuesday, 2nd Period
School Cafeteria
See Mr. Garner to sign up

Russell Simpkins walloped me in the back.

"Get outta the way, Mildred," he shoved. "You're clogging up the works."

I stood to the side, letting the throngs of lunch box-carrying kids fly past me, my eyes fixed. Tomorrow, 2nd period. A play. A real play. And a chance to be in it! Mr. Edwards at Prosperity Elementary hadn't believed in plays for the elementary kids. "The kids are too little," he used to say. "Plays are for teenagers."

But now.

I eased into the crowd, heading toward Miz Dingle and Room 32. I would sign up with Mr. Garner today. Even the sight of Violet Griffen sashaying down the hall in a new pink skirt couldn't dampen my spirits. In fact, I really didn't see her at all.

I saw a stage. It was wildly decorated with fall foliage, a long table full of turkey and corn, and I was brave, strong, Pocahontas, stunning the audience with my story of Capt. John Smith's gallantry and my courage in the face of my great chieftain father, Powhatan. It didn't bother me that Pocahontas wasn't really around during Thanksgiving. I think Miz Dingle would call this poetic license. Ladies in the audience would weep as I declared my love. Men would stare in wonder, forgetting they sat in the school cafeteria. I would transport them all to the wild woods of early America with my gripping portrayal.

Just at the moment that I was being swept into Capt. John Smith's arms, I ran right into Miz Dingle's huge backside, catching the scent of lilac water and talcum powder. My nose pressed into her shoulder.

"What in heaven's name?" Miz Dingle's sharp eyes cut around. "Mildred. Watch where you're goin', child."

"Yes'm," I mumbled, embarrassed. I'd better pull my head out of the clouds.

The bell rang at 3:15 and I hustled out as quick as I could. Deb's Chicken was waiting on me, and I couldn't wait to test out my new-found freedom.

Kids scattered into the waiting buses, looking like a long line of yellow and black caterpillars, inching into a garden row. Cars rolled out slowly as well, and within only a few minutes of the bell, the schoolyard was practically empty, a few homework sheets blowing ownerless in the breeze.

I hitched up my books, preparing to walk the few blocks to Deb's, which would take me past the Piggly Wiggly and a couple of other businesses down Main Street. Once I bought the chicken, I'd come back toward the school and hang a right into the shortcut, getting home before Mama and Daddy, most likely. But I'd stick the chicken in the oven on warm and get my homework done before they drove up – if all went well.

I had walked only a little ways when I saw a group of kids hanging out in front of the Piggly Wiggly. It looked like one of them had bought something – maybe candy – and the others were begging for a portion.

Keeping up my pace, I didn't pay much attention until I saw Gregory's fuzzy brown head and familiar blue and grey t-shirt. Of course. He was right in the middle of the cluster of kids. I cut sharp to the right, crossed the road again, and ambled up to the group. Nobody even noticed me until I spoke.

"Hey Gregory. What's goin' on?" I was almost laughing, watching him try to wheedle for some jelly beans from a scrappy looking kid.

Seven pairs of chocolate eyes looked toward me, jolted out of their bargaining. The air hung heavy and all laughter stopped. Gregory's wide smile collapsed as he saw me, standing there expectantly in my purple high-tops, balancing books and lunch box.

"Well? Cat got your tongue?" I asked.

Suddenly, there was a shift in the air and a tall, black boy with thick glasses jerked his head toward me while talking to Gregory.

"Hey, Gregory. Looks like a little white girl here wants to talk with you. You got anything to say?"

My mouth dropped. Little white girl? Who did he think he was talking to? I started to ask Gregory who this goof ball was when one of the girls broke in.

"What's a' matter, Gregory? Us colored girls not good enough to be yo' friends? Got to go find white trash?"

The parking lot started to close in on me. The air became hot, thick, and I felt all color drain from my face. Gregory was frozen, mouth working silently as I waited. Some of his friends began to giggle and nudge him.

"Well, like the girl said. Cat got yo' tongue?" The boy with thick glasses grinned weakly, elbowing Gregory hard. I saw his Adam's apple bob as he swallowed, then Gregory turned toward me fully. His eyes said one thing while his mouth spoke something different.

"Naw," he spit out. "Cat ain't got my tongue. Go on home, little white girl. I ain't got nothin' to say to you."

"But Gregory..." I stammered.

"I said, 'Go on home, white girl!'" Gregory shot out the words like arrows, each centering on its target. His friends stared at me, laughing, punching one another. The small girl propped her hand on her hip and said, "Didn't you hear him, girl? You got broke legs or somethin'?" Her plaited pigtails swung back and forth as she spoke, driving each word deeper and deeper.

I took one last look at Gregory, standing straight and tall, and spun on my heels. I began to run as fast as I could, feet flying over the parking lot pavement, beating across the road, slamming into the dirt path on the shortcut. All thoughts of Deb's Chicken flew out of my mind and I didn't stop running until I had jerked open the door to our trailer and collapsed on my bed.

Surely my sobs would be loud enough to drown out the words that chased me all the way home. But as I tried to catch my breath, I realized I could still hear them, along with the sound of Gregory's laughter leading it all.

I heard Mama and Daddy talking in the yard before they got to the front stoop. My eyes were crusted with dried tears and my mouth felt all dry and cottony. The screen door banged open, slapping hard against the cheap, tin siding on the trailer.

"Mil? You home?" Daddy hollered from the door. "Need some lights on in here. Come on, honey, plop down in your chair for a rest and I'll check on that chicken.

"Mil?" Daddy yelled again as I stumbled into the living room. He glanced toward me in the twilight, not really seeing me. "Honey, did you put the chicken in the oven? Your Mama and me are starving and I'm sure you are too."

"What'd the doctor say?" I shifted the imaginary cotton balls in my mouth.

"Good things. We'll talk about it while we eat." Daddy tugged open the cold, dark oven door, then looked at me more carefully. "Where's the chicken, Mil?"

"I didn't get it," I mumbled.

"Didn't get it? Why not?" His voice began to rise as he straightened up. Mama's sixth sense kicked in and she spoke calmly from her chair.

"Mildred Juniper, come here please." She sounded weak, yet held all the other-worldly power of a mother. I dared not hesitate. As I drew closer, she leaned toward me, her green eyes peering steadily into my blue ones.

"What's the matter, honey. You look like you been drug through the ringer."

"I just had a bad day, that's all." I looked away as I answered. It was so hard not to spill the beans when Mama looked at me like that. But this time, this time, my Mama came back. For the first time since June, she wouldn't let me slide by. I didn't need the doctor's report. I knew she was better.

"Sam?" Mama called to Daddy with that no-nonsense look. "Why don't you hop in the car and head over to Deb's. Mildred and me need some girl talk."

Daddy opened his mouth, then shut it real fast. He grabbed his keys and walked out the front door, leaving me and Mama in the living room together. She smiled, motioning for me to join her in the big recliner and I gladly slid in beside her. As I laid my head on her shoulder, I realized how good it felt to not have to be strong for a while.

Me and Mama talked the whole time Daddy was gone. I broke down and told her all about the terrible scene in the Piggly Wiggly parking lot and she cried with me. Mama said she understood betrayal in a friendship, and that's what Gregory had done. She told me about two different friends she had growing up in Prosperity. How one of them had pretended to like her just to get closer to Mama's older brother. And how the other had been her friend since elementary school, but started hanging out with the popular kids in high school

"It does hurt, Mil," she stated again after our crying spell was over. "And sometimes, no matter how hard we try, we can't get those friendships back. It takes two people to hold a relationship together – whether you're friends or even married. Both have to work at it. If only one tries to keep things going, it's sure to fail."

"So what do I do now? I don't even think I could look Gregory in the face. He was horrid!"

"I know. He was pretty horrid," Mama raised her eyebrows. "What do you think you should do?"

The question hung there in the air like a stinking, dead cow. I wanted to hurt Gregory back. I wanted to never speak to him, but I wanted to slap him hard first! All the scenes played across my mind while Mama scratched my back gently. She waited.

"I reckon I ought to try to forgive him." I gave Mama the answer I knew she wanted to hear.

"Um huh."

"But I just don't know how, and I don't even want to!" I sputtered.

"Well, why don't you try this? Spend some time prayin' about it and ask Jesus to give you a heart that's ready to forgive. Then, just wait and see what happens next time you run into Gregory."

Mama shifted a little in the chair. "'Course, you know forgiveness will have to be given, whether he deserves it or not?"

Yep. I knew that. One of the Rhodes' house rules. We Rhodes always forgive – or at least try to. This was going to be a real tough one, though.

"Mama?"

She leaned back, obviously tired from her long day. "Do you have to forgive Daddy for dragging you to Piedmont Ridge?"

I'm not sure what I expected, but she chuckled quietly. I saw headlights reflect off the back walls and knew our time was short.

"Yeah, Mil. I guess I have had to forgive your Daddy – and God, too. I'm working on that. Some days I get it right, some days I don't."

The timid knocking on the screen door made us both jump. We expected Daddy to barrel in and weren't ready for so quiet an interruption. I leapt up and squinted through the tightly-knit wire. Miz Wanda Broomer stood on the porch stoop and she looked awful! I just stared.

"Hi Mildred Juniper," she whispered. "Is yo' Daddy at home?"

"Mildred, honey, who is it? Tell them to come on in," Mama was tucking away stray wisps of hair behind her ears, wiping the tear streaks from her face and biting her lips. She always did that to get the color up when she needed it.

"Please come in, Miz Broomer," I said, quickly opening the door. "Daddy oughta be home any minute now."

I couldn't stop the gasp that forced its way out as Miz Broomer stepped into the light. Mama echoed as we both stared in horror. She was a shambles. A big clump of hair was stuck to the right side of her face; it looked like it was stuck with blood. Her left eye was swollen almost shut, and her top lip looked like somebody shot a truckload of air into it. She kept her face turned away from us somehow, almost like she was ashamed to be here.

"Good Lord, Wanda!" Mama pulled herself up, moving quickly to her side. "What in the world happened? You need to be at the hospital! Mildred. Get some wash rags, a pail of warm water and the medicated cream on my bathroom shelf." Mama shot out directives like a drill sergeant.

I pulled my eyes away from Miz Broomer's swollen face and ran back to Mama and Daddy's room. I could hear Mama making soothing noises while Miz Broomer began to sniffle and cry. Finding the cream and three clean wash rags, I hurried to the kitchen for a container to hold warm water. It always took forever to get the water hot in this stupid trailer, so I turned the tap while I dug through our junk tupperware drawer. My hand clutched the red bowl with the handle as I listened.

"What? Wanda. You don't mean it? He wouldn't have," Mama's shocked voice pierced into the kitchen.

"He did," Miz Broomer wailed, "and it ain't the first time. I just don't know what to do." And the sobs grew louder. I got the bowl filled and began hauling Mama's first-aid kit into the room. Mama waved her hand to the side table where I placed each item within arm's reach. Headlights once again filled the room as the Malibu swung into the driveway. Daddy was finally home from Deb's Chicken. It seemed like he'd been gone forever.

"Mil, go help your Daddy get the chicken in and let him know Miz Broomer is here, okay?" Mama gave me a knowing sort of nod and I knew my job was to catch Daddy and fill him in before he saw her in this disastrous state. I dashed out the front door and met him as he shut off the motor.

"Hey monkey. Everything alright?" Daddy questioned as he eased out the driver's side door.

"No, sir. Miz Wanda Broomer's here and she's all beat up."
"What?"

He stopped and looked from her truck to the trailer. You could see Mama through the window leaning over, wiping blood off Miz Broomer's forehead. Night had come completely now and the living room lights looked like beams from a lighthouse.

"Somebody beat her up and Mama told me to come let you know ... and help with the chicken."

Daddy thrust a brown paper box into my arms as he dashed past me to the door of the trailer. I followed slowly. My stomach growled as the smell of chicken floated to my nose, but I wasn't sure if I could eat. I felt a little nauseous. Maybe I would head into my room. I tiptoed through the living room, trying not to listen as Mama and Daddy asked Miz Broomer what had happened to her.

I set the box on the stove top, went on back to my room and shut the door tight. Poor Miz Broomer. And I thought I had a bad day.

Chapter 22

Dot

Dot waited on the front porch with her ankle propped on the extra rocking chair. She thoughtfully scratched Parthos behind the ears, figuring Mildred Rhodes should be coming around the house in the next ten minutes or so.

Sam had called last night, confirming that Mildred was needed today. Dot grimaced as she shifted in her chair. Yep. She was needed this afternoon. Daryl Thomas did the bulk of the milking all day yesterday, and Dot had managed this morning. But the pasture work – filling water troughs, checking fence rows for breaks – hadn't been tended to since Sunday morning.

The afternoon sun dipped low enough to shine its laser-like rays into Dot's eyes as she scanned the road. Maples boasted in their glorious color now and Dot thrilled in the season. Sunlight only enhanced each shade of yellow and orange, making the dynamics more distinct. She looked past the tree line to the dust-covered highway, watching for the four o'clock school bus. Sure enough, like clockwork, Bill Parson's bus careened down the highway, carrying its fill of hyped-up kids ready to be home.

Dot only caught a glimpse of the mustard yellow color from her front porch but easily saw clouds of red Carolina dust piling into the air. She coughed just watching it, but the cloud dissipated before it could roll over Dot's white farmhouse. She stared at the evaporating image, vainly longing for a long-legged girl to emerge.

Years ago, Leslie would have been skipping down the road by now, empty lunch pail clattering a drumbeat to her singing voice:

Oh, would you like to swing on a star?
Carry moonbeams home in a jar?

Leslie's clear-pitched voice rang in Dot's memories. Days and days of joy and adventure, and stories from school.

"Mom! Guess what? Today, Gertie Floss passed a note to Gerald Butler and Miz Kitchens intercepted it!"

"Oh yeah?"

"Oh, you shoulda seen Gertie's face. I so hoped Miz Kitchens would read it out loud to the class." Leslie's eyes would leap at the prospect. "But she didn't." With a quick breath, "but she should have! Don't you think, Mom? Anybody who writes notes like that oughta be embarrassed. I mean, really embarrassed."

Echoes of yesterday' laughter bounced through the rafters of Dot's front porch. She allowed her mind to continue to move through the memories like a child on a breadcrumb trail. Crows cawed from the deserted cornfield, and somewhere in the distance, she heard a car door slam. In less time than it took to form the thought, Dot envisioned Leslie's mom, Dora, standing by the driver's door of her Oldsmobile. She could never forget that day: July 26, 1951. The day Dot's dream began to shatter.

Leslie had just bounded into the house holding a jar of tadpoles when they both had heard the car. Dot didn't recognize the blue, rust-stained car, but Leslie did. She began screaming, running frantically out the back door. Dot had no idea. She walked out on the front porch, squinting into the sun, catching the shadowy figure of a woman with light auburn hair. She seemed to be swaying – or maybe Dot's eyes were playing tricks on her.

"You Dot Harris?" the woman screeched, her voice high-pitched.

"Yep. Who are you?"

"Me?" the woman almost crowed. "Me? I'm the real mother, you witch. I'm Leslie's mama and I come to git her back whar she belongs."

Dot felt the porch move and shift. She groped for the rocking chair and sat down hard. Where was Tom when she needed him?

"Wh-what do you mean? Leslie doesn't have a mother."

"You bet your sweet butt she does, and I'm it! I mean her. I'm her!" the woman flung her arm crazily and a brown glass bottle spun out of her hand, falling into the ditch. It was empty.

"You're drunk," Dot declared, still wrestling with the confusion in her mind. "You're drunk and you're a liar."

"Ha! I may be drunk, but I ain't no liar. I done heard you and yo' husband done took in Leslie and I'm here to tell you she's comin' back home."

Dot never was very good at thinking on her feet, but one thing she knew for sure. There was no way she was letting Leslie go anywhere with this woman.

"Leslie says her mother died and until you prove to me that's who you are, she's goin' nowhere," Dot stated adamantly. "So you might as well get back in that car and go back where you came from."

"Like heck I will!" the woman shouted, spitting across the car hood. "She's comin' with me."

Dot casually leaned over and reached behind the pie safe on the right side of the porch. Pulling out Tom's 12-gauge shotgun, she raised it, pointing the barrel directly at Dora's skinny face. Some things speak clearly, even when you're drunk. Dora shut her mouth abruptly and glared at Dot.

"Fine. That's the way you want it. I can play hardball too. You ain't heard the last of me." She reeled back to the door and snatched it open. The eight-cylinder motor roared to life and Dot's first meeting with Dora Haskell was history.

She had lowered the gun, feeling an unusual shaking in her arms. The car barreled down the driveway, leaving a trail of blue-grey exhaust, slowing fading into the sky.

Dot had placed the gun back behind the pie safe and went to find Leslie and Tom. She had found them together in one of the back fields. Tom was off the tractor, holding Leslie while she wept in his arms. Dot had lots of questions – the first being why Leslie had lied about her mother. Because there was no doubt that the ragged sot of a woman in their front drive had been her mother. She looked like she had spit Leslie out. But Tom met Dot's frown with a quick nod and she knew this wasn't the time.

It had taken weeks to get the truth out of Leslie, but having finally heard it all, Dot couldn't much blame her for lying.

Looking back, Dora's visit had been the harbinger of what was to come – and in reality, Dot knew it but refused to consider the consequences.

Bill's now empty bus clattered back down Route 56, heading to its shed until tomorrow's morning run.

Dot glanced at her watch. Mildred ought to be here by now. She knew that the draw she felt toward the child most likely came from her similarity to Leslie. Mildred was about the same age, height and even had the same personality as Leslie, although she was somewhat harder to read. But that's where the likeness ended. By all accounts, Mildred seemed to have a stable family life, albeit a semi-invalid mother. Yet Dot knew, since the Rhodes came to town, her preoccupation with Leslie was growing and she didn't like it.

Parthos eased up and stretched, grunting as he moved over and flopped between Aramis and Athos. The crows had flown to another field and the silence grew. No, she didn't need to keep digging and picking at memories that were best left forgotten. It's just that, for the life of her, Dot couldn't figure out how to stop. She found herself enjoying the thought of having another girl around. Familiar feelings of protecting, guarding, rose in her heart. It was terrifying. It was wonderful.

A chanting, lilting voice floated ever-so-quietly into Dot's reverie. She drew in a quiet gasp. It couldn't be ... but yes, there it was:

> *Oh, would you like to swing on a star?*
> *Carry moonbeams home in a jar?*

The strength of the voice grew until it met up with Dot's wide eyes as the singer skipped around the corner of the house. Clad in purple, high-top tennis shoes and blue-jean overalls, Mildred Juniper Rhodes had arrived.

Chapter 23

Mildred

In spite of Gregory (My Betrayer) and Miz Wanda Broomer's beat-up face, I still found myself excited to start my first real job. It's true, Dot Harris wasn't exactly a warm, cuddly boss, but I figured I wouldn't have to talk with her much. Chit-chat wasn't her style.

Daddy told me Miz Dot would be waiting on her front porch, and I was running a little late. Mr. Garner had try-outs after school for the Thanksgiving play. There were only a few girl parts – some pilgrims, the narrator, one or two kid's roles and the Indian princess, Samoset's sister. Hers was the part I longed for, but Mr. Garner said he would audition all parts, then decide who would fit each role best. Just to increase my chances, I had braided my hair this morning into two pigtails. Mama looked at me funny when I came out of my room, but with Miz Wanda sleeping on our sofa, Mama didn't bother with me.

I jumped off the big rock to the path that ran by the creek bed and on up toward the Harris farm. Miz Broomer's swelling had gone down when I dropped my books by the trailer this afternoon, but her bruises were turning deeper shades of yellows, purples and blues. I didn't know how long she'd be sleeping on our sofa, but I hoped not too long. With all the showers and baths, I barely had enough hot water to wash my face this morning.

And, thank the good Lord, Gregory's parents didn't come over last night. That was a real worry! With Miz Broomer falling apart in the living room, Daddy could've called Elder Thomas. If he had come ... and brought Gregory, I mean, My Betrayer... I slapped a branch out of my way; it snapped back and popped me across the bridge of my nose. Dang! My eyes watered, but I kept walking fast.

Still, Mama and me had such a good talk last night that I didn't think she would've let Gregory come over. She's all about forgiveness, but she also can be counted on to give a girl time to think things through.

Fall leaves crunched under my feet, sounding like wrinkled grocery bags, as I tramped out of the woods and into the back pasture. I hoped Miz Dot would understand about the auditions. Daddy had said she wouldn't mind, but I felt sure showing up late for your first day of work wasn't responsible.

When I barreled around the side of her house, I was completely out of breath and I think my nose was bleeding where that branch got me. Maybe that's why she stared at me. I stared back. Her grey hair was mussed more than usual and not covered with that ridiculous-looking fishing cap. Her foot was propped gingerly on a rocking chair, and when she turned to look my way, her eyes widened and her face grew pale. Maybe there was more blood than I thought. I reached up to my nose.

She seemed to come to life then, her eyes re-engaging.

"Well, it's about time, Mildred," she said slowly.

"I'm sorry, Miz Dot. I ran as fast as I could, but we had Thanksgiving play auditions today at school and Daddy said you wouldn't mind and I was so hoping to get a part. But I ran hard and I'm ready to work." I paused. "Is my nose bleeding bad?"

"Bleeding? Nope. And don't worry 'bout explanations. Play auditions are an important part of life, but I do have a list and I need you to get moving to beat the dark."

Miz Dot stood up and winced as she set her swollen foot on the planked front porch. Blue paint chips shifted, revealing much-used places that were worn down to the wood. I wondered if, when I finished this week's chores, Miz Dot might hire me to repaint her porch. I made a mental note to ask...depending, of course, on how we got along.

She hobbled over to where I stood and leaned toward me; I

eased back, unsure what she was about. I almost had to dodge as she stuck her arm out and pointed behind me to the shed where her truck was parked.

"Head on over there and you'll find a pair of work gloves in the bucket next to the right wall. It's the white bucket. Grab those and then go back toward the field, where you came up from the creek. I need you to begin at the gate and follow the fence row completely around the field. You're looking for breaks in the barbed wire or missing nails from where the wire is attached to the posts. Tug a little on the wire as you go 'cause you'll feel the slack if there's a nail out. Once you finished that pasture, head on over to the other pasture. I'll be in the barn, and you can come back when you're done."

My head was swimming. "What do I do if I find a break?"

"Mark it or note it somehow so we can come back to fix it. 'Course, if it's a big one, you'll need to find some way to close it up until you come get to me."

"Close it up?"

"Yeah. Use a bucket or stick or something to scare the cows away from that spot." I must've looked panicked because Miz Dot threw a short smile my way. "Don't worry so much about it, Mildred. I'll have the cows in the barn most of the time. They won't be working their way around the fence for a few hours."

Relieved, I turned to head back toward the pasture, but stopped short. It occurred to me Miz Dot might need some help getting to the barn. She didn't seem to be doing so good on the porch. As I paused, she read my mind. "I can get there on my own. Don't you worry 'bout me. You got a lot of ground to cover before dark. You best get on it."

So I did. I was surprised at how long it takes to walk around pasture fences, pulling, tugging and judging wire. Made me appreciate farmers more, that's for sure. And it was almost dark when I made my way into the milk barn.

I had been watching the barn as I made the rounds. It was like a soft, glowing haven from the darkness falling in all around me. I could hear the cows gently mooing as they were led in to be milked and the world felt warm and safe and complete. I could see why Miz Dot might like this sort of life. I hadn't thought about Gregory or Miz Broomer or Thanksgiving plays all afternoon.

I kept the barn door from slamming as I eased into the light. Miz Dot was propped up on a wooden stool, watching from a corner of the concrete-covered floor. It looked like about eight cows were harnessed in stalls, and all of them had milking machines attached to their bellies. The swish, swish sounds reminded me of a quiet washing machine. Miz Dot glanced up as I entered and put her finger to her lips.

"Always talk in whispers around the girls when they're giving milk," she said quietly. "They're particular and don't like to be disturbed."

I nodded, taking in the scene.

"This is the last group and then we can begin clean up," she continued in a whisper. "Why don't you go on into the milk room" – she waved toward the concrete-floored room I'd just passed through – "and start some sudsy water in the right side of the sink. Get it good 'n hot. Hot enough to almost burn. Got it?"

I nodded.

"Once I begin freeing up the machines, I'll set aside nozzles for you to wash. There's scrubbers and sponges hangin' over the sink that'll fit in every crevice you got to clean. Just look them over and use 'um. If we don't keep clean milkers, we'll have bad milk and diseased cows."

A horrible sucking sound began to shriek from one of the cow's machines. It broke into the stillness like a thunder boom in a gentle rain. Miz Dot eased off her stool, limping over to the offending machine.

"Sounds like Mose is empty for the night, aren't 'cha girl?" Miz Dot just yanked the suction cups off Mose's teats and I winced. Ol' Mose didn't even bother to lift her head out of her feed trough.

"Here, gal," Miz Dot unplugged the suction cups from the wiring and handed them to me. "Take these with you and get that water going. Ten more of these are comin' your way. Just take it completely apart. See? It all pulls off and separates. Use those scrubbers I told you about. Then rinse them in hot, hot water and prop them on the drainer. When you finish that set, come back for more."

It all seemed so complicated.

"Just go and look at it, Mildred. You'll figure it out and I'll be there in no time."

I reckon all those years of washing dishes paid off that evening. I did figure it out – and there are a million things to wash in a milk barn. Thank the good Lord, Miz Dot had been able to dump the milk into the giant, silver-cylindered tank by herself. I couldn't believe she did all this work, twice a day even. And as skinny as she was.

I picked at my red, chapped hands as we walked together back to her house. My stomach was growling and I hoped Daddy would be here soon. Who knew what I'd face back at Big Star Drive. Would Miz Wanda be moved in? Had she taken my room? And Gregory. What to do with Gregory?

I must've sighed or something because Miz Dot looked at me funny as I held open the screen door for her. She slid her boots off, going as slow as molasses on her hurt foot. It was still tightly bandaged, but not as big as it had been a few days ago.

"Your Daddy oughta be here in a second, Mildred. Would you like a glass of tea?"

Would I ever!

"Well, then, why don't you get us two glasses and pull up a chair? We might as well sit a spell." Miz Dot's face looked pinched and tight as she slid into the wooden, slatted chair. She dragged the left chair closer by using her good foot, then propped her hurt foot up again. Finding the glasses took no time, and I quickly filled two tall cups of iced tea . Sitting felt wonderful, but my hands hurt.

"So, how are things going?" She tugged her fishing cap off and fluffed her matted hair.

"Um. OK, I guess." I swigged the tea and glanced at the clock.

"And how's your little friend ... Gregory ... right?"

I almost choked on an ice cube. Surely she didn't just ask me about Gregory, My Betrayer? The has-been friend. The Judas in my life. I felt my face flush as I tried to think of some way to answer.

"He's ... uh ... he's ..."

And then the very worst possible thing happened. I started to cry. And it wasn't even a pretty cry like those blonde-haired movie stars do. My lips started to quiver and then the dam busted. Before I knew it, my head was on my arms, lying on the table, and my nose was running. I didn't really see Miz Dot, but I felt a table napkin being pressed into my hands. Thankfully, I took it and had a long blow – then another one.

I reckon being around animals all the time kept a person from yakking at the wrong times because Miz Dot didn't say a word during my unseemly outburst. She just sat there and let me cry. Finally, I dried up. I didn't have the courage to lift my head though.

"Anything you wanna talk about?" She handed me one more napkin.

"I'm sorry," I sputtered. "I didn't mean to. I mean, I had no idea. It's just that..."

"Mildred, why don't you just slow down and tell me what happened."

So I retraced my steps from Monday, leaving out no detail of the humiliating experience. "Mama and me had a real good talk about it and I thought I was okay, but ..."

"But now you don't know what to do or how to act next time you see him."

How did she know? I pulled up and looked at her. Surprisingly, all I saw was compassion in those tired eyes.

"Oh, I've had my share of bad encounters in my life, Mildred. Lots of folks that I wished I wouldn't have to face again, but I did have to face them. That comes with living in a small town."

"So what'd you do?" I sniffed.

"Well, 'course the first thing is to make sure your heart is right."

"Yeah. That's what me and Mama talked about."

"Good. That's the hard part. Once you've decided to forgive, it gets easier from that point on."

"How's that?"

"Well, now you can really do something about it. Like maybe wait after school one day and beat Gregory up."

My eyes bugged out. Miz Dot busted out laughing. This didn't seem the appropriate time to make a joke. She must've thought different. She snorted.

"It's just a joke. Of course you can't beat up Gregory, but it sure would feel good, wouldn't it?"

She had me there. I can't pretend I hadn't thought of at least fifteen different ways to make him pay – 'course, that was before my intent to forgive. But even this morning, I still was fighting those thoughts. It was like Miz Dot could read my mind!

"Nope. Unfortunately, I can't give you an ABC answer on how to handle him next time you see him. It's always different. Different folks require different responses." She was staring over my head now, looking into something I couldn't see. "Some folks keep on spewin' their poison – even good church folk. Just like the Bible says in the Book of James, their tongues wag and set a fire to everything they touch. Poison pours from their mouths and touches everybody who hears them, almost like ripples in a pond. Then those words are carried to others who fall under the spell of the poison. And it continues on down the pike until just about everybody you see begins to avert their eyes, to look anywhere – anywhere at all except at you. No matter how hard you hope people will believe truth, especially people who've known you their whole lives – they choose to believe the lies about you. And there's not a dad-nabbed thing you can do about it."

I wasn't sure what all that had to do with Gregory. I don't think he had said ugly stuff about me around town, but I reckon you never know. My ice shifted in the tea glass, making a soft clinking sound in the stillness of the room. I glanced at the cuckoo clock swinging silently over the kitchen sink, wondering when Daddy would show up. Gravel crunched on the driveway at almost the exact same time.

"Reckon that's your Daddy," Miz Dot said quietly. "Why don't you run on out to meet him and I'll see you after school tomorrow."

I felt a strange reluctance to go, but I didn't want to stay either. For someone who was older and, well, odd, I couldn't escape the notion that Miz Dot understood me ... better than most people.

I put my glass in the sink and said my goodbyes, my mind turning to the question of whether I'd sleep in my own bed or would Miz Broomer get first dibs?

The screen door popped behind me as I tramped down the porch steps. I ran to the passenger car door with the headlights gazing steadily at me. They seemed to be trying to see into the depths of my soul.

I wondered, if they could see, what would they find there?

As Daddy turned left into Big Star Drive, I found myself thankful he hadn't started Wednesday night services and that Miz Broomer had decided to go on back to her house. I was pooped.

"What in the world?..." Daddy dragged out the words. Darkness had fallen quickly, but ahead, near the end of the circle, a bright light was burning – almost like a campfire.

"Did Mama build a fire outside?"

"Not that I know of. No reason to do that," Daddy responded.

As the car eased into the driveway, the fire took shape and I realized it was not even on the ground – it was hanging from a pine tree; it looked like a giant, dangling marshmallow on fire. As I rubbed my eyes trying to clearly see what it was, Daddy threw the car into park, jerked open his door and started yelling.

"Laura Lee! Are you alright?"

I got out of the car confused. Why would a burning clump make Daddy so scared? As he ran toward the trailer, I moved a little closer to the fire. By now the brightness of the flames had dimmed a little, casting strange, moving shadows across the trees. If I didn't know any better, I'd say it looked like a person on fire. I heard Mama talking to Daddy as they hurried my way.

"No, I haven't heard anything. What is it, Sam?"

Daddy didn't answer her – "Mildred, don't get too close!" he hollered as he came up to my side. Mama looked confused.

"What is it?" I asked, pointing.

"I'm not sure..." Daddy hesitated.

"Look!" Mama pointed to the base of the pine that was draped in shadow. Barely visible was a propped up, sloppily painted sign that read:

> *Black and White Don't Mix.*
> *Shut down your church, or else!*

"Dear Jesus," Daddy breathed as he brushed back his hair from his forehead. About that time, the biggest part of the burning mass hanging from the tree fell to the ground, slinging sparks wide around. We all jumped back, checking feet and legs for burn spots. "Well, there's nothing much to do now," Daddy continued.

"Reckon we oughta go to the police?" Mama shivered, pulling her sweater tighter around her shoulders.

"I suppose, but I don't see them doing much about it. Heck, it could've been anybody who did it – even one of the cops," Daddy's voice was hard.

"Now Sam, there's no sense in going there. You get on down to the police station while Mildred and me douse the fire. We'll be fine. People who do these kinds of things are too cowardly to face us head-on. I'm sure they're long gone," Mama smiled reassuringly, gently steering Daddy toward the Malibu. I watched him drive out, a frown on my face.

Chapter 24

Dot

By the end of the week, Dot had transformed Mildred into a first-rate milking assistant. She now moved into the milking parlor with quietness and ease, and her dishwater was almost hot enough to scald a cat. Dot was pleased – so pleased, in fact, that she was toying with the idea of keeping Mildred on for about three afternoons a week. The ankle was good enough to walk on – Dot had even made deliveries on Thursday – but having the clean-up help was awfully nice. Best of all, Mildred Juniper didn't chatter. Motor mouths drove Dot crazy.

She shoved Bess out of the barn as the sun just dropped below the horizon. Early morning had shown a light frost – wouldn't be long before ice would have to be broken in water troughs every morning, and water spigots would have to be re-insulated. Dot shielded her hand over her eyes to block out the sun's rays as she squinted, looking out over the pasture. The cows moved slowly toward the back field, their tails swinging loosely, synchronized with their gaits. It never failed to move Dot to see the beauty of creation, the simplistic outline of the trees against a darkening sky. Tom had always loved this spot, morning and night. Dot would bring coffee to the barn and find Tom standing right in this place, watching the sun rise over the barn roof, calling cows in for their morning milking.

She didn't cry anymore over these memories. The crying days had long since passed. Now Tom's absence had settled like a dead weight in the pit of her soul. There was never a day she didn't think of him, miss him. Probably the worst part was not being able to share what was happening on the farm. Just last week, Jo had a hoof infection, yet Dot knew it wasn't hoof rot. It had her stumped, but Tom would have known what to do. He always had a knack for vet care and they would've worked together on the animal. As it was, Dot ended up having to call the vet, spending money she didn't have.

The last machine clicked off as Mildred flipped the switch and took the suction tubes to the washroom. *Tom would have been just as overwhelmed by Mildred's similarities to Leslie as I am,* Dot thought. She wished he were here to tell her what to do now. She felt her heart being pulled toward the Rhodes family, but the risk of loving again, and losing, almost took her breath away.

Unconsciously, she put her hand to her heart as she watched the bright circle slip behind the trees completely.

Dottie, you know it's better to have loved and lost than never to have loved at all.

Tom, don't quote me cliches.

If they're true, why shouldn't I? Tom would have used his gruff, no-nonsense voice.

But you never really lost. Leslie left, and I know that was heartbreaking, but we still had each other. You left me alone. Ten years of alone. How can you expect me to love anyone again?

The crickets and tree frogs began their nightly serenade. Dot stood still a moment more, knowing she had to get back in the barn. The floor had to be swept and washed early tonight because she had to pack up that extra single mattress and box springs that were in the barn and haul them to the Bingo Hall. Sam Rhodes asked if she had an extra bed. He was bringing Bobby Caldwell home from the hospital tomorrow and needed some furniture for his room in the Bingo Hall. Dot was to take it tonight as she drove Mildred home.

Letting folks borrow things, giving away items – none of that ever bothered Dot. She had found you can easily give away your stuff. It was giving away her heart she avoided.

Chapter 25

Mildred

Saturday morning came carrying lots of emotions. Piedmont Ridge Police had moseyed on out to the trailer Wednesday night, said something about teenagers and pranks, then left about as fast as they had come, assuring Daddy that they'd do a careful investigation of the burning dummy and threatening sign.

"Humph!" Daddy responded as the police cruiser disappeared out of sight. "Won't hold my breath on that one." He had called Elder Crenshaw and Elder Thomas, just to make sure nobody else had a flaming surprise in their front yard. No one had any word of such doings since the fire at Pecan Holler Church a few weeks before. "Reckon we're just special," Elder Thomas had said, laughing wryly.

On the bright side, Mr. Caldwell was officially well enough to move into the Bingo Hall and begin work for the church. That made me excited.

But I would probably see Gregory today in the midst of the afternoon picnic celebration in Bobby's honor.

Not so good.

Miz Dot Harris had actually agreed to join us at the picnic and bring brownies and fresh milk.

That was good.

But Miz Wanda Broomer had gone back home Wednesday afternoon and no one had heard from her since.

Bad. In fact, Mama was concerned. I could hear every word of the conversation through the paper-thin trailer walls.

"Look, Sam," Mama's voice showed surprising strength. "You've hauled me all the way up here to be a pastor's wife. Now I finally begin to feel a little better, feel like stepping into this role, and you're slamming the door in my face."

I stopped moving around, willing myself to be totally silent.

"That's just not true, honey. You know I value your advice. It's just that I think Wanda needs a little more time. I don't want to offend her husband by being too pushy a pastor."

"Too pushy?" Mama's whisper rose a pitch higher. "You call checking in on a woman who was beaten till she was almost unrecognizable being pushy? No sir, Samuel Rhodes. How do we know her husband hasn't done something worse since Thursday? We haven't heard a word from her in two days! You've got to go by her house – today! If you don't, I will."

"Now, honey. You know you're not well enough to drive. You can't just pick up and ..."

"Oh yes I can. And I will!" I could feel the built-up tension through the wall, but suddenly all got quiet. I counted to ten before I heard Mama speak again, more softly this time.

"Sam, you're the one who told me that if God was calling you to be a pastor, He's calling me to be a pastor's wife. I've been fighting it for months – and I'm still none too happy about it most days. Everyday I tell the Lord Jesus I'll do what He wants, and everyday it's hard. But I'm making it! And now I begin to act like what I'm called to be and you're shutting me down. You're gonna have to make up your mind as to whether you really want me involved in this. God knows, I'm trying. I'm trying to do what I can. Even around the house, I'm trying. I hate that Mildred has to work so hard. I hate that I can't cook you a good supper. I hate that I have no real friends. I hate, I hate..."

My ears strained to hear, but all I could catch were rustling noises and Mama blowing her nose. Finally, Daddy spoke.

"I'm so sorry, honey. I just didn't realize you were still this unhappy. I thought we'd been getting along good, just like the doctor said. The rest is bringing about your healing."

Mama heaved, breathing in deeply. "I'm not all that unhappy, really. It's just so hard sometimes. I can see where we can have a good life here – except for threats and fires in the yard! — but I have to be a part of the ministry. You've been treating me like an invalid, not your wife. I deserve better than that. I'm your partner, not your patient."

"I hear you," Daddy's voice was closer to the wall that had my ear plastered to it. He was pacing the room. "Alright. We'll be partners again ... and Laura Lee? I'm so sorry." His footsteps continued their steady emphasis. "I guess that means I'd best check on Wanda on my way to the hospital?"

Mama's chuckle warmed my heart and sent my fears flying. "You'd better! And bring me a full report."

Chapter 26

Dot

Dot couldn't say why she agreed to meet Sam Rhodes at Piedmont Ridge General when Bobby Caldwell was discharged. She didn't necessarily see the sense in it, but Sam thought it would make Bobby more comfortable to have someone there who had known him longer than a few days. Dot figured it was another one of Sam's bait and switches – he'd get her there then pull her in even deeper. Even though she had him figured out, she played the game. She just couldn't help herself.

She pulled her truck into a parking place as close to the entrance as she could. Pete Griffin's gray Cadillac was two spaces down. Dot hoped she wouldn't have the pleasure of running into him again. There were few things more likely to bring on a bad day than encountering Pete Griffin. Sam's Malibu was also in the lot. "Looks like the gang's all here," Dot mumbled as she limped toward the glass double doors. The ankle was almost a hundred percent, but Dot was still taking it easy. She didn't need a setback.

Before she even rounded the corner to Room 115, Dot heard him. Pete Griffin in all his glory. And sure enough, he was standing outside of Bobby's door, talking loudly to Sam. Dot hesitated, wishing she could break away, but Pete had already spotted her.

"You might as well come join the party, Harris. I done give Mr. Rhodes here the bad news," Pete looked like he was doing anything but delivering bad news. He obviously was headed out to the golf course this morning. His button-down collared, neatly creased pink shirt was tucked into sandy brown golf slacks. A few sprigs of hair were plastered over to one side of his bald head, giving a semblance of a part.

Dot noticed Bobby's door was cracked and she heard voices inside – sounded like Mildred Juniper. Whatever discussion that had happened between Sam and Pete must not have flowed into the room. She stepped up, waiting for Pete to spill his news, purposely not asking for any details. She knew he wouldn't be able to hold it in, and sure enough, he cleared his throat and smiled a slow, subdued smile.

"It's like this, Harris. I was a'tellin' Mr. Rhodes here that it's awful nice of his little .. ahem ... church to offer to put Bobby Caldwell up in the Bingo Hall, but it seems to me that'd be an infraction against City Codes. The one where nobody can dwell in a place of business."

Sam stood to the side, trying to inconspicuously check Pete's fingers and fingernails for soot residue. Although he doubted Pete would actually do the dirty work of burning a cross at a church – or a bundle of rags in front of his trailer, – he figured it wouldn't hurt to be observant.

Pete continued his rambling. "Now, you realize I wouldn't want to make no trouble or nothin', but me being a long-standin' member of City Council and all – I'd have to let the council know or it'd be like I was shirkin' my duty."

Dot rolled her eyes. "Well, good grief, Pete. Since when did a church get to be a business?"

Pete's adam's apple dipped.

"As far as I know, a church is more like a family or community. There's no buying or selling going on there. Is there, Pastor Rhodes?" Dot crossed her arms and waited.

"No ma'am, Miz Harris." Sam perked up. "In fact, we are considered a not-for-profit organization and I'm sure having someone living on the premises of that kind of group would be just fine."

"Like at the Red Cross headquarters," pointed out Dot as she turned back toward Pete.

"I don't think that at all," he blustered. "It's my duty as a councilman to get to the bottom of this and I mean to do just that. You'd best take my advice and put Bobby Caldwell somewheres else. I feel sure my fellow councilmen will agree with me on this issue.

We've got to protect the public – keep public nuisances away from good, honest townfolks. We're the good guys, Harris, and you know it!" Pete's finger wavered in front of Dot's eyes. She'd about had all she could take.

"Pete, did you come all the way to the hospital in your best golf clothes to tell Sam he couldn't move Bobby into the Bingo Hall?" Dot questioned.

He sucked in air and glared at Dot.

"No, I'm here to pick up Violet. She's candystripin' this morning."

"That so?" Dot replied. "Shouldn't you be finding her then? I'm sure you don't have the time to keep jabbering with us."

Pete paused then threw up his hands, red-faced. "You'll hear from me one way or another Mr. Rhodes," he said as he walked toward the nurse's station. "Tell Bobby not to get too comfortable."

Sam and Dot watched him stride away, both feeling the day brighten with every step he took in the opposite direction.

"That's the best view I know of Pete Griffin," Dot said quietly. "His backside, walking away."

Sam snorted, laugh lines creasing the corners of his eyes. "You got that right." He pushed the door into the room, talking to Dot over his shoulder. "Do you think he's right? Can he make trouble for us?"

"Make trouble for who?" Bobby shouted from across the room. He was just deaf enough to give everybody else ringing ears each time he talked.

"Aw, nothin'," Sam assured him. "I'm just running my mouth. Have you two about packed everything up?"

"Just about. Mildred Juniper here is about the best help I seen in many a day."

Mildred raised her eyes, brushing back a loose strand of brown hair. Her ponytail flipped high on the back of her head while a pink ribbon dangled loosely from the knot. Dot took note. She'd bet ten-to-one that Laura Lee worked a little on the girl before she left this morning. Dot glanced down. Sure enough, Mildred's trademark purple tennis shoes had been replaced with brown loafers. She suppressed a smile when Mildred glanced up and saw Dot's eyes travel from her feet to her head. She smiled back and shrugged.

"Mil, have you spoken to Miz Harris yet this mornin'?" Sam said, while reaching for a duffle bag by the door.

"Mornin', Miz Harris."

"Mornin', Mildred Juniper...Bobby," Dot cast her eyes around the empty hospital room, assessing. There was a pillow and a blanket sitting on the food tray and a wilted bunch of flowers still perched in the windowsill. Dot would be glad to get out of this antiseptic-smelling building. She always hated hospitals.

"Daddy, should I pack this up, too?" Mildred opened a cabinet and found a half-opened box of paper towels and another box of soaps.

"Hm. Sure, honey. I reckon..."

The door slapped open. Pete stood, blocking the way, with Violet quickly coming up alongside. Her red-and-white striped pinafore was crisp and clean, making her look like the poster-girl for a perfect candystriper. Mildred concentrated on not seeing her, pulling out boxes and stuffing them into Bobby's brown paper bag.

"Just thought I'd let you know, Mr. Rhodes, that I run into Ed Crouch down the hall. He's checkin' in on his mama, being that she's got the gallstones. Anyway, he's on the City Council too, and he feels mighty sure that Mr. Caldwell here," Pete derisively swept his gaze over the skinny, disheveled man, "will not be able to stay in the Bingo Hall."

Bobby's cottony ears were able to catch this without any interpretation needed. Rage flared in his eyes, then his face fell and his head lowered. Sam's hands clenched in tight fists, a slow red wave crawling up his face. Violet took a step back, then seemed to take notice of Mildred who was steadily packing the bag. A slow smile spread across Violet's face and, as if nothing else were happening, she spun on her heels and ran back down the hall. Her father didn't know she had left.

"I don't recall anybody invitin' you in here, Mr. Griffin," Sam stated through clenched teeth. Dot fingered her truck keys, wondering how this might play out.

"Well, excuse my interruption," Pete replied with sugary sweetness. "I just figured you'd want to know where things stand."

"You figured wrong. Why don't you go ahead on out," Sam pointed to the door. "If anybody from the council wants to deliver any papers about specific church business, they know where to find me."

Mildred stood up, picking up the paper bag and sliding closer to Dot. Just then, a lady's voice raised in alarm from the corridor.

"What?" the woman screeched. "Where? We need to call security!"

Yet again, the door was jerked open and Violet's eager face peered around her daddy's girth. "There she is," Violet pointed at Mildred gleefully. "And I'll bet that's the stuff in her hands."

Mildred's mouth gaped as she stared at Violet, then her daddy, confusion rolling like waves on the seashore. An overbearing nurse with a masculine voice pushed Pete to one side. Her neatly creased cap sat askew on a hornet's nest of gray hair.

"Is this the girl?" she spun toward Violet.

"Yes, ma'am. I saw her puttin' the hospital materials in that there brown paper bag." Violet was all innocence, rosy cheeks and ruby lips, painting a portrait of sweet, Southern charm.

"Let me see what's in that bag, girl." Nurse Simpson snatched the bag out of Mildred's hands, dumping the contents out on the mussed bed.

"Now, look here..." Sam began.

Two boxes of soap and the half-opened box of towels rolled out.

"I told you so," Violet crowed from the doorway.

"You tryin' to steal hospital merchandise, girl?" Nurse Simpson grabbed Mildred's wrist, squeezing tightly.

"Ow, you're hurtin' me," Mildred squirmed. Dot raised her hand – she wasn't sure if she planned to punch Livvie Simpson or just knock her out of the way, but Sam beat her to it. He shoved past Bobby and threw himself between Mildred and the nurse.

"I said, Look here," Sam pulled Mildred aside, stashing her behind his back. "Mil's only packing up what I told her to get. We didn't know it wasn't supposed to come home with Bobby."

Nurse Simpson picked up a box of soaps, waving it slowly in front of Sam's face. "So, these big words right here. The ones that say: Piedmont Ridge Hospital Sanitary Soaps, wasn't a give away that they belong to the hospital and not Mr. Caldwell?"

"We were interrupted by Mr. Griffin," Sam explained. "We were just packing up and I would've caught it, but it's been like a zoo in this room!" Sam waved his arms wildly. "Honestly, all we want to do is check out Bobby and it feels like the whole world is against us." Frustration oozed from Sam's pores and Dot echoed the irritation. Bobby was silent and cowed on the other side of the room.

"Looks to me like you're wantin' to check out more than Mr. Caldwell," Nurse Simpson tossed the soap back on the bed.

"Livvie, for cryin' out loud," Dot spoke up.

"What about it, Harris?" Livvie spat the name. "You gonna weigh in here too?"

"Why in God's name would Bobby want to steal hospital soap?" Dot reasoned. "Or even this girl, for that matter? It's an oversight and we would've caught it before we left. No harm's been done and if you'll just let us get out, we'll be out of your hair completely."

Nurse Simpson put her hands on her broad hips, standing tall in her hospital-issued, stocky nursing shoes, exulting in the power of her position. That's where the elderly security officer found her as he tapped on the doorframe.

"You people call fer security?"

All eyes looked to Nurse Simpson who slowly relaxed her stance. "It's alright, Frank. I think it was just a misunderstandin'. You can go."

She turned back toward the room with the sound of Frank's slow, steady feet padding down the hall. "I want to see all Mr. Caldwell's things at the front desk as you leave. I will take it as my prerogative to search the bags to make doubly sure no other hospital contraband is being stolen. Do I make myself clear?"

Mildred felt sure this was really a man in a woman's body, but she wanted no more time to have to find out. Sam and Dot nodded.

"Fine. I'll see you at the front desk." She spun around to march off in her efficiency and ran right into Pete. "Mr. Griffin," she charged. "Please leave this room so these people may check out."

Pete effusively agreed, smoothing his hair tighter to his head.

As the entourage vacated Bobby's room, Violet turned back one more time. Her eyes found Mildred and she smiled a wicked grin. Blond curls bounced on her shoulders as she swaggered out the door with her father.

Vengeance isn't the Lord's, thought Mildred, *vengeance is Violet Griffin's.*

Chapter 27

Mildred

I must've been gnawing on my gums because Mama said, "Mildred, stop bitin' your cheeks." It was hard to stop. I stood at the front screened door, watching for the Thomas's truck to come down Big Star Drive. Everything was set for the celebration picnic. Daddy, Mr. Caldwell and Miz Harris were still unloading Mr. Caldwell's stuff at the Bingo Hall. They'd already been there two hours since we got back from the hospital. Our picnic tables were set and Daddy had hauled out the kitchen table to stack food on. Mama was finishing up pimento cheese sandwiches in the kitchen, and I had managed to get those blasted brown loafers hidden in my closet. I hoped Mama wouldn't notice my bare feet, but I knew she noticed my nervousness.

She padded into the living room wearing a late summer dress, finally out of the bathrobe. I thought she looked more and more like her old self lately. Her thick hair was knotted in a tight bun with loose curls falling on each side of her face. Daddy especially liked it.

"Whew! I'm 'bout worn out!" she flopped in her chair. "Anybody show up yet?"

Of course, she knew they hadn't but was trying to make conversation.

"No, ma'am."

"Now, are you sure you saw Wanda this mornin' when you and your Daddy went by the house? She look alright?" Mama's brow twisted in worry.

"Yes, ma'am. She came to the door and waved at me. She seemed all happy and excited, and the bruises were almost gone.

'Course, it did look like she was wearin' a lot of makeup – maybe to cover up."

"Hmm." It was Mama's turn to chew her lip. "Well, at least she's comin'. Between me and Mary Rose, we'll get the story out of her." Mama's eyes got that far-away look, so I turned back to the road.

My heart leapt when I caught sight of a vehicle, but it was just Miz Mary Rose's old gray sedan. She and Mr. Stew had promised to bring his famous catfish stew and, I admit, I was looking forward to that. We had bought several loaves of fresh white bread to sop in the thick, brown soup. My stomach rumbled just thinking about it.

"Looks like Miz Mary Rose is here," I reported from my watch.

"Good. Why don't you go ahead and see if you can help them unload? I'll rest another minute then come on out. I want to conserve my energy."

I stepped out into the late October sunshine, feeling the warmth on my face. The sultry September heat had evaporated into something more like a heat lamp than a ball of fire. It was welcomed.

"Hi there darlin'," Miz Mary Rose boomed across the yard. "Come hep me get this food outta the car while Stew works on that fish pot in the trunk."

Mr. Stew looked like the Jolly Green Giant getting out of a toy car. His short-cut afro added an extra inch or two, but what did it matter? He already had to duck to keep from knocking his head on the tree limb. He threw a hand up toward me and took two giant steps to reach the back of his car. As he disappeared behind the trunk lid, I wondered how big the furniture in their house had to be to hold these two up.

"Here, sugar, why don't you put this sweet tea over there for me, then come on back to grab the deviled eggs? You alright today?" Miz Mary Rose stood up straight, gazing thoughtfully into my eyes. It felt like time stood still and she was inching her way into my soul. Scary. I was glad to hear Daddy hollering from the Bingo Hall parking lot because it broke the spell – just as I was about to spill my guts again. I just had to get better control of myself. I couldn't keep falling apart when these grown-ups asked me a simple question.

I grabbed the tea and made my way toward the table, stepping gingerly to keep from tripping over the pine tree roots weaving through the yard. Twisting, hiding, reappearing, lumping up, they formed a treacherous path to my destination.

So my back was turned when I heard the tell-tale sputter of Elder Thomas's truck changing gears. Gregory was coasting down Big Star Drive and I wanted to keep walking, straight past the trailer, through the yard and into the woods. Lucky for me, Mama heard the truck too and chose that moment to come out on our stoop, carrying a humongous platter of quarter-squared pimento cheese sandwiches. She winked at me, smiled an encouraging you-can-do-it sort of smile and said, "Mil, can you put these sandwiches on the table, please?"

My almost-wayward feet turned obediently toward her and carried me to the side of the stoop. Leaning down to hand me the platter, she whispered, "Hang in there, honey. You can face him. Remember, God is bigger than Gregory Thomas!" Her bright eyes sparkled and I saw boldness and something like the tied end of a rope, a rope that had a knot for me to hang onto and not fall into this deep pit of worry. I took the platter and turned back toward the table. As I glanced up, I saw Miz Debbie hand Gregory a plate and point the way to where I was. His face followed her pointing finger, saw me a moment, then he deliberately avoided my eyes. Ha, I knew he had to feel bad! He sure should. The scoundrel. I decided then to make it hard on him. I mean, I forgave him of course, but he still deserved a little punishment. He wouldn't find me to be such a pushover. I deposited the sandwiches and sashayed back to Miz Mary Rose, passing him with barely a glance. He'd know before this day was over just how horrible he had been!

Surprisingly, Gregory didn't get close to me all afternoon. I have to say, I was confused. The Lewis family arrived, toting their three little ones; Miz Broomer was dropped off by her disappearing husband and, of course, Miz Dot and Mr. Caldwell walked over from the Bingo Hall. They pronounced his room "livable," and he looked worn out but happy.

I found my job was babysitting the Lewis children while Mr. Stew took his big black cauldron out of the trunk of the car and lit a bonfire under it. The stew had already been cooked, he explained, but it was always better dipped out of his pot – "has all sorts o' herbs and onions soaked in the iron of the thing," he explained. "It's always best on the open fire." Miz Mary Rose nodded knowingly, swatting at a late-season mosquito.

While I was watching Bobby Jr., Jimmy and Lily, Gregory hung out with the men-folk, avoiding me altogether. Mama glanced my way and shrugged, being just as confused as I was. I reckoned he just felt so bad that he couldn't bring himself to even talk to me. I gave him two or three chances by "just happening" by, or asking him to throw one of the kid's balls back our way. He pretty much ignored me — it was driving me crazy.

The thick, full smell of catfish stew hung low under the trees by the time Mr. Stew pronounced it ready and we all sidled up to the pot. I found a spot next to Mama under the big pine and sat on a root, laying two sandwiches, two deviled eggs and some white bread to the side of my sweet tea. Mr. Caldwell was given the place of honor in the big chair next to one of the picnic tables, and as I glanced around, I realized everybody seemed to be having a great time. Even Miz Dot took off her fishing hat and laid it to the side as she sat down at a table. Gregory was the only blemish on this day. I cut my eyes to the right. Yep. There he was. Still stuck to his daddy. I thought he was acting like a silly, little girl, and I planned to tell him as soon as I could. After all, I deserved an apology, and a good one at that!!

It was about the time that the Lewis' were packing up to go home when Elder Thomas glanced my way and said, "Gregory, go on over there and play with Mildred a little. You two been so preoccupied with children and grown-ups all day, you ain't had no time to be together. We'll take care o' the dishes. Get on over there."

A hush fell over the scene and the sounds of Miz Lewis cramming Bobby Jr. in the car seemed amplified. Miz Dot turned a curious gaze my way, and Mama's reassuring smile seemed to waver. I was glad...sort of. At least now he'd have to fess up and apologize, but the tension was still tight and uncomfortable. Plus, I figured the grown-ups wanted to pow-wow on the whole flaming "marshmallow" we'd had in front of the trailer last week. I'd read about the Klan, of course, in newspapers and stuff, and I'd overheard lots of stories about coloreds being hurt or having burning crosses in their yards. In fact, it happened once in Prosperity a long time ago, and Gregory had mentioned the cross that was burned at Pecan Holler Church back in August. But I'd never really known anybody personally who had that problem – until now. My heart skipped a beat. What if we were on the Klan's list now? What if it got worse? Gregory's rude mumblings interrupted my train of thought.

"Ah, that's awright, Daddy. Mildred's probably tired o' playing with the young'uns all afternoon."

"No, she's not, son. Now get on. Let us grown-ups have a little time. Git!" Elder Thomas swatted Gregory's behind while I crossed my arms and waited. Gregory dragged his feet across the ground, still not meeting my gaze. Good! Make him feel as rotten as possible, I wanted to yell. That's right. Force him to apologize.

"Yeah, kids. Why don't y'all head to the creek and wade a little before it gets too cold. Won't have many more wading days this year," Mama added. Daddy was deep in conversation with Miz Broomer and had that pastor-look on his face.

"Yes, ma'am." I responded, turning toward the back yard. Gregory followed at a distance and we didn't speak until we were out of earshot. When I was sure I couldn't be heard, I spun around, confronting him.

"Well, I guess you gotta do it now," I challenged.

"Do what?"

"What do you mean, do what? Apologize, of course." I felt my face flush, the anger and humiliation of that afternoon haunting me.

"Uh? Apologize. Me?" Gregory took on a defiant look. "Why in tarnation should I apologize?"

"What?" I couldn't believe my ears. "Because you treated me like dirt, that's why."

"Well, I wouldn't have treated you like dirt if you'd had half a brain and hadn't tried to talk to me. What's tha matter with you, anyway? That was the stupidest thing I ever seen!"

His earnest brown eyes drove me right over the edge. I'm not proud to admit it, but I lost my temper. Before I knew what was what, I tucked my head and ran straight at Gregory's stomach. I caught him with a full, frontal head butt and sent him pounding to the ground.

"Ow! What you doin' you crazy girl?" he sputtered, then flipped me over, putting me into a headlock. I was upside down and fighting for all I was worth – punching, jabbing and kicking until he had to let me go. Then I grabbed his legs and dragged him back to the ground. We began to tumble down the hill toward the creek. We must have hit every rock between the trailer and the creek by the time we stopped rolling. Heaving and breathing we lay there for a second, tangled up in each other's legs and arms, hair covering my face. All I could see were patches of blue sky between shoots of brown hair. Gregory moaned, trying to disentangle his legs.

"Good gosh, Mildred. You 'bout killed me," he panted.

I pulled a leaf out of my mouth. "You think I care? You are a mean boy, Gregory Thomas." I sat up, brushing off my shirt. A long, brown mud streak was planted across my chest, and one of my sleeves was torn at the wrist.

"I ain't mean. I live in the real world, Mildred. You think just 'cause we're friends you can just walk up to me on the street and chat about yo' day?"

"Well, sure. What do you think?" I shot back.

"It don't work that'a way. If you hadn't noticed, yo' skin is white. My skin is black. The two don't mix, especially in Piedmont Ridge." He sat up, grimacing as he shifted his back. "Dang, I think you busted up my shoulder."

"We're together right now and you're still black and I'm still white."

"This is different and you know it. Yo' Daddy's already stirrin' up enough trouble in town without you havin' to come messin' with me around my friends."

"Messin'? You call sayin' 'hello' messin'?"

"Yep. Sayin' 'hello' can get us both into trouble." Gregory sighed deeply, leaning back on a sycamore tree trunk. "Look, Mil. We can be friends at church and at yo' house, but not anywhere else. It's just too dangerous. I'll get beat up, called an 'Oreo' and won't have nobody to play with at school."

"Yeah, but true friends stick up for each other, Gregory. No matter what. You sure as heck didn't stick up for me the other day."

Gregory hesitated. "Let me ask you somethin'. Do yo' white friends at Piedmont Ridge Elementary know about me – yo' colored friend at the county school?"

Now it was my turn to hesitate.

"Naw? I didn't think so. I don't expect you go 'round tellin' yo' white girlfriends that you hangs out with a colored boy every weekend, now do ya? An' if I walked up to you on the street, while you chattin' with yo' white girlfriends, as I says to you, I says, 'Hey Mil. What we gonna do this weekend?', you gonna answer me back like I'm just another friend?"

He waited. Admittedly, I didn't have any real friends at school, but a few of the girls who managed to talk to me sure wouldn't put up with me having a colored boy for a friend. Suddenly, things looked an awful lot different.

"Yeah," he said.

And so we sat there, together, in the quiet of the trees, picking at dried leaves, not talking. Is this what our world was making us? Weekend friends only? I felt very old then, old and not wise enough to work out the things of this world. Mama always said when things didn't make sense to talk to Jesus 'cause He always made sense. But I couldn't exactly do that right then. Gregory was watching me.

"Where does that leave us, Mil? Are we still friends?"

I thought about that long and hard. I mean, who had been there for me ever since we moved from Prosperity...well, except for in town? Gregory, of course. I didn't want to lose his friendship, even if it meant only having it half-time.

"I reckon so, but I sure don't know how to do it."

Then the old smile was back, teeth shining brilliantly in the fading light. "I figure we just pretend we don't know each other if we see each other in town." He stood up, offering a hand to help me to my feet. I accepted. "Hey, we could even work out a secret code to talk around others. You know, like I pick my nose and it means we need to meet at the Bingo Hall or somethin'."

"Oh, ugh! That's gross."

His laughter rang out. "Yeah, but it's a swell idea."

We started inching our way back up the hill, taking care to step on rocks as much as possible. We both were still barefooted and the light was getting so low that we couldn't see the stinging nettles. Gregory must've devised fifteen different codes between the creek and the trailer – from coughing three times, which meant one of us needs rescuing, to scratching an armpit, which meant to meet at the creek. I already couldn't keep it all straight and told him so, but he just laughed and kept on talking.

It felt good to be with him again, like a long-lost friend had come home. We rounded the trailer and found the Thomases, Mama and Daddy, Miz Mary Rose and Mr. Stew and Miz Dot sitting around a small campfire. Everyone else had already gone home. Mr. Stew had moved his pot and they had pulled up chairs, propping their feet on rocks to feel the heat from the fire. They were laughing at something Miz Mary Rose had said, and suddenly, I couldn't wait to join them. I ran up to Mama, who took a long look at me (and my clothes) but didn't say a word. I knew I'd have to report in later, but I was let off the hook for now.

Daddy slid over and made room for me and Gregory. We found two buckets, flipped them upside down and pulled them up to the fire. It felt good on my feet and hands. October nights had a way of getting really chilly once the sun went down.

Miz Mary Rose had asked Miz Dot about someone named Leslie when we walked up, and I think me and Gregory were a diversion of some sort 'cause they all got real quiet. Once we were situated on our buckets, Miz Mary Rose looked at Miz Dot and asked the question again. "What did ever happen, Dot? I never heard and you seemed to disappear to your farm. I've missed ya. Can you tell me now?"

I've never seen Miz Dot at a loss for words, but she was then. Her face puckered a little, almost like she might cry, but I knew that couldn't be right. Must be the fire playing tricks on me. Daddy got real quiet and motionless, which he always did that when he was hoping somebody would talk some more – almost like he was afraid a noise would shut them down. The fire crackled and spit while Miz Dot wrestled with whatever demon she had, then it was like a tap was on and water flowed out. She began to talk and I wasn't sure if she'd ever stop.

Chapter 28

Dot

Mary Rose's initial question dragged Dot into a narrow vortex of emptiness. She heard nothing, couldn't focus, couldn't breathe. It was as if all life had been vacuumed into a blackness so deep she couldn't find her way out.

"Dottie, it's time to talk," Tom's voice echoed in the cavern.

"But I can't. Can't even say Leslie's name out loud."

"These folks care about you. The lid's been on too long. It's time to release it."

"Help me, Tom. I don't even know how."

"Cry out to Jesus, Dottie. He is your strength in your weakness. He is your stronghold. He is the power..."

The flames came into focus as Dot watched Mildred and Gregory find a spot by the fire. Fresh air blew in from the west carrying a sweetness that felt life-giving, and Dot greedily sucked it in. Finally she found her voice. "It's been a long time, Mary Rose. I try not to think about it."

But Mary Rose was persistent.

"You have to think about it," Mary Rose leaned into the fire. Shadows flickered on her dark skin, accentuating the creases and edges. Small, curly gray hair framed her round face. "You and Tom adored that girl. Have you heard from her at all since she left?"

"She didn't leave; she was taken!" Dot's barely suppressed pain shot to the surface. The air around the campfire became charged and Sam gently held Laura Lee's hand. Their eyes met, but neither said a word and even Mildred and Gregory were as still as tombstones. It was Debbie Thomas who found the courage to speak.

"Whatever do ya mean, Miz Dot? Yo' girl was taken? Taken by who?"

Dot's gaze swept over the faces in the dim light, then she sighed deeply. Tom was right. The time had come.

"Maybe I'd best start at the beginning." She took a long drink of tea then put her cup on the ground next to the chair. Dot leaned back and seemed to brace herself and began to speak. "It was seventeen years ago when a stringy haired, six-year-old gal showed up on our doorstep hauling a brown paper bag full of clothes. Tom and I were dumbstruck. We had no idea who she was or how she got there." Dot chuckled, shaking her head. "But there she was, Leslie Doreen Smith – at least that's what she told us. Even at six, she knew to lie about her real last name.

"Of course, we let her stay the night, and Tom began checking around town early the next day to find out who she was. Leslie herself said she had no daddy and her mama was dead. Said she had no idea where to live and she'd always wanted to see a farm, so she picked our place. Tom headed straight to Sheriff Dabney's office, but there was no record to be found of a six- year-old Smith girl in Piedmont Ridge. Thank goodness, Dabney had another idea. He knew of a slum area near the river where a few families lived in makeshift shacks. He seemed to remember seeing a little girl there.

"So he and Tom went down to Shacktown – that's what the locals called it – and Dabney asked around. Sure enough, there was a young woman who had lived there with a girl, but she was gone. Cleared out the week before."

Daryl poked at some embers, piling them back toward the center of the fire. Dot watched, her mind drifting.

"Nobody knew their full names – said the girl went by Leslie and the mama was called Dora. We figured we had the girl, but Dabney had no idea what to do with it all. Tom told him we'd keep an eye on Leslie until Dabney found her mama. 'Course, Dabney wasn't crazy about the idea, but I think he was willin' to let it slide 'cause he sure as heck didn't have a better plan. Tom came home later that day and told Leslie she could stay a while."

Dot broke into a huge smile. "Well, that's all the encouragement Leslie needed. Within two days she was callin' us Mom and Dad and we began to love her like..."

Dot's voice broke and Laura Lee finished for her, "Like the daughter you never had?" Dot nodded, staring blankly into the fire. Pine cones cracked and popped as Gregory threw more into the flame, waiting for her to continue.

"Tom and I weren't stupid. We knew our happiness was on borrowed time, but Leslie kept insisting her mama was dead, and the woman never showed up. Years passed. First grade, second, third. We made it all the way to fifth grade before Dora drove into the yard, demanding her daughter back."

Debbie Thomas gasped, clapping her hand over her mouth, while Daryl gently placed his hand on her knee.

"Leslie went ballistic when she saw the car and there was no way on God's green earth I was sending Leslie with Dora. But the woman was persistent. She sobered up and went to Sheriff Dabney's a few days later, trying to press charges on us for kidnapping!

"'Course, Dabney didn't go for that, but unfortunately the woman did have a birth certificate for Leslie and some cockamaney story about leaving Leslie with a friend and coming back to find her gone. Said it took her six years to find the child..." Dot choked out a hoarse laugh. "Six years to find her – in Piedmont Ridge? Go figure."

Sam broke in. "But what about Leslie? Did she want to be with Dora?"

"Leslie?" Dot smiled wryly. "Oh no. All heck was breaking loose at our house because Leslie was so afraid of Dora. Seems Dora had a steady flow of ...," Dot glanced at Mildred and Gregory, "...of boyfriends while Leslie was young. Some of them treated her badly and she didn't want to go back. She was terrified."

Mary Rose heaved herself out of her lawn chair to walk to the stack of wood scraps. She grabbed a few branches and tossed them into the fire. "Good Lord, Miz Dot. What a mess you and Mr. Tom was in. No wonder you two wasn't seen in town much."

"Nope. We pretty much hunkered down with Leslie and our lawyer, trying to do anything we could to keep Dora Haskell out of the picture."

"But it didn't work?" Laura Lee whispered, afraid to hear the answer.

"The law was on Dora's side," Dot answered. "Didn't matter that she deserted her own flesh and blood; she was the mother. There was nothing we could do." Dot rubbed her forehead in frustration. "Sheriff Dabney and Dora showed up one Saturday morning and we had to say goodbye to Leslie."

The horrified faces staring at her across the fire barely registered with Dot. Tears streamed down Laura Lee's and Debbie's cheeks. Mary Rose and Stew pondered with troubled eyes, but Dot had no tears. Just a hard, set pain that rarely ebbed.

"It hurt me beyond measure," she said, "but it almost killed Tom."

Stew had been sitting on a wooden crate, leaning against the big pine throughout Dot's account. Carefully, he rubbed his finger across the sharp tip of a poplar stick he had been whittling while his deep voice resonated into the dark night, echoing in gentleness and warmth. "Reckon it did kill Mr. Tom. Tweren't too terrible long after that he passed."

"I've often thought the same thing, Stew," Dot confessed.

Silence crept into the circle of confidants and even Mildred and Gregory felt the weight of the burden Dot had been carrying. In the recesses of her memory, Mildred saw the photograph of Dot's family. The thin, smiling man, the happy young girl holding wildflowers. It was Leslie, she now knew, and she felt her heart twist for this girl she had never known. Once again it was Debbie who broached the question they all had been thinking. "But just because Dora took Leslie shouldn't have meant that you'd never see her again," she insisted. "Didn't you keep in touch?"

"Oh we tried. Dora took her back to Charleston with her, and Tom and I began writing letters before they got outta the yard good. We also had talked with Leslie, and she had promised to send us something – even if it was just a postcard – from every place they went. Dora had a habit of staying nowhere for long. We got two letters in the next three weeks, then they stopped coming."

"Did you keep writing?" Sam asked.

"You bet we did until the letters started coming back with a 'Return to Sender' stamp on them. We tried directory assistance – even hired a PI a few months after, but Dora – and Leslie – had vanished."

"Sweet Jesus," whispered Mary Rose. Stew just shook his head as he sliced another bark shaving into the air.

"How long ago was that, Dot?" Sam asked.

"She left July 26, 1956. That'd be about twelve years ago. Tom passed two years later."

"So Leslie has to be in her mid-twenties by now," Sam was thinking out loud. "Why do you think she hasn't come back?"

For the first time, Dot's hard, impenetrable eyes blurred with tears. "I have no idea. I don't reckon I'll ever know."

Chapter 29

Mildred

November 15, 1968

Dear Martha Claire:

It seems hard to believe that you've been back home for so long! Sorry I didn't write sooner. There's been so much happening that I haven't had one spare minute. I guess Uncle Goose told you that Mrs. Dot's ankle got better? Did he tell you I work on her farm now? A real job. She pays me 75 cents a day, and I usually work three days a week. She's real nice now, not half as scary, and I like the cows and cats. Maybe next time you visit you can come help me at her house?

Gregory is doing pretty good, but I'll have to tell you about our big fight. It's too long to write — anyway, we are still friends, but it's all weird. Ha. Just like Gregory. Weird.

And there's Mrs. Broomer too. Remember her? The lady with the giant polka-dotted dress and red hair? Well, looks like her husband might be beating her up. Don't tell nobody. I'm just figuring that by all the bumps and bruises I've seen on her face. We might need to pray for her.

Mama's doing better and better, but Daddy's been awful quiet lately. He acts like he's got something on his mind. Maybe blue potatoes? Ha!

Mama says we might drive down to Prosperity over Christmas break, depending on how she feels.

PRAY HARD FOR THAT!

OK. I gotta go. Write soon.

Love, your best friend,
Mildred Juniper

p.s. Did I tell you I got the Indian girl part in the Thanksgiving play? I can't wait!
P.s.s. Did your Mama get to vote for the president? Mine did and Miz Dingle, my teacher, talks about President Nixon all the time now. You know he's sorta like a Yankee?

It had been four weeks since Miz Dot unloaded her burden and four weeks of craziness. Between working at the Harris farm in the afternoon and play practice, I hadn't had time to think of much. And Daddy had been right. We hadn't heard one word from the police about our burning "marshmallow." Gregory and me had decided it couldn't have been the Klan 'cause nothing else had happened. Still, I always had a question mark in my head and found myself watching for men wearing white pointed masks late at night.

Anyway, after Miz Dot told us about Leslie at the campfire, I had dragged myself back to school on Monday and – lo and behold – heard my name announced over the intercom as Samoset's sister in the Thanksgiving play. There was a God – and I think he finally found me in Piedmont Ridge! Mama poo-pooed me when I told her that.

"Mildred Juniper, you know better than that," she fussed. "God has not left or forgotten you."

"It's just a joke, Mama," I said as I threw my lunch box on the counter. "It's just been so awful here that I can't believe something good has happened."

She looked up then from the stack of bills she was paying on the table. "You really wanted this part, didn't you?" Pieces of eraser stubble dotted her cheek where she had absentmindedly scratched an itch.

"More than anything." I flopped in the chair, kicking off the dreaded famolare leather, wavy bottomed school shoes. She had demanded I find them this morning before school. Mama had gotten more and more perceptive lately, which was a good thing, but it did have its drawbacks.

"Is Samoset's sister the lead female part?"

"No, ma'am, but she's the keenest part in the play. Oh, and Mr. Garner wanted to know if you have time to sew my costume? It won't be much – just a brown sorta dress. He said maybe we could thread colored ribbons on it and tie them with beads. Mitchum's Drug Store has beads. What do you think, Mama?"

She flashed a big smile and said, "I'd love to pull out the sewing machine. I need a challenge."

And so Mama had been steadily sewing and Miz Dot's ankle was pretty much well now. I was her No. 1 milking assistant, she told me. I really liked the time we had to drink tea at her table before Daddy picked me up. She knew all about my Indian part in the play and even promised she'd come to see me perform. I hadn't brought up Leslie again, but every once in a while, I'd go into her bathroom and stare at the photograph on the half table. Mr. Tom, as I had come to call him in my mind, always stared back at me – laughing, but also begging me, it seemed, to be Miz Dot's friend, to keep her from being lonely.

The only thing messing up the perfectness of my life was my nemesis, Violet Griffin, and her sidekick, Mary Beth Connelly. Wouldn't you know? They both had parts in the play – so I was forced to talk to them – but only on stage.

Miz Dingle was the director. She never mentioned the lizard in the pencil case incident — neither did I. Instead, I tried hard to be a good helper and ignore the cold, hard stares and menacing looks from Violet and Mary Beth. I have to confess that once we started real rehearsals, I didn't pay much attention to them or their pilgrim dresses. The stage became my world.

"Samoset!" I yelled breathlessly as I dashed on the stage. "Our Father, Chief Powhaton, say you no smoke peace pipe with white man!" Then Fred Marley – Samoset – would argue with me and I got to drag him off stage. The dragging part was the best, although

I don't think Fred liked it much.

Act III was where I had to talk to Violet who was playing Mary, the pilgrim. We were to pass a plate of fake deer meat at the big Thanksgiving dinner feast, then we had to smile and say, "Happy Thanksgiving," as the platter was passed. The audience would only see a sweet, pretty blonde-haired pilgrim girl, properly passing the platter. They couldn't see her fingers pinching me under the table or her eyes flash in anger when I kicked her shin – hard! And this wasn't even dress rehearsal yet! Who knew what would happen on play night? But I was determined not to let her get to me.

Today was our last practice before dress rehearsal and Daddy promised to pick me up for a special ice cream treat at Marley's Store to celebrate. Mama put the last stitch in my Indian dress last night, and I planned to add a few more colored beads tonight after homework. It was Monday – not my day to work on the Harris farm. Dress rehearsal was Thursday, then the play was Friday. I could hardly wait.

I grabbed my books, yelling goodbye to Miz Dingle over my shoulder, as I dashed out the side doors of the cafeteria. Wonder if I should use yellow beads with the red and green? Or would an early American Indian princess not want all those colors? I almost tripped over the curb as I opened the car door.

"Hey, pumpkin," Daddy smiled. "Ready for some ice cream?"

"Been thinkin' about it all day," I flashed a smile back. "I want chocolate with nuts sprinkled on top."

"Oh yeah?" Daddy eased the car out from the school parking lot. "I'm looking forward to just plain ol' vanilla."

About that time a long, gray Cadillac turned into the lot, pulling next to us. Mr. Pete Griffin's sweaty forehead gleamed in the sun's reflection as he rolled by, his face turned away from us. I knew he saw us 'cause I saw his expression change as he turned into the lot. He was trying awful hard to not see us now. Violet would be waiting for him at the door to the cafeteria, her pink book satchel in her hand. Yuck. I know I'm supposed to love everybody, just like Jesus says, but just thinking about loving Violet made my stomach hurt. I glanced at Daddy. He had seen Mr. Griffin too. I could tell because he got that little furrow between his eyes that he gets only when he's thinking real hard or not happy about something.

I think he saw me watching him, so Daddy pushed whatever ugly thoughts he had out of his mind. I figured I should do the same, so I pushed Violet right into my "Does Not Exist" world – at least for now. Daddy and me had some ice cream to eat!

The "ice creme" sign on Marley's General Store peeked over the horizon, looking just as rickety as it always did. I reckon Mr. Marley wasn't ever gonna fix it. The spelling part sorta drove me crazy, but everybody knew he had the best ice cream in Piedmont Ridge, so I'd let it go.

Dried oak leaves floated down to the sandy driveway as we got out of the car. I looked up, realizing that fall was all-the-way gone now and the look of winter had set in. The trees waved, looking naked, while the missing leaves revealed a complete view of Mr. Marley's house tucked way back behind the store. You could still see a well-worn path through the stretch of woods leading from the back of the store to the front door of his gray-clapboard house.

A bell hanging over the door rattled when Daddy went in, it being too old to hold a tone anymore. A musty store smell snuck up my nose as I entered, something like old shack competing with ammonia and bleach wash. Still it was clean and I knew Mr. Marley took pride in having a neat business.

"Howdy folks," Mr. Marley hollered from the back. "Come on in an' I'll be with you'uns in a sec." Daddy winked and led the way to the ice cream freezers.

They sat like monuments in the back of the large room. We moved between shelves of canned goods and dodged the closed-up pot-bellied stove in the middle of the room. Shining silver cases held eight different kinds of ice cream to tempt even the most picky eater. I had tried the strawberry and pineapple earlier in the fall, but had not tasted Marley's chocolate yet. Polished glass kept any greasy fingerprints from blocking my sight to the tubs of creamy dessert. I sighed in contentment, thinking I could stand here all day dreaming about each flavor, almost tasting it on my tongue.

"What kin I git fer you folks?" Mr. Marley rounded the corner. His store apron was crisp and clean as was his hair and neatly trimmed beard. His brown eyes sparkled as he spotted Daddy.

"Whalll, if it ain't Preacher Rhodes. It sho is mighty good to see you again. How's the pastorin' goin'? Needin' a bit o' ice cream to he'p freeze up some of those folks who git all hot-headed?" He laughed loudly at his own joke and I giggled too...but mostly at Mr. Marley. His belly jiggled when he laughed, and if his beard had been white, I'd have been tempted to think this was where Santa Claus spent most of his year.

Daddy didn't seem to enjoy the joke as much as the teller, but he put up with it and began discussing the finer points of ice cream flavors. I watched Daddy with interest as Mr. Marley talked and scooped. He just didn't seem to be himself lately – especially ever since Miz Dot had spilled the beans about Leslie. Maybe it was church troubles, I thought. The services seemed to be going alright. Not many new folks coming, but we only started three months ago. Maybe he was worried about Miz Broomer...or Mama, even though she looked more and more perky every day. Could be that he felt sorry for Miz Dot.

"What'll it be fer you, Little Lady?" Mr. Marley's intense gaze focused on me – eyes magnified behind his thick glasses.

"Chocolate with nuts, please."

"A fine choice, fine choice," he chuckled, dipping his silver scooper into water to clean it off.

Daddy went for vanilla, as he had promised, and we moved outside to the weather-worn picnic table beside the store. I don't reckon many folks ate ice cream outside in November, but me and Daddy didn't mind. We talked about Thanksgiving, the way winter eases in, milking cows and who was better at Scrabble. We didn't talk about Mama or church or flaming threats with rude signs that people put outside your front door.

After about an hour at Marley's Store, Daddy announced he needed to make a quick trip to the co-op. Would I mind?

Well, far be it for me to throw a wrench in his works! I always loved the smell of fresh feed and leather, plus I might get to say hey to Gregory if he was working this afternoon.

So as the deep blue sky grew more brilliant, we packed up and headed down the road again. I checked my mouth in the side mirror, and sure enough there was some chocolate stuck in the corners.

"Why didn't you tell me I had chocolate stuck to my mouth?" I asked, looking reproachfully at Daddy.

"Didn't notice, monkey. Sorry."

Men! I licked my finger and rubbed the smudge off. He probably wouldn't notice if I had a giant horn sticking out of my forehead. I giggled just thinking about that and stole a glance at Daddy, but he was intent on driving.

The dust rose in clouds as we turned into the co-op, so we waited a few seconds until it settled before we got out of the car. Business wasn't booming on a late Monday afternoon. Only a rusty green pickup was in the parking lot and it was pulling out as Daddy parked.

"Want to come in while I look around?"

Of course I wanted to look around. We saw Miz Mary Rose's huge body stretching up to twist in a lightbulb as we entered the vast building. Her ladder didn't look like a top-of-the-line, co-op specialty ladder. It was weaving and wobbling, its wooden legs straining under the weight. One of her co-workers, a skinny, short man with orange hair, looked pretty worried. We could hear him clear across the store.

"Lawdy, Miz Mary Rose. You be careful up thar. Mr. Anderson'll have my head in a noose if I let somethin' happen to you."

"Oh, stop yer badgerin', Jeremy. If the mornin' crew would'a done their job right, I wouldn't have to be hangin' up here, standin' on a ladder made of toothpicks, and you wouldn't have the terrifyin' job of havin' to keep me from fallin'!" Miz Mary Rose's booming laughter echoed over the rows of suspenders and dog food bowls, drawing me and Daddy toward her like two magnets that have no choice but to suck up to the metal. She spotted us just as we passed the nuts and bolts aisle.

"Glory! It's Pastor Rhodes and Mildred Juniper," she bellowed, the ladder leaning dangerously to the right. Jeremy jumped quickly over, leaning into the side of it as he desperately tried to keep the thing from tipping. It scared Daddy enough to jolt him into action; he dashed the last few feet and grabbed the other side of the ladder, pulling it toward him. Miz Mary Rose looked at the two men like they had no sense whatsoever.

"You two think I ain't learned how to climb a ladder in my last fifty years?" She eased down the three steps, the broken lightbulb in her left hand. She sighed heavily once she reached the concrete, and I think – if I had been the ladder – I'd have sighed too. "Now give me a hug and tell me what you two been up to today."

I moved in for the obligatory Miz Mary Rose hug, which – truth be known – I had come to enjoy. The key was to twist your nose upward a little so that her bosom didn't cut off your airflow. I smelled the familiar jasmine scent as she released me. "You comin' just to visit me, or you got co-op business?" She was wearing a red Marion County Co-op cap today, but her grey hair snuck out from the brim, curling every which-a-way.

"Oh, I'm always ready to visit," Daddy said as he smiled, "but I also need to get some metal hooks for that coat wall we want to put on the back of the Bingo Hall. Bobby said he thinks he can set up a good place for our winter coats and all it'll cost us is a few cents for hooks. Think you can help me out with that?"

"So I can hang up my coat this Sunday and not have to set it on my chair? You bet I kin help," she laughed. "Come on over here and let's see what might be best."

Daddy followed Miz Mary Rose like an obedient child and I realized that I was feeling a little bit tired. Guess school and play practice had taken more out of me than I thought. I turned back to the front door and peeked my head out. Sure enough, the big wooden rockers were empty, slightly tipping in the breeze. As soon as the sun went down, the temperature would drop, but it still felt pretty good outside. I walked on out and grabbed the chair on the right starting off with a good, hard rock, pulling my feet under my legs.

Leaning my head back, I watched a Beetle Bug car pull into the parking lot, but I stayed put figuring whoever it was came on co-op business and wouldn't want a rocking chair. Sure enough, an extra large lady with an extra-large straw hat unfolded herself from the tiny yellow car. She toted a brown shoe box filled with multi-colored tubes. I had a feeling this might be the Coon Creek lady ... what was her name?

"Well hi there, sugar," her deeply Southern voice interrupted my remembering. "You sure picked you a good spot to watch the world go by."

"Yes, ma'am," I agreed, smiling in spite of myself.

"I would be inclined to join ya if I didn't have business to see to. The days just don't git much prettier than this." She bustled off seeming very busy with her clattering tubes and vague odor of honey. I wondered how you actually made chap stick from beeswax – and do the bees mind? I felt sure we'd be buying more of her product – Mama had said it worked better than any chap stick she ever had.

Two crows noisily flew over the road to the dried up cornfield across the street. I reckon the farmer had stripped the corncobs and left the stalks in his field till they withered up. Shading my eyes, I looked across the field as far as I could see. Rows and rows of dead corn stalks fell on each other. Made me sad somehow. What had been so green and full and alive just a few months ago was dead and gone. So fast.

The two crows landed on a stalk toward the middle of the field, cawing back and forth. I closed my eyes, listening and making up words for them.

"Hey Fred! Where's the corn?" one might say.

"Don't know Bob. I thought Farmer John had left more than this."

"Yeah, maybe you just ate it all."

"Me? Me? Do I look fat to you?" The caws sounded repetitive, echoing back and forth, *"Me? Me? Me?"*

I laughed out loud, opening my eyes again. One of them was staring right at me, and he did look bigger than the other one. Maybe he was a pig – for a crow, that is.

The cash register drawer slammed shut and voices made their way toward me. Didn't take Daddy long to find his hooks. Moving to pull my legs down and get ready to go, I heard Miz Mary Rose ask Daddy a question.

"Well, I know how the church is doin', Pastor, but how are you?"

"'Scuse me?"

"You. How are you – in yo' soul, yo' spirit. How is Sam Rhodes?" Miz Mary Rose's jasmine scent wafted out the door and tickled my nose. I could see the red of her vest by the corner, but she had stopped walking. Daddy's footsteps halted as the silence crept in.

"I reckon I'm doing pretty good, Mary Rose. The church seems to be fairly solid, though there ain't many of us. Laura Lee is slowly getting better and Mildred seems much happier now that she's working for Dot Harris. I am looking to find some part-time work," he hesitated, then continued. "I'm just not sure if the church can support us enough – not that y'all can't or wouldn't give us more money if you could. I just hate being such a burden."

"Uh huh," Miz Mary Rose dragged out. "Like I asked. How are you?"

Daddy shifted his feet. "I reckon I'm not sure what you mean, Mary Rose."

"I been watchin' you, Pastor. You don't smile as much as you should and you look more worried lately than you were when you first came to town. You havin' second thoughts about pastorin'?"

"Second thoughts? No, not second thoughts." I heard Daddy sigh real deep. "It's just not quite what I expected when I first heard about the work here. Not that I'm not glad to be here," he quickly reassured, "I guess I'm just trying to find my footing."

"Uh huh," she said again. "Well, I believe I got another question for you. If the good Lord said to you, 'Sam Rhodes, this church body will never grow any bigger. I'm callin' you to pastor this tiny, little flock and no other. That's your call.' Now, if the good Lord said that to you, would it be enough?"

"Well, sure Mary Rose, if the Lord said that ..." Daddy paused and I saw his hand move across the doorway. I knew he was running his hand through his hair, which is what he always does when he's perturbed. "I mean, the Lord wouldn't say that though. He wants His kingdom to grow and bear fruit. He wants our community to grow and be a family that is adding on all the time."

Miz Mary Rose changed gears again, throwing Daddy around in the conversation like a truck on a curvy road.

"You aren't happy with the size of the church?"

"Well, no. Of course not. Like I said, the Lord wants His church to grow and ..."

"And so you're sayin' you ain't happy with where the church is right now. The size. The people. And you're worried about money?" she pressed.

"No, that's not what I said," Daddy's frustration began to grow, but he was still being real polite. "What I'm trying to say is that I know the Lord wants this church to grow and be a vibrant part of our community. We need to get bigger and pull in more folks so the kingdom of God can expand. As far as our people, you know I love them all – we just need more of them."

"Uh huh." I still got the feeling that Miz Mary Rose hadn't heard what she wanted to hear. "I'm goin' back to my other question," she said. "If the Lord said we weren't gonna grow any more and you would spend the rest of your life pastorin' fifty people, but that's what He wanted you to do, would that be enough?"

I wish I could have seen Daddy's face so I would know more of what he was thinking. He had gotten awfully quiet, not even shifting his feet. I felt the air grow still and silent, waiting for something – I just wasn't sure what.

"You're thinking it's all about motive, aren't you?" Daddy asked. "What's my motive for what I'm doing? Am I doing it for God or for me – or some other reason?"

"Maybe motive," Miz Mary Rose responded slowly. "But even more — to get you to the root of who God is and what it means to serve Him. Sam, can I tell you a story?" Daddy must've nodded cause she kept on. " I remember when me and Stew were newly married and we had such high hopes for a big family with lots o' chil'ren crowded around our dinin' room table. Then one year went by, two years, then five years – and no babies were comin'. Stew didn't make much money in his job at the Court House, but we saved and scrimped enough for a few doctor visits, but no doctors could help us. We tried everything. Then it was seven years and no babies and the Lord and me had a sit-down talk. That's when He asked me a hard question like I'm askin' you."

Miz Mary Rose paused a second, then took a deep breath.

"The Lord, He says to me, 'Mary Rose, if I choose – in my Sovereignty – not to give you and Stew chil'ren, will you still follow me? Will I be enough for you?'

"Well, I'm here to tell you I had to think long and hard 'bout that one. I took days – prayin', cryin', beatin' my pillow. Poor Stew didn't know what to do with me. He finally tossed up his hands and let me be." Miz Mary Rose chuckled then. "I reckon the Lord and me was wrestlin'. And you know who won?"

Somewhere in the back of the store, a phone rang, but Miz Mary Rose made no move to get it. Daddy finally cleared his throat.

"I wasn't sure if you and Stew just didn't want any children or ... what," he said softly.

Miz Mary Rose's voice rose, almost with joy, which really made no sense to me. "Me and the Lord wrestled and I finally come to that place where whatever He wants is what I want. And He chose to not bless my womb, but over the years, He has blessed me and Stew in so many other ways I can't count 'em. We gots tons of chil'ren – and grandchil'ren – all over this county. They may not be from my body, but they's our chil'ren. I reckon I had to start thinkin' outside my box and lookin' at things from His point of view."

"I see," Daddy said slowly. "You know, Mary Rose, you are

something else."

Her laughter rang through the store and I think the birds began to sing again, too. Miz Mary Rose brought life everywhere she went. "I get told that a lot, Pastor. I reckon I am somethin' else. I'm just not so sure what that is!"

They both began to laugh as they walked through the entrance doors. Daddy saw me and motioned for me to follow, but I don't think it registered to him that I'd been listening the whole time. Probably a good thing.

Miz Mary Rose gave my shoulder a hard squeeze, and Daddy and me piled back into the car to head home. The bee lady's car looked forlorn and lonely as we pulled out of the dusty parking lot. Wonder if she was getting a lecture from Miz Mary Rose now.

Dusk was coming and Mama had assured me this morning that she was going to fix supper all by herself tonight while Daddy and me were out and about. Sure seemed like it'd been a long time since we came home to the smell of cooking.

Daddy was different on the drive home – happier somehow. Maybe Miz Mary Rose's words helped. I sure hoped so.

Chapter 30

Dot

Just because she was short on time didn't mean Dot would be sloppy in her cleanup. She stacked her milk boots neatly by the back door, as always, then moved to the kitchen sink for one final handwash. The afternoon milking had begun earlier today – the day of Mildred Juniper's Thanksgiving Play – to give Dot time to spruce up and get to the school by 7 p.m. She had laid out some slacks and a blouse last night – had to dig nearly to China in her dresser to find something that wasn't overalls or blue jeans. If she remembered right, she'd last worn these slacks at Tom's viewing, but she didn't abide by sentimentality when it came to clothing.

She rounded the corner to her bedroom, glancing at the bedside clock and figuring she had fifteen minutes before she'd have to jump into the truck and head toward Piedmont Ridge Elementary.

The tight schedule is a help, Dot thought as she pulled off her overalls. She didn't have much time to brood... didn't really want to. She had thoroughly enjoyed becoming a small part of Mildred's life and knew the Lord wanted her to see the child in the big play, but Mildred had no idea how difficult this was. Delivering milk to the school kitchen was one thing. Walking into the cafeteria, sitting with an audience to watch a performance, that was a whole different can of worms. Leslie's last play had been "Little Women" where she had portrayed Beth.

Dot walked into the bathroom, running water to brush her teeth. She gazed at her deeply lined, tanned face, seeing instead a younger Dot pulling her hair up in a bun.

Leslie had been beside herself with excitement over the play, practicing her lines with the calves every afternoon. That was why Dot had named the next set of milkers after the Little Women cast.

She figured the calves already had a soaking in the story, might as well make them players. Leslie's costumes, memorization, make-up — Dot had walked through it all with her. And Leslie had been stunning, of course. She and Tom knew she was an actress the first time they heard her story.

And now, Mildred.

Dot had been thinking about her all during milking, especially since Mildred had informed on Violet Griffin and her tricks under the table. She didn't know which was more sad – that one as young as Violet was already picking up mean tricks from her daddy, or that the Griffins truly thought of themselves as God-fearing people.

"Not for you to judge, Dot old girl," she mumbled to herself as she dried her mouth. "That's the Lord's work."

Tom's face smiled up at her as she hung the towel back on the rack. *He'd be proud I'm going,* she thought. Funny how Tom's voice still directed her, even after not hearing it out loud for so long.

Quickly, she ran a brush through her hair, knowing there wasn't much she could do with this gray ball of mess, but at least it was clean. She looked over at the vanity drawer that held twenty-year-old make-up, but shrugged off that idea. Arriving clean and not in overalls was about all she could muster.

Dot grabbed her truck keys off the hook on the wall and let herself out the front door. Porthos wagged lamely as she clopped down the steps and headed for the shed. It was 6:45 p.m. She'd just make it.

Already the cafeteria was packed with parents, children and grandparents. Dot had parked a ways off, walking quickly to catch the start of the play. Even though Laura Lee and Sam had promised to save her a place, she didn't really want to make a scene by coming in late. Had Sam not been waiting by the door, she wasn't sure she would have ever found them.

"What a zoo!" she said with a grimace. "Now I remember why I hate comin' to things like this."

Sam held out his arm with a wry smile and one eyebrow lifted.

"Hate it? Why Miz Harris," he drawled with an exaggerated Southern accent, "I heard you most always attend every social function in Piedmont Ridge."

Dot snorted as she tucked her hand under Sam's arm.

"You're a piece of work, Sam Rhodes," she retorted.

He led her along the back wall and down the last aisle to a row of folding, aluminum chairs. Laura Lee sat gracefully on the end seat, her purse laid out over the chair to her right. Farther down the row were Elder Crenshaw and his wife, his body crammed into the dimensions of a chair too small for his frame. He smiled briefly at Dot, waving her into the row.

"Come on down, Miz Harris. I ain't been bitin' nobody tonight," he joked. Dot eased by Laura Lee with a brief smile. "Course there's always a first for everything," he continued with a wink. She elbowed him. She taught Ben Crenshaw Sunday school about a million years ago and she never put up with any nonsense then. Didn't figure she'd start now.

"I'm so glad you could come, Miz Harris," Laura Lee leaned over Sam to touch Dot on the arm. "It just means the world to Mildred to have you here."

Dot nodded in response, amazed at how beautiful a woman she was. Without the rose-colored housecoat and with some life in her green eyes, she was breathtaking.

The lights dimmed and the room erupted with "shhs" and "hushes" from front to back. Children were placed into the metal chairs while grandparents adjusted their spectacles. The spotlight fell on an velvet crimson curtain, and Mrs. Dingle paraded out on stage in her finest school wear, a baby-blue, polyester dress with modest brown pumps. She cleared her throat and tapped the microphone.

"Good evening," she attempted. A few more children were being rounded up near the entryway. She cleared her throat again. "Good evening, ladies and gentlemen," she stated with authority. All extra noise ceased.

"We are thrilled to have you at our annual Thanksgiving play.

The children have been working very hard for weeks and have pulled together what we think will be the best Thanksgiving play you've ever seen." She hesitated, waiting for the applause to die down. "Without further ado, I present to you Mary Beth Connelly, your narrator for the evening."

Mrs. Dingle stepped off to her right, taking care not to trip over the microphone cord, while Mary Beth approached the podium from the other side of the stage. Dot watched her carefully, knowing that this was Public Enemy No. 2, as far as Mildred was concerned.

Mary Beth didn't much look like a villain. Short with matching bobbed blonde hair, she pranced on the stage wearing a fluffy purple dress with stars imprinted in silver. Once again, Dot tried desperately to withhold judgment. Mary Beth began speaking in a sing-song voice, telling the story of that Thanksgiving long, long ago.

Thank the Lord, they had an intermission forty minutes into the play. Dot dashed to the girls' room, the same one she'd used fifty years ago – even looked like the same bar of soap at the sink

So far, Mildred had appeared on stage several times in her cardboard-brown-colored Indian dress and painted face. Hollywood was safe from any stars budding out of Piedmont Ridge, Dot considered as she washed and dried her hands. One more scene and the evening should be over. A toilet flush in the far stall interrupted her thoughts as the door swung open. Out stepped Corella Dean, wife of Deacon Jason Dean, Piedmont Ridge City Church. Dot's eyes widened in disbelief. Somehow she had managed to avoid all Deans since Tom had passed, a seemingly impossible task in a town the size of the Ridge, yet she'd done it. That last meeting in the church – the one when Jason crucified her for not tithing from her inheritance money – was enough of the Deans for Dot. She had seen them in town – from a distance – but had not faced either one. Ten years was a long time.

Corella saw Dot's face a split second after she swung the door, a startled reflection in the bathroom mirror. As always, Corella was dressed immaculately, sporting an orange-brown, floral dress, her cream-colored hat sitting atilt on her head, matching ribbon falling gracefully down her back. She could have stepped out of a Sear's catalog, but the shock on her face was anything but glamorous. Her previously hurried steps faltered as an array of emotions swept across her face. Dot decided not to wait around to find out which emotion Corella settled on. She jerked a paper towel from the dispenser and turned toward the door. Corella's voice halted her in her tracks.

"Dot ... wait." Corella sprang to life, grabbing Dot by the forearm. "Wait. There's something I want, I need to say."

Dot turned slowly, feeling as if she was caught in a surreal daydream.

"I, uh, I've always regretted our last meetin' – or the last time we talked," Corella stammered. "Jason, well, you know men, he has his own thoughts on things, and I just usually go along with him, but ..."
Corella released Dot's arm then patted her shoulder.

"What I guess I'm tryin' to say is I'm sorry for the awful way you were treated. I've never thought it was right, but ..," she glanced around as if to make sure no one else was listening, "but I know a good wife follows her man and I just didn't want to make any waves with Jason. You know how men can be?" She smiled a sugary smile, but it didn't quite reach the corners of her eyes.

Dot hesitated, wanting to rant and rave and drive her words like nails into this Southern porcelain doll, but she had her integrity and knew what was right.

"It's alright, Corella. What's done is done and there isn't any going back. It's best just to forget about it." Dot smiled briefly and reached toward the doorknob.

"Dot, wait, one more thing," Corella reached out again. "There's been talk in town that you're joinin' up with that Georgia preacher who's startin' that colored church in the Bingo Hall."

Dot drew in a breath, ready on the defensive, but Corella waved her hands frantically.

"No, no, I don't care about any of that, my concern is Wanda Broomer. Isn't she part of that group?"

Dot nodded slowly. "Yes, she's been with Pastor Rhodes."

"Well, maybe you can tell that Pastor Rhodes that he might need to check on Wanda tonight. Jason and me were drivin' here for the play and I happened to see Wanda and Joe Ray outside of Deb's Chicken. Joe Ray was yellin', like he always does, but then I saw him grab Wanda hard and yank open the truck door. I promise, Dot, it looked like he was tossin' in a little ol' bag of potatoes. I saw her head hit the dashboard as she fell in, then he went on around and got in on his side and they drove off."

"Did you tell Jason?" Dot questioned.

"Well, of course, but Jason says what happens in a man's home or with his wife is his own business," Corella parroted. "I just thought you might want to know."

The door flew open, and Corella quickly turned toward the sink, grabbing the slick bar of soap as if to vigorously wash off any stain of the past five minutes. Dot smiled briefly at the child entering, took one more look at Corella and made a beeline back to her seat. She had to grab Sam before the play started again.

Sam's response to Dot's news was to draw Ben Crenshaw to the side and huddle in a corner, whispering and gesturing feverishly. Ben nodded, ran his fingers through his tight curls, and nodded again. Alma Crenshaw and Laura Lee had scooted together to chat during the break, and Dot didn't want to dampen their party, so she slid in her chair and waited. Sure enough, Ben came back over, whispered something to Alma, and left by the back door. Sam slid back into his aisle seat just as the house lights darkened and Laura Lee moved back beside him. A question lingered on her brow, but Sam put his finger to his lips, smiled and pointed to the stage. Dot figured the ladies would be filled in later on.

Mary Beth again took her position as narrator, laying out the final elements of the historical Thanksgiving celebration. As she spoke of hunting and fishing and the different ways both pilgrims and Indians obtained food, actors and actresses entered and exited the stage, dragging fishing poles, BB guns brought from home and whatever other props they could to bring life to the story. Mildred traipsed across carrying a feathery bundle over her shoulder — supposedly a turkey — laughing with Chief Powhaton.

The finale had arrived. Prop carriers moved out a giant table and set out plates and cups. Mary Beth exited the podium, and action again returned to the stage. All players moved out, chatting and pretending to enjoy each other's company. Dot noticed one of the smaller pilgrims got his hat snagged on some of the stage rigging and was desperately trying to release the hat while ambling gayly to the table. Mildred eased out from stage left, patting another Indian on the back, making her way to her seat. Chief Powhaton stood up to address the guests – waiting for a slight moment for the small pilgrim to give up on the hat and take a seat bareheaded. The hat dangled uselessly for a second, then disappeared as a hand reached out from backstage and removed it.

The chief thanked the pilgrims for their great friendship – a speech Dot felt would have been better served coming from the head of the pilgrim group – and the pilgrims responded with humility and gratitude. Governor Bradford stood up, toasted the group, and proclaimed the day "Thanksgiving," which Dot also knew was taking quite a bit of liberty with the original story. Ah well, these things had to be expected with a stage full of third, fourth and fifth-graders.

As Dot checked her watch, she remembered to keep an eye on Violet, although it seemed the girl was simply trying to act her pilgrim part. She had scooted in next to Mildred, adjusted her hat and shifted some of the cups around on the table. Everything looked fairly normal; she could see no signs of under-the-table pinching or kicking. Mildred just might escape this unscathed.

The toast was proclaimed across the table now with actors nudging one another to remember the next part. Almost simultaneously, they raised their glasses. Strains of a muted "Star-Spangled Banner" floated up from the school band, which Dot found amusing for a Thanksgiving celebration while the Governor and the Indian

Chief each signaled to their parties to drink a toast to the New World and new friendship.

As Dot glanced toward Mildred, she saw that the girl looked thrilled to seal the grand finale of her first performance with a toast. Violet appeared sweet, genteel and ... somewhat smug.

Uh oh, Dot thought. *This can't be good.*

All pilgrims and Indians drank heartily. Suddenly Samoset's brown-dressed sister, with the fake tanned skin and colorfully beaded dress, sputtered, gagged, retched and stood up. Liquid shot out of Mildred's mouth, covering the table, the plastic turkey, the fake corn and the pumpkins. A few drops even somehow made it into the school orchestra pit, and Dot saw a flute player frantically wiping off her instrument, a look of horror etched on her face. A collective groan filtered from the audience to the stage, and all players froze in shock — all players except Violet Griffin, Dot noticed. She definitely had a self-satisfied smirk on her face for a split-second before she put on the more expected, shocked expression. The cafeteria fell silent and everyone waited, although no one was sure why. Mildred still stood, eyes wide open, wiping her mouth with the back of her wrist.

Dot prayed, looked over at a frozen-faced Laura Lee, and prayed some more.

"Well, for heaven's sake, Governor Bradford," Mildred's voice rang out, a bit weak but with some underlying determination. "That's some mighty strong firewater you pilgrims concocted. It's a bit much for us Indians, isn't it Samoset?"

Mildred turned toward Fred Marley, waiting for his response, begging him with her eyes to follow up to her lines. Fred only hesitated a moment before he replied, "Indian agree, Governor Bradford. Strong drink is hard on Indian. Makes Indian stomach queasy." The audience broke out in applause and laughter while Mildred flopped down, visibly unnerved, but trying to maintain her composure. Violet appeared frustrated.

Mary Beth soon returned to her narrator perch as the cast stayed seated on stage. She wrapped up the story while the school band began playing louder and louder, and everyone rose to sing the "Star Spangled Banner," thus ending the Piedmont Ridge Elementary Thanksgiving play for 1968. Dot sighed in relief. It could have been much, much worse.

Chapter 31

Mildred

I don't know why it surprised me. It's not like Violet and me ever called a truce, but I didn't think she'd do something so ... evil ... in front of all those people. "She takes the cake!" I muttered, stomping around backstage. Violet had disappeared to who-knows-where, and even Miz Dingle had made herself scarce. I looked around and only saw Mr. Price's fourth-grade boys cleaning up stage props. As for me, my pigtails were still intact, but a few of the yellow beads dangled helplessly from the fringes of my dress, dropping in spots all over the wooden flooring. The laughingstock of Piedmont – that's what they'd all be calling me. I just didn't see how I'd ever live this one down. Maybe the headlines would say: "Girl Spits All Over School Orchestra." Or maybe: "Indian Princess Throws Up During Thanksgiving Play." Yep. That'd be the one.

As I opened the door to the cafeteria, searching the crowd of grown-ups looking for Mama and Daddy, I heard a voice yell out: "Hey! There's that Indian princess who drank the firewater!"

I winced, my stomach knotting up, but much to my surprise, people started clapping and cheering.

"You were just wonderful, honey," a sweet-smelling lady gushed in my ear.

"Wonderful? Why, she made the whole play worth comin' to see," her loud, cigar-smoking husband laughed, crinkles folding into his forehead as he smiled. "Wish I had me some o' that firewater!"

The crowd parted as I worked my way through with lots of back-slapping and "atta-girls" along the way. I felt like the winner of the Kentucky Derby; all that was missing were the flowers. Then I spotted Daddy, grinning like a schoolboy. His hair was slicked back, picture-perfect, and the brown on his slacks matched perfectly with a thin tan stripe in his plaid shirt. Mama had done well.

"Mil, over here!" he waved.

I elbowed and shouldered my way over to our Bingo Hall crowd – Mrs. Crenshaw, Mama ... I wondered where Elder Crenshaw had gotten off to?

"You were super, honey," Mama crowed as I joined them, her eyes sparkling in laughter. "I can only imagine what must have been in your drink, but you recovered awfully good." Mama, of course, knew all about Violet's under-the-table pinching tactics, and so did Miz Dot. Where was she? I looked around, wondering if she'd made it.

When I saw her, I about dropped my teeth. She actually looked nice, like a regular older lady. She had some silky looking black slacks on and a colorful sweater with pearl-like beading around the collar. I think she might have been wearing shoes that actually had a little heel on them and her hair was brushed neat and tidy. Mama started laughing when she saw me examining Miz Dot – top to bottom.

"Hardly recognized her, did you?"

"No ma'am. She looks real nice."

"Yes, she does," Mama muttered, half to herself. "I think it's been good for Dot Harris to come out to the play tonight. I'd like to know how long it's been since she's participated in town doin's." Mama's green eyes flashed then and she turned and smiled at me. "I reckon you're thinking that it's been quite a while since I participated in any doin's at all, aren't you?"

"Oh no, Mama, I know you've just been lounging away at home, feet propped up, loving me and Daddy waiting on you hand and foot."

Then we laughed together, loud, and everyone around us stopped a second to see what was up, but I didn't care. Mama had made it to the Thanksgiving play and the firewater fiasco turned out way better than I ever thought it would.

The crowd had started to thin out when Daddy walked over, sliding up to grip Mama loosely by the elbow. "Laura Lee. We need to ease on out the door. There's something I need to tell you about Wanda." Miz Dot must've heard or either just knew the look because she stopped her conversation with her friend quickly and walked over to where we were. Miz Crenshaw had slipped away.

Beads kept dropping off one by one, and I had a pocketful by now, jingling and clanking as I walked. Mr. Price's boys were shutting off stage lights and I caught sight of Miz Dingle ushering people out like she was closing down a big party, grabbing coats, patting people on the back, hugging children – all the while pushing them toward the gaping double doors that led to the parking lot. She was almost to our group when Mama gathered her evening bag and coat. Miz Dot echoed her steps as Daddy urged us toward the exit.

"Mr. Rhodes? Mrs. Rhodes?" Miz Dingle once again used her megaphone voice, this time halting us all in our steps. I always stopped when she used that tone, but it made me giggle to see Mama and Miz Dot stop on a dime as well. Daddy spun around in mid-stride.

"Thank you so much for allowing Mildred to participate in this year's play," she stated briskly, striding toward us like a drillmaster stepping off. "She was a real asset and such a huge help during practices." Then she turned all of her teacher charms on me. "And Mildred Juniper, you had all the nerves of a seasoned actress out there tonight."

Uh oh. Here it comes. I held my breath.

"I can only assume you drank too fast and choked up, but your reactions were marvelous and, in fact, added life to the show. Bravo, my dear!" Her trademark glasses bounced against her bosom as she stretched toward me, grasping me in a tight, warm hug.

So she had no idea of Violet's part in the whole rotten mess.

What to do? The right thing would be to keep quiet. But it would be so much fun to tell all and watch in satisfaction as Miz Dingle grew livid with the injustice of it all.

She released me and as I rocked back I saw Daddy, smiling and nodding at me, and I knew what I had to do.

"Yes, ma'am," I responded. "Thank you, ma'am. I'll try not to let it happen in the future though." I heard Miz Dot snort behind me and felt Mama's hand rest on my back. Daddy's eyes said, "Well done, Mildred," and together we all walked to the doors, buttoning coats and putting on hats along the way.

Yet even as we said our goodnights, I was completely aware that Daddy still had news of Miz Wanda that wasn't going to wait. He allowed the doors to bang shut behind us before he turned to Mama and Miz Dot, apparently forgetting I was there – or not caring that I heard.

"Laura Lee, Dot ran into a friend in the bathroom who said she saw Joe Ray hitting Wanda tonight downtown." Mama sucked in air, preparing to let loose, but Daddy waylaid her. "I've already sent Ben to her house to find out what's up, and Alma has gone on home. I need to meet Ben over there, so I was hoping Dot wouldn't mind taking you and Mil on home?" Daddy glanced at Miz Dot, but before he could take another step, Mama's hand came down on his arm, hard. I don't know if Miz Dot knew what was up, but I sure did.

"Sam. I'm goin' with you to Wanda's." Mama's voice said there would be no debate.

"Now Laura Lee..."

"Sam." Mama's fingers tightened. "Remember what we talked about the other night? Wanda needs a woman and I'm going."

"Well, then, that's alright I reckon, but you gotta stay in the car until I find out where Ben is and what he's learned."

Miz Dot had been awful quiet for a long time, but I could feel her body tensing up the longer we stood there and I knew she was about to bust. I backed up a little, turning to her determined, deeply lined face.

"I'm going, too," she stated.

"What?" Daddy croaked. "Oh, come on, ladies. I can't have half the towns' women coming out to the Broomers. I have no idea what I'm gonna find there, and somebody – somebody's got to take Mildred home!" Daddy's voice had risen in agitation and I felt a little sorry for him. Mama had been down for so long, he'd almost forgotten what kind of a force she could be when she felt good. And Miz Dot was like a bulldozer. There was no moving her. I just kept real quiet, knowing I just might get to go along on this ride.

Daddy's hands were on his hips, legs apart and he was breathing hard. Mama, on the other hand, looked as cool as a cucumber and Miz Dot started walking toward her truck. I reckon she figured it was all worked out.

"Oh for cryin' out loud. Get in the car!" Daddy turned on his heel and stomped toward the Malibu. I followed Mama quietly, half glad she won, half not. I didn't much want to see Miz Wanda if she was all beat up again, but I sure hated to miss an adventure.

We piled in quickly, following the taillights of Miz Dot's truck. As we turned left, Deb's Chicken was just closing up and I could barely see the night lights at True Value Hardware. The tall columns of the Piedmont Ridge City Church were lit up by specially placed lights which made the building look even more fortress-like than usual. As we turned away from it down a darker road, I wondered what it would be like to go in that church, just to see what it looked like on the inside. I'd never been in a church that big. Wonder if your voice echoed when you talked in the halls? And was it more worshipful to sing hymns while gazing out stained glass windows?

The ride out to the Broomer farm took about five minutes. I'd guess it was only a mile or two past the turnoff to Miz Dot's. Speaking of Miz Dot, she was driving the speed limit, as usual, which about sent Daddy to the loony bin. He griped the whole time about letting her go first, but we eventually made it. I'd never been there before, but even in the dark, I could see it was a house that needed some work. Daddy's headlights raced across two tottering sheds and an old car propped up on cinder blocks. The Broomer's front porch was spotlighted for a second, revealing some painted metal porch chairs and two geraniums in concrete urns. I remember their name because they always looked so pretty but stank something awful.

We saw Ben Crenshaw's old car and Elder Crenshaw himself stepping out of the driver's side. Daddy pulled in next to Miz Dot, headlights finally resting on a small, greenhouse-type building, which looked neat, sturdy and spotless. I could see the outline of thriving plants and a rock-covered walkway. If I had to guess, I'd imagine that this was Miz Broomer's and hers alone. Joe Ray didn't seem the type to grow anything beautiful.

Daddy cut the car off.

"You girls stay here for a second and let me find out what Ben has to report." Daddy leaned over and pecked Mama on the cheek. As he slammed the door, Mama spun around, propping her arm across the back of the seat

"Stay put, Mildred."

She opened her door, swung her legs out and slammed it shut. Daddy heard her but kept walking. Yep. Things were getting more and more normal in the Rhodes' household.

They weren't that far from the car – Elder Crenshaw, Miz Dot, Mama and Daddy – so I rolled down my window and hung my head out. It was one of those crystal clear, cold November nights where sound carried from three farms down the road. I had no trouble hearing what was said and who was saying it.

"She's in the house, Sam, but won't come out," Ben Crenshaw reported as Daddy approached.

"Why not?"

"She's afraid Joe Ray'll find out she talked to us and get even madder."

"Where is Joe Ray?" Mama asked, glancing uneasily around the moonlit yard.

"Not here. She thinks he's headed to Mel's Bar over near the railroad tracks."

Miz Dot leaned against the hood of her truck, arms crossed.

"Well, it's ridiculous for us all to be out in the yard and not talking to her," Mama ventured, moving toward the front door. Daddy grabbed her arm gently.

"No, wait, honey. Let me think for a second. Wanda's fear is real. Joe Ray easily could beat her for talking with us tonight, but unfortunately, our simple presence in her yard will be enough grounds for that. He'll come home drunk and angry anyway – certainly not in any mood to believe that Wanda didn't talk to us."

"But how will he know we were ever here?" Mama asked.

"Men like that always find out somehow," Dot spoke up. "Neighbors keep eyes open around here. He might not hear about it tonight, but he'll hear it soon enough."

"But surely Wanda's neighbors won't take up for Joe Ray? They've got to know what's been goin' on here," Mama turned toward Dot. "Won't they cover for Wanda?"

Miz Dot shook her head, looking like she wanted to answer differently.

"Seems like there's an unspoken code with the men in this town. No matter how horrible you're actin', you stand up for one another. Nope. The neighbors will tell Joe Ray what he wants to hear."

"...which puts us between a rock and a hard place," Daddy said thoughtfully. "There really is only one good solution. We convince Wanda to come home with us tonight and leave a note for Joe Ray. Maybe I can talk some sense into him tomorrow after he's sobered up."

The group contemplated this silently and seemed to come to some sort of agreement as they moved together toward Miz Broomer's front porch light. Crickets and tree frogs chorused louder and louder as they stepped closer – maybe it was a warning.

I looked intently at the drawn curtains over her front window. I didn't see any movement, like I half expected to, but I was sure Miz Broomer must be watching from somewhere. Poor Miz Wanda. Stuck in the middle of deliverance and fear.

Daddy led the way up the concrete-block steps and knocked hard on the door. It didn't open, but I could hear Miz Broomer yelling from behind it.

"Go away, Pastor! I done told Ben I can't be seen talkin' with you now. Please, please, just go away!" her voice cracked like she'd been crying.

"Wanda, it's too late. We figure the neighbors have already seen us. Joe Ray won't believe you when you tell him you didn't talk to us."

"I'll just have to take that chance," the muffled voice responded. "Now, please, I'm beggin' you. Leave!"

"Wanda," Mama spoke up in her most persuasive voice. "You know you can't stay here tonight. We'd love to have you at our house. Mildred would be glad to give up her room; it would be so much safer. Sam'll try to talk to Joe Ray tomorrow when he's good and sober. He can explain things. Come on out, honey. You know you can't stay."

Miz Broomer took no time at all to respond.

"There ain't no explainin' nothing to Joe Ray. If I go with you, he'll find a way to make me pay. It might not be tomorrow or even the next day, but it'll happen. It always does. Now for the last time, I ain't going. Please leave!"

She cut the porch lights out on her last word – and all the lights in the front room soon followed. The dark house seemed cold and naked now in the bald light of the moon. Four shadowy figures eased off the porch stoop quietly. I reckon they all figured she wouldn't be persuaded.

As Daddy drew closer to my rear window view, I could see he was scratching his chin, a sure sign of deep thought. Mama's eyes were tight and her skin looked pale, and I wasn't sure if I saw tiredness or fear. Then Elder Crenshaw clapped his hands loud and we all jumped three feet; I even hit my head on the roof. He did have the grace to look ashamed.

"Oops. Sorry 'bout that. I was just thinkin' we might as well head on home. I can't figure anything else we could do for Wanda tonight. That woman's mind is made up as far as I can see." Daddy nodded slowly, but stopped short of agreeing.

"I think we ought to stop and pray."

"Right here?" Miz Dot looked alarmed.

"Absolutely," Daddy continued. "No better time nor place. Come on. Let's gather in a circle ... and Mildred?" His voice raised a note higher as he leaned back to look around Elder Crenshaw's wide shoulders, eyeballing me. "You might as well get on out and join us. Wanda needs all the prayer she can get."

Mama opened the circle and held her hand out as I walked over. I took care not to slam the car door. It was an eerie scene, what with the moonlight playing across the yard, making normal things like a tool shed look like a witch's cottage. I couldn't shake the feeling that the very air smelled creepy.

"Lord God, we stand in this circle tonight, on this property, in agreement that you would send your protection around Wanda. Your Word says when two or three are gathered in Your name, there you are. Well, there's five of us here, Lord, and we agree that Wanda needs heavenly help to keep her husband from ..."

Daddy paused then, glancing my way.

"...from being mean to her tonight or any night. Cover her with your wings of protection and hide her from the plans of the evil one."

"And show us, Lord, how to help her," Mama added.

Miz Dot and Elder Crenshaw said a hearty "Amen" as they dropped hands, although Mama kept holding on to mine — for which I was grateful. I did notice the yard didn't seem as spooky anymore. Daddy ended the prayer and immediately began looking around. He stopped, squinted and turned around a few times before Mama had had enough.

"What?" she said, a little grumpily.

"I'm just thinking. If I could find a place to hole up and wait, I could watch Joe Ray come home and make sure Wanda would be okay – at least tonight."

"Not a bad idea," Elder Crenshaw nodded. "That fir tree over there might be just the spot. You can park the car in the vacant lot around the corner. Joe Ray won't come that way from Mel's – and I'm thinkin' two men could hide easy in that shadowy part."

"Two?" Daddy repeated.

Elder Crenshaw hitched up his pants and puffed out his chest. "You don't think this here logger's gonna let his pastor take a risk while he goes home, do ya? Heck no!"

"Dot?" he asked. "Would you mind runnin' by the house on your way home and lettin' Alma know what's up?"

"No problem," Miz Dot said, turning toward Mama. "Why don't you and Mildred hop in my truck. Mildred can squeeze in the middle, and I'll drop you off at the trailer?"

Well, I could tell this was killing Mama. She wanted to stay. She didn't want to stay. She was afraid for Daddy, for Miz Broomer. Finally, her worried eyes lit on me and she smiled – a real, honest-to-goodness smile – and tugged at one of my braids.

"Yep, my Indian girl. I do think it's time me and you set up the wigwam and hit the sack." Daddy kept his mouth shut, probably glad Mama wasn't making more waves. And as much as I didn't want to miss any excitement, the activities of the night were beginning to wear on me. All the beads on the right side of my dress were now gone and I was beginning to feel like a girl who was going to miss the end of the ball. I yawned.

"I reckon that settles it then. Laura Lee, don't worry about me and Ben," Daddy squeezed Mama tight. "With two of us here, one can light out after the sheriff if there's a problem. We won't take any unnecessary chances."

"I know. I'll just pray," Mama said, her voice muffled by Daddy's thick, corduroy jacket.

Miz Dot didn't bother saying goodnight to Daddy or Elder Crenshaw. She walked over to her truck, climbed in and slammed the door. Elder Crenshaw watched her, looked back at me and winked while Daddy gave me a quick hug and a kiss.

"Goodnight, Mil. I'll see you in the morning. Alright?"

I buried my head in his chest, drawing a deep breath of Old Spice aftershave and starched shirt. It smelled of security and home and safety. Pulling away and walking to the truck took more strength than I thought I had at the moment. As Miz Dot drove us away, I watched Daddy climb into the car, hoping I'd see him tomorrow. Mama looked straight ahead, her lips set in a firm line.

Chapter 32

Mildred

I woke smelling bacon frying and coffee brewing. The lure dragged me out of a part- dream, part-awake place where I was an investigator, just about to crack the case of Leslie's disappearance – it was one of those weird dreams that I could actually direct with my thoughts. But it stopped short of giving me any clues, so I laid there for a minute or two, wondering about the girl with the sideways grin and wildflower bouquet who stared so intently at me in Miz Dot's bathroom.

Then I remembered what happened last night and hopping out of the bed, I dashed into the kitchen to see what was up.

It was Daddy — up to his elbows in flour and milk. We must be having biscuits, too. He laughed as soon as he saw me.

"Whoa, there, girl. You act like a cattle driver, done worked all night and needs to eat her breakfast," he drawled out the words in a slow, John Wayne sort of way. I ran up to him, hugging him from behind, kicking up flour dust all over the counter.

"You're okay," I said, burying my head into his back.

"Of course I'm okay. What else would I be?"

"I don't know. I was just afraid..."

"Not to worry, Mil. The Lord always takes care of His own. Always." He slapped the dough ball down, right in the middle of the flour, dusting the counter. As he reached for the rolling pin, I glanced around, wondering where Mama was.

"She's sleeping in, honey. Last night was a long one for me and you, but felt like eternity to your Mama. I'm hoping it won't set her back any."

"What happened?"

"You mean after you girls left?"

"Yes, sir."

"Well, it was pretty dull, actually. Ben and me sat under that fir tree for — oh I don't know — probably two or three hours before Joe Ray's truck came rolling down the road. He got out, stumbled to the door and practically fell into the living room. I reckon Wanda helped him in 'cause the front door shut and we didn't hear a word. We stayed another hour or so before we gave it up and came on home." I handed him the biscuit cutter, and Daddy began slicing round circles of dough, placing them on a tin sheet nearby. Then he opened the oven door, sliding in twelve perfectly round biscuits.

"So now what?"

Daddy turned to me, ruffling my hair with his white hands. "I think Ben and me might take a quick trip out to see Joe Ray later today, about the time he might sober up. We'll have a nice talk with him and see what happens, but I'm not worried about it. We're doing what the Lord would have us do. It's the safest place to be."

I suppose he was right, but it sure didn't feel real safe to me. I figured I'd just pray a lot and hope for the best. After all, what else could I do? And I knew we had a big planning day ahead of us. Thanksgiving was only five days away and Daddy announced a church Thanksgiving Dinner in the Bingo Hall last Sunday. You'd a thought he told them they were winning the bingo jackpot. People screamed and clapped their excitement. Me and Gregory rolled our eyes – the grown-ups could be way more crazy than we were. Still, I have to confess I was excited too. People like Miz Mary Rose and Elder Thomas were beginning to feel like family to me – colored skin and all. Maybe the kids at Piedmont Ridge Elementary were right; maybe I did love coloreds. Could be worse.

Today was grocery list day. Monday we'd do the Thanksgiving Day shopping after school, and Wednesday we'd start preparing the birds with stuffing – chopped onions, green peppers, lots of butter. Mmm. Made me wipe my mouth just to think about it. Now that the play was over, everything else felt like a skate down a hill.

I came home early from our half-day of school on Wednesday to find Daddy unscrewing the hinges on our rickety screen door.

"What's up?" I asked, emerging from the wooded path.

"What's that?" Daddy turned to face me, his brow furrowed, sleeves pushed up on his arms. "Oh, hey hon. I'm takin' the screen door off for the winter. Your Mama is tired of it slamming every time we walk through the front door, and there's no need for it till spring anyway." He smiled and winked. "And she's anxious over the Thanksgiving cooking and trying to find something to get me out of the kitchen. I reckon this'll do."

I laughed, dropping my book bag on the stoop. "I thought you and Elder Crenshaw were gonna be putting up tables today anyway." I leaned over and scratched yet another mosquito bite on my right arm. Seems I couldn't walk through the pines without getting bitten at least once.

"We'll do that later. Meanwhile, I'll try to find something to keep me occupied outside of the trailer. But you – Mildred Juniper Rhodes – *you* are the chosen one!" Daddy swept his arm wide, pointing to the door with his Phillips screwdriver. "Your presence was requested by the Queen of the House as soon as you appeared on the horizon. So I say to you, 'Enter at your own risk. Be strong and be brave. You may be facing untold peril, sweeping away roasting pans with a giant flourish, cornering ears of corn to be shucked, pushing aside all thoughts of yourself to conquer the field of...'"

"Mildreeeeeeeddd!" Mama's harried voice rang from the trailer. "Is that you?"

Daddy mouthed "good luck" and turned back to the last drooping hinge, screwdriver ready. I sighed, picked up my bag and walked in – knowing I might not escape the kitchen until the sun went down. Mama's "exhaustion" seemed to be disappearing more and more now that the holidays were upon us, and it was killing me!

Daddy had somehow managed to be missing for the next two-to-three hours when I heard a car pull into the gravel on the edge of our driveway. Mama had gone to lay down thirty minutes earlier, leaving me with soft, boiled pumpkin and a mashing spoon. She had planned on bringing four pies to tomorrow's festivities, along with the two turkeys, one cornbread casserole and sweet tea. I thought she was going a bit overboard, but she insisted that the preacher's family ought to bring more than their share and so prove to be a good example. I wasn't sure how her working me to death the day before Thanksgiving would be a good example, but I had managed to keep my mouth shut so far.

I washed the pumpkin mash off my hands and grabbed the dishtowel as I trotted to the door, hoping to catch whoever it was before they woke up Mama. A long, grey Cadillac had pulled under the pine tree in our front yard, and Mr. Pete Griffin was easing out of the driver's side door. Across the parking lot, Daddy and Elder Crenshaw walked slowly from the Bingo Hall, chatting as they went. I saw Daddy laugh really hard at something Elder Crenshaw said, then his smile froze when Daddy saw Mr. Griffin getting out of his car. The air was brisk, standing with the front door open, but I decided it was worth it. I did shut it enough so that Daddy wouldn't notice me, but I peeked out and turned my ear toward the yard. This could be important. Luckily, Pete Griffin's gravelly voice was also loud, especially when he was all hyped up about something, so I had no problems hearing him.

"Howdy Preacher," he bellowed across the parking lot. Hope Mama left her fan running in the room. "I have a little something here from City Hall that I thought you might want to see." Mr. Griffin hitched up his black, polyester pants and ran his free hand through his thinning hair. Part of it lifted in the breeze like a struggling flag on a flagpole. In his left hand, a brown envelope dangled ominously.

"Oh yeah?" Daddy had on his friendly face, but I knew better.

"Yep. Some of the gentlemen at City Council think, just as I do, that Mr. Bobby Caldwell living in the Bingo Hall is a violation of City Codes. In fact, I have the documentation right here. I know it's the day before Thanksgiving and everything, so in the kindness of our hearts, we decided to give you five working days to get Bobby packed up and moved out. Uh, but I do need to tell you ..."

At this point, Mr. Griffin's voice dropped a little lower and I had to hang my head out farther to hear. Mr. Crenshaw stood quietly to the side, watching both men intently.

"...well, you know the whole Bingo Hall being a church thing came up in discussion as well." Mr. Griffin stood a little taller. "We're not sure where the approval came for the switch- over – from a business to a non-profit location – but we're pretty sure that wasn't cleared through the city office. It may just be...well, it's too early to tell...but it could be that the church itself won't be able to meet here. After all, you have to admit, a church in a Bingo Hall is highly irregular," he forced a laugh that sounded more like a snarl to me.

Daddy opened his mouth to speak, while a flaming red creeped up Elder Crenshaw's face. It hit the roots of his hair, which in and of itself, should've sent Mr. Griffin running back to his Cadillac. I got the feeling you just didn't cross Elder Crenshaw. But then Daddy gathered himself, clamped his mouth shut and forced a fake, but broad, smile. "Mr. Griffin, you do what you gotta do and we'll do the same. Now, I appreciate you bringing this paperwork all the way out here the day before Thanksgiving. That was a real sacrifice on your part, but Ben and I need to grab a few more tables from the storage shed, so we'll be seeing you."

Mr. Griffin's poking-out chest sagged and the red on Elder Crenshaw's face was replaced with confusion. He looked at Daddy like he grew three heads, and I couldn't say that I blamed him. He wasn't the type to take this lying down.

Yet Daddy waited and watched. Looking somewhat smaller, Mr. Griffin turned his back on the two men and thoughtfully walked toward the car. Suddenly, he spun around one more time, all friendliness gone.

"I don't know what your game is, Rhodes, but your days as a

preacher in this town are numbered. If I can't run you out of Piedmont Ridge, I'll at least run you out of the Bingo Hall. You might as well head on back to Georgia; you ain't wanted here."

Daddy continued to hold his plastered smile, but Elder Crenshaw had enough.

"And I reckon you don't have no knowledge of a burning done right over there on that pine limb, do ya?" Elder Crenshaw's voice boomed like a bolt of thunder. "If'n you can't run the man out by one method, you'll grab you another, won't you? You ought to be ashamed of yourself, calling yourself a Christian. Ha! I seen more Christian-like behavior from my coon dog. At least he stands by a man."

Daddy must've thought this wasn't going nowhere 'cause he grabbed Elder Crenshaw's arm.

"It's alright, Ben. Let's just go on and get those tables. Mr. Griffin has business elsewhere, I'm sure."

Mr. Griffin looked ready to say more to Elder Crenshaw, but I reckon the sight of that tall, burly, curly-headed log cutter zipped his mouth shut right quick. He swallowed it down, turned and stomped back to his car, slamming the door. Cranking the engine, he sped down the road, kicking up a mixture of gravel and dust in his wake. He wasn't even out of sight before Elder Crenshaw threw up his hands, exasperated.

"What was that, Sam? Since when do we roll over for the likes of Pete Griffin?" Elder Crenshaw's normal, sweet expression was gone and I almost felt like closing the door – almost. I had to see what Daddy would say.

"Don't let it bother you," Daddy returned, placing his hand on the big man's shoulder. "The Lord's been teaching me quite a bit about accusations and frontal assaults. Don't reckon I need to ask Him why He's showing me all this," Daddy sighed, shaking his head. "The reality is that when you defend yourself, you place your accuser in the position of a judge. Do you see what I mean?"

"Not really," Elder Crenshaw was still mad.

"Think of it this way. When Jesus was brought before his accusers prior to the crucifixion, did he ever try to state his case or answer the questions?"

"Naw, exceptin' that one time ..."

"Right, when the High Priest adjured Him by the living God to speak. At that point, the highest authority was named, forcing Christ to answer the question."

"Yep. I recall that." The two men began walking toward the trailer again.

"But that was the only time he defended himself, and even then, he simply answered a question. Christ never tried to refute the accusations against Him. I believe that if we do the same then we make a place spiritually for the real judge, God, to come into the situation and judge fairly. If I answer to Pete Griffin, I'm giving him a place of authority in my life that he simply doesn't have."

Well, I could tell that, like me, Elder Crenshaw was going to have to let his brain soak on this awhile — like dried beans in a pot of water.

"Does this mean we're just gonna let them kick us out – and Bobby too?"

At that, Daddy threw back his head and laughed loud enough to scare the squirrels high in the pines.

"Of course not. I'm gonna have Dot start digging into City Codes come Monday morning. That's not answering Pete Griffin in my mind; that's just getting the facts. Meantime, we got a lot of praying to do."

Daddy tromped around the trailer to the storage shed, leaving Elder Crenshaw scratching his head. I eased the door shut, completely understanding how he felt.

Thanksgiving Day finally arrived and I was making my last trip to the Bingo Hall with the food. Gregory opened the door for me, the cardboard turkey decoration snagging the sleeve of my coat. I jerked it free, making the cardboard Tom Turkey careen wildly back and forth.

"That all, Mildred?" he asked with a sideways grin.

"Yeah. No help from you in getting it here! What have you been doing while I had to run back and forth in this weather?" I shook the rain off my coat and handed him the last of the pumpkin pies. Gregory laughed. You would think with the rain pouring down and all the food we had to transport from the trailer to the Bingo Hall that Daddy would have piled it all in the car and made one big trip. In all fairness, he did start out this morning with that sort of a plan, but then people started arriving. He had to get Mama over without getting her dress wet and I ended up having to make three trips back and forth.

"I been helping Mr. Stew unload his car while Miz Mary Rose ordered us both around. Don't be thinkin' you got off the hook or nothing. It's been crazy in here," he rolled his eyes back in his head when he said that and, as I gazed around the room seeing all the umbrellas, raincoats and children running between chairs, I realized he was telling the truth. The Lewis children were usually fairly well-behaved, but I reckon the joy of two days off of school and the tempting smells of baked turkey and cookies were about more than they could handle.

"Bobby Jr., get down off that table right now," Miz Lewis screeched across the room. Little Bobby paid no attention as he jumped to the end of the table and bounced on the floor before it could flip on him.

"Good gravy," I mumbled, hanging my coat on the back of a metal chair, "who let all these folks out of the loony bin? I don't think I even know some of them."

"Yeah. I noticed that too 'cept I seen that family before." Gregory pointed across the room at a tall, skinny man with spiky black hair and his short, wide, curly haired wife. She held a dark-haired baby close to her chest, rocking and jiggling him as she chatted with Elder Thomas. Miz Debbie stood to the side, half listening and half not. "I think they come into the co-op last week and got a good dowsing from Miz Mary Rose. You know how she don't let no newcomer go without invitin' them to church or some such thang."

I could well imagine. Wonder if they got "The Mary Rose

Hug?"

"Have you seen Miz Broomer," I questioned.

"Naw. Been watchin' for her and Joe Ray, like you said, but I ain't seen 'um. You sure they comin'?"

"Daddy said she wouldn't miss it, and Joe Ray promised him a day or two ago he'd try to come see if he might like us church folk. I don't think Daddy's holding his breath, though. Joe Ray sounds like a piece of work. Daddy said he was all nice and polite when he went to visit him, but he wouldn't trust him as far as he could throw him."

"Is that what he say?" Gregory's eyes got big and round.

"Daddy? Well, yeah, that's what he said...but he said it to Mama and I overheard it when they were talkin' in their bedroom. Don't tell!"

"Uh huh," Gregory was trailing off, looking back behind me, his face all puckered and thoughtful. I turned in time to see the back end of the Broomer truck pull out of the parking lot, and Miz Broomer struggling to open the glass double doors while hauling a picnic basket about as big as she was.

"Lord, Gregory, come on!" I dashed to the door, pushing it open while Gregory reached for her basket.

"Well, you sweet boy," Miz Broomer gushed, handing her basket over. "You make a lady feel mighty welcome." She patted me on the head as she sashayed by in a long, flowery skirt. She wore a pretty brown cape over her shoulders, and her strawberry hair was swooped up in some sort of sideways bun. I had no idea how she managed to keep herself all together – I mean, with nothing falling out, down or off. Today her lips were painted a bright, full orange, which of course, matched the brooch fastened on her cape. She swept through the room in a flurry but try as I may, I couldn't spot any bruises on her face. I saw Gregory cutting his eyes at her as he lugged the basket toward one of the food tables. He was doing the same thing.

"Wanda!" Miz Mary Rose screeched out, barreling toward her with arms outstretched. I swerved a hard left, heading toward Mama to avoid a serious collision. Mama sat at the front table, folding napkins and laughing at something Miz Crenshaw said. I slid into the chair beside her. She glanced sideways at me and winked, a gesture that flooded my heart with joy. There hadn't been much winking going on with Mama since we moved. I watched her carefully crease, then fold twice, then stack, each dinner napkin while enjoying Miz Alma's story about a coon in a neighbor's trash can. Mama's green eyes sparkled and the dullness that had lived behind those eyes seemed to be gone forever. She had woken early this morning to paint her fingernails and fix her hair – it was swept up in a bun, loose strands hanging around her face. I glanced toward Daddy who was sliding another table end-to-end to make room for *more* food (heavens to Betsy!). He was deep in conversation with Elder Thomas – my guess was it had something to do with the Bible.

On the other side of the room, Gregory unloaded the last casserole dish from Miz Broomer's basket, under the ever-watchful direction of Miz Mary Rose. She had shed her co-op vest for a large brown sweater with three round pumpkins embroidered on the front. It was hard not to see the strong resemblance between the shapes on her sweater and the shape of her body, but I tried not to let my mind stray there.

My eyes continued to sweep the area – over Mr. Bobby carving one of the big birds, Elder Crenshaw pulling Miz Wanda to the side for a chat, the Lewis children throwing a plastic ball to each other in the corner. They were finally calmed down somewhat, thank goodness! It was almost a perfect scene. And then I saw it. The rusty old truck sputter into the parking lot. Mr. Bobby saw it, too, and hollered out, "There she is! 'Bout time she decided to grace us with her presence." Small bits of spit sprayed between his teeth every time he hit a "p." I wondered if it was falling on the turkey.

Gregory hit the double doors at a run, most likely prompted by Miz Mary Rose. He dashed out in the rain to help Miz Dot get her food from the passenger side.

Miz Dot Harris was here, and I leaned back in my chair, sighing in contentment. Now it was the perfect Thanksgiving.

Two hours and two plates full of food later, I wondered if I would ever need to eat again. "Ohhhhhh," moaned Gregory beside me as he unbuttoned his striped vest. "My belly won't fit behind this ol' vest no more. I can't even think about movin'." The metal chair groaned as he leaned on the two back legs, stretching his feet into the chair across the table.

"I'm not so sure I ever want to see turkey again," I agreed, pushing my plate away, the turkey leg bone wobbling in protest. Mama and Daddy were at the adjoining table, still laughing it up with Miz Mary Rose and Stew, Elder Thomas and Mr. Bobby. The Lewis' were already packing up for the baby's afternoon nap, and I was so thankful I wouldn't have to play Ring Around the Rosy anymore with their kids. Me and Gregory had spent an hour playing with them, and with my stomach protruding (I sneaked and unhooked my top button on my pants.), I sure didn't want to run around the room. I leaned back next to Gregory and we rested without talking. Voices from around the room drifted into my mind.

"...so I'm wondering what we can do to try and find Leslie."

Gregory started to bolt up in his chair, but I pinched him real hard on the tender spot of his underarm. He jerked back toward me, but it was enough of a distraction to get him to keep his trap shut – well, except for him mouthing, "I'll get you for that."

I shrugged and put my finger over my lips. We began to listen in earnest.

"I'm not so sure Miz Dot would want us diggin' up her past," Elder Thomas offered.

"The way I see it, she doesn't have to know unless we find something out," Daddy responded thoughtfully. "I admit it's hard for me to let a mystery like this go without investigating, but I've also prayed about it some and keep getting the same feeling – why not?"

Mama was unusually quiet, a sign that she was either thinking hard or holding back from saying something she might regret later.

"I think Sam is right," Miz Mary Rose spoke up. Gregory shot a smile at me. "Dot ain't gonna try no more to find her, but if we could put this to rest somehow for her, well, just imagine how wonderful it would be for Dot to have some answers."

"And that's what I'm afraid of," Mama broke her silence. "What if the answers are horrible, even worse than not knowing? I feel like Dot is finally breaking out of her shell and if we go and do this, we might lose her forever. It's just not worth it. Sam," Mama looked at Daddy with pleading eyes. "You know this. It could go well, but more than likely, it won't. And the type of lady that Dot is..."

"Laura Lee, you are assuming many things. I don't even know how to begin looking for Leslie. We'd probably hit a brick wall right at the get-go. And if we got a lead or two, it'd most likely fizzle out."

"So why bother?" Mama shifted her empty plate to the side, leaning into Daddy who was sitting directly across from her. "Why take the chance of losing Dot over this whole thing?"

All eyes shifted back to Daddy, but he remained silent.

Out of the corner of my eye, I noticed Mr. Stew chewing a little faster on his toothpick. His forehead wrinkled up as he frowned thoughtfully – sort of reminded me of an elephant's skin. He finally slid his chair back and slowly removed the toothpick.

"I find myself agreein' with Miz Laura Lee here," he drawled. "Seems to me that we seen Miz Dot make some mighty big strides in takin' to folks again. I'd sure hate to see all that washed down the drain due to our meddlin' in places we ain't welcomed. My Daddy always said I was to mind my own business and not poke my nose in places I ought not be – lessin' you was asked, o' course."

Elder Thomas spoke up as he leaned on the tables with his elbows.

"You know, my brain agrees with ya, Stew, but my heart says to take the chance – that the other end of this here journey just might bring Dot Harris to a place of real peace – whatever that might be for her."

Daddy slapped the table so hard the plates jumped, and Gregory about fell backwards. I grabbed his arm, holding him steady.

"That's it, Daryl," Daddy said. "You said it just right. I can't put my finger on why I keep feeling led to pursue this, but my heart – maybe the Spirit of God in me – won't let it go."

Mama's mouth opened, but Daddy didn't see her.

"I know it just as easily might not be the Spirit of God. Could be just my curiosity or inability to let things go. I'm not sure, but my heart says we have to see what we can find out. If nothing turns up, then nothing comes of it. But if something does – well, then, we'd have to decide what to do with the information and how to let Dot know."

Mama shut her mouth. Anytime Daddy threw in the Lord as a possible element, Mama always shut her mouth. She'd told me before that she's learned to keep to herself until she's talked to the Lord in her own way. I reckon that's what she had in mind now, although her face still had a healthy looking red glow to it, and I don't think it was the heat in the room.

"Pastor, did you know I done some investigatin' in Korea?" Mr. Bobby jumped into the conversation.

"What kind of investigating?"

"Well, I was low man on the totem pole, you might say," Mr. Bobby cleared his throat, "but in my unit, we'd sometimes have to dig up information on some of our men. Maybe financial records if a Joe was in money troubles. Shoot, sometimes I even had to interview men after battle situations so my higher ups could compare accounts. I didn't do no judgin' on my own, 'course. Just gathered intel. The officers took it from there, but I did learn a few tricks on finding things out. I reckon I might could use some of that know-how to dig in some local records. Never know what I might turn up."

"Can you do it discreetly?" Daddy asked.

"Come again?"

"Quietly. Can you do your digging without lots of folks finding out about it?"

"Oh sure," Mr. Bobby's front tooth shone in the light and his blue eyes sparkled. "My cousin Lucille is the records clerk for the county. She's about the only family I got that don't turn the other way when I walk down the street. She'll help me out."

"Stew, Daryl, what do you think? Should we go for it?"

Mr. Stew picked up his soggy toothpick and stuck it back in his mouth. He nodded with his head, but he didn't look overly confident.

"I ain't that comfortable with the idea, but I sho can pray about it," Elder Thomas put in. "Meantime, I jus' hope nobody gets wind of it, especially Dot Harris!"

Right then, Miz Dot busted out laughing; it must've been something Miz Broomer said. She didn't notice the two groups on the other side of the room – one filled with worried-looking grown-ups and the other one with two equally worried kids.

Chapter 33

Dot

Dot fell into her broken recliner, air squeezing from its cushions under the weight. Pulling the ottoman closer with her foot, she slipped her boots to the side and lifted both legs, stretching them out in relief. It had been a busy morning, a hectic week, and she wasn't sure how much more she could do physically.

"Aaaaaa, chooooo!" she bellowed, reaching for the tissue. Two strong honks and she was again at rest, glancing at the clock. Mildred would be over in about two hours to help with the afternoon milking. Dot had a chance to sit a spell, and she needed it.

The stack of books beside her chair beckoned as she glanced that way, but even she had to admit, she didn't feel like reading. Unfortunately, she didn't feel much like napping either, although that certainly would be good for her cold.

Truth was, Dot was a little uneasy. She hadn't slowed down enough to figured out why, but she had known there was something ... unsettled ... in her heart. And even though she didn't know what that was, she also hadn't been in the mood to find out. Maybe in her subconscious, she knew it was something she didn't want to consider.

But those familiar, odd sensations began rolling in the minute she sat still. If she had felt better, she would have pushed herself up to go work on the chicken coop before winter really set in. There were a thousand things to be done on the farm during the slower, winter months – like shoveling manure from the coop to the garden – but the thought of work made her ... "Aaaahhhh choo!" She shook her head and reached for the book, a who-done-it that she would have solved by the third chapter. But before the book was in her hand, she strongly felt a stillness in the room. It almost took her breath away, the intensity behind the presence. She halted, hand in mid-air, and suddenly she knew she couldn't run any longer; that's exactly what she had been doing, running. It was time to stop because God was calling.

With resolve, Dot pulled her hand back, leaned back in the chair, and said matter-of-factly to the empty room, "Alright, Lord. You're right. I've been avoiding You. And now I'm sick and tired – and sick and tired of running. What is it You want to say?"

The steady ticking of the Pepsi-Cola wall clock was her only answer, but it allowed her mind to open to the still, quiet voice of the Lord as she recalled her reading that morning. She had reread the parable of the lost son in the book of Luke, Chapter 15, about the son who had squandered his inheritance, then returned home to a welcoming father. Dot had ruminated on the reaction of the other brother in the story, the one who had been consistently with his father, working the farm. His response to the wayward brother had been anger, possibly a feeling that his father was a pushover. Dot completely understood that reaction. Sort of had that feeling herself. She knew the principle behind the parable, that of a father's forgiveness when true repentance occurred, but she also sympathized with the responsible son, wanting the younger brother to at least get punished. It just didn't seem fair.

She allowed her mind to play over the parable again, picking apart pieces of detail that she had noted. She recalled the extensive way the father had celebrated the arrival of the lost son – he gave him a ring, sandals, the fatted calf, a huge party. No wonder the older brother, who was in the field working, came home a little frustrated. Dot blew her nose again. She knew she would feel the same way. After all, she, of all people, understood the steadiness and perseverance of a hard worker.

Dot.

She sensed more than she heard the voice.

You are the lost son, not the older one.

What? Dot almost sat straight up in the recliner. This made no sense.

You are the lost one, the prodigal, the one who has left the warmth of relationship, the church in Piedmont Ridge. Now as you dip your toe into Sam Rhodes' fellowship, you are turning towards home. I am placing a ring on your finger, sandals on your feet and killing the fatted calf for the return of my daughter.

Dot's eyes filled with tears as the truth of this word sank in.

And yet ... you haven't fully decided whether to stay in the church. Will you stay, Dot? Or will you return to the land of isolation?

The question dropped into the room like a hammer, its ring rebounding and echoing. *Will you stay?*

Just then, Dot knew and understood the weight of the question. She had been toying almost, playing with the idea of returning to church. In fact, she had spent Thanksgiving Day with the Rhodes' but hadn't been attending regular services. One foot in the door, one foot out.

Tears continued to flow and great, heaving sobs stole out of Dot's mouth. She saw it all so clearly.

She had felt justified to leave the City Church after they demanded a tithe of her inheritance money after Tom's death. What they didn't know was that there was no inheritance. It took all her savings just to pay for the funeral. They had been living month-to-month and had cashed in everything just to make it. But no one, not one elder, pastor or deacon, had bothered to ask her if she was alright financially. They had assumed she was cashing in and waited for their payoff. When it never came, she was taken to task for it.

Dot had never told any of them that there was no money. She figured they didn't deserve to know anything after the way they had acted. She had pulled away, pulled her membership and left the church with her pride and justification intact. Never again would she be presumed upon.

For ten years she had lived alone, justified in her judgment, and now she saw clearly. She had been living among her own set of pigs – a self-imposed isolation. Her weeping began to recede and, ironically enough, Dot chuckled. She was living among the pigs –

and the cows and chickens and dogs. It was lonely but it had been what she thought she needed, until now.

The question still hung in the air, pushing, probing, seeking. Was she willing to return? To be a part of Piedmont Ridge Community Church? The clock chimed three beats as the electric heater beside her chair flipped on, a dull, steady hum. Dot knew she couldn't be flippant about this. The Lord was asking for a firm commitment, which equated to a no-turning-back policy. Dot knew if she planned to continue walking with Him, she couldn't say no. As afraid as she was of people and their ability to hurt her, she was more afraid of God and the thought of not having His presence to greet her every morning and sustain her every day. There really was no choice. You either walk ahead with God or say no and drive a wedge in your relationship with Him that will render your faith weak and frail.

The empty room waited.

"I reckon You know You've got me between a rock and a hard place," Dot spoke out loud. "Now that You've shown me my heart, I can't go back. And the only way forward is to join in and begin to love again, come what may. And yet, I don't even like some of these people," Dot wiped her nose and grabbed a fresh tissue. "But I do like Sam and Laura Lee and Mildred ... God help me, I love them and I'm afraid ..." Dot began crying again, admitting freely her fears of losing, hurting and being pushed away. She continued to speak to the room, sometimes loudly, sometimes in whispers, all while the clock continued its steady, even course around the dial.

It was about the time Mildred came in view of the backside of the milk barn that Dot got up from the floor. At some point during the past hour, she had eased out of the recliner, lowered herself down on her knees next to the ottoman, and fully committed to join again with other believers, specifically those at the Community Church. She promised to love them, with God's help, and to try to forgive those at the City Church that had treated her unfairly so long ago. As she stiffly pulled herself up, she thought she could pinpoint every aching bone in her body. But in her heart? Dot Harris felt as light as a feather. She found herself smiling as she wiped the last tears from her eyes.

"I wonder, Lord. What's my fatted calf gonna be?" she asked as Mildred knocked on the front door.

Only a week had passed since Dot's newfound commitment to God and to the Community Church. She hadn't mentioned anything to Sam Rhodes yet, didn't want to belabor the issue is what she told herself. In reality, she knew she would have to come clean soon and let Sam know about her conversation with the Lord and the steps He was asking her to take. As she watched Sam pull his brown, dusty car into the city government parking lot, she figured God must've gotten tired of waiting on her and was throwing her like a football, a sort of "Hail Mary" pass.

"Do you have the paperwork?" Sam asked quickly as she walked toward him. The winter sun was low on the horizon, just about to dip below the roof line of Deb's Chicken, and Dot knew it must be close to 5 p.m. City Council would start right on time and she and Sam would need to be inside, ready to present their findings about Bobby living in the Bingo Hall. Their turn would come right after the review of last month's minutes.

"I've got everything right here," she replied, shoving the manila folder toward him. "I still say you need to be the one to address the council. It's your church and your responsibility," Dot said in a no-nonsense voice. Almost everybody in Piedmont Ridge would have obeyed her, especially with that tone, but not Sam. Exasperated, he shoved his hand through his thick hair, leaving furrows from his fingers lining back to his collar.

"We've already discussed this, Dot, and you know the council will listen to you more than they will to me. You did the digging in the record's office, you found the old rulings that Pete Griffin ignored, you know this information backwards and forwards. It's got to come from you." Sam began striding to the glass front doors, waving the folder back toward Dot, but even as his steps fell, he started to lag. Eventually, he stopped and swung about, facing her directly. "You know, come to think of it, I refuse to push you anymore on this. You're not a child. If you don't believe you are to do the presentation, then give me the paperwork and I'll do it."

Dot hitched up her overalls – she purposely hadn't changed following the afternoon milking – and took a deep breath. She was certainly tired of Sam's attitude and she'd let him know about it...and yet she knew in her heart that she was supposed to do this. It was about more than whether Piedmont Ridge Community Church could meet in the Bingo Hall or whether Bobby could live in a back room. No, tonight was about Dot Harris and a face-to-face with her persecutors. Not only was Pete Griffin on the City Council, so was Jason Dean. He had chaired the council for the past twenty-plus years. When she had agreed to research city codes and records for Sam and the church elders, she had no idea it would lead to a showdown.

Sam stood impatiently, ignoring the brisk wind that stirred the dead leaves all across the parking lot. It took Dot a few seconds to corral her emotions, but she did – shoving all the frustration and anger at Sam aside. She knew in her heart that the Lord was setting this up and she had to walk through it. It wasn't enough to forgive and move on; sometimes giants had to be faced.

"Alright, fine. Give me the folder." She took it from Sam's hand, pushed past him and jerked open the doors before he could reach them. If she had to do this thing, she wanted to get it over with.

The chamber room hadn't changed since Dot had last been in it. Same staid brown carpet, same folding chairs that made up the gallery, and the same faux leather seats for the six people who sat on Piedmont Ridge's illustrious City Council. Pete Griffin's name plaque sat on the far left, and of course, Jason Dean was front and center. Dot knew that four of the members attended the city church; but the other two fellowshipped in one of the small churches that filled every community holler between here and Greenville.

Dot only knew those two men by reputation. Never had the chance to meet them personally, but she had heard decent things about them. In fact, when she and Sam had discussed their case earlier in the week, she told him these two men – Simons and Bullock – would view their information without prejudice and would concur with them. They both felt sure that Pete Griffin would fight them to the death, and Dot told Sam that Jason Dean couldn't be counted on to be impartial either. That left J.C. Reynolds and Ed Crouch. Both men attended City Church but weren't in leadership. Dot didn't know if they knew why she dropped out of circulation and they probably didn't care. She and Tom had known them in a casual way but had never really mixed with them in any way outside of church activities – and that was years ago.

Years and years, Dot thought, looking around. She wondered if she had aged as much as everyone she noticed here. Jason, in particular, looked almost haggard. He hadn't seen her yet, and Dot wished she didn't have to see him.

"You alright?" Sam asked, watching her with curiosity. He knew this would be hard for Dot to stand up and speak before the council, even though he didn't know her history with these people. Now watching Dot's countenance change, he wondered if he had pushed too hard in insisting she make the presentation. It didn't occur to him that there might be more going on than just nerves over public speaking. He felt his frustration with her float away and compassion pour in. "You know I can do this if you need me to," he whispered as they found two seats near the middle. "We've talked about it enough so I can probably pull it off just fine."

"If there's anything I hate worse than being pushed, it's being pitied," she snapped. "Just back off and let me be." Dot didn't intend to be harsh, but Jason Dean had just spotted her. He had been moving slowly toward his seat, eyes scanning the room over his reading glasses, and with a jerk, his gaze met hers. She didn't know exactly what she had expected, but certainly not this...this resignation. The hard, unmoving, righteous Jason Dean merely lifted his hand in a small acknowledgment, smiled briefly and settled into his swivel chair. He lifted the gavel and, for Dot, those raps moved in slow motion while Tom's voice eased into her mind.

"Time does strange things to us, eh Dottie?" Dot could only numbly stare as the secretary stood to read last month's minutes.

"The ones that persecute, that spew hatred, that intimidate – they become bigger than life in our imaginations." Tom's gentle voice rang clearly. *"Then what's the end of it all, Dottie? He's just a man, that's all. Complete the circle and extend forgiveness even to him. He has no power over you."*

"He has no power, no power," she whispered to herself.

Dot felt Sam's elbow in her side and she roused herself enough to hear Jason mention new business on the night's docket. Straightening her back, she sat tall in the rickety folding chair, demanding justice by her very stance. She met Jason Dean's eyes once again as she rose and walked toward the podium.

Five minutes was all it took to outline the City Code's allowance of a non-profit to lease the Big Star property and to allow a resident gardener on the grounds as a live-in employee. Dot mentioned the local Masonic Lodge's takeover of a closed-down shoe store. She also spoke of the community clothing closet leasing property from Shaker's Mill and having a person living in the store to supervise and oversee donations. She pulled the code Pete Griffin and his cronies had used to start the whole mess and fully related how that did not apply to Piedmont Ridge Community Church and Big Star Drive. She mentioned Bobby, but never by name. She was well aware that all members of the council knew it was Bobby Caldwell, former drunkard and "murderer" (by their standards), who lived in the Bingo Hall, but she purposely withheld his name to try to keep personalities out of it. That was the main reason Sam told Bobby to stay home tonight. His presence would have been like kerosene on a brush fire.

Sam was impressed. He'd never seen an old lady in overalls take the stage the way Dot Harris did that night, but he was thankful and proud. He squeezed her arm as she sat back down.

Other new business came up and several folks approached the podium in hopes to sway the council to their way of thinking, but Sam found it all trivial compared to the pins and needles hidden in his seat. He had uncrossed and crossed his leg for the millionth time when Jason Dean banged the gavel to close all new business. There had been little discussion overall, even when Dot finished her allotted time. No one had raised any real issues with the evidence, but now the time had come to vote.

"Mr., uh, Rhodes, is that right?" Jason Dean peered from under his glasses, glaring at Sam from across the room.

"Yes, sir. I'm Sam Rhodes," Sam spoke hesitantly, wondering why on earth he was being singled out.

"I see that you are the head of the Community Church here in town. Is that right?"

"Yes, sir. Moved up from Georgia earlier this year."

"Well, I don't know about my fellow councilmen, but I'd like to hear a word from you as to the situation here. Apparently Mr. Griffin feels very strongly that you folks using the Bingo Hall is not pursuant to City Regulations; however, Mrs. Harris seemed to make a strong case tonight as to how Mr. Griffin may have unknowingly misread the aforementioned code." Sam felt Dot's body tense up beside him. "Since I haven't had the pleasure of meetin' ya, why don't you just take a minute or two and tell us a little about yourself and what you see this church lookin' like in our community?"

Sam glanced at Dot who had a worried furrow between her eyes, but he could see no way to tactfully weasel out of this. He stood self-consciously, tucking in the back of his plaid shirt, and walked slowly to the podium. There were probably only about eight townspeople at the council meeting, but Sam could feel all sixteen eyes burrowing into his back. The six councilmen in front of him were just as brooding.

"Mr. Dean, I appreciate you allowing me a chance to address you all," Sam smiled his broadest, most engaging smile, looking individually at each man. "I don't feel I need to go into the codes discussion anymore since Mrs. Harris did such a super job explaining our perspective on the situation. But I would love to have the chance to tell you what I see this church looking like in this county and this area.

"First off, you have to know that I am a simple man – a mill-worker out of Georgia who moved to Piedmont Ridge because I felt God called me here. I didn't move here because the people are nice – even though they are. I didn't move here to make lots of money – although that'd be alright too." J.C. Reynolds laughed out loud at that. "I didn't even move here to make trouble for the City Council or to cause Mr. Griffin frustration." At that, all eyes turned toward Pete Griffin who had been sitting quietly in his seat. His face was a mass of convoluted emotions - - first blanching, then turning red – yet he remained silent. Sam continued. "I moved here to start a church and as I found out more about the people, I realized this church would be different from any other church in the area or even the state. I reckon people might use words like 'integrated' or 'mixed' or 'bi-racial.' Well, we just call each other brother and sister. We don't care much about skin, we care about the Gospel of Jesus Christ being proclaimed on the streets of Piedmont Ridge and serving and loving one another in our church body."

Dot didn't budge and neither did anyone else in the room.

"So my question for you – and really for the town – would be this: Can you look past color and just love one another? Can we live together without prejudice?"

"Now wait a minute here, Rhodes," Pete Griffin half-rose out of his seat, unable to contain himself any longer. "I don't recall anybody askin' you to start criticizin' or accusin' folks of wrongdoin'. I really don't give a smarmy rat's tooth what you hope to see or want to become in our town. I think we've all seen enough of that in the past months." Pete turned toward his fellow councilmen. "Ever since this man come to town, they's been all sorts of unrest and unquiet in our streets. We got folks who ain't got no business bein' together meetin' and greetin' and doin' all sorts of foolishness. Why, just the other day I seen Bobby Caldwell walkin' downtown like he was somebody and we all know he don't have no rightful place in our town! None of this happened till Sam Rhodes came here. I think he just needs to pack up and head on back to Georgia where he come from."

Dot rose out of her seat, anger lighting in her eyes, while chatter and arguments erupted in the small chamber room. The sound of Jason Dean's gavel finally rose above the din.

"Order, order in chambers," he demanded. The room slowly began to quiet down while Sam stayed at the podium, unsure what to do next.

"Mr. Griffin," Dean turned to his right, addressing the man directly. "If you recall, I asked Mr. Rhodes to tell a little about himself, which he is doing quite admirably. We all know where you stand; I'd appreciate it if you would quiet down and let the man finish speaking."

Pete Griffin sputtered, reddened and sat with a thump, glaring ferociously at Sam.

"Please continue, Mr. Rhodes."

Sam glanced around the room, trying to get a feel for the crowd. He really just wanted to finish up and get home. Dot smiled encouragingly.

"I think I'll just close with the idea that Jesus came to bring peace to those who would accept peace. I echo that. The Piedmont Ridge Community Church wants to bring peace to this community and to dwell in peace. I would ask you to consider yourselves: Are we for peace or division? If having colored and whites worshipping together causes you a lack of peace, then I'm sorry but we're not changing. We are who we are. No apologies. But you can't ever accuse us of not loving this town or these people – all of them."

And Sam sat down quickly. He felt a little like he hit a brick wall and should have exited his plea in a more gentle manner, but he was out of words and had nothing else to say. The atmosphere in the room was charged and waiting. Pete Griffin opened his mouth but a quick, decisive glance from Jason Dean stopped any words he might have spoken.

"Well, gentlemen, I advise that we take Mrs. Harris' information under consideration before we make any move toward evicting Mr. Caldwell out of the Bingo Hall – as well as the Community Church," Dean intoned. "We will meet in private session on Dec. 29, then plan to have a final decision at next month's meeting." He lifted his eyes toward a frazzled Sam and Dot seated back in the center of the room. "We will keep you posted on our decision."

"Thank you," Sam managed. He didn't hear any more of the city business that was raised in the last twenty minutes of the meeting. His mind wandered and his stomach was knotted. When the final gavel sounded, he excused himself from Dot and made a beeline for the men's room that was adjacent to the lobby. Dot found herself standing next to the doors, waiting with manila folder in hand. The few remaining townspeople left quickly, some smiling briefly at Dot before allowing a gust of chilled winter air in as they exited. Every time the chamber doors opened, she could hear Pete Griffin's voice rising from the room, still arguing and bellyaching to some poor soul. Dot was glad it wasn't her. Then the chamber door opened again and Jason Dean walked out, a little stooped over and somewhat frail. She began to wonder if he was sick.

"Ah, Mrs. Harris," he spoke slowly. "I was hoping to catch you before you left."

Dot tilted her head and waited.

"I understand the burning in Mr. Rhodes front yard is a crime that remains unsolved?" Dean paused.

"You understand right," Dot replied.

"Yes, well, please let Mr. Rhodes know that he won't have to worry about any such event happening again in his front yard. I feel sure the culprits will have a change of heart – in fact, a conversion of sorts." He laughed, a hoarse, choking laugh that ended in a cough. "It's probable that word will get out that times are changin' and our city needs to change with them. Of course, I can make no promises on the outcome of the codes dispute, but I do think we have a few men on council who might just see past bitterness and might judge more ... let's say, impartially ... than others. In the interim, Corella and I hope you have a very, merry Christmas."

The men's bathroom door swung open and Jason Dean disappeared in the same moment. Dot never had the chance to respond, which, as she considered later that night, was probably a good thing. She had no idea what she would have said.

Chapter 32

Mildred

As I skipped down the familiar trail from school, which had become a well-worn footpath in the past three months, I felt like my insides were about to bubble out all over the pine straw. The last day of school before Christmas vacation had been all I'd dreamed of – Christmas cookies, all the punch you could drink, no real classwork to finish and Miz Dingle had even given every student a brand-new book, "The Year of the Christmas Dragon." I reached to my side, touching my book bag one more time to make sure I hadn't accidentally left it under my desk. Nope. Still there. I couldn't wait to start reading.

A squirrel dashed in front of me, stopping me short in my skipping. I watched him climb the pine closest to me, a nut stuck securely in his mouth. Sure enough, high up was a pile of leaves and twigs – his winter nest. I squinted into the sky, wanting to stay and watch, but there was no time to dawdle.

Daddy had said we should have our new phone installed by this afternoon. Finally! A chance to call Martha Claire because Mama and Daddy both said I could call Martha Claire on Christmas Day. 'Course, I'd have to call her at Uncle Goose's, seeing as how Martha Claire and her Mama didn't have a phone either. But Uncle Goose lived right next door, and he'd be able to run over and get her to the phone. Boy, would she ever be surprised! I giggled out loud, just imagining her shock and amazement.

"Mildred Juniper Rhodes!" she'd drawl over the phone. "What chue thinkin' 'bout, callin' me all the way down here in Prosperity? Have you lost yo' ever lovin' mind?" And I would tell her that, of course, I never had an ever-lovin' mind, so I sure didn't have one to lose. And we'd laugh and talk and tell each other what we got for Christmas, although I might have to be careful there. You never could tell if Martha Claire would get much of anything for Christmas, except maybe some oranges in her stocking by the wood stove. Maybe I'd let her go first. That way, if she didn't mention presents at all, I wouldn't either.

I broke through the woods at the side of the trailer and stomped up the front stoop. First goal was to find out if we had the phone in. I knocked off my shoes, left them to the side of the door and walked in.

The first thing I saw was Mama, sweeping the kitchen. More and more of the real Mama was returning.

"Well, good afternoon, Mildred," she sang across the room. "You, my dear, are just in time to grab that dustpan and give me a hand here. Oh, and welcome home!" she smiled a lovely smile and I knew Mama was having another good day. I picked up the dustpan as I tossed my bag in the chair.

"Who's Daddy talking with?" I asked as I squatted next to the pile of dirt.

"He's on the phone with Mr. Caldwell," she said, matter-of-factly. She laughed when she saw my expression. "That's right. We have a phone. The telephone people were in and out in no time. You'd think something like that would take a while, but it didn't. I even offered them a little lunch, but they had to leave on another call."

I could tell Mama was disappointed at that. She loved nothing better than to feed people, when she felt good, that is.

"I just can't wait to use it," I gushed. "But how is he talking to Mr. Bobby. There's no phone at the Bingo Hall."

"Mr. Caldwell, (Mama stressed the Caldwell. She never took to me calling adults by their first names, even if the person asked me to, as Mr. Bobby did), is at the County Records Office. He's looking up some information for your Daddy and decided to try out our new line at the same time. Isn't it exciting?"

I wasn't sure if Mama meant the information Mr. Bobby was getting was exciting or the phone was, but I opted for the phone.

"What color is it? Does it have a black numbered dial or white? Can you hear a hum over it or is it clear like the phone in Prosperity?"

"Whoa there, girl. You'll just have to find all that out after your Daddy gets off the line. Good heavens, Mildred. You'd think neither one of us had ever seen a telephone before!" We laughed together at that, realizing she was right. We'd always had a phone at the mill house but just now got enough money to have one put in here. I reckon it was the extra money Daddy earned from helping Elder Crenshaw at the sawmill last week, but I didn't ask. Then I showed Mama my gift from Miz Dingle and told her all about my day. Might have been the best day ever at Piedmont Ridge Elementary.

Daddy stayed on the phone only a few minutes more. Mama and me heard him hang it up, muttering. When he came into the living room, his hair was standing on end again and his plaid shirt was untucked on one side.

"Well, Bobby lost the trail," Daddy said, sighing.

"I suppose I am disappointed too, honey," Mama began hesitantly. "But I also still am anxious as to what finding – or not finding — Leslie might do to our relationship with Dot. We have prayed about this, so don't you think this might be the Lord's will?"

Daddy rubbed his eyes fiercely, apparently listening to Mama but I'm not so sure he liked what she was saying.

"I suppose so," he glanced up finally, "but I still have a hard time believing it. There's such a hole in Dot, an emptiness that we can't help her fill. I just know the Lord wants to heal her."

"But we all know there's more than one kind of healing," Mama persisted. "Maybe the Lord simply wants to take care of her himself and fill in that hole with His presence. It could be that getting Leslie back would only drive her away from God. He's all about relationship with Him first. I think He's good enough to know what will keep us from Him and we just have to trust His decisions."

Daddy laughed then.

"I reckon God has blessed me with one of those wise women out of Proverbs 31," Daddy leaned back, wrapping his arm around Mama's shoulder. "You are right, of course, but I can't help being disappointed and He can't stop me from praying more about it all. Maybe He'll change His mind."

"Mm hmm, and in the meantime, don't forget you promised to help Wanda get her aluminum Christmas tree out of the attic this afternoon. That'll keep your mind off Dot and Leslie."

Daddy groaned and the moment was over, so I got up to head to my bedroom and unload all my school stuff. My book from Miz Dingle was calling my name, but as I stood up, Daddy saw me.

"Ah ha!" he pointed with a smile. "Just the tree helper I need. Pack up, Mildred girl. We're off to the Broomer's."

"Sir?"

"Miz Wanda can't get that tree out of her attic by herself and Joe Ray isn't, well, hasn't been home to help her. He's been gone for days." Daddy turned toward Mama then. "Should I call her to let her know we're on the way?"

"No. No use. Joe Ray pulled the phone out of the wall last week," Mama looked up and her face twisted in a funny way. "I mean, it's disconnected right now."

I wasn't a dummy. I knew what was up, but for some reason Mama and Daddy kept trying to talk around the whole issue with Miz Broomer and her no-good husband. And now the tree in the attic? "I'm thinking he's on some drunken binge," I muttered as I went to change shoes and pants. At least it would be sort of interesting.

Besides me telling Daddy about my day, the drive over to the Broomer's house was quiet. Low, gray clouds filled the sky, in fact, we hadn't seen the sun all day. It had been a fuzzy ball of light at one point, but that was about it. I'd seen this a lot in Georgia in the wintertime. Martha Claire and me called them No-Snow Clouds. All our science books showed pictures of clouds heavy with snow which looked just like today's sky, but it was almost never cold enough to snow in mid-Georgia in December. I'm figuring this 45-degree South Carolina weather would be the same way, but I'd still keep my eye on it. We Southerners always watch our weather.

Our car sped past Miz Dot's black mailbox and I saw smoke rising out of her barn chimney. She'd have the wood stove going by now to warm the barn for her afternoon milking. Part of me wished I was there, but most of me was glad I didn't work on Fridays.

Daddy flipped the blinker and turned down Coates Road. Miz Broomer's would be ahead on the right.

"Looks like it'll be dark soon, Mil. Sky is overcast."

"Yes, sir. No-Snow Day."

He raised an eyebrow at me as he slid the car into the yard.

"No snow?"

I smiled mysteriously as I jumped out of the car and walked toward Miz Broomer's front stoop. Her geraniums had been replaced with some sort of evergreen tree and a worn cornshuck wreath hung neatly on the front door. It had a funny little sign that read: "Christmas Memories" stuck in the middle of the brown husks.

Daddy glanced around the empty yard and tapped on the door. You'd a thought Miz Broomer was perched on that knob by the speed that she opened the door. Her fire-engine red lips parted in the widest hello I ever saw. Maybe we were the only people she'd been around that day.

"Welcome, Preacher! And Mildred, darlin', what a happy surprise to have you come as well." She stepped aside, motioning us into a decent-sized, tidy room. Daddy and me shrugged off our coats, hanging them on a coat tree next to the front door while I looked around with interest. Daddy and Miz Broomer did the usual "How are yous?" At first, nothing struck me as unusual. Joe Ray's chair was in the right corner, facing an old television set with a crooked antenna hooked at the top. I knew it was his because of the stains all over the arms – bet it was beer or some such bad drink. Plus I didn't see a person like Miz Broomer content to have dirty furniture in her living room, just like I couldn't imagine Joe Ray letting her clean his stuff.

"Mildred, can I get you a Coca-Cola?" Her green eyes smiled warmly, pulling my gaze away from Joe Ray's world.

"Oh, yes ma'am, if it's okay?" I turned to Daddy.

"Sure, why don't you sip on that while I climb up in Miz Broomer's attic. Stay on stand-by, though, in case I need a hand."

Miz Broomer pointed to the attic stairs she had already pulled down into their narrow hallway. "You'll find it toward the back left. It's the biggest box up there. Can't miss it." Miz Broomer kept walking the whole time she talked to Daddy, her plaid, wool skirt swishing with every step. I followed out of the front room through a swinging door into the kitchen area. A dining room branched off from another kitchen door and I caught sight of lots of knick-knacks on shelves. I think they were salt and pepper shakers of all kinds. Maybe I'd have a chance to investigate later. The kitchen captured all my attention for now. Bright, sunshine-yellow curtains waved over the sink and I was hit with a powerful feeling of light.

"Oh my goodness," I gasped.

Miz Broomer turned on her heel, catching my expression.

"It is lovely, isn't it, dear?" She waved her arm as if to encircle the daisy dishtowels, yellow tile on the walls and bright, white floor tiles. Fake sunflowers sat in a can in the corner of the room, stretching almost as tall as me. "This is my happy spot. I figure that as much as I love to cook, well, a body ought to be comfortable in her favorite place. I keep all my necessary things right here at hand." She pointed to her oven, a line of canisters and a lazy susan filled with spices. "Cooking is a real joy for me. Joe Ray ...," a shadow moved over her face, "he never really comes in here."

She laughed then, tugging at a piece of loose hair and chewing her lip.

"I reckon this is my girl spot, a place I can let my hair down."

For a minute, I saw what Miz Broomer must have been like when she was younger, before Joe Ray. So pretty and so happy.

"Well, I best get you that Coca-Cola before your Daddy's all done and you have to leave. Oh, and I made some wonderful fudge for Christmas Day. Would you like a piece?"

"Oh, yes, Miz Broomer!" Christmas fudge and Coke all at the

same time. It was almost too much to take in.

"What's this 'Miz Broomer' stuff? You'd best be callin' me Wanda if ya know what's good for ya," she laughed. It was a warm, happy sound.

So Miz Wanda popped the lid off the bottle and sat it on the counter where two tall stools were kept beneath a ledge. She laid two pieces of fudge on a tiny glass plate and placed a white napkin to the side.

"There now," she said, hands on hips to survey her work. "That looks like a tasty treat for a hard workin' gal." She smiled again then tilted her head, sort of like a bird does when he catches a sound on the wind. All I heard was a truck muffler popping. Sounded a ways away.

"You know, honey, I ought to check on your Daddy. Lord knows he could fall out of that attic and kill himself with that tree. It's a booger. Be right back." And she was gone, leaving a swish of skirts and a lingering smell of rose. I pulled out the stool and perched myself up to fully enjoy the fudge. It even had nuts.

The window revealed a backyard filled with birdfeeders and birdbaths. That had to be Miz Wanda's doing as well. On the other side was a half-way broken-down shack filled with old tires and auto parts. Looked like two or three junk motors propped against the outside wall. One bird flying into the side of that thing could knock it over in a skinny minute.

I must've heard a truck door slam, but I was too absorbed in fudge and Coke to pay much attention at the time. I did hear the front door open though. It almost knocked me off my stool.

"Wanda! Wanda! Who the hell is in my house?" The voice was raw with anger, yelling so loud that it hurt my ears. Joe Ray!

Footsteps clicked rapidly down the hallway and onto the front room carpet. "Joe Ray! It's just the preacher. I needed help with the tree and..."

"Help with the tree?" the voice roared. "What tree? And since when do I need any help in my own house?"

"I just didn't know, I mean, you hadn't been home in days and, well, Christmas is two days away and I couldn't..."

He bellowed again followed by a loud crash, a noise which propelled me to the door. I peeked through just in time to see Daddy jumping off the attic stairs and round the corner. The coat tree lay sprawled out in the middle of the room.

"Wait Joe Ray, it's just me. No need to get all uptight." Daddy held his hands out, talking real quiet and nice, walking slow, but I don't know if Joe Ray even heard anything. I've never seen a man so scary – and so sad – at the same time. He wore an old dingy undershirt underneath his overalls. His curly hair was wet and sweaty and his eyes, oh my, his eyes were black and wild and glassy. He reminded me of that rabid dog Daddy shot back in Georgia. He even had flecks of spit stuck in his mustache. He held a fireplace poker in one hand and was reaching on top of a bookcase with the other. Daddy kept talking nice and quiet while Miz Wanda stood there, crying and crumpling her skirt pocket in her hands.

"Remember when we talked a few weeks ago about how you wanted to change and be a better husband? We had a real good talk and a good prayer. Remember that?"

Joe Ray's right hand finally found what he'd been grabbing for and he pulled the biggest shotgun I ever saw off the top of the shelf. Miz Wanda lurched forward. "Joe Ray, honey, what're you doin'?"

"I'm protectin' my wife from this man who comes to my house when I'm not home. Any man who visits another man's wife when he's not home is no friend of mine," Joe Ray growled. He answered Miz Wanda but stared down Daddy the whole time. I began to push open the swinging door, but Daddy must've seen me out of the corner of his eye. He waved me back and I stopped.

"It's not like that, Joe Ray. Wanda wasn't sure when you'd be home and Christmas is just around the corner. You know how these girls can be? I just got here and was pulling the tree out of the attic. It's a monster," Daddy laughed loud, trying to reassure Joe Ray, but it didn't seem to work. By now, a strong smell of beer had floated my way and Joe Ray's bloodshot eyes only added evidence to my suspicions. He was drunk as a skunk!

He popped the barrel of the shotgun in place with a quick flick of his wrist. He breathed hard then, shook his head and wiped his nose on his arm. He did not lift the gun. Daddy tried again.

"Joe Ray, why don't we step outside and discuss this like men. This really has nothing to do with Wanda."

"I ain't steppin' outta my own house to chat with no preacher in my own front yard," he spit out. "If anybody's leavin', it's gonna be you." Joe Ray pointed toward the gaping front door with the poker. "Git out."

"Baby, please put the gun down," Miz Wanda begged. "Preacher Rhodes will leave, but there ain't no need for the gun. Please, darlin'," she tried for a warm, loving smile, but her lips were trembling.

"Yeah, you'd better believe he's leavin' – now!"

Daddy began moving toward the door slowly, still smiling in the face of it, but his eyes had that steely look I knew so well. Daddy wasn't about to leave Miz Wanda in a house with an angry, drunk man, swinging a poker and a shotgun. "Oh sweet Jesus," I whispered. "This just can't end good."

Surely my heart was beating loud enough to be heard in the living room. I could barely breath because it had climbed into my throat, almost gagging me. In fact, the more I watched, the more nauseated I got. With my whole self, I wanted to dash in and rescue Daddy, but his hand wave – and my heavy feet – kept me where I stood, watching through a crack in a door, wishing we were anywhere but here.

Daddy was still easing around Miz Wanda, drawing closer and closer to Joe Ray and his poker.

"I am leaving, Joe Ray. Just like you said," Daddy said softly. "I'm just gonna ease right past you here and ..."

Wham! Daddy jerked around to the left, grabbing Joe Ray's right arm and twisting it up behind his back. The shotgun fell to the floor, hitting a side table on the way down. I covered my ears and closed my eyes, expecting a loud boom. When it didn't come, I looked again and saw total chaos. Somehow, Joe Ray had managed to twist back around and knock the poker against Daddy's arm. He blocked it and returned blow-for-blow by punching Joe Ray hard, making his nose spurt blood, which added fuel to the fire. With a roar that shook the curtains, he lunged back at Daddy – and at that point, it all looked like a blur of fists, arms and legs, with a black, iron poker flying around in the middle. Miz Wanda had backed up into the hallway, out of the way of the two men rolling around on the living room floor. I kept hearing Mama's voice telling me to never get in the middle of a dog fight – I could get bitten. I knew this would be even worse, especially with that poker flying around. My eyes searched the room for anything that would be a help. Then I saw the shotgun lying to the side.

Miz Wanda and me were thinking along the same lines 'cause I saw her edging her way toward the front door. Daddy had managed to pin Joe Ray down and both men rested a second, breathing hard and sweating.

But that was short-lived.

Joe Ray spotted Miz Wanda and, I swear, the strength of a hundred buffalo came into him. He heaved Daddy off like a sack of potatoes, pushed past the sofa to reach Miz Wanda and jerked her back by the hair. She screamed in pain about the same time Daddy hit the edge of the coffee table. His head snapped in a funny way as he landed and his body went completely still.

"No!" I cried out, but the sound of my voice was lost in Miz Wanda's babbling and sobbing.

"Oh Lord, Joe Ray. What have you done?" she wailed, but her husband didn't seem to care. He picked up the shotgun while hanging on to her hair, then tugged her toward the door.

"You know, Wanda honey, I'm feelin' the need for a little drive. Why don't we just head down the road a piece together. Let's go to our favorite little waterfall near the bridge. Wouldn't it be nice to be there together – just husband and wife?"

The sound of his mocking voice and blood smeared all over his face made him look like a crazy man. But I didn't have time to think about that. Daddy lay crumpled on the floor and – as scared as I was for Miz Wanda – I just wanted them to leave. With lots of dragging and crying, they finally did.

The minute I heard the truck start, I pushed through the swinging door and fell beside Daddy. He was moaning and his head already had a huge bruise and a nasty cut. There was blood, but not much; I shook him as gently as I could.

"Daddy, Daddy, are you alright?"

His eyelids fluttered but nothing else.

"Please, Daddy, can't you wake up?" I began to cry then; just couldn't bottle it up anymore. But Daddy wasn't budging. I eased up and looked around at the upturned furniture, broken coffee table and attic stairs still hanging out from the hallway ceiling — and realized that I was alone. Utterly, completely alone. Which meant, of course, that it all hung on me.

I took one more look at Daddy, lying there all crumpled up and decided I had to get help. My mind raced with a thousand ideas all in one second, but the easiest answer was to take the Broomer's backyard trail to Miz Dot's house. Miz Dot had told me weeks ago that it wasn't a far piece to her house and barn and I knew she'd be milking. There was nothing else to do. No phone here. No neighbors close by and I sure as heck couldn't drive the car. It was Miz Dot's or nothing.

I wiped my eyes on my shirt tail, kissed Daddy on the cheek, shut the front door, and began running as fast as I possibly could. Daddy had to have help — fast!

I found the trail immediately and was engulfed in the woods within seconds. The trail was clean and clear. I ran faster.

Chapter 35

Dot

Over mooing and bellowing cows, Dot couldn't have heard a siren, much less Mildred's reedy voice calling from the trail. Head down, Dot continued to herd the cows toward the barn door, pushing the first ten toward the stalls that held their food and relief, but as Mildred drew closer to the Harris farm, her yells became more distinct and intense

"Miz Dot! Miz Dot! Help! Daddy needs help!"

Mildred's neat purple high tops were caked with mud and her ponytail half dangled in her face as she rounded the corner. Dot saw the unmasked panic on her face and found herself running toward her in the paddock, boots squishing and sucking through the mud and manure.

"Mildred, what is it?"

"It's Daddy! Joe Ray beat him up ... and he's out ... on Miz Wanda's living room floor ...and Joe Ray drug Miz Wanda ... off by her hair," she panted out, leaning over and gripping her side. "We have to get help!" Mildred's words tumbled around in Dot's mind like bingo balls in a cage. Even as she listened, her feet began moving toward the back door of her house, while she quizzed Mildred further, ignoring the pleading moans of her cows.

"Are you alright, child?"

"Yes, ma'am, but we gotta get to Daddy now. He's hurt real bad."

"Was your Daddy conscious at all?"

"No, ma'am. He's got a goose egg on his head and a cut. He just crumpled up when he fell and ..." Mildred's voice cut out and Dot realized she'd better keep the girl on task or she'd lose Mildred's cool sensibilities.

"Alright, that's fine. He'll be fine," she asserted quickly. "We'll get there. Now I need you to go find my truck keys and my jacket while I get on the phone and call the sheriff's department. We'll head over there right after we get some help on the way." Mildred stared, wide-eyed. "Now go!" Dot waved, and Mildred dashed into the house, rummaging around while Dot kicked off her manure-covered boots and yanked the phone off its nest on the wall. She dialed rapidly.

"Doris? Yeah, this is Dot Harris. I got no time for chit-chat. We have an emergency at the Broomer farm. That's right, Broomer. Joe Ray's place. We got Pastor Sam Rhodes unconscious and Joe Ray has hauled Wanda off to God knows where. What's that? Oh, because Rhodes' daughter saw the whole thing and she's here at my house. Right. She's fine." Mildred came running from the bedroom carrying a heavy coat and dangling the truck keys in her hand, "Just pretty upset. Yep. We're heading over now." Dot listened for a moment, furrowed her brow, then spoke sharply. "Nope. We're going over. We're in no danger and I'll not leave Sam Rhodes by himself one minute longer. Doesn't matter what you suggest. Just get the sheriff out there, alright? Oh, and Doris, call Sam Rhodes' wife, Laura Lee. They just got a new phone in. She needs to know. But be sure to tell her Sam is going to be alright!" Dot slammed the receiver down with the sound of Doris's voice still rattling on, demanding her not to go to the crime scene. Dot smiled briefly at Mildred as she shrugged on her coat. "Don't worry 'bout her. Doris always did fret too much. Let's go."

As the Harris truck sped out of the driveway, Dot didn't give one thought to the swollen cows – neither did Mildred.

It took only a few minutes to drive the roundabout way to the Broomer's house. Mildred was out the door before Dot had fully stopped, dashing toward the house like it was on fire. She jerked open the front door and disappeared inside, leaving Dot to hurry after her, almost afraid of what she might find.

A tornado, Dot thought at first glance, *that's what I'm finding. The total upheaval of a tornado.*

The room had maintained its upside-down shape, and Dot immediately saw Sam's twisted body lying by the broken coffee table. Mildred's hair hung over his face, blocking her view, as the girl begged her father to wake up. Knowing a little about shock and first aid, Dot quickly scoured the room for a blanket of some sort. A multi-colored afghan hung over the back of a recliner and she grabbed it to drop over Sam's inert body.

"Mildred, tuck this in around your Daddy's legs and under his side. We need to keep him warm until the ambulance gets here."

Mildred obeyed without a word, her tear-streaked face set and determined. Dot leaned down, looking intently into Sam's pale face, noticing the gash along his forehead. She lightly tapped his cheeks.

"Sam? Sam? Can you wake up?"

He didn't move, but a slight moan cracked his lips. Mildred began to whimper while Dot leaned closer, felt his warm breath on her face and allowed herself a short smile.

"Shouldn't we try to straighten his legs out?" Mildred asked.

"No, child. There may be something broken there and we'd do more harm than good. The ambulance should be here any minute now. Let's just pray and wait." Dot looked hard at the girl, covered in grime and tears. "Mildred, do you have any idea where Joe Ray took Wanda?"

Mildred shook her head.

"He didn't mention any place that you heard or any item at all that might help?"

"No, ma'am." Mildred spoke almost before Dot finished her question, so Dot reached out, pulling Mildred's face – and focus – toward her.

"Think, Mildred. Stop and really think."

Slowly Mildred's blue eyes acknowledged Dot's presence again as she blinked.

"He might have mentioned something about a waterfall – and a bridge."

Dot frowned grimly. "Did he now?" Shrill siren horns could barely be heard in the distance but soon blared down Coates Lane as Dot stood up to go out into the yard. She needed to meet the sheriff and send him on to Brazier Falls. There was no doubt in her mind that's where Joe Ray took Wanda. A popular hangout with the teenagers, it was also one of the steepest drops in the area. Might even be 150 feet from the top to the river at the bottom. Dot didn't like the sound of that at all – and Joe Ray's anger had only been exacerbating in the past weeks. She glanced back at Mildred who was settled back by her father.

"I'll be right back. I'm gonna meet the sheriff and the ambulance."

The girl didn't look up as Dot hurried out the door to meet Sheriff Dabney's cruiser whipping into the yard.

"Harris! Where's Rhodes?" he demanded, his breath creating short clouds of mist.

"He's inside, Sheriff, but there's no hurry." His face dropped in dismay and Dot quickly interjected, "No, not that. He's unconscious and is as comfortable as he can be until the ambulance arrives."

Sheriff Dabney strode toward the house, a man on a mission, until Dot fastened onto his arm.

"Dave, Sam Rhodes' daughter overhead Joe Ray tell Wanda he was taking her to a waterfall and a bridge."

The sheriff stopped short. "Brazier Falls?"

"I think so. It doesn't sound good at all. Mildred says Joe Ray dragged Wanda out of the house by her hair."

Dave Dabney spun on his heel as the whir of the ambulance siren came racing down the lane. "I'll call backup and get Houston Fields headed toward the falls. He's over in that area of the county already," Dabney shook his head. "I've been waitin' for Joe Ray to push it too far – I hope to God I didn't wait too long."

Dot sidestepped as the long-bodied, blue-lettered ambulance slid into the yard, kicking gravel out on the dirt road. Monroe County Ambulance Service was printed in bright red letters on the door. She listened as Dabney radioed his request to the dispatcher,

Gladys Peoples, then slammed his car door to head to the house.

"What's with the Monroe County ambulance? Surely they aren't gonna carry Sam all the way to Exeter?" Dot questioned.

"Yup. Seems the Marion County Hospital ambulance is on another call – you know we only got one workin' right now. So the Monroe County folks said they'd help out. It's a pain, but better than nothin'." He scratched his gray-flecked beard as two gurneymen raced by, entering the house through the well-traveled front door.

"Is the girl inside?" he asked as they quickly followed.

Dot nodded wordlessly. The ambulancemen had tubes, needles, machines and stethoscopes out before Dot could find a clear place to watch. Mildred had moved toward the swinging kitchen door, chewing her fingernails feverishly.

"Is she okay?" Sheriff Dabney whispered to Dot, looking Mildred up and down with doubt.

"Uh huh. She's pretty tough, but it's been a hard afternoon. Be nice to her, Dave."

"I'm always nice, Dottie. You know that. Besides, I don't see me interviewin' the girl without you hangin' over my shoulder like a dang vulture."

"You got that right, and I told you before – stop calling me Dottie."

Sheriff Dabney ignored the older woman, pulling a used toothpick out of his shirt pocket and gnawing slowly. By now, the ambulancemen had Sam strapped on the stretcher and were maneuvering to get him out the door and down the three steps of the stoop. Tears tumbled down Mildred's face, but still she said nothing.

"Will you boys be taking Mr. Rhodes to the Monroe hospital in Exeter?" Sheriff Dabney asked.

"Yes, sir. That's what we're told."

"Does he look alright to you?" Dot interjected.

"We ain't no doctors, ma'am, but I can tell you his breathin' is good, his color is gettin' better and the cut ain't that bad. Don't look like he broke no bones or nuthin'. Even if I ain't no doctor," the man smiled and winked at Dot, then glanced toward Mildred. "I'm thinking he's had some pretty good care here and he'll be out o' the woods afore you can whistle 'Dixie.'"

Mildred almost smiled then. "Can I come in the ambulance, too?" she squeaked out from across the room. Sheriff Dabney waved the ambulance on, turning toward Mildred.

"How 'bout I ride you to the hospital in the sheriff car and we talk on the way? I'd sure like to hear you tell us what happened here today. Think you can do that for me?" He shifted his toothpick to the side of his mouth and let the full force of his charm hit Mildred head on. It was known all over Piedmont Ridge that nobody could deny Sheriff Dave Dabney a thing when he unleashed that smile. People said every four years that he was just too darn nice, handsome or winsome to not be re-elected. Mildred silently checked with Dot; she nodded almost imperceptibly.

"Yes, sir," Mildred picked her way across the overturned furniture.

"I'd like to ride too, Dave," Dot said, tossing the afghan back on the recliner. "But I need to call Daryl Thomas to see if he can get over to the farm. I left the girls bustin' at the seams."

"No problem, we can do that from the car."

Chapter 36

Mildred

My mind went ape. There I was, worried sick about Daddy, eyes straining to watch the ambulance in front of us, being asked a million questions by the sheriff, and all I could think about was how jealous Gregory was gonna be when he found out that I got to ride in the front seat of the police car. It was gonna kill him!

The siren blared and important sounding information kept popping out of the police scanner. Numbers and letters that made no sense but surely added to my dream-like moment. Like I even needed more craziness in my life. I was beginning to feel like one of those radio drama shows that Mama told me about, but I wasn't allowed to listen to.

Empty fields shot past my window, one after another, as we flew by people who stopped and stared at the two vehicles racing back-to-back. If I'd been by the road, I would be swept up in the excitement of it all. As it was, my stomach hurt – a sure sign I had bad nerves.

The sheriff had used his police radio to call the station and found out that Miz Alma and Mama were on the way to Monroe Hospital, that Elder Thomas would take care of Miz Dot's cows, and that Deputy Fields was trying to track down Miz Wanda and Joe Ray.

"Sweet Jesus," I closed my eyes fervently, whispering, "please, oh please, keep Miz Wanda safe."

I saw her in my mind again smiling, all excited about the Christmas tree, popping my Coca-Cola bottle, then later pale-faced in fear, screaming while Joe Ray dragged her out the door. Tears dribbled down my chin and I realized I was crying again. Was it just a few hours ago that I had the best day ever at school?

We shot into the hospital parking lot, practically hanging onto the bumper of the ambulance. I saw Mama right away, walking toward the door with Miz Alma Crenshaw and I bolted from the sheriff's car.

"Mama!" I yelled, racing her way, "Over here!"

Her head snapped up as she recognized my voice, and before I could think, I was in her arms, folded and tucked into the lovely warmth that was my Mama.

"Oh sweetheart, are you alright?" she breathed into my ear.

Just those few words unplugged me like a tub of bath water. Looking back, I'm a little embarrassed about wailing in the hospital parking lot, but at the time I didn't care. I could have cried a river and taken my own sweet time doing it except for the sheriff, who didn't know anything about twelve-year-olds needing a moment to gather themselves. As he and Miz Dot came up behind us, he was already talking, explaining to Mama in a real quicky way what had happened. Honestly, I was so glad he did. I just didn't want to tell the story anymore. Didn't want to see Daddy's body crumpling or Miz Wanda being dragged across the floor again. I wished I could erase it from my mind.

Mama kept her arm close around me, her red, woolen coat adding warmth to my cold body as she angled me toward the emergency room doors.

What an odd group we were. There was Miz Dot, still in her milking overalls (but thankfully, not the boots), Mama with her best coat pulled over her tacky, brown house slacks, Miz Alma with her apron still on, the string bean-shaped sheriff and me. Mildred Juniper Rhodes. Mud-caked high tops, dirty school clothes and messy hair. I reached up to untie my ponytail and try to neaten it up a bit.

Warm air rushed out of the doors to greet us as we filed in to the information desk. Mama took over, leaving me standing by Miz Dot and Miz Alma as Sheriff Dabney said his goodbyes.

"Dottie, hate to leave you stranded, but I gotta git on over to Brazier Falls. Houston's almost there and he'll need me, I reckon. Pray for us all, will ya?" he smiled in a sort of sad way, the wrinkles at the corners of his eyes looking deeper and longer. Miz Dot put her hand on his arm reassuringly and he was gone.

"Not to worry, Dot. We'll git 'cha home," Miz Alma said reassuringly. "I'll be right back. Got to move my car outta the ER parking lot."

The rest of us were sent to a lonely corner of the giant waiting room with instructions to wait for a nurse to come get us. They had already wheeled Daddy in the back somewhere – Mama still hadn't seen him. But the lady at the desk reassured us that we'd be the first to know anything and we'd just have to wait a spell till the doctor had a chance to do his examination.

I could've told her Mama doesn't wait well.

I held my breath while Mama's eyes flashed and she gnawed on her lip. I'd seen her and Miz Dot in action at the Broomer's after my Thanksgiving play and I thought the poor receptionist best fasten her seat belt, but Mama surprised me. She stomped to the metal-backed chair and sat down, straight up, purse in her lap, looking directly ahead, obviously trying to be obedient. Even Miz Dot seemed quiet. I sat too, knowing this wasn't a good time to keep talking, but Miz Dot had more gumption than I thought.

"Laura Lee," she spoke, leaning forward with her mouth set firm. "We need to pray. Right now."

I didn't see any angels walking up and down a ladder right there in the waiting room, but surely heaven had fallen in on us! Miz Dot? Saying we need to pray? There? In the middle of all humanity? I think it was mostly surprise that kept our mouths shut, but Mama and me bowed our heads and listened as Miz Dot prayed the loveliest, most beautiful prayer anybody has ever heard. When she finished, I felt like those angels floated all round Daddy, all around Miz Wanda (maybe even Joe Ray) and that we had some Godly protection in the waiting room. Peace and warmth settled over us like a cozy blanket. Then she quietly said, "Amen."

A whoosh of disinfectant alerted us to open double doors where a tall nurse burst through looking in our direction. Her shoes squished evenly on the floor as she had the very appearance of nurse perfection in action. I was impressed. Somewhere on my right, I heard a sharp gasp. I glanced up to Miz Dot, wondering why on earth she was surprised.

All color had drained from her face and her lips quivered. Miz Dot's hand reached out for something – what? – and grabbed ahold of my wrist, squeezing it so hard I yelped. Must've been my cry that took the nurse's eyes away from Mama to settle on me and Miz Dot. Then the nurse stopped short and gasped, her hand going to her chest like she was trying to hold her heart inside. Everything froze until she finally found her words.

"Mom?" her voice quivered. Miz Dot slowly pulled herself out of the chair, suddenly looking her age.

"Leslie?" she gasped. I jerked my head to look again at this nurse. Her name tag read: Leslie Haskell. My eyes trailed up to her face and I strained to see the carefree girl who smiled at me from an old picture in Miz Dot's bathroom. I could see it. I saw her. The same quirky mouth and eyes, although they weren't smiling this time. Tears trailed down her cheeks.

She threw her clipboard into an empty chair, reaching blindly for Miz Dot and the two fell into each other's arms, much to me and Mama's surprise.

I was aching to know how Daddy was, but Miz Dot and Leslie – the nurse who held all the information — were locked together, crying and crying. Folks all around the waiting room had stopped to watch, without trying to appear to, of course. After all, they probably thought somebody just died – not that somebody just came back to life.

Mama reached over and grabbed my hand across the now-empty chair between us.

"Oh Mil, isn't our God so good and amazing?" Her face glowed and I suppose mine did too. In jerking sobs, Leslie told Miz Dot bits and pieces of her story, enough to satisfy for now.

Another whoosh of disinfectant and another important-looking hospital person headed our way. He had "doctor" written all over him. Thick glasses, frowny face, all serious. *Oh Lord, don't let him be serious about Daddy.*

"Mrs. Rhodes?" he walked straight up to Mama, barely glancing up from his clipboard. Mama stood up, while Miz Dot and Leslie tried desperately to stop crying.

"Yes?"

"I assume Nurse Haskell told you your husband is stable?"

"Yes," Mama lied, but I didn't blame her.

"Well, he's certainly out of the woods. Had a nasty knock on the head resulting in a full-blown concussion. Had to put in about fifteen stitches. Next few days will be crucial in the sense that we'll have to keep an eye on him, but overall, it could have been much worse." Every word hit like machine gun fire – short and fast – but I didn't care; they were good words. He finally looked at Mama, wrinkling his face like his huge glasses wouldn't focus on faces, only on written notes. Miz Dot had pulled out her handkerchief and blew hard. I think the sound scared the little man. He jumped and suddenly noticed the heap of crying, waded up women on the chairs to his left. His brow furrowed again, then he dismissed the whole incident.

"Right. Well, then. If you have any other questions, just ask Nurse Haskell here. Mr. Rhodes will be placed in a room within the next thirty minutes. The receptionist will call out your name and direct you there."

He spun on his heel and was gone and I wondered if Mama's stomach felt as swimmy as mine did.

I was in the bathroom when Nurse Leslie found out where they had put Daddy. After all this excitement, I reckon my body couldn't take anymore.

"Mildred? They've got your Daddy in Room 313. I'm gonna leave Nurse Leslie here at the door to take you up when you're done," Mama's voice echoed all around the tile-covered bathroom walls. "See you in a sec!"

I was actually already at the sink, but I didn't stop Mama. I know she hadn't seen Daddy at all.

Staring at my own white face in the silver-edged mirror, I scrubbed my hands. Right above my cheek was a smudge. Grabbing a paper towel, I wet it and began rubbing and watched it come off pretty easy, leaving a reddish-brown stain on the towel. Then it hit me like a ton of bricks. It was blood. Had to be. Off of Daddy's forehead. I watched myself in the mirror, my hand moving slowly into sight, touching the place on my forehead where Daddy's cut was, touching my cheek – the door cracked open and the friendly face of Leslie poked through.

"Mildred? Are you ..." She must've seen me, must've run to me. All I remember is feeling her strong arms catch me before I hit the floor.

Something cold, soggy and wet clung to my forehead as bright light worked to force my eyes open.

"Ugh," I moaned. "What happened?"

"I reckon your day finally caught up with you," Miz Dot stated matter-of-factly.

I cracked my eyes open enough to see that I was in a room, stretched out sideways on two chairs pushed together with Mama, Miz Dot and Leslie anxiously hovering over me. To my left, I glimpsed a bed, lots of machines and a man's body lying still.

"Daddy?" I tried to raise up and immediately regretted it as the room swam and dipped. "Oh, ugh," I groaned again.

"Honey, lie still. Your Daddy's fine – he's just sleepin', that's all. And you passed out in the bathroom." Then Mama laughed. "Like mother, like daughter."

Jokes? Mama making jokes at a time like this? I suppose that was a good thing, but it sure didn't keep my stomach from flipping.

"Here, Mildred. Can you sit up and swallow these pills?" Leslie's anxious face came out of nowhere, hanging over me. "They'll settle your stomach and your head."

I raised up, popped them in my mouth and drank deeply of the water, then I leaned back, already feeling a little better. The blinding lights had sunk to a normal brightness and I could see that several ugly chairs had been moved into Daddy's tiny room. Leslie bustled back and forth, turning knobs, reading equipment, generally situating all of us. I stole a look at Mama. She had turned back toward Daddy and seemed to be content, at peace. All Miz Dot could do was watch Leslie and ...

"Miz Alma?" I croaked.

"She's fine, honey. Had to run back to town, but she'll come back soon," Mama answered with a pat on my leg. It was getting too confusing keeping up with all these people. I sighed, suddenly feeling deep-down, bone-weary tired. I felt myself start to sink back to that warm resting place.

"Wait!" I forced my eyes open. "What about Miz Wanda?" I practically shouted, pulling up to run to who-knows-where.

"Easy, Mildred. We don't know yet. Sheriff Dabney will let us know as soon as he can. We're all prayin' and that's about all we can do. Rest, darlin'. Just close your eyes and rest." Mama's voice faded.

And so I did. With Mama and Miz Dot keeping watch over us, Daddy and me slept the sleep of the dead.

I woke because of the sausage. Juicy, slightly greasy, delicious-smelling sausage frying somewhere in the hospital. My stomach answered with a loud grumble and I sat up, stiff and sore.

Daddy lay still and breathing peacefully while Mama had crawled up into his bed sometime in the night. She was curled next to him, an expression of happiness on her sleeping face. Miz Dot's chair was empty and the door to the hall hung open. I could hear beeps and low voices, early morning hospital sounds. Leslie popped her head in the door just then, but she wasn't wearing her hospital whites this morning. She looked fresh and clean in navy slacks and a gray sweater – a bright red headband holding back her hair. I suddenly felt mussed and wrinkled.

"Oh, good. You're awake," she whispered. "Think you can join me and Mom in the cafeteria for breakfast? I think your Mama and Daddy will be fine."

I agreed. They looked as snugly as bears and I was starving! I mouthed a "yes" but pointed to the bathroom. Maybe I could wet my hair a little and smooth it down. If I was a mess yesterday, I had to be a monster today.

I left the room a little more presentable, at least the mud had dried on my shoes so I didn't track wet dirt down the hallway. Leslie made chit-chat as she led me through more halls than I cared to count. On the bright side, the sausage smell grew ever-stronger and at last we rounded a corner into a small cafeteria. The Garden of Eden of food! Three rather large colored ladies stood behind eggs, sausage, bacon, grits, sawmill gravy and the biggest, roundest, fattest biscuits I'd ever seen. Next to the biscuits were breakfast corn breads baked in the shape of corn-on-the-cobs and off to the side were boxes of all kinds of cereals and even hot water for oatmeal. The sight was so heavenly that I felt myself sway with the wonder of it all. Leslie led me by the hand to a rack of trays.

"Here ya go, Mildred. Just grab your tray and start movin' down the line. Tell Miz Clarice what you want and she'll fix you right up," she encouraged. "Don't worry about going to the cashier. We've already got that taken care of. Mom and I are sitting over there," she pointed to a quiet corner of the room, away from talking hospital employees. Miz Dot waved and smiled, nursing a white ceramic cup full of something hot. She looked better this morning.

It took me no time at all to fill my plate to the brim and make my way over. Leslie had placed a carton of milk at my place as well as a small glass of orange juice. Surely I had died and gone on to be with my Maker. I couldn't remember when I'd ever had this much scrumptious food to choose from.

Neither Miz Dot nor Leslie really talked to me until I had cleaned my plate. Mostly, Miz Dot was telling Leslie what had happened to the people Leslie knew from her time in Piedmont Ridge. They laughed a lot, remembering old stories and tales. What they didn't talk about was the past twelve years, not even Mr. Tom. It seemed like they had some sort of agreement to not discuss these things. I was curious but more hungry than anything.

Finally, I pushed my plate back and sighed happily.

"Well, girl. Now that you got the rest of the pig down, are you ready to join us in the land of the living?" Miz Dot joked. I wiped the grease off my lips.

"Only if I get to have another plate in a minute."

"Ah, then I need to tell the cook to kill another hog. I'll be right back." And Leslie got up from the table without missing a beat, walking back toward the kitchen.

"Wait, I ..."

Dot burst out laughing. "She got you, Mildred. Don't worry. She has some other business to attend to in the kitchen. She's just pulling your leg."

Leslie turned back and winked at me as she disappeared behind the swinging door, her red bandana the last thing I saw.

"Miz Dot? I'm so glad you found Leslie and all." I started folding my napkin into fours then eights. Fiddling, Mama called it. It always drove her crazy. I put it down quickly and smoothed it back out. "It's just that, well, have you talked to her yet to find out where she's been?"

"I have," Dot answered firmly. "And it's some story, but I want to wait on it till she can tell it and until your Mama and Daddy can hear it. Stew and Mary Rose, too. The whole church community if they want to. I almost feel like it's just as much y'all's story as it is mine. But I can tell you more about Mrs. Broomer, if you'd like to know that."

"Oh yes!" I almost leaped up from my seat. "Tell me! What happened?"

"Well, the sheriff arrived here late, late last night, carrying Wanda in his car. She's gonna be fine but is in a room recuperating."

"Have you seen her? What'd he do to her? Where's Joe Ray? Is he dead?"

"Whoa there!" Miz Dot held her hand up, trying to stop my rapid-fire questions. "One question at a time, and if you'll give me a minute, I'll bet I'll answer them all. Just let me tell the story.

"Sheriff Dabney and Deputy Fields apparently arrived at Brazier Falls — that's the place where there's a waterfall and a bridge.

They heard Joe Ray yelling toward the top of the falls, so the sheriff went on up the path. Houston crossed the river, trying to ease up on the other side and come up behind Joe Ray. The sheriff said he could hear that Wanda was still alive, but it sounded like Joe Ray was still trying to hurt her. So he hotfooted it up the path, yelling for Joe Ray to stop.

"When he got to the top, sure enough he found Joe Ray holding Wanda around the neck, yelling and threateng to throw her off the falls if he came any closer." Dot shook her head and started laughing softly. "Joe Ray really is a dummy if he thought Dabney was gonna let him get away with that. Anyway, Sheriff Dabney began talking him down – which he said he thought he was doing alright with, but Joe Ray still wasn't budging.

"In the end, it took Houston – I mean, Deputy Fields – coming up behind the two of them and whopping Joe Ray over the head with his billy club. Wanda fell loose and the sheriff picked her up and brought her on here. He said he knew she'd rather be in the hospital where her family is."

"Her family?" I asked, a little confused.

Miz Dot's eyes got all watery, "That's us, Mil. Wanda's family."

"Oh." Now my eyes were getting all watery. "But what happened with Joe Ray? Is he in the hospital too?"

"No, well, not this one. After Deputy Fields stunned him, he tried to run. In the end, Houston got his man. The sheriff is thinking that Joe Ray has a broken arm – oh, lots of cuts and abrasions, but they took him on to Marion County Hospital. Once he's well, I'm sure he'll be in jail."

"Poor Miz Wanda," my eyes felt wet again.

"Ah Mildred, if it weren't for you, Wanda probably wouldn't be with us today. You have been a brave, brave girl. We all are so very proud of you." Miz Dot's sharp eyes stared deeply into mine and I felt warm and hopeful all over. I didn't see where I did anything that amazing, but I was just so thankful that my ... my family ... was alright.

"Hey you two. I need some help carrying these trays. Think

you can give me a hand? I'll bet I know of two other people in this hospital that might like a big, hearty breakfast," Leslie had magically reappeared juggling two trays loaded with food. I grabbed one while Miz Dot took the other. Leslie went back for milk and coffee, and the three of us made our way back through the maze of halls, bringing Mama and Daddy the best meal of their lives.

Chapter 37

Dot

Only four bulbs were out on Dot's string of Christmas lights – two blue, a red and a yellow. She shook her head in amazement. "You'd think after ten years in the attic, none of them would work. Miracles continue to fall, don't they, Porthos?" The hound thumped his tail from his nest on the rug at the front door. Dot wasn't sure why she let the dog in; maybe she needed the company.

It was Christmas Eve. 1968. The day Leslie would come home.

Sam Rhodes had been dismissed from Monroe General the day before and Dot, Laura Lee and Leslie had concocted a combination Christmas Eve/Welcome Home celebration. Dot insisted it be at her house. The Bingo Hall would have provided the space they needed – especially since the Thomases, Crenshaws and Stew and Mary Rose were invited as well – but no, Leslie had to come home, even if it wasn't permanent.

Pulling out a small box from the bag of ornaments, Dot stood up with an "Ah ha!." She held four large replacement bulbs up to the light. They looked perfect. Quickly she unplugged the cord, screwed them into place, then jammed the cord back into the wall socket. The three-foot-tall tree glowed and transformed her humble living room into a cozy space of joy. She surveyed her work, pleased at the results.

It certainly hadn't been a slow morning, up at 4:30 milking, then hurrying back in to finish tidying up and pop the ham in the oven. Cutting the small cedar out of the woods behind the house had been a last minute addition. She'd had her eyes on it for years, knowing it was a perfectly- shaped Christmas cedar but dismissing such thoughts. No use to let her mind dwell on such drivel. Dot had never expected to have the joy of a Christmas celebration again.

The rich smell of baked ham trailed into the room, reminding her to put in the meat thermometer. She calculated it would need another thirty minutes before it was done, giving her just enough time to finish setting out dishes and sweeping the porch. They all had agreed to meet at noon. Leslie would arrive about thirty minutes early; she thought she would need a few minutes with just Dot at the Harris farm before the rest of the crew descended.

"Joy to the world, the Lord is come. Let earth receive her King," Dot hummed as she closed the oven door.

"Welcome home, Dot." The still, quiet voice echoed in her head. She stopped folding napkins, hand in mid-air.

"Welcome back into family, into my family."

"Is that you, Lord?" Dot placed the napkin on the table. She felt Him laughing at her gently, as a mother might over her child.

"When someone's been a prodigal for so long, coming home means everything, doesn't it? You don't even care if I throw a feast; it's just so good to be with family again."

Dot's face broke into understanding and added joy.

"Oh yes, I had forgotten ..." Ironically, her eyes filled with tears as a wave of sadness swept over her, "...forgotten how lovely home with You can be. I just didn't realize what I had cut myself off from. Please forgive me!" she dropped her face into her hands, weeping. Then the other-worldly warmth fell into the kitchen and Dot stopped crying almost immediately.

"No tears, Dot. And you've already repented, remember? Today is a day of joy and celebration – a day of feasting for the prodigal. Let the peace of Christ rule in your heart." The presence in the room lifted somewhat and Dot realized it was later than she thought. Almost simultaneously she heard the crunch of gravel under tires. Leslie was home.

Dot clasped her hands, feeling suddenly afraid. What if it wasn't the same for Leslie? What if she found that "home" really wasn't home anymore? Hearing the car, Porthos yawned and stretched, standing up expectantly at the front door.

"Dot?" she cocked her head, listening. *"You might want to go greet Leslie. You might call her your 'fatted calf'."*

Before the front door was flung open, Leslie heard Dot's laughter. She stood on the bottom step, listening and wondering who had made her Mom laugh so hard.

By two o'clock the members of the Piedmont Ridge Community Church who were crammed into Dot Harris's clapboard house felt they were so stuffed they might not make it out the door.

"Lawd, I can't remember a better tastin' ham. It sho' wadn't store-bought. Was that one of yours, Dot?" Mary Rose leaned against Stew whose legs stretched far into the middle of the room, ankles crossed. She stood beside him, one hand on the back of his chair, the other rubbing her stomach in sweet agony. Stew grunted agreement and switched his toothpick to the other side of his mouth.

"Yep. Hog killin' last January," Dot answered from the kitchen. Sam had been given the place of honor – and most comfort – in Dot's recliner. He lay back contented with Laura Lee settled at his feet, her head leaning on his thigh. A rectangular gauze bandage covered part of his forehead, but his eyes were sharp and clear.

Gregory and Mildred Juniper found a spot on the floor near the front door. They'd convinced Dot to let Porthos back in after lunch, and the children sat on each side of the dog, alternately scratching behind an ear or under a paw. Porthos had given up staying awake quite a while ago – his hound dog ears flopped over one eye as he quietly snored.

The Crenshaws and Thomases lounged around in other areas in the room as Dot wiped her hands on a soggy, much-used dishtowel and dragged a kitchen chair into a corner of the living room. Easing it next to Leslie, she slid in, enjoying the easy banter of the occasion.

As if on cue, voices ebbed, each one knowing in the unspoken Code of the South it was time to talk. The food had been plentiful and perfect, the kitchen cleaned. There was a story to be told and it was time.

Dot glanced at Leslie as if to say, "You first," and Leslie responded with a slight nod of her head. Today she wore a Christmas red sweater with stylish black boots tucked under the hem of her long skirt. The multi-colored scarf tied loosely around her neck gave her just enough color to reflect the rosy glow from her cheeks. Her brown eyes sparkled with life. Mary Rose crossed the room and settled onto the sofa with a deep sigh. In the midst of contentment, there was an intensity present in the room. No one was anxious, yet most held their breath – if only for a second or two.

"Mom has told me that she filled you all in on her side of the story – of our story – just last fall. That she's been quiet and, in her words, trapped all these years with the memories of those days." She looked sideways at Dot, who briefly nodded and smiled. "Well, if Mom was trapped, I suppose I died in my heart and soul. I left here with my natural mother that summer day when I was twelve years old and I began to die.

"She took me straight to Charleston where we lived with her boyfriend in a nasty trailer in an RV park. I suppose he worked – to this day I don't really know what he did, but he went somewhere most days and sometimes came home with food. Mostly he came home with liquor, which he and my mother drank every night. I began writing letters to Mom and Dad," Leslie waved her hand toward Dot. "When I could scrape enough change together for a stamp, I would put the letter in the RV park mailbox and pray to God that I'd get a letter back. I never did," her face sagged at the memory.

"Then right before the week school was to start, mother woke me early one morning and dragged me to the bus stop. Apparently she and Bruce had an argument and she had decided Charlotte, North Carolina, was our new home. She gave me enough time to pack one bag and we were gone. I never knew what happened to Bruce and honestly never cared to find out."

Leslie drew a deep breath, the work of the telling evident on her face.

"So we got off the bus in downtown Charlotte on a Saturday afternoon. I assumed mother had a plan – she was always good for some sort of plan – but she didn't have one that day. She tried to bluff and pretend her friend stood us up at the station, but by nightfall, I had figured out there was no friend. We slept on benches outside the library."

She paused for a moment, staring at the wall clock, silent.

"Maybe I should explain that my mother was a real piece of work. She wanted a daughter, but she didn't. Not really. There was no way she was a real mother except for her uncanny ability to keep up with me and know where I was at all times. Maybe she had just determined she would never lose me or let me go again. I don't know, never could quite figure that out. But I can tell you I lived under her thumb and all I knew was what she told me – that was my only truth.

"So when mother found a job in a bar – which she did the next day – we moved into an upper room in the bar where several other bar workers lived."

"You poor baby," Debbie sighed from the other side of the room. Leslie responded with a sad smile.

"Yeah. Not exactly a Norman Rockwell home. I could tell you lots of stories that would curl your hair, but the worst part for me was my final cutoff from Mom and Dad here in Piedmont Ridge.

"I began writing letters immediately, leaving them on the bar counter in the going-out mail stack. It was years later before I realized they were never mailed, but at the time, I just assumed Mom and Dad weren't responding. Of course, a twelve-year-old can come up with lots of reasons why that might happen, especially one who hears her mother say everyday that she's not worth anything. It broke my heart. In fact, I had started school and my teachers kept pressing me, wondering why I wasn't applying myself to study, but I closed up.

"Then came the morning a few weeks later that I had decided I'd get back to Piedmont Ridge no matter what," Leslie reached out for Dot's hand blindly. Dot grasped it and squeezed while

Leslie stared fixedly at the wall clock, lost in time. "Between digging in sofa cushions, picking up money that had dropped in the bar and earning a dollar or two by running errands for the owner, I had gathered what I thought might be enough for a bus ticket to Greenville. I figured I'd walk from there. Mother knew nothing about it, but I had already checked all the schedules and planned to leave on a Thursday morning at 6:30. I was going to give her some excuse for going to school early, pack a few clothes in my school bag, and get back to where I belonged!" She laughed harshly, her throat catching. "It was a perfect plan, except that Mother had seen the bus schedule hidden under my bed and figured the whole thing out. Imagine how I felt when I arrived at the station, only to find her – and her new boyfriend – waiting for me there."

"Oh Lawd, sweet, precious Jesus," Mary Rose muttered from the sofa.

"I guess I should be thankful they didn't kill me, but they might as well have," Leslie said, shrugging. "Mother had it all worked out. She simply told me, while her scary, tough boyfriend stood there, that if I ever tried to go back to Mom and Dad in Piedmont Ridge, she'd kill them."

All semblance of quiet and peace left the room. Sam leaned up in the recliner, readying to get out, while Daryl jumped out of his seat, his face covered with conflicting emotions. Even Stew pulled his legs in and sat up straight. Dot held out her hands, shushing the righteous indignation. "Let her finish, people. It's alright."

With great effort, the men sat back in their seats while the women reached for their handkerchiefs.

"It would give me great pleasure to tell you she was bluffing, but I knew she wasn't. Her latest boyfriend won bar room fights every night – he was big, mean and terrifying. I had no doubt he could do such a thing. So my choice became apparent. Leave for Piedmont Ridge and face that threat head-on. Or stay put and know that Mom and Dad would always be safe." Tears fell freely down Leslie and Dot's faces as they looked at one another again. Although they'd already had this discussion, it made it no less painful in the retelling.

"It was obvious, then, that I had to turn my back on Mom and Dad forever in Piedmont Ridge; at least that's how I felt. Mother and Roger – the boyfriend – hauled me back to the car and took me straight to school. I knew I'd get it when I got back to the bar that afternoon, and I did but I had lost all hope so it just didn't matter."

She stopped, taking a moment to blow her nose and wipe her eyes. Mildred and Gregory had long since stopped scratching Porthos, their eyes as wide as moons and their mouths hanging open. A death threat wasn't something you heard about every day. Leslie drew a deep breath, willing herself to finish the tale.

"And so I went on in that way for quite some time. Mother ended up working her way up to bar manager at The Easy Tavern and I began to find a haven at school. Eventually one of the teachers, Mrs. Baxter, took me under her wing and began to teach me more than just academics. She worked with my speech and pronunciation, she gave me a love for learning, she gave me ... well ... hope again. Always in the back of my mind were Mom and Dad but I never spoke of them again. Didn't have to. I knew nothing had changed and Mother's threat remained.

"She decided Charlotte was a good place to stay so we didn't move again. Thank God! Mrs. Baxter continued to push me and all I knew was I wanted out of The Easy Tavern and into a better life. The drugs, the alcohol – none of it ever appealed to me. My life consisted of washing dishes at the bar, going to school and studying," she laughed ruefully. "Mother didn't care as long as I stayed there and kept out of her way. We reached a truce, I suppose.

"Again thanks to Mrs. Baxter, I received scholarships for college and knew nursing was where I wanted to be. By that time, Mother's hold had lessened, but it just made sense to keep my dishwashing job and no rent while I studied nursing. So I did. Then a year ago I graduated and it was time to break away regardless of the consequences. I confronted Mother and Roger, who believe it or not is still around! It's funny really," Leslie paused a moment. "Somewhere along the road Mother became more like the child and I found the strength to say, 'Enough!'

"Anyway, she begged and pleaded. Roger even cried, but I

heard none of it. I packed my bags and headed off to be a nurse on my own terms."

Laura Lee pulled her stocking feet from under her legs where she'd had them tucked. As she stretched them out and shifted back up against Sam's recliner, she gently interrupted. "But Leslie, why didn't you come straight back to Piedmont Ridge, especially since it sounds like your mother wouldn't or couldn't make good on her threat anymore?" Heads nodded in agreement all over the room as Leslie shrugged.

"Well, I did - sort of. You have to remember that even before Mother's threat, I hadn't received any letters from Piedmont Ridge. As far as I knew, I had written dozens from Charleston as well as Charlotte and never did I hear one word in return. Mother was like a record player, repeating over and over that I wasn't wanted by the Harrises. That they had actually begged Mother to come and take me back with her. They were just too nice to tell me themselves, Mother would say. After years of lies, you begin to believe them, so even though I wanted to call or come here, I was also terrified – absolutely petrified that I might find out it was all true. Then where would I be?"

"So you were almost paralyzed with fear of the truth," Sam stated, absentmindedly rubbing Laura Lee's shoulder, "even though the truth could set you free."

"That's from the Bible, isn't it?" Leslie said. "Well, I suppose that's one way to put it. Mrs. Baxter, my beloved teacher and friend, kept pressing me to take the bull by the horns and call Mom and Dad, but I wavered. Ultimately, I decided that taking a job at Monroe General would be like dipping my toe in the water, so to speak. No one there would know of a Leslie Haskell that had lived at the Harrises twelve years ago, and yet I would be close enough to chat with the locals and get a lay of the land." She squeezed Dot's hand harder. "That's where I found out that Tom Harris passed ten years ago and Dot now lived on her own, in a sort of self-imposed seclusion, as far as I could tell. I had just reached the place where I was thinking of driving out one day soon when Mom walked into the ER, and you know the rest of the story."

Leaning back in his chair with a satisfied smile, Daryl announced, "The hand of the Lord is a mighty thang to behold. His ways are far, far above our own."

Leslie shifted, focusing on him with a half-smile on her lips. "I...I suppose so although I have to admit I hadn't put much stock in God. He never seemed to be around."

Again heads bobbed in understanding, all of them knowing that the journey of finding the Lord was an individual one, directed by the hand of God himself and the searching of the seeker.

Afternoon sun warmed the room through slanted blinds while the Christmas lights grew brighter in the slowly ebbing day. A sense of completeness settled over the room, the feel of a full circle among all who were present. Sam and the others would have called it the presence of the Lord, but Leslie just felt safe and secure for the first time in a long, long time. A monotonous thumping from Porthos' tail broke the spell, and Mildred Juniper slowly rose to her feet, stretching tall and yawning. She was wearing her favorite blue snowman sweater, which clashed terribly with the purple high tops.

"I feel the need to think in the outdoors," she announced, then turned to Laura Lee. "Can me and Gregory go down to the creek for a little while?"

"Child!" Laura Lee chided. "Please, cover your mouth when you yawn. For heaven's sake!"

"Oh, sorry," Mildred clamped her mouth shut.

"By all means, children, go to the creek," Sam commanded from his chair. "You've been with grown ups way too long on the day before Santa Claus comes. You need to go be kids."

"Daddy," Mildred moaned, "Santa Claus? How old do you think we are?"

"What 'chu talkin' 'bout, Mildred Juniper?" Gregory's round, chocolate eyes peeled wider in pretended ignorance. "Santa Claus is comin', ain't he?"

"Oh for Pete's sake, Gregory!" Mildred tossed her hair while opening the front door and kicking Porthos out. Gregory spun back toward the family in the living room, flashing an exaggerated wink. Laughter burst out as he shut the door.

The remainder of the afternoon was spent swapping stories and sampling the cider Dot had simmering on the back of the stove top. Each time someone lifted the lid on the oversized cooking pot, a rich aroma of cinnamon, oranges and cloves floated into the air and out toward the open living room. An AM radio station was dialed into easy listening Christmas music and Dot thought there couldn't have ever been a more perfect scene. The only thing missing was Tom, but today even that thought didn't trouble her mind as it usually did.

Daylight began to dwindle and even though no one seemed to want to go home, the loud stomping of Mildred and Gregory's boots turned several heads toward the wall clock and, thus, toward gathering things together. Dot knew she was running late with her milking, but it was a Christmas Eve prerogative. Besides, Leslie brought her jeans to stay behind and help, so they would head out as soon as everyone had started on their way. With both of them working, it wouldn't take long.

"As wonderful as this has been, Dot, we really must be leaving," Laura Lee announced as she slowly ambled toward the kitchen. "Would you like some of this leftover sweet potato casserole for your Christmas dinner?"

"Oh Lord, no," Dot held her stomach. "I'm stuffed and I've got enough ham here to choke a mule. In fact, why don't you all take some of it? I'll never get it all eaten."

As the women crammed into the tiny kitchen to divvy up leftovers, Sam pulled Daryl, Stew and Ben aside. He had eased up from the recliner, taking care to not rise too quickly, and stood gingerly leaning against the back of the chair.

"Fellas, I just want to say ..." his eyes grew moist. "Well, I just don't know what I would've done without you these past few months."

"Ah, no pastor, you don't have to worry..." Daryl began.

"But I do, Daryl. I need to let you know that you three are the best friends, the truest pillars a man could have beside him. And to think that you are the foundations of this church and you care enough about us, about me, to join alongside and pastor and lead – well, it's overwhelming," he brushed his hand lightly over his forehead, taking care not to knock off the bandage. "I'm so thankful, so very thankful."

The front door banged open as Mildred and Gregory dashed through the living room to get to the kitchen and the tea pitcher. "I'm parched," Gregory gasped, slinging his coat to the side.

"Whoa there! Hold it! Wait a minute!" Shouts of women with casseroles spread all over the counters added to the chaos. Smiling at one another silently, the four men moved in unison to the front porch, two supporting Sam as he walked slowly but steadily.

A cold breeze greeted them, the temperature dropping quickly as the sun dipped on the horizon. Naked trees encircled the sides of Dot's house, looking like giants just waking up from a long winter's nap. As the men stood and stared out front at the empty field, a line of starlings flew over, finding no place to settle.

"You know, we still have this thing with Pete Griffin and the City Council hangin' over our heads," Sam spoke low. "And Wanda oughta be released from the hospital by tomorrow evening. I know she really wants to be out before Christmas is over. Joe Ray is in the city jail, and Wanda'll need support. Then there's Bobby who'll be with us tomorrow for Christmas dinner."

"Sam," Daryl broke in. "Don't worry 'bout all these folks. We got cha covered. Between the three of us – and other folks at church – they'll be taken care of. It's a blessed season and we are a blessed people," his deep brown eyes flashed as he spoke. "We gots lots of unknowns and I reckon we always will, but we just keep listenin' to Jesus, doing what He says, and we gonna be alright."

"It's that simple, is it, Daryl?" Sam said softly.

"I think so."

Ben nodded without saying anything, the tall, heavy-set lumberjack gently patting Sam's back. Stew watched the starlings disappear behind the trees, his arms crossed. Streaks of color from the sun's reflection on the clouds shot across the sky, starting pale and turning brilliant before their eyes. Then he spoke.

"You know, Sam, I ain't never had no preacher, no pastor – no white man – treat me the way you do." Sam pulled his eyes away from the sky to watch Stew as he continued. "We all on a journey; that's the way I see it. Some of us got long journeys through pretty green forests for most all our lives. Everythin' jest seems awful easy. Others of us got a path through a desert and it seems like it don't matter what you do or how hard you try, you ain't never gonna get outta that desert. Most of us, I reckon, got somethin' in between, where we feel like we in the desert part of the time, in the forest part of the time and," Stew laughed, "we don't know exactly where we are." He fully smiled then, turning toward Sam while Daryl and Ben listened quietly.

"Yo' journey could'a been pretty easy, I figure, but you chose to leave yo' home and come on up here where you don't know nobody, to try to pray for, preach to, and love on a group of misfits the likes of us. What's worse is yo' misfits come in all shapes, sizes and colors. Most any man I knows would 'o walked out the first week. Any other man I know would 'o fer sure left the first month. But you done stayed with it. It didn't matter what nobody in this town said to you, you was determined to stay and watch over blacks and white folk."

Stew reached across Daryl and turned toward Sam, holding out his hand. Sam met him halfway as the two men shook. "I'm proud to know you, Sam Rhodes. Proud to have you as my friend. You done proved to me that there are folks out there that don't care nuthin' 'bout color or money or the likes of that." Stew pulled Sam in closer, embracing him with his huge, bear-like arms. "Thank you, Sam. You done give me hope again," Stew finished, his words muffled in Sam's coat. Then the giant shoulders lifted as Stew gathered control and leaned away. Sam didn't know how to respond, then realized he didn't have to. All four men turned back toward the field, watching the sky ease its way into dusk.

Suddenly, the door flew open and their repose was broken with the sounds of coats being pulled on, women chatting about Christmas, children grabbing boots. But Sam knew there was one more deed that had to be completed before they left. He spied Dot following Leslie out onto the front porch, carrying his coat over her arm. He cleared his throat to try to gather everyone's attention but there was too much noise for that. After a few tries, Sam stuck two fingers into his mouth and blew a sharp, shrill whistle. All activity stopped.

"Thank you," Sam said, smiling broadly. "You people sound like a stampeding herd a buffalo!" As good-natured arguments began to be raised, Sam held his hand up. "Truce, truce," he cried. "I actually have one more thing to present before this wonderful day is closed and before poor Dot and Leslie have to go herd in cows!" Everyone laughed quietly, glancing toward the two women.

"Dot, this is actually for you." Dot shifted closer to hear, placing Sam's coat on the back of a rocking chair. "As I was praying this morning, I felt like the Lord led me to the book of Isaiah. I was reading through and it was as though a giant light fell on one verse and it impacted me so much, I memorized it. If I heard anything from the Lord today, I heard that this verse was for you. May I quote it to you now?"

The Dot Harris of a few weeks ago would have run from the moment and she knew it. But now? She was back in family, back in community, and she knew that whatever Sam had to say was what she wanted to hear. She smoothed back her untidy gray hair and tugged her sweater lower on her hips. The sun had completely disappeared and the golden light that remained shot a direct beam under the eaves of Dot's front porch. The air looked golden, like it was filled with stardust.

"I'd love to hear it, Sam," Dot replied as Leslie came alongside, tucking Dot's arm into the crook of her own.

Then Sam took a deep breath and spoke clearly and loudly, "It's from Isaiah, Chapter 54, verse 1. It says, 'Sing, O barren woman, you who never bore a child; burst into song, shout for joy, you who were never in labor; because more are the children of the desolate woman than of her who has a husband, says the Lord.'"

A ripple of God's presence wafted across the porch as the she soaked in the words. Dot Harris, the desolate woman, the barren woman. She felt Leslie squeeze her arm as she looked over at Mildred leaning against the front door. Her girls. She knew she was desolate no longer.

A sudden stillness and peace descended and almost as if on cue, all of them turned back toward the field, watching the colors blend, merge and burst into violent light before darkness completely overtook the day. They stood side-by-side, silent and yet full of joy. It was the loveliest of Christmas Eves.

Epilogue
Three Months Later

Mildred

    A round, plastic bowl of dirt sat on my right and an empty egg carton on my left. A bag of corn seed was in my lap and I was about to embark on planting, the great tradition of seed sowing in the South. Apparently, we'd had the last winter frost and the ground would be warming up soon.

    Miz Dingle had told us to plant one seed in each pocket and bring our egg cartons (with names clearly printed on them!) to class on Monday. When I dragged the dirt bowl into the kitchen, Mama pointed to the front stoop and said "Out!" in that no-nonsense voice of hers. I reckon all the important scientists didn't have mothers who smothered their creativity.

    I began drizzling enough dirt in each pocket to support my seed. It was to be our spring project, Miz Dingle had announced Friday in her usual demanding tone. Just lately she had changed out her plain brown shoes for cream-colored pumps with a strap and a snap. That, along with a new pink pastel sweater, announced the coming of spring better than anything I knew.

    As if to echo my thoughts, a robin landed on the ground a few feet in front of the stoop. It pecked at a corn kernel then gave up and moved on. I'll bet it was too big for his tiny throat.

    The screen door that Daddy reattached last weekend slapped lightly as he slid in beside me, knocking off a pile of dirt to give him a clean spot to sit on.

    "What a mess — you having any fun with this?" Daddy asked.

    "It's not so bad, if you gotta do school on a Saturday," I responded, glancing up at him through squinted eyes. All that was left of Joe Ray's violence was a thin, white line across the top of his forehead. As Daddy stayed outside more, working part-time at the saw mill, it turned whiter and whiter; the rest of his face was tanned and strong-looking. He wore an old pair of overalls and work boots, but I noticed his socks were purple and yellow checked. I stiffled a giggle. Obviously, Mama didn't lay out his clothes today.

Daddy grunted his understanding of schoolwork and Saturdays as he stared vacantly out toward the front yard. I kept pouring dirt, hearing only birds chirping and mucking about in dead leaves. It was a nice, peaceful moment; Daddy sighed contentedly.

Thankfully, life had slowed down considerably since Christmas time. Maybe it was all a test from the Lord, Daddy had said last week, to see if the Rhodes' would stick it out in Piedmont Ridge. Apparently, the Lord likes to test those He loves. I wasn't so sure how I felt about that, but I reckon we had passed.

We were still here -- Bingo Hall and all.

I glanced toward the old grocery store, amazed that I even cared about it. Miz Dot had come over last month telling Mama and Daddy that the City Council bru-ha-ha about our church being in the Bingo Hall had dried up and died. She said something about Pete Griffin, the Klan and white sheets and and hood being found in the trunk of his car. Mama and Daddy had raised their eyebrows and shared one of "those" looks, then Daddy asked a question about planting spring lettuce. Lettuce! I wondered when he was going to realize how grown up I was.

"So what's up with the daffodils? Has your Mama said anything about them?" Daddy waved his hand widely, drawing my eyes back to the trailer. It was a good question. It had been about a week ago when we realized that the bulbs Gregory and me planted in the fall actually did come up. Even Miz Mary Rose, who had poo-pooed the whole idea, was amazed when we pointed them out to her last Sunday.

"What?" she had asked incredulously, drawing her large brimmed hat on as she prepared to leave after the service. "You mean those old bulbs we got outta the storage room last year? Lawd, it must have some Jesus blessin' on 'em 'cause them were some sad lookin' bulbs!"

They sure weren't sad looking this morning. Daddy was right. They were popping out everywhere and surely they'd be opening up soon, blooming yellow pathways across the yard.

"Didn't we buy about a hundred bulbs, Mil?" Daddy asked as he stood up to look around both sides of the trailer.

"Yes, sir. I know 'cause I counted as me and Gregory planted."

"Did you plant any over there?" he pointed toward the pines where we held our campfires.

"No, sir."

"How 'bout over there next to the Big Star parking lot?"

"No, sir. We just planted on each side of the stoop, working out in a path to where we park."

"Huh. That's what I thought."

He settled back on the stoop as I looked back toward the Bingo Hall and saw Mr. Bobby coming our way. His old, lanky body ambling across the parking lot made me smile. Funny how scared Gregory and me had been of him; he was nothing but a big teddy bear. Daddy and me squinted and watched as he drew closer, his baggy trousers dragging a little on the ground.

"Mornin' Mildred Juniper. Preacher," he said, tipping his hat. "What cha'll got goin' this morning?"

"Not much, Bobby. Mildred and me were just commenting on the proliferation of daffodil buds and plants in our yard. Mil planted about a hundred last fall but this seems like way more than that."

"What's that? Oh, yeah. Why that'd be because this here trailer was put on Miss Mabel's old homestead location." Mr. Bobby grabbed a five-gallon bucket from under the big pine and moved it over. He flipped it and expertly sat on the bottom. Reaching deep in his pockets, he took out a beat-up looking knife and out of the other pocket, a small chunk of wood. He began to whittle and talk at the same time. "See, Miz Mabel Mathis used to have a big old house right here. Fact, before there was a Big Star, there was Miz

Mabel's farm. She was a widow who tried to keep things runnin' but it was awful hard on her. Finally, when she got old enough that her children had to put her in the home, they sold the house and land. Big Star bought it all up and just tore down the house." He shook his head at the thought. "I always did say if Miz Mabel had any idea what they was gonna do to her house, she'd a never let them drag her out. A shame, it was. A cryin' shame.

"Well, the grocery moved in and left this parcel empty. They had knocked down the house fer nuthin', it looked like, 'cause they didn't even end up usin' this piece of the land. Still, every year I lived around here Miz Mabel's daffodils kept bloomin' – all around where her front porch had been and down the sides of where the old house was. I reckon when the church put you a trailer in here, they positioned it right where Miz Mabel's front porch must've been. Huh. Imagine that, still bloomin' after all these years," he shook his head again, kicking out wood shavings as he quickly formed the rectangular piece of wood into something more oval and smooth.

I wondered what he might be working on and was about to ask when I heard the screen door creak open behind me. Mama's head peeked out, her eyes crinkling in pleasure when she saw Mr. Bobby; he had become one of her favorite people. She came out looking like a spring flower herself. Last week she had fished around in boxes marked "Summer Items" and found a few short-sleeved, flowered dresses. She had one on today even though it wasn't hot yet – not by Carolina standards. I reckon she couldn't help herself. Matching green sandals completed her outfit; it was nice to have Mama back.

"I just got off the phone with Wanda. Her phone's hooked back up and she's feeling more settled than she has in years," Mama reported. "If Joe Ray gets as much jail time as they say he might, she'll have a good chance to get herself together. Who knows? Maybe he will, too."

"Well, we're sure gonna work on him," Daddy promised.

"What are you three gabbing about anyway?" she asked, sliding in beside Daddy on the stoop. "I sent Mildred outside with her dirty mess, not knowing I was starting a party without inviting myself."

Daddy reached out and grabbed Mama's hand, holding it and squeezing tight. "Actually, Bobby here was telling us the story of our daffodils."

"Oh, what's that?"

So while Daddy filled Mama in, I finished planting my corn, mashing each kernel at least a half inch down in the carton, then taking care to sprinkle dirt over the top. He was wrapping up the story about the time I grabbed my cup of water and gently dampened each seed. I slid the carton to the side of the stoop so as to keep it in the sun but not where we might accidentally kick it over.

"What you're saying is that," Mama hesitated, "that for fifteen years I slaved over those daffodils in Prosperity, working my fingers to the bone, digging, uprooting, re-planting, and all we had to do was pack up and move to Piedmont Ridge?" Her green eyes sparkled mischievously as she laughed but her voice was strong and getting louder as she continued. "I 'bout killed myself over that mill house and the Lord brings us to this stinky, brown, no-color trailer in a po-dunk town and he gives me more daffodils than I ever could've planted or imagined?"

Daddy had been slowly leaning away from Mama as her voice squeaked higher and higher, and I was beginning to worry that she might just end up screaming and break down into wails, right there in front of God and everybody.

But I was wrong.

She sucked in a deep breath and began to laugh. Hard. Hysterically. She laughed so hard she slid sideways off the stoop and landed on the ground. Daddy jumped up to make sure she was alright, then he started laughing. It was contagious and I found myself holding my sides, just wishing I could catch my breath. Poor Mr. Bobby didn't know what to make of any of it – and that was so funny it made me hiccup. I tried to tell Daddy that Mr. Bobby couldn't understand, but I couldn't talk by then. Tears rolled down Daddy's face, and Mama finally buried her head in her hands, her shoulders shaking as she continued her hysterics.

Had anyone been driving by that afternoon, they would've thought the Rhodes' family had finally lost it. I could hear them now, "Must've been that knock on the head that finally got to Sam Rhodes. I seen him and his wife and daughter laying all over the trailer stoop t'other day, laughing at nothin, nothin, I tell ya. And that crazy homeless Bobby jest sittin' on a bucket watchin'. I always knowed them folks weren't quite right in the head."

It would be all over Piedmont Ridge before nightfall, and I wouldn't even care! The more we laughed, the better I felt. Mama would say I was being melodramatic — a word I just learned last week — and maybe she'd be right, but I felt free for the first time since I heard about the mill closing.

Finally, we all caught our breath, which gave Mr. Bobby a chance to clear his throat and scratch his jaw. I could see he didn't know quite what to say, so he just picked up where he left off, talking about the daffodils and pretending nothing ever happened.

"I'm expectin' them to bloom any day now, more'n likely tomorrow seeing as how we got us a bushel load of sunshine in the forecast," he stated. "Up to now, it's been so cloudy that nothin' has been bloomin' like it regular would, but I'm really thinkin' that tomorrow that'll all change."

I still had the hiccups and Mama was breathing hard as Daddy helped her back up on the steps. "Oh, that felt so good," she sighed. "I haven't laughed that hard in a long time; I might've pulled a muscle." She rotated her shoulder, winced, then straightened her dress around her legs as she settled back down on the stoop. Daddy pulled her close while I leaned into his other shoulder. Every once in a while, one of us would shudder, still trying to recuperate, but we began to quiet down. I felt a little like a wrung-out sponge.

"You know, it really is just like the Lord," Daddy broke the silence.

"What is?" Mama kept her head on his shoulder.

"To bring blessing where there was emptiness. To bring bounty where there was need. To bring joy where there was sadness. To surprise us with his love where we least expect it."

"To bring daffodils where there were none," Mama added.

Mr. Bobby sort of grunted as he continued to carve and I stared across the street at the Bingo Hall. Funny. I hadn't called it the God-Awful Place in a long time. Now that Mr. Bobby had planted some bushes, and even had a rose bed started, it didn't look so bad. Just last week, Daddy had a man in town come paint a new sign over the door: Piedmont Ridge Community Church stood out in bold, blue letters with a drawing of flames of fire beside it. Underneath, in smaller letters, were the words "Our God is a Consuming Fire." For a church sign, it was alright I reckon. I mean, it wasn't all lit up like the City Church sign, but then again, the Bingo Hall didn't exactly have columns lining the front area either.

Nope. The Bingo Hall was who we were and that was alright with me. We had hundreds of daffodils waiting to bloom, a church filled with colored folks and white folks, and friends like Miz Dot who had found her family. Piedmont Ridge, South Carolina, might not be anybody else's idea of home, but for me?

It would do.

With Gratitude

"I thank my God every time I remember you." Phil. 1:3

How in the world can I possibly thank everyone who has held my hand, prayed for me, encouraged me in the midst of this project? I'd like to say it's been a short drive, but in reality, I've written on this book for years, in the midst of homeschooling our boys. (Maybe that's why the edit took so long. It was as choppy as a tumultuous sea!) And yet, friends and family have listened and supported me way beyond the time "required" for such a thing.

At the risk of leaving out someone, I would be remiss if I didn't say "thank you, thank you, thank you" to David and Teresa Elder, editors, publishers and friends; to my Tuesday Night Writers' Group -- Ellen K., Ellen T. and Sharon -- the input was almost as good as the hot tea (smile); Miz Audrey, the Holmes' "girls," Tami, Myrna and others who read over drafts and made **ColorBlind** so much better; and, of course, Byron, the webmah-ster who worked so tirelessly on my behalf.

My husband, Landon, put up with me throughout -- not an easy task -- and the boys didn't get terribly outdone with me when I told them to "wait five minutes" before I helped with their studies.

And many of you "just prayed" for me.

Just prayed ...

How much love does one person have for another when they spend the time and effort to pray?

Thank you to all.

And to my Lord and Savior Jesus Christ, who heard their prayers -- and mine -- and gave me the idea to write the precious story of Mildred Juniper Rhodes. If there is anything good in this book, it's because of Jesus.

To Him be the honor and the glory, forever and ever.

For More About
ColorBlind

To find out more about Melanie Meadow and her next project or to download **ColorBlind** on e-book, go to

www.MelanieMeadow.com
or
www.ColorBlindthenovel.com

Melanie also loves "snail mail,"
so feel free to write her at:

Melanie Meadow
P.O. Box 104
Adams, Tennessee 37010

Paperback copies of **ColorBlind** and e-book

are available via the websites listed above
or at Amazon.com

Made in the USA
Charleston, SC
21 May 2011